CW01514068

A True and Perfect Knight

A True and Perfect Knight

Jeffrey Robinson

LITTLE, BROWN AND COMPANY

A *Little, Brown* Book

First published in Great Britain in 1999
by Little, Brown and Company

Copyright © 1999, Jeffrey Robinson

The moral right of the author has been asserted.

*All characters in this publication are fictitious
and any resemblance to real persons, living or dead,
is purely coincidental.*

A CIP catalogue record for this book
is available from the British Library.

ISBN 0 316 64472 2

Typeset by
Palimpsest Book Production Limited,
Polmont, Stirlingshire
Printed and bound in Great Britain by
Creative Print and Design (Wales)

Little, Brown and Company (UK)
Brettenham House
Lancaster Place
London WC2E 7EN

For Adrian Shire and the memory of Sue Shire

A True and Perfect Knight

Prologue

If I ever find a bottle on a beach, you know, the kind that has a genie trapped inside, I'm gonna rub it, and if a genie actually does pop out and says I'll grant you one wish, I'm gonna tell him my one wish is to have a dozen more wishes, and if he tells me sorry chump you get one and only one wish, I'm gonna tell him, okay, here it is – my one and only wish is to have that Monday back again so that this time I can get it right the easy way.

Chapter One

He tries to be unconventional and winds up ticking like a clock, was what that fella Too Right Tel had explained to me, adding, *just stand outside his office on a Saturday or Sunday and eventually he'll show up.*

So that's what I did.

And sure 'nough, that's what he did.

'Cept by the time he got around to showing up it was already Sunday afternoon, which meant I'd been standing there for the better part of two days – which went real slow – even if it had taken me almost a full three weeks just to get this far. Still, the moment I spotted Thomas d'Aquin Whitestone – his bald head now glistening in the rain – taking four giant steps from the back seat of his baby-blue Rolls-Royce to the front door of his office building, I was long convinced that even if he didn't care much 'bout me till now, the time had finally come to make him care.

He was juggling a huge bouquet of long-stemmed red roses and a magnum of champagne in one hand, and trying to unlock the large antique mahogany door with his other hand, but he couldn't manage it and the champagne started to slip out of his grasp. Somewhere in his mind he must have realized he'd have to make a decision – save the flowers or save the bubbly – and he chose the bubbly.

The flowers crashed on to the wet pavement.

'Bloody hell,' he said loud enough that I could hear him where I was hiding, clear across the street.

His chauffeur jumped out of the car but Whitestone waved him off, unlocked the door, bent down, grabbed the flowers, shook the wet off the plastic wrapping paper, signalled that it was all right and stood there – his six foot, three inch frame slightly stooped – forcing one of his Buddha-like smiles, until the chauffeur climbed back into the car and pulled away.

As soon as the car was gone, the smile disappeared too.

The little voice inside my head urged, *let's go, he's there, we got him where we can get to him.* But my brain didn't send the message to my legs fast enough 'cause, by the time I moved away from the side of the building at the corner of the square, he'd already stepped inside and, as soon as he did, the door shut firmly behind him.

I stopped and sighed, and thought about myself getting soaked on a rainy Sunday afternoon in the middle of deserted downtown London England, and thought about him all decked out with roses and champagne. Knowing what I already knew about him, which by this time was one helluva lot, I didn't have to work for NASA to understand that he didn't bring that stuff 'cause he was expecting me to show up.

I checked my twenty-buck Cartier to see that, even by knock-off watch time, it was just 2 p.m.

So now I asked the voice, *do we wait until after he scores or do we get in the way and hope that just to get rid of us he comes to terms with the fact that he's not gonna get rid of us this time?*

The voice didn't hesitate a bit. *If nothing else, getting in his way is drier.*

Right. I stepped off the kerb, crossed the street and marched up to his locked tight front door. There was a bell, I thought about ringing it, then noticed the security camera staring down at me. 'Cause there was no way he'd answer the door if he knew it was me, I put my finger on the bell and pushed it seven times. That's a little trick I worked out when I was flogging stocks and bonds. I'd need to get into a building where I don't know anybody and if I rang any bell at random just once, the guy at the other end would want to know who was there. If I answer, I'm sorta Wall Street's equivalent of the Fuller Brush man, he wouldn't let me past the welcome mat. So to make the person at the other end think he knew who was there, I'd push his bell to the beat of 'Shave and a haircut, two bits!'

Which is what I did with Sir Tommy's bell – *dah dah dah dum dum, dah dah!* – before scurrying out of camera range.

Sure 'nough, a few seconds later, his familiar voice came over the speaker to say, 'Bon jour, bon jour, top floor.' The door buzzed, I opened it and hurried inside.

What I hadn't rightly expected was that the damn door would swing shut behind me so fast that I couldn't find the light switch, leaving me in the dark like that. All I could see was the thick Persian rug I was standing on and outlines on the walls of some very large paintings.

Just then, the grinding noise of an elevator broke into the silence. It moved down, as if in some kind of pain, from all the way up on the top floor, until it arrived on the ground floor. When it stopped, casting a feeble glow at the end of the hallway, I walked there, opened the main door only to discover another door – this time a real fancy, old-fashioned gilt cage door. Inside, a pair of long narrow light bulbs, flickering like candles, just-about lit a dark red leather seat for two.

I told the little voice, *when you have more money than God you get a better elevator than him, too,* and sat down. The outer door closed automatically, I leaned forward to pull the cage door shut, then pushed the top button – which I counted, would take me up to the fourth floor – crossed my legs and waited while the motor that powered the elevator coughed and jerked a couple of times, before starting its groaning rise upwards.

The light bulbs flickered a couple of times, shut off, then just as quickly came back on.

I passed the second floor, then the third floor – the lights went off again and the elevator gave out a real sickly wail – then finally came to an abrupt halt.

I stood up.

The outer door opened from the other side at the same time that I yanked the cage door open, and standing right there was Whitestone himself. Wrapped smartly in a blue blazer, grey slacks, lemon-yellow shirt with a yellow and blue silk tie, he had the roses in his right hand, a glass of champagne in his left hand and his best Buddha smile on his face.

I waved, 'Howdy.'

His smile instantly evaporated. 'What the bloody hell . . .'

I grinned, 'Hope I'm not interrupting anything.'

'Mr Doone . . . you again?'

'Sir Tommy . . . me again.' I acknowledged, 'Nice tie.'

Staring at me, he shook his head back and forth several times – 'You are indefatigable' – put the champagne glass on an antique table next to the elevator and tossed the flowers on to an antique chair next to the table. Behind him, I could see what looked like the living room of a fancy hotel suite – you know, a lot of dolled-up English furniture and a real comfortable overstuffed couch filled with tapestry-covered pillows. Behind that, I presumed, was a bedroom. There was music on the stereo which took me a few seconds to figure out. 'What on earth . . . Mr Doone . . . what are you doing here, now, this time?'

I had to ask, 'Julio Iglesias?'

He ignored my question. 'Mr Doone, would it be too much to ask that you kindly find someone else's house to haunt?'

'Problem is,' I confessed, 'I've been looking but there are no other houses. Least I can't find any. Just yours. And then, you're not home most of the time.'

'But why,' he demanded, 'why, Mr Doone, why are you here now, this afternoon?'

'Now? This afternoon? I'm here 'cause you're here. Which you weren't in New York two weeks ago when you said you would be. Or in London after that when you said you would be. Or last week in Paris when you said you would be. And cause I almost gave up chasing you when you escaped to . . . where the hell was it, India?'

'Mr Doone . . .' He took a gentle grip on my elbow, moving me back into the elevator. 'Mr Doone . . . please excuse me but I have a previous engagement this afternoon . . .' He stepped into the elevator with me, closed the cage door and pushed the button for the ground floor.

'Perhaps tomorrow, Mr Doone . . .' He shook his head several times, then checked his watch – a huge, gold Rolex Oyster with diamonds imbedded all 'round the face of it where numbers should be – then shook his head again. 'You see, this is a most awkward time . . .'

'Actually, Sir Tommy, it is the perfect time . . .'

The elevator jerked, the lights went out, and the cage suddenly fell a couple of feet.

'Jeezus!' I screamed.

Then it stopped.

'What happened?'

'Perfect, indeed,' he mumbled, pushing the button once, then twice, then a third time. 'Yes, absolutely perfect, Mr Doone.' He tried opening the cage door, which wouldn't open, then banged the buttons again. 'I don't believe it . . .'

'Are we stuck?'

'What does it seem like to you?' He spun around to ask, 'May I please borrow your mobile phone?'

I could just about see his face in the dark. 'My mobile phone?'

'Yes, please, Mr Doone, your mobile phone, or cellular phone, or whatever Americans call them? Because, yes, Mr Doone, we are stuck.'

'Ah . . . you see, I used to have one, but they cut me off when I got fired and I never got around to reconnecting . . .' I stopped. 'Yeah, well, what about your mobile phone, or cellular phone, or whatever Brits call them?'

There was a long pause before he started banging on the elevator buttons again. 'Perfect . . . perfect, indeed.'

I dared to ask, 'Does this happen often?'

He snapped, 'You mean, do I often get trapped in a lift with someone and have no way to ring for help?'

The little voice in the back of my head suggested, *if we don't admit we're trapped we won't be trapped*, so I told him, 'Just keep pushing the button. It will work.'

He did. But nothing happened.

'Well . . . ah . . .' I suggested, 'how 'bout we start shouting for help?'

He fell on to the red leather seat. 'This is Sunday afternoon. No one will be anywhere within earshot until around eight-thirty or nine tomorrow morning. But . . .' he gestured, 'please, Mr Doone, be my guest.'

I tried to force open the cage door but it wouldn't budge for me either. Then I hit all the buttons several times.

'Indeed, Mr Doone,' he repeated dejectedly, 'please . . . be my guest.'

First I hit the buttons real hard. Then I pushed them real soft, thinking maybe they didn't like being hit hard and would only work if I took the gentle approach. Then I settled into the seat next to him. 'Your guest? Sir Tommy, yeah, well . . . I think I finally am.'

Chapter Two

The Monday that actually turned out to be the first day of the rest of my life – the one that dawned exactly twenty days before I stepped into that elevator with Sir Tommy – began usual enough.

I was up at 5.20, on my running track by 5.30 and teasingly kissing the inside of Lorilee's ear by 5.40. At first, she purred. I whispered, 'Don't start without me.' Then she turned over, grabbed two of our dozen pillows, rudely tossed one at me, stuck another over her head, and mumbled, 'I'm asleep.'

All as usual.

I got the fast train from Stamford, sat where I always sit, sorted through my newspapers – the *Wall Street Journal* for the markets, *USA Today* for the late West Coast basketball scores, and the *Daily News* to see how badly the Knicks were playing – scurried along Platform 35 in Grand Central Station, jumped on the shuttle to Penn Station and changed there for the express downtown. I got off where I always get off, deep inside the bowels of the World Trade Center, made my way to the news-stand where I always bought my morning's supply of M&Ms, stepped into an elevator in the east tower and was whooshed upstairs. Two minutes later, I sauntered past Garrison-Cotton-Braddock's glass doors – inscribed GCB sideways in huge gold letters with speckles of tiny green dollar signs – ducked under the imitation McDonald's arches of the floor-to-ceiling glass wall at the far end of the still empty reception area and entered the 'War Room'. Just as I did, the digital clock on the back wall labelled New York – clustered in the middle of a group of digital clocks labelled London, Paris, Tel Aviv, Moscow, Singapore, Hong Kong, Tokyo, Honolulu, Los Angeles, Denver and Chicago – clicked over to 7.29.

Everything still usual enough.

Taking up the entire south half of the 76th floor and covered in gold carpet with more of those tiny green dollar signs – if you squinted hard you could see that they formed a running pattern to spell out GCB – the War Room offered the world's greatest view of Staten Island, which would otherwise be okay if it wasn't an oxymoron.

We were about a hundred and thirty traders in all, pretty minor league by Wall Street standards, but old man Garrison – recently deceased – designed it that way cause he believed that medium-sized fish in a medium-sized pond were the dine-ers, whereas medium-sized fish in big ponds were the dine-ees.

Philosophy was his strong suit, followed, only just, by his fondness for all things soldierly, like the way he'd personally designed the War Room.

The first bank of computer consoles is where everyone starts their GCB careers – he insisted they be referred to as buck private foot soldiers – unless you happened to have married into G's or C's or B's family, like the schmucks who were presently running the company.

Next level up are the sergeants. Then there are the lieutenants, the captains, and the colonels. Finally, along the far wall, just under the clocks, are us six generals.

All this was the brainchild of a man whose particularly brilliant army career consisted of five months' active duty during the late 1940s stationed in an air-raid tower on the beach at Point Lookout, Long Island.

Again, just like the army, he dictated that promotion should come to those who showed bravery in battle, which translated to mean that in order to move up the steps you had to bring in new clients, which is the way I moved up, much to the eternal chagrin of the management. Most everyone else had to wait for someone higher up to leave. A lieutenant would get promoted to captain, a sergeant would get promoted to lieutenant, a private would get promoted to sergeant and a new private would get hired. Garrison preached that this created a neat and orderly system of advancement. The rest of us knew that, more often than not, it simply created an excuse for knocking off the guy one work-station higher.

Garrison also dictated that just like in the army, here too, rank would have its privilege. In the case of us generals, privilege meant a side-table with room enough for telephones and lunch pails, which was his subtle way of trying to get us to eat lunch at our desks.

What he knew that we knew was that this military crapola was just a sneaky way of capping trading limits so that the firm wouldn't have to pay all the traders the same level of commission. What he didn't know that we knew was that he'd acquired the side-tables for free, and couldn't figure what else to do with them after picking up a pile of office furniture for the directors' conference room from a bankrupt trader ten floors below us. What we knew that he knew was none of us generals ever intended to eat lunch at our work-stations 'cept on days when the market was going to hell in a handbag.

Lunch, he would mumble on slow days as we all filed out at 12.30, is for losers. But that obviously didn't include him or any of the G's, C's or B's cause they had lunch catered in and served by a waitress in a skimpy black dress, which is what used to go on every day at 1 o'clock behind the closed doors of the directors' conference room with the used furniture.

'Though the place took a little getting used to, I'd been there just over seven years now and little by little, had assembled my own creature comforts, like using my secondhand side-table to hold a NY Giants football helmet bowl where I kept my M&Ms.

'What's with London?' I asked a private on my climb up the steps of the still very quiet War Room.

He fidgeted with his hands but kept his nose buried in his screen. 'Ah . . . I think it's up a couple.'

'Frankfurt do its thing yet?' I called out to a sergeant.

'Yeah, hi,' he said sheepishly, avoiding any eye contact.

'Hong Kong?' I turned to a captain. 'Hang Sang?' But either he didn't hear me or he didn't want to tell me.

'What's going on here this morning?' I asked a particularly idiotic colonel named Binterman, whose work-station was just one rung below mine.

'Yeah . . . well . . . that's for me to know and you to find out.'

'Find out what?'

'What I know.' He forced a nasty smile, then made a huge effort to turn back to his screen.

'Have a nice day,' I said, searching to find at least one friendly face in a still sparse crowd.

Little Debbie wasn't in yet.

And even though Pinky's tent-sized jacket was hanging over his chair, he wasn't anywhere to be seen.

Falling into my chair, which squeaked loudly as I swung sideways, I pushed a button to open a phone line to Snack Attack Central – Maynard had to wait for Garrison to die before he could change the name from 'The Mess' cause he thought Snack Attack Central was cool – ripped loose my tie, called into the speaker, 'One coffee and one bialy please . . . Doone. And please, this time, not butter . . . margarine.'

That done, I was just about to pour my bag of M&Ms into the football helmet when I noticed my screen was blank.

'What the hell?' I hit the reboot button but nothing happened.

Suddenly I realized that most of the eyes in the War Room were staring at me. But when I looked up, every eye abruptly turned away.

'What?' I shrugged. 'You're all long on butter? How about going short on cholesterol?'

It was as if no one heard me.

My work-station was on the west side of the building, which is where the Hudson River and New Jersey used to be before someone decided to put the twin tower right there. If nothing else, it kept the afternoon sun from melting my M&Ms. Though, from where I sat I did have a panoramic view across the War Room. So now I glanced to the East River side and the glass-walled offices of the 'chiefs-of-staff'.

Miller Maynard, chairman and CEO, was in a huddle with Hogan Cotton, the youngest of his two partners. Cotton had his hands on Maynard's shoulders, and their heads were very close, 'cept instead of looking at each other while they conferred, they were glaring across at me.

I broad-grinned them, mouthing the words, 'Up yours.'

Maynard's grey hair was set back off his forehead, accenting his pointed nose, making his face look something like the front of a supersonic jet fighter plane. He seemed flustered.

Cotton, two inches taller and emaciatingly thin, had been born with a silver spoon, 'cept instead of having it in his mouth, it was rammed up his butt. He immediately turned away.

The easiest one to stomach was D. Whitt Braddock – there was no doubt in my mind that the D stood for dim – but only cause he spent most of his time travelling and therefore proving the old adage, outta sight, outta mind.

Being fifteen years my senior made Maynard ten years older than Cotton, which made Cotton five years older than me, which, frankly, is one of the few non-derogatory things I can think of saying about either of them. 'Though to give the dogs their due, it wasn't an entirely unholy alliance. Both were Yale. Both were rabid WASPs. Both were borderline incompetent traders.

As far as I could tell, Maynard's only bankable asset was to know more dirty golf jokes than anyone else on earth. *Did you hear the one about the midget caddie who says to the lady golfer about to make a putt, what's the difference between a mashie niblick and cream soda?*

Cotton's claim to fame was to own the world's worst collection of neck-ties, most of which came straight out of the Disney Store – a grown man pretending to be a force to reckon with while wearing pure silk images of Goofy.

The only other thing I give them credit for is that when it comes to women they're both smarter than me. What did it really matter that Marylou had a mouth like Bianca Jagger? Or that Carrie in a bikini could bring a beach to a standstill? Or that sex with Lorilee deserves to carry a government health warning. 'Cause Maynard married one of Garrison's twin daughters – Braddock married the other – and Cotton married Maynard's kid sister. Blood being thicker than Evian – a bottle of which gets delivered with the directors' compliments to each trader's desk every morning – the chiefs-of-staff pick up a million bucks a year for a thirty-hour week, get a secretary and a chauffeur-driven Lincoln Continental, not to mention the real good view – meaning Brooklyn and the harbour – while I'm making a quarter as much for a sixty-hour week, can't deduct my subway fare and have to choose between looking at Staten Island or sitting with my binoculars, staring into the other tower's windows, hoping no one over there starts complaining to the cops about some voyeur at GCB.

Not that I'm saying I'm underpaid. But I'm a trader and traders have to earn their M&Ms every day. Maynard, Cotton and Braddock only had to earn theirs once, on their wedding night.

Anyway, there I was that morning, sitting all the way back in my chair, looking at them – watching them stealing glances at me – wondering what they're talking about. That is, until the little voice inside my head screamed, *it's us, idiot.*

So after my screen failed to light on the third reboot, and after my bialy and coffee failed to show, even though I phoned for breakfast two more times, and even after I picked up my binoculars and focused on them and still couldn't read their lips, I summoned up my nerve, pulled myself out of my chair and trekked along the War Room mezzanine, then down the steps to Maynard's glass wall.

As I did, every eye in the room was back to following me.

'What's going on?'

Maynard and Cotton were clearly perplexed, but I didn't take that to mean anything cause I'd long ago written them both off as terminally perplexed.

'Mr Doone? We, ah . . .' Maynard motioned for me to come inside his office.

'You can call me K.C.,' I reminded him. 'Only my friends call me Mr Doone.'

He didn't get it. 'K.C. . . . okay . . . yes . . . you see . . . it's that Mr Cotton and I . . .'

I didn't budge. 'Mr Cotton? Gee, Mr Maynard, you promised that as soon as I was eighteen I could call him Hog.'

'I meant Hogan,' he corrected himself. 'Hogan and I . . .' He turned to Cotton who clumsily pushed Maynard close enough to the glass that his nose was touching it. 'Hogan and I . . . K.C., would you please be kind enough to step inside?' He pointed to the glass between us. 'It's that . . . this is a metaphorical barrier standing between a meeting of our minds . . .'

'But this is . . .' I rapped it with my knuckles, which startled him . . . 'metaphorical glass.'

'A meeting . . .' he stammered, '. . . about your future here. K.C., I don't have to remind you that you've never been a team player and I'm afraid that . . .' He turned to Cotton, as if he was a man desperate for moral support. 'It's that the TransMare-Telco incident . . .'

This time it was me who didn't get it. 'What TransMare-Telco incident?'

Cotton joined him at the glass in a show of moral support. 'TransMare-Telco. They're supposed to run telephone cables under the oceans . . .'

'What do you mean, supposed to?'

'They don't,' he said. 'You mean, you don't know? They've gone under.'

'Huh?' That stopped me. 'Impossible.'

'One o'clock this morning,' Maynard said.

Cotton nodded to confirm it. 'That was eight o'clock Hong Kong time.'

'Hong Kong?' I swung around, marched over to the nearest empty desk and punched up our real-time headline news service. 'What the hell does Hong Kong . . .' Halfway down the list I spotted the words 'HK Police Raid Kow-Tig-Tun – TransMT sinks'.

'Oh . . . shit!'

Grabbing the mouse, I double clicked on the headline to bring up the story.

'HK Police raid premises of broker Kowloon-Tiger-Tung. Six Chinese nationals, three Japanese nationals among 19 arrested, charged with money laundering, stock manipulation. TransMare-Telco hollow in pump-'n'-dump scheme washing Triad gang drug cash. Assets disappeared or non-existent. Shares suspended. SEC notified.'

My head started spinning.

Dow Jones had the same story.

So did AP.

I wanted to scream but the little voice was already doing it. *Chump, we've been had.*

All I could manage was a feeble, 'Son of a bitch . . .' cause the little voice was right.

Not that I was ever going to admit this to Tweedle Dee and Tweedle Dum staring at me from inside their glass house, but what really pissed me off was that I should have known better.

'Oh . . . Shit!'

I knew that Kowloon-Tiger-Tung was slightly suspect. But if a trader like me stopped dealing with every broker on the planet who was slightly suspect, Wall Street would be a parking lot and there'd be no one left to play with. So it wasn't that air-raid signals should have blasted when I discovered that Kowloon-Tiger-Tung was involved. It was that I didn't recognize a 'chop' when it was stuck like a Post-It on the very end of my nose.

Been had, the little voice repeated, *been had good and stupid.*

A gang of crooks had infiltrated a brokerage, hit on a stock that didn't trade much and bought into it. They'd cold-called and hard-sold the shares, run the price up twenty-thirty-forty times, strong-armed legitimate brokers to keep from bailing out too soon, then dumped the shares on an otherwise unsuspecting market at the inflated price. That sent the shares back to a rock bottom. Presumably, the gang had also shorted the shares, so that when the roof caved in, they stood to make another wad.

It was a phenomenon becoming all too familiar around Wall Street, along with the presence of guys in small brokerage houses with shoulder-holster creased shirts and broken noses. By owning their own pipeline into the markets, organized crime easily washes whatever dirty money they have.

Still, if I was gonna be honest about this – which I was decidedly not gonna be to anyone else, 'specially Maynard and Cotton – I didn't get done by some tattooed Chinamen playing at the NASDAQ, I got done by my own greed.

I'd first read about TransMare-Telco in a tip-sheet I liked a lot called Cassandra. Apparently she was some sort of Greek princess given the power of prophecy by Apollo. The guy behind the sheet was a two-dollar-window player named Dimi Ionides, whose grandfather came from some island with an unpronounceable name in the Mediterranean and had opened a coffee shop on 9th Avenue, off 57th Street. Dimi inherited the coffee shop, which turned out to be his only qualification for picking stocks. Personally, I liked the guy. As a coffee shop owner, he committed the worst imaginable offence – selling bad coffee and yesterday's pastries – but as a stock picker, he was sometimes pretty good. He had a feel for penny shares and I'd made some dough off him for my clients. Sure, he was one of a ballpark full of guys forever touting the next Microsoft and Intel. But he'd spotted Durango Dairies five years ago at $2 and today it's at $42, and he'd spotted PharmaChem-Noga at $1.50 a year ago and today it's $18 and he'd spotted Crestiles two years ago when it looked flat on its back at 75 cents and today it's $11.50.

He was the one who put me on to TransMare-Telco, touting them at half a buck.

That was a month ago when trading on the shares was invisible. I got in at $15/16$ths, they went to $1\frac{1}{4}$ in two days and I sold at $1\frac{1}{8}$. When it slipped a bit, I bought at 1, sold at 1¾, bought in again at 2 and held on until I could sell at 3⁵⁄₁₆. It dropped to 3 and this time I got in big.

Too big.

Shit . . . much too big!

I didn't have a doubt in the world that the shares would hit 5, so I leveraged a bunch of portfolios – as a general I had big limits – brought in some of the firm's money and, to protect myself, put in a stop at 2⅞. Ionides said he was buying too and forecast $10 before the year was out.

Enough guys read his tip-sheet and it looked like enough other guys like me got in while the getting was really good because buying sent the shares straight up to $6. When they hit $7.50, I reckoned this was going to be my career maker, so I moved my own pension fund into TransMare-Telco.

What I never considered was how much of that buying was being done at gun point.

Everyone knows it's a gambler's market, which normally suited my short-term interests just fine. In the past, I'd say hey, if the Chinese want to punt and I can make a bundle on the way up there's no way I'll get caught still holding on when it nose-dives down.

But this time, obviously, it wasn't normal.

My golden rule has always been, don't gamble, trade. And following that golden rule, I normally live with trailing stops, meaning that at each stage I move my sell-orders just that much higher to keep protecting my downside. But this time I figured it different. I told myself, if I sell at $8 I can retire to Connecticut. The thing is, I was already living in Connecticut. I convinced myself, wait till it hits $15 and retire on the moon.

Instead, the Hong Kong cops broke down the door of Kowloon-Tiger-Tung and found the floors covered in worthless TransMare-Telco paper.

'You understand, of course, that we have no alternative but to reconsider your employment . . .' Maynard came out from behind the glass barrier to stand a few feet from where I was still staring blankly at the news on the screen. 'The firm's funds were not suitably protected . . .'

Associated Press was reporting, 'This was just one of eighteen separate enquiries currently being pursued by the Hong Kong authorities. The threat posed by globally organized crime is real and must be met.'

'No alternative, I'm afraid, whatsoever,' Cotton agreed, although he was staying on his side of the glass.

A spokesman for the FBI commented that while the extent of the influence of organized crime on Wall Street was not known, the TransMare-Telco case demonstrated how 'Mobs looking to launder drug profits in the world's stock markets are like buzzards circling over a herd of starving cattle.'

'Under the circumstances,' Maynard went on, 'I regret that compensation will not be forthcoming from the firm . . .'

A spokesperson for the Securities & Exchange Commission was quoted as saying that they too would be looking into the TransMare-Telco dealings. 'We cannot allow organized crime groups to edge into the canyons of Lower Manhattan, which they are doing now that their long-time control of traditional rackets has weakened.'

'We are confident,' Cotton said, 'that you understand the sensitivity of our position . . .'

Huh?' I looked up at Maynard, then at Cotton. 'What?' Out of the corner of my eyes I noticed Binterman sizing up my work-station for himself.

Cotton concluded, '. . . and that your position here has become untenable . . .'

Maynard cut in. 'If you'll check your contract you'll see that . . .'

'My contract?' That's when I finally understood. 'You're cutting me off?'

'I'm afraid,' Maynard said, 'you have left us no alternative . . .'

'Cutting me off? No alternative? Am I supposed to tell you it's too late to fire me cause I already quit?'

'Perhaps if you would prefer . . . for the sake of your résumé . . .'

'Took you long enough, didn't it?'

'What did?'

'Finding a way to get rid of me.' The little voice demanded, *kick 'em both in the balls*, but the best I could muster was a meek, 'Couldn't just do it to my face . . . no, not you guys, you needed to find some excuse.'

Maynard backed away. 'This is hardly just some excuse . . .'

'Yeah, right. We'll see about that.' I stormed out of the War Room.

We'll see about that, I repeated over and over again to myself

– quieter and quieter each time – as I went down in the elevator, through the maze of shops and out the West Side Highway door. *Yeah, we'll see about that* . . . I stopped, looked around, then had to ask myself, *now what?*

My clients had lost a fortune. My firm had lost a fortune. I was unemployed.

And I was broke.

If only the day had ended there.

Chapter Three

'I think we might be able to get out of here,' Sir Tommy said, surveying the grated hatch at the top of the elevator cage. 'If one of us could fit through that, then climb out of the lift, just past the motor, he might be able to get back through the door.'

'Sounds like a plan,' I said, sitting right where I was, motioning for him to go ahead.

'Fine. Then let's begin by shoving the grating aside. You're smaller and lighter, so if you will step up here on the seat I shall try to boost you high enough to get to the grille.'

'Me?'

'Yes, you.'

I looked up at the trap door. 'Hey, this is . . . like, dangerous. I don't want to climb on top of some elevator cage. What happens if I fall?'

'If you fall,' he pointed out, 'you will land on the roof of the lift.'

'Yeah . . . well . . . what happens if . . . I don't know, let's say I get up there and the door won't open and the elevator suddenly starts moving. What happens if the elevator crashes?'

'If it starts moving down, we shall be saved. If it crashes down, I see no practical difference between being inside the lift cage or outside. If it crashes, I suspect we'll both be killed, either way.'

'Charming,' I mumbled. 'And what if I'm up on top and the thing starts going up? I'm the one who gets squashed.'

'If it starts moving upwards, then I shall help you get back inside before it reaches the top.'

'Yeah, well, how about if I help you get back inside before it reaches the top and that way you'll be the one who doesn't get squashed?'

'Mr Doone, might I remind you, I would not be in this

predicament if it weren't for you. I am therefore asking politely, please step up here on the seat and I shall try to boost you high enough to get you through the grating.'

'Funny, but the way I see it, neither one of us would be here if you hadn't kept giving me the slip.'

'I have done nothing of the kind.'

'No, of course not. All you've done is shown enormous care and concern . . .'

'Care and concern? Mr Doone, at the risk of overstating the obvious, my concern at this very moment is about our predicament and I would be grateful if you would at least pretend to show equal care . . .'

'Care? I care about my own butt. How 'bout I boost you high enough to get you through the grating?'

He must have realized I wasn't going to give in cause he took off his blazer and handed it to me – 'If you'd be so kind' – then stepped on to the leather settee. At his height he had no trouble reaching the trap door, but almost as soon as he poked it, the grating flew up, clanked into something above it and sparks flew.

'Bloody hell,' he howled, and came off the settee, landing squarely on his feet in the middle of the elevator cage. 'What was that?'

I suggested, 'A warning that we shouldn't be fooling around up there.'

He studied the grille as if he was waiting for flames to shoot out – the possibility of which was definitely going through my mind too – then stepped back on to the settee and very gingerly pulled the grating into place.

'Be careful,' I said, cause I figured I had to say something.

Without responding, he stepped down, mumbled, 'So much for your bright idea,' brushed off the settee and sat down.

'My bright idea?' I might have argued that point had I not noticed an acrid odour. 'Do you smell something? Like burning electrical wires?'

'Ironic,' he muttered, 'having spent the morning looking forward to an afternoon of romantic pleasure, only to find oneself spending the afternoon looking forward to dying in a lift fire.'

'You always this cheerful?' There didn't seem to be any smoke and, 'cept for those sparks, there didn't appear to be anything glowing up there. 'I suppose if there's some sort of short circuit, the fuse will blow . . .'

'How comforting, Mr Doone, to know that among your many talents is electrical engineering.' He drew in a few long breaths, then volunteered, 'The odour isn't getting worse, which I take to mean that it came from those initial sparks.'

'Smoke rises,' I said. 'So does heat. If there is some sort of fire about to happen . . .'

'Would you please hand me my jacket.' I did. He hung it on the elevator door handle, slipped out of his tie – folding it meticulously before putting it in one of the blazer's pockets – then unbuttoned his collar.

When he was finished, I took off my raincoat and hung it on the door handle too, over his blazer. I dared, 'Now what?' And just as I said it, a buzzer rang upstairs.

'She's here,' he announced in a soft, almost forlorn voice. 'That's her, ringing the bell.'

'Help,' I screamed towards the bottom of the elevator shaft. 'Help. We're trapped in the elevator. Help!'

He didn't budge.

'Maybe if we both shouted . . . I mean, you're trapped in here too.'

He shook his head. 'The door is antique Hungarian oak. It's thirty feet down to the ground floor and another thirty-five or forty feet to the front of the building. The door weighs . . . I don't know, probably three hundred pounds. It's this thick.' He gestured about four inches with his fingers. 'Even if we were standing just the other side, it's doubtful that anyone would hear us.'

She rang again.

'Well . . .' I tried to think of something. 'When you don't answer, she'll get concerned. She'll phone. There won't be any answer. She'll figure that something is wrong.'

He looked at me. 'Do the women in your life worry about your health when you don't answer the door? If they do, you must be a very lucky man, Mr Doone. Unfortunately, I'm afraid, at least in my case, when I don't answer the door, women get angry and plot ways of making me pay for it the next time we meet.'

We both listened as the bell rang another eight or nine times.

I had to know. 'You stand them up once and they're willing to give you a second chance so that you can do it to them again?'

He asked me, 'Did you ever know anyone who had a dog that would bite without cause?'

'Huh?'

'Some friends of mine,' he explained, 'used to have a shih Tzu named Charlie. You know, one of those tiny Chinese dogs about the size of a large rat. Well, Charlie would bite anybody and everybody without cause. Nobody could get close. Everyone knew it and yet everyone tried. Despite all sorts of growling from him and warnings from his owners, everyone who ever met Charlie invariably got down on his or her knees and attempted to play with him. True to form, Charlie never failed to take his pound of flesh. Literally. Everyone knew he would and yet everyone always tried. Do you know why?'

'Why he bit people?'

'No. Why everyone disregarded the warnings and opted to play with him.' He didn't give me a chance to respond. 'Because everybody wanted to be the one Charlie didn't bite.'

I was expecting the woman at the front door to ring again, but she didn't.

'Do you see the point?'

I told him the truth. 'Not really.'

'Everybody wanted to be the one to claim to have tamed Charlie.' He said quietly, 'It's precisely the same with women and me.'

'What, you mean, the more flesh you rip from them, the more they come back hoping to be the one to have tamed Sir Tommy? How admirable.'

'Tell me, Mr Doone, do you always treat women admirably?'

'Admirably?' I didn't have to think about that very hard. 'I've more than my share of problems dealing with women. So maybe admirably isn't quite . . .'

'You've had problems dealing with them? Or might it be the other way around?'

'Nope. I've been the victim.'

'Mr Doone, men always see themselves as the victim. No matter how much, as you put it, flesh we rip from them, it is we who suffer. Just as it was with Charlie.'

'How did Charlie suffer?'

'Everyone wanted to stroke him. He'd bite. So he wound up never getting stroked. Sound familiar, Mr Doone?'

'Sounds pretty morbid, Sir Tommy.'

He confessed, 'I tend to get morbid when I worry, Mr Doone. And right now, thanks entirely to you, I am a very worried man.'

Chapter Four

Sue the bastards!

'Hi.'

That's what we're gonna do, the little voice kept prodding me, *we're gonna sue the bastards!*

'Happy Monday . . .'

I've got a contract, I reminded the voice, *so they can't do to me what they're doing to me.*

'Hello?'

That's right, we've got a contract so we're gonna get us a lawyer and we're gonna despatch the bastards into penury.

'I said . . . hell-o-ho . . . anybody home?'

'Huh?' I turned around to find Little Debbie standing there, grinning up at me through dark bangs that poured past her over-sized bright red glasses.

She was waving. 'Did I wake you?'

People pushed past us on their way into the building. 'Hey . . . howdy . . .'

'Are you going upstairs? Good. Let's go up together. If you let me ride upstairs with you, I'll even buy you a packet of M&Ms.'

'Ah . . . thanks . . . listen . . .' With rush hour in full swing, it seemed as if all 25,000 people who worked in the twin-tower complex were pushing past us to get to their offices. 'I'm not going upstairs.' I took her hand and moved us a few steps out of the way. 'From now on you're on your own with the Three Stooges,' I said, referring to Messrs. Maynard, Cotton and Braddock. 'I've already been upstairs and . . . I think I've just been fired.'

Her mouth opened wide. 'You think?'

'I know.'

Now her eyes got red. 'Oh my God.' And then she started to cry.

That's when Pinky rushed out of the building. 'I just heard . . .' He fought his way through the traffic. 'I missed the elevator you were on . . . I tried to catch up to you.' He threw his big flabby arms around me and squeezed tightly.

'It's okay,' I lied.

Neither of them believed me, so I stood there for a short while, getting bear-hugged by a six foot, three inch, 265-pound gay twenty-two-year-old wearing a thick black beard and a pale green yarmulke, while at the same time trying to comfort a five foot, one inch waif of a twenty-one-year-old with tears streaming down her face.

'It's okay . . . really it is.'

'They can't do this to you.' Now Pinky was crying too.

'Listen . . . guys . . . this is not going to solve anything . . .'

But neither stopped, and after a few seconds Debbie disappeared into Pinky's huge arms.

'They can't do this to you,' he wailed.

'To us,' Debbie cried from somewhere inside the huddle.

'Really, guys . . .'

Just then one of the building's security guards appeared, wanting to know what was going on.

I assured him, 'It's . . . kinda like a death in the family.'

He said, 'The thing is that they're blocking the way in and out of the building, so these two persons must desist from crying right here. If you want, these two persons, accompanied by yourself, can go off the property and cry there. But I can't have people crying at the entrance, it's against the rules.'

I had to ask, 'Against what rules?'

He decided, 'It's a fire hazard.'

'A fire hazard?'

'That's correct,' he nodded confidently. 'A fire hazard.'

'Gee . . . officer . . . we wouldn't want people in mourning to 'cause a fire . . .' I obligingly tugged Debbie and Pinky out of the way. 'No problem, officer . . . come on, guys . . . just over here . . .'

The guard waited until we were halfway down the block before he nodded contentedly and went back inside.

'They can't do this to you,' Pinky kept saying.

'They just have . . . but everything's gonna be okay.'

'You know what I'm going to do?' Pinky decided, 'I'm going to quit in protest.'

'Me too,' Debbie said. 'We'll all walk out. The entire office.' Her tears quickly turned to indignation. 'I'll organize it. I know how to do that. I led a protest once in high school. They didn't want us to have a cola machine so I got everyone together.'

'That's it,' Pinky agreed. 'We'll organize the entire office to walk out. That will teach the *gonifs* a lesson. My cousin Harry is a lawyer. I could talk to him . . .'

'They're not just *gonifs*,' Debbie cut in, 'they're also . . .' She hesitated, then blurted out, 'Schmucks.' She said it loudly and confidently, almost as if she was proud to have come up with an adult expression. 'Schmucks,' she repeated.

'*Gonifs*, maybe.' That was one of the few Yiddish expressions I knew. But then, no one could work on Wall Street for more than fifteen minutes and not know that *gonif* means crook. 'Schmucks . . . definitely. But worse than that, they're vindictive. If they knew you guys were down here plotting against them, they'd fire both of you.'

'They can't fire us,' Debbie said, 'because we're going to quit. We're coming with you. Wherever you end up, we're going to work there too.'

'Yeah, well, I haven't ended up anywhere yet this morning 'cept out on the street. So go on, get upstairs and pretend like nothing happened. Keep your jobs. I'll be all right. And I'll be in touch.'

Pinky started shaking his head. 'You got me named Rookie of the Year. I don't want this job unless you're there.'

'I didn't get you anything,' I corrected. 'I just fought your corner when the Three Stooges said they wouldn't give the Rookie of the Year Award to anyone who was . . . well, you know . . .'

All six generals sat on the Promotion and Awards Committee, the theory being that the generals would rubber stamp all decisions by the chiefs-of-staff, that way giving the impression that the landlords consulted the serfs. But when Pinky's nomination as Rookie of the Year came up – which he deserved by being able to out-trade any of the other privates – everyone chimed in with an emphatic no. 'Cept me. I knew that in their eyes Pinky had a couple of strikes against him, but that they could never come out and say one of them was the skull cap. Overt anti-Semitism along Wall Street was tantamount to suicide. So they side-stepped the issue by going after the softer target. I figured I could box them into a corner by saying that if they refused Pinky on the grounds of being gay, I'd not only phone the papers, I'd also see that the New York Association of Gay Traders moved their protest machine into the War Room. Suddenly, Maynard, Cotton and Braddock had no place to go. It didn't keep me any friends in the upper echelons at GCB, which wasn't really a problem 'cause I didn't have any friends there to begin with.

Anyway, the Chiefs-of-Staff gave Pinky the award. That was something I was proud of 'cause old man Garrison never concealed his feelings when it came to minorities of any kind, the only exception being the ultra-rich.

If God didn't want them to be minorities, he once explained, *then he would have made them like us.*

'You won it,' I reminded Pinky, ''cause you deserved it.'

'Well, you got me my job,' Debbie said.

The problem with her was totally different but absolutely typical. Old man Garrison had a loudly-enunciated but otherwise unofficial policy against hiring young single women. It had to do with fertility. Mirroring the then popular argument about admitting women into the military academies, he sincerely believed that young females were biologically unable to control their own sexual appetites and, as they were naturally wanton, their presence was not only disruptive of discipline and decorum, it also inevitably led to pregnancy.

When I first started there it was an all male shop. Just before he died, he hired half a dozen women. But they were all married and with children.

No sense training some young filly, Garrison preached, *if she's only going to be here long enough to get pregnant.*

When Maynard took over, he hired four more, two of whom were already at the tail end of their biological clock. *Their field is drying up*, he explained, *so it's time for us to plant our own crop and take advantage of the female's genetic sense of intuition to reap hearty profits.*

Then Debbie showed up.

Maynard's initial reaction was to refuse hiring her on the grounds that women were 'anatomically unruly'. Almost as soon as he said it, I threatened to bring the entire women's movement into the War Room. Luckily Maynard didn't call my bluff. Instead, he passed the buck to Cotton who, genetic coward that he was, hired her.

That Debbie had a talent for trading was never a consideration. Cotton confessed, by whispering in my ear with Maynard standing a few feet away for moral support, that he'd given her a job 'cause he felt guilty. He told me that Debbie told him she needed the money to support her ageing mama who'd once been a dancer but had broken her leg. 'Cept Debbie swore she wasn't interviewed by Cotton and that her mama is not a former dancer with a broken leg.

Still, Maynard wanted me to understand that their pity had limits, and that if Debbie didn't make the grade quickly, or wound up 'parturient' – I hurried to the dictionary and found out it means 'with child' – she'd be fired and I'd be held personally responsible.

As it turned out, Debbie was a fast learner and with each small trade gained just enough confidence to get her through a bigger trade the next time. She worked hard and made real progress real fast. And yet, she was automatically passed over for promotion to sergeant in the first round. I knew she was hurt, though she never said anything about it to me. And it bothered me too, 'though I never said anything about it to her 'cause the only reason for not promoting Debbie was to prove a point to me.

'You guys need to keep your jobs,' I insisted. 'Ya'll don't understand that if you walk out, they win.'

'But they've already won,' Debbie said, 'because they've gotten rid of you.'

'We'll see who's won,' I said, turning them both towards the door. 'Now go on upstairs.'

Debbie hesitated, then threw her arms around me and started crying again. 'I'm going to miss you.'

'Me too,' Pinky said, his arms big enough to toss around both of us. 'Me too.'

It took me several more minutes before I could disentangle myself and get them both heading back to work.

Once they'd gone inside, I asked the little voice, *now what?*

Now what? We're gonna sue the bastards.

Right. I headed for Lorilee's brother's office 'cause Duke had drawn up my contract with GCB and Duke always knew what to do.

I walked there – he was only a few blocks away – and when I got upstairs I told the receptionist that I had to see him immediately. She was reluctant to interrupt his meeting, I insisted, she went to the conference room and after a minute or two Duke came out.

He was wearing a thousand-dollar blue suit and silver snake-skin boots. 'What's going on?'

'I've just been fired.'

An odd look crept across his face. 'They can't fire you. Contract says so.'

'They think they can. And they just did.'

'I'll have to look at it real close, but if memory serves . . . let's think here a minute . . . the only thing they could possibly get you for is some sort of breach of fiduciary trust.' He wanted to know, 'Ya'll haven't breached anyone's fiduciary lately, have you?'

'No.' I shrugged. 'No . . . I mean, I haven't. It's just that, well, we had a little trouble with a company I got us into called TransMare-Telco.'

'Insider type trouble?'

'No. And I wasn't really all-that-over my discretionary limits, 'cept that I kinda fudged a few figures in order that I could get in fast and get the hell out fast . . .'

'But not fast enough?'

'Guess not.'

'So it must be fiduciary . . .'

I snapped, 'I don't know what the hell a breach of fiduciary trust is . . .'

'And I don't have time to explain it,' he said motioning towards the conference room. 'Those guys in there pay me real money so that comes in front of free advice. Look, ya'll go home. Tell Lorilee what's happened and don't worry. They're going to have to pay you a whopping big amount of money to get rid of you.' He stopped, then added, 'Unless, of course, there's been that breach of fiduciary . . .'

The voice inside my head urged, *go for blood*, so I told him, 'I want blood.' Turning on my heels and heading for the door I said, 'A whole blood bank full of blood.'

Back on the street, I tried to recall where I'd put my copy of my contract. A couple-a-three years ago, we rode a big wave for several months and my bonus was nearly as much as my salary, so I bought a little one-bedroom place for Lorilee uptown just off First Avenue. That way we'd always have someplace to stay in the city when we wanted to go to dinner or a show. I assured myself, it's probably there, and headed that way to get it. But after a few minutes I decided, the hell with it 'cause Duke must have a copy and I just think I want to go home.

Long before the opening bell sounded at the NYSE, I was on the express train back up to Grand Central and waiting for the next thing smoking to Stamford.

I bought two jumbo-sized bags of M&Ms but wound up sitting on some snail-slow local, which stopped everywhere, which meant I went through both bags. During that time, when I wasn't mumbling about how laggard the damn railroad was, I was trying to figure out how I was going to break the news to Lorilee.

The little voice inside my head stayed quiet.

By the time I got off the train, I'd decided that my best defence was a strong offence. I even rehearsed it out loud in the car as I drove home.

We're gonna fight this thing together, Lorilee. And Duke is gonna get us one mama-of-a-huge settlement. Don't you forget that I know where all the skeletons are buried at GCB . . .

I reckoned she'd fall into my arms and swoon, *course Duke is gonna do that for us 'cause he's my big brother and you're my husband and I feel safe knowing that you're both gonna protect little ol' me.*

I'd reassure her, *you bet I'm gonna protect you . . .* and then, just maybe, we'd fall into bed for a minor matinee.

A blue Porsche was parked on my side of the driveway.

Huh?

I pulled in behind it – 'cause Lorilee was real sensitive about me using her side of the driveway and not being able to get her car in and out of the garage without having to ask me to move mine – climbed out of my car, walked to the front door, unlocked it and was just about to call out to her when I heard loud pounding music coming from the back of the house.

What the hell . . .

I followed the music all the way to my bedroom, opened the door and stood there staring at some young stud pumping away bare-assed naked on top of a writhing Lorilee.

'What the hell?'

He looked up, spotted me – I recognized Manuel, her personal trainer – and froze in mid-stroke.

Then she looked at me, screamed, bucked him away – sending him over the far side of the bed, crashing to the floor – and rushed to find some sheets. 'What are you doing here?'

'Goddamn, Lorilee.'

'Get out,' she demanded.

I turned to Manuel and motioned towards the door. 'That means you.'

'No,' she screeched, 'I'm talking to you. Get the hell out of here.'

'I live here.'

She reached over to the night table, grabbed a clock and tossed it at my head. It missed.

Without saying a word – the little voice screamed, *bitch!* – I swung on my heels and stormed out, heading straight back to my car, driving straight back to the station, and getting on the first train going straight back to New York.

Long before anyone on Wall Street even started to think about lunch, I was in Grand Central Station, marching along Platform 37, heading for an uptown subway.

For the next two hours I couldn't focus on anything.

I just kept pacing through the apartment. Going from the bedroom to the living room. Then back to the bedroom. Picking up all of my ten pillows off the bed and throwing them down again. Then marching into the living room. Before returning to take my vengeance out on my pillows.

The only thing that interrupted my routine was the phone. I guessed it was Lorilee, so I marched over to the answering machine and switched it on.

Instead, it was my mama sobbing uncontrollably.

'What's going on?' I grabbed it, got an earful of feedback from the answering machine, snapped the damn thing off and now got another earful of weeping. 'What are you crying about?'

She couldn't talk sense for nearly five minutes, until I convinced her to take a shot of bourbon – she always kept a bottle in the kitchen cupboard on the same shelf as the peanut butter – which shortly calmed her down enough to string a couple-a-three words together. 'It's my apartment.'

'What happened?'

'It's the bank.'

'What bank?'

'The bank.'

'Your bank?'

'The other bank.'

'Mama, I don't understand what's going on.'

'Wait.' She put the phone down and I heard her traipse back to the kitchen. A few seconds later I heard her slam the cupboard door shut and knew she'd taken another hit of bourbon. When she finally picked up the phone again, she was better, but only just. 'It's the bank. The one who owns my apartment.'

'No bank owns your apartment. It's all paid off.'

'Not the mortgage . . .'

I started to say, 'There is no mortgage . . .' when, suddenly, a terrible thought dawned on me – she was only sixty-eight and if this was a first sign of Alzheimer's . . . 'There's nothing to worry about.' I'd spoken to her two days before and she was fine. She'd always been fine. Now, the thought of her starting to go loony . . . I needed to get my own life back together before figuring out what the hell to do about hers. 'Mama, listen to me . . . your mortgage is paid off. 'Member, after we sold the house in Boston, we used what was left of papa's pension fund to buy the apartment . . . 'member the house in Boston?'

'Don't ya'll go on treating me like I'm some sort of crazy old woman, hear?' That second belt of booze had clicked in – now she was angry. 'Course I remember the house in Boston. But I'm telling you that the bank . . . I don't know its damn name . . . it's just a bank . . . something Federal . . .'

'Mama, we paid off your mortgage a long time ago. Like ten years ago. It was at—' I tried to recall '—Barnett Bank. Ya'll know the one . . . just off West Lantana Road? 'Member we went in there together . . .'

'Not that bank,' she snapped. 'Federal something. The bank where I had to put the sweepstakes . . . the money I won . . . that bank.'

'What money you won?'

'The money I won that I never told you about 'cause I didn't really win it . . . 'cause it's kind of like a mortgage . . . I don't know, your papa always took care of these kinds of things and then you used to and when they told me I had to sign, I did what they all said I had to do. Now they're telling me that I gotta get out within ninety days.'

'Who's telling you that?'

'The bank,' she said loudly. 'They're the ones holding my damn mortgage.'

'You signed another mortgage?'

'That's what I just told you and now they're telling me . . .'

Alzheimer's Light struck me as a much better alternative. 'Mama . . . I need to look at all the paperwork. You got copies of everything, don't you?'

'I don't know.' She was crying again.

'It's going to be all right, mama. Is there a Kinko's somewhere near you? Or any place where you can make photocopies and where they also have a fax machine? You gotta find one of those places and take whatever paperwork you have, including whatever letter says you have to get out, and fax it to me. And you gotta do it today.'

'If I can find someone to fax it for me . . .'

'They'll do it for you at one of those photocopy places. Now, get a paper and pen so I can give you my fax number.'

'I've already got it jotted down somewhere . . . your office . . .'

'No. Fax it to me at the apartment.'

'Why? Where are you now? 'Cause I couldn't find you when I phoned your office and there was no answer at home . . .'

'I'm at the apartment.' I didn't feel like going through all the explanations I'd eventually have to go through. 'Got that paper and pen?' When she had it, I gave her the number. 'Now tell me exactly who it is who wants you out of your apartment.'

She said the fellow who signed the letter was someone called Alexander George and that his company was called South Florida Island Federal Finance. She gave me his address, which was a post office box in Miami, and an 800 number.

After spending a few more minutes reassuring her that everything would be all right, I decided she was calm enough to drive to a fax machine. I only hoped no cop would ask her on the way to blow up a breathalyzer balloon.

Hanging up with her, I dialled the 800 number, heard a woman answer – not using the name South Florida Island Federal Finance but instead repeating the phone number – and asked for Mr George.

Right away she said, 'I'm sorry Mr George is not available.'

I tried, 'When will he be available?'

She said, 'I'm sorry, I can't tell you that. If you would leave your name and phone number, someone will get back to you.'

I did.

No one ever bothered.

I said to the voice, *I'll be damned if I'm gonna call Lorilee.*

The voice suggested, *try Duke instead.*

I thought about that, figured maybe telling Duke what had happened wasn't such a bad idea, and phoned him.

First, his secretary said he was on another call. Then, after a few minutes she said he was out. From the way she said it, I got the distinct impression he wasn't gonna take my call. I didn't know what he knew so I left a simple message. 'Please tell him that I need to speak with him. I'm uptown at the apartment. Please ask him to phone me as soon as possible.'

She said he would.

He didn't.

Waiting for the phone to ring wasn't going to stop me from getting on with my life, so I booted-up my laptop computer, typed in 'Celtics' which was my entry code, and went to a file I called 'Contacts'. One by one, I went through an entire list of folks around town, looking for where I held markers. At some time or other I'd scratched a few backs so now, I reckoned, it was time to get mine clawed.

It took about an hour but after going through a couple of hundred names, I settled on an even dozen, banking that my dart-board theory of life would see me through yet again.

It goes like this: If you want to hit a bull's-eye, don't get bogged down worrying 'bout how far away the dart-board is or where you're standing or how good you can aim. So long as you can see it and reach it, the most important factor is how many darts you have 'cause, eventually, if you throw enough darts, you'll hit the target.

I'd worked it out during my senior year of high school, a logical extension of my never-ending string of fantasies for cheerleaders, though I didn't get to put the theory into practice all that much till I started at Boston College. For the sake of science, I had to give up on cheerleaders – I hated to concede that the college kind were too old for me but they never hesitated to point out that I was too young for them

– and decided to limit my test sample to blonde, blue-eyed freshmen.

I walked around the campus during my first few months, going up to total strangers – always of the blonde, blue-eyed freshmen variety – asking outright, ya'll wanna have an affair with me? Not surprising, I got turned down a helluva lot. Not surprising, I also got slapped a helluva lot. But, to the utter amazement of my pals, I scored more than they did.

Just keep throwing darts, the little voice was forever reminding me.

Since then, I've lived by the theory.

Now, looking at my list of a dozen solid contacts, I told myself this was more than enough to hit at least one bull's-eye.

'Hey, Harry, it's K.C. How ya'll doing?'

'Word's out on you, man,' he said. 'Sorry but there's nothing here for you.'

'Hey, Mick, it's K.C. How ya'll doing?'

'Heard you flamed out,' he said. 'Hope you find something else.'

'Hey, Suzie, it's K.C. How ya'll doing?'

'Wow, man, rumour going around that you've become the plague.'

'Hey, Abe, it's K.C. How ya'll doing?'

'I gotta tell you, old boy, when you piss someone off, you truly do it with style.'

I changed my tack.

'Sam, this is K.C. Doone. What about lunch one day this week?'

'Sorry, pal, I'm busy for the rest of my life.'

'Hey, that Caroline? This is K.C. Doone. Ya'll up for a couple of drinks one evening this week?'

'Too bad but I think I just quit drinking.'

'Hey, Billy, it's K.C. Doone. How about a couple of good old southern boys doing some barbecue one lunchtime this week?'

'Sorry pardner, my job ain't secure enough these days.'

'Paddy, this is K.C. Doone. How about a couple of die-hard Red Sox fans getting together for some baked beans and a discussion about life?'

''Fraid life isn't long enough.'

I changed my tack yet again.

'Listen, Arnie, this is K.C. Doone and I'm calling to ask a favour.'

'Wish I could help you but there's nothing open with us. Hope you find something.'

'Hello, Joyce? It's K.C. Doone. Once upon a time, when the world was long on Intel, I talked you into going short and you made a lot of bucks for your clients, so I was figuring, 'cause we were such a good team that we ought to find a way to put our heads together again.'

'I'll tell you, K.C., right now the world is long on me and short on you, so I think I'll pass.'

'Tony, this is K.C. Doone. 'Member when you and I set our sights on those Canadian mining shares and moved enough, single-handedly, to put the price up by nearly a nickel?'

'Those were good times, my man, but I ah . . . I think I'd better pass . . . you understand.'

'Bobby, if my memory serves me correct, when you moved into that big office of yours, ya'll said to me, K.C., I've got you to thank for this so if you ever need anything . . . well, I need.'

'Yeah, sure, K.C. I remember . . . but . . . well, it's like this . . . there's nothing open here . . . I mean if anything comes up . . . maybe we'll do lunch some day . . .'

I was just about to say, 'How about tomorrow?' when he hung up.

The little voice chimed in, *looks like the chances of finding something right away are slim to none*, and after thinking 'bout all those folks who didn't want to know, I had to admit, *and slim just left town. Sunnuvabitch!*

Gotta just keep throwing darts, the voice urged me on.

Screw you, I said, grabbed the phone and dialled GCB.

If Yolanda, the smart operator, answered, I'd try to disguise my voice. But Frannie, the dumb one, took the call, so I didn't bother. 'Debbie Adjmi, please.'

There was a click and she picked up the phone. 'This is Debbie.'

'This is the guy you bumped into on the street,' I said. 'Go to a pay phone and call me back. I'm at my apartment.'

'Everybody here is talking about you . . .'

'Call me straight back,' I said and hung up.

It took nearly ten minutes before she did. 'I couldn't get out right away . . .'

'Where are you calling from?'

'Downstairs. I took a break and came down to the pay phones near the bookstore.'

'Never call me from the office.' I didn't have to remind her that dealing rooms record phone calls on the pretext that all trades must be verifiable. In reality, very few trades are ever questioned to the point that someone has to dig through millions of hours of taped conversations. The real reason is, taped phone calls keep traders in New York from romancing their girlfriend in Hawaii on the company's time. 'What's going on in the office? What are the Three Stooges saying?'

'They've been locked in meetings and making calls all morning. They must be talking about you because everybody is.'

'What are they saying?'

'I don't know because no one is saying it to me. Except a few people near my work-station who said that you'd gone over your limits. And that creep Binterman who keeps saying he saw it coming and has already moved into your work-station.'

'Binterman . . . what a surprise.'

'I got your Giants helmet with the M&Ms. And your binoculars. But I couldn't get your cell phone or anything else. They confiscated it all right away.'

'Thanks,' I said, 'cause I didn't want her to think I wasn't grateful. 'Listen . . . I need a favour.'

She was the first one all day to say, 'Sure.'

'I need you to find out what they're telling people. Can you do that for me?'

'How?'

'Good question.'

'Should I ask one of them?'

'Bad idea.'

'Then how?'

'Well, maybe you can quietly ask a few other people what they've heard. See what some of the people you trade with have heard. I need to know what the word is on the street.'

'Okay, I'll try.'

Then I added, 'Don't call me at home. Only here at the apartment. Got that?'

She didn't ask why. 'Okay.'

'Oh . . . and don't let anyone at GCB know we've spoken. Be very careful. If they find out you're talking to me, they'll fire you.'

'Is that all?' She put on her best bravado tone. 'Who cares if they do?'

'You should,' I said. 'Take it from someone who's becoming an expert on the subject the hard way. It's worse than you think.'

After a while, I decided I was hungry and 'cause there wasn't anything in the fridge – just one stick of butter and a couple of bottles of Cold Duck champagne – I went down the block to the Korean market on the corner where I picked up a turkey on lettuce with tomato and Russian dressing, a Dr Brown's Cel-Ray tonic, a big tin of pretzels and a jumbo bag of M&Ms. As long as everything else in my world had gone to the dogs, I figured my diet could as well.

By the time I got back to the apartment, the fax from my mama – nine pages worth – was waiting for me. I sat down on the couch, spread out my lunch and tried to figure out what was going on. But even after I read the whole thing three times, I still couldn't make hide nor hair of it.

There was one letter about a sweepstakes – saying that her name had been chosen to go into a multimillion-dollar draw – then a bunch of letters from South Florida Island Federal Finance Company confirming her acceptance of what looked to me to be some sorta re-mortgage terms. But there was no contract. Another letter, a medley of double-talk, came from a company called Padre Island Finance Management Services with a post office box in Brownsville, Texas. Finally there was a letter – the gist of which was that they were calling in her loan and converting it to a receipt of sale – from a company called Eton Island Finance Management and Trust Company. Their address was a post office box in Freeport, Grand Bahama.

It didn't take a cop's kid to know a scam when he saw one.

Or a nuclear scientist to know that I had to act fast to protect my mama from whatever sharks were out there.

So I got Information on the phone and asked for the number of the Lantana District Attorney's office and when I dialled it I eventually got through to a fellow who told me that any serious wrongdoing in a case like this would probably be handled by the

State Attorney General. He gave me that number in Tallahassee. I dialled it and a woman there said that the best thing I could do was contact their office in West Palm Beach.

The man I spoke with in West Palm was helpful, but after hearing my mama's story, he said 'cause the Eton Island address was foreign, the best thing I could do was call the US Attorney's office in Miami. So that was the next thing I did. A woman there suggested that 'cause my mama lived in Lantana, any complaints should be filed with their office in . . . she hesitated, then suggested, how about Fort Lauderdale. I never thought to ask if there was a US Attorney's office any closer to my mama's place 'cause I naturally assumed the woman would have told me if there was. So after she gave me the number, I called Fort Lauderdale.

I explained to the woman who answered there what the problem was – that took nearly fifteen minutes 'cause she asked all sorts of questions that I didn't really know the answers to – before putting me on to someone who introduced himself as Assistant US Attorney Ira E. Babcock. I told him as much as I knew of the story, and he listened attentively, but after almost twenty minutes, all he could suggest was that, either I put my complaint in writing and forward it to his office or stop in and fill out the usual forms. I asked, 'Have you ever heard of South Florida Island Federal Finance or Padre Island Finance Management Services or Eton Island Finance Management and Trust Company? Or—' I checked to find the name of the guy who'd signed that first letter . . . '—how about someone called Alexander George?'

His response was, 'I'm afraid I cannot give out any information over the phone.'

I said, 'Well, can ya'll give out any information if I show up?'

He said, 'Your complaint will be appropriately dealt with.'

I said, 'I don't know what that means, but how's tomorrow afternoon?'

He said, 'You don't need an appointment. Someone will see you when you get here.'

I said, 'Okay, I'll be there tomorrow,' hung up with him and dialled Delta Airlines.

In the old days – meaning life that morning – I could afford to pay for first-class tickets, which I usually wound up doing 'cause

Lorilee reckoned that only peasants flew tourist class. Looking back, maybe that's one of the reasons why, after I married her, I never had more than nine bucks in my pocket. This time I had the presence of mind to convince myself it might be prudent to be a peasant. I asked, how much, and blanched when they told me what steerage from LaGuardia to Lauderdale costs. I'd forgotten all that stuff 'bout having to book a seat three weeks in advance, stay over a Saturday night, wear a green baseball cap, bring your own lunch and change your name to Walter.

Putting the phone down with them, I tried to recall where I'd once seen a list of bucket shops bragging 'bout cheapo tickets to anywhere, decided it must have been the Travel Section of the Sunday *New York Times*, but didn't have the paper and couldn't think of anywhere else to get the numbers 'cept the Yellow Pages. So I wound up sifting through them.

Some guy named Hassan said he could get me to Lauderdale tomorrow for $68 return, but only if I changed planes in Winston Salem, North Carolina. Another guy, this one named Hussein, said he had pull with all the airlines, could do anything I wanted and offered me a seat to Lauderdale later tonight for $73 round trip. Unfortunately, he said, he couldn't guarantee getting me back to New York tomorrow, or ever – 'Some things, mister, are only in the hands of God' – though he said he did know of a way to get me priority on the stand-by list for any flight into Newark, over in New Jersey. A guy named Prakash said he could get me to Miami tonight for $55 one-way, and then probably get me back to New York from either Miami or Orlando the following day for the same fare, but only if I didn't mind using someone else's name. Eventually I found an American called Joe who said he'd happily backdate a ticket for me to Lauderdale for $135 return, which sounded great, till he remembered to add, 'But, oh yeah, you got to stay a Saturday night.'

I wound up putting my faith in my new friend Hussein. 'When does that flight leave?'

'Mister, when do you want to leave?'

'How 'bout some time in the next half-hour?'

With only enough time for a fast shower, and only enough clothes at the apartment for one change, I did thirty seconds under a hard spray and stuck a couple of things into a gym bag, headed out the door, got a taxi to the airport and was climbing on to the six o'clock for Lauderdale when I realized I left the sandwich half-eaten on the coffee table, left the pretzels and the jumbo bag of M&Ms unopened on the couch, forgot to turn the answering machine back on, left the computer on, forgot to take my razor and toothbrush, and left my fortieth birthday present to myself – a Vacheron tank watch – sitting on the shelf under the mirror in the bathroom.

With that simmering near the boil in my mind, I found myself on a totally full plane, stuck in the next-to-last row between an old lady who needed a bath and a very fat man who, as soon as we took off, pulled three melted cheese sandwiches out of his carry-on and proceeded to eat them all.

Then, somewhere over Georgia I realized that I didn't have any place to stay. So when we landed, I phoned my mama and told her I was going to drive up to Lantana, which was a pretty dumb way of arranging this 'cause it would have been simpler to fly into West Palm Beach, stay with her and then drive down to Lauderdale. Anyway, I rented the cheapest car I could find, stopped at an all-night Eckerd's drugstore to buy a toothbrush, a razor and some shaving cream, and finally got to her place just before 11 p.m.

She constructed a fried peanut butter and banana sandwich for me, I reassured her that everything was going to be all right and by the time she made up the couch and I lay down, it was past midnight.

I shut my eyes and told myself, *today it is Tuesday.*

The voice reminded me, *Monday is finally over.*

I promised myself, *Tuesday is when everything starts to get better.*

The voice agreed, *sounds like a plan.*

I have seldom been so wrong.

Chapter Five

He sat perfectly still.

So did I.

'Cept he was gnashing his teeth.

I tried to ignore the noise but when you're stuck in an elevator with someone and they're sitting right next to you, gnashing their teeth like that, after a few minutes it's downright impossible to ignore. 'Hey, what do ya'll say we get one thing straight?'

He glared at me. 'I beg your pardon?'

'How 'bout, as long as you and I are gonna be here for a while, how 'bout we agree that this isn't my fault and ya'll stop making that noise just to annoy me.'

'But it is your fault.'

'The hell it is.' I pointed my finger in his chest. 'If ya'll hadn't been avoiding me, leaving town every time I showed up . . . did you really think I was going to give up . . . ? I'm warning you, get it through that shiny bald head of yours or . . .'

He opened his eyes very wide. 'Or?'

I admitted, 'I'd just love to knock your over-gnashed teeth down your damn throat.'

He paused. 'However?'

I took a deep breath and pulled my finger out of his chest. 'However . . .' I had to concede, 'the object of the exercise is not to send you to the dentist.'

'Surely not,' he said calmly.

'So would ya'll do me a favour and please stop grinding your teeth?'

He shrugged, then shook his head to show me that he was fed up with me. 'Mr Doone . . . you are a pain.'

But at least he stopped.

I waited for several minutes before I wondered, 'Don't ya'll have a lot of people hanging 'round? Won't somebody figure out that you're missing?'

'Except that I am not missing,' he insisted. 'I am stuck here with you.'

'What happens when you don't show up . . . I don't know . . . like for dinner or something? Your chauffeur . . . what time is he supposed to come back here to get you?'

'I have more than one chauffeur and more than one residence, and when I'm not in one place the people at that residence naturally assume I am at another.'

'How about all your wives?'

He raised his eyebrows as if to tell me I obviously didn't understand much. 'It's the same thing.'

Now I had to ask, 'And just how the hell can you live with more than one wife?'

'How the hell can you live with only one?'

'It's called bigamy.'

'Bigamy is merely a word.'

'Where I come from bigamy is also a problem.'

'Bigamy is only a problem if one of the people being bigamized bothers to complain.'

'I've always had my hands full keeping one from complaining. And you've got . . . three?'

'How do you know that?'

'I've done my homework.'

'Homework?' He wanted to know, 'Have you memorized me the way students cram for an English exam?'

'More like the way I learned Shakespeare.'

'Play by play?'

'Cliff Notes,' I said.

'What does that mean?'

'Crib sheets. You know, summaries. Outlines. No sense reading the whole thing when you can whip right through the abbreviated version.'

'Hamlet in six paragraphs?'

'Thomas d'Aquin Whitestone in three wives.'

He grinned. 'It's true that I have, over the years, had several.'

'Paragraphs?'

'Those, as well. But I'm referring to wives. At the moment I have only two. Although I maintain three families. It appears that there is currently a vacancy in the wife department.'

'But no vacancy in the girlfriend department,' I reminded him. 'Or was the lady scheduled for this afternoon here to audition?'

'Vacancies occur from time to time,' he explained, making it understood that he took this very seriously. 'When one marries one's mistress that creates an obvious vacancy. The lady this afternoon was . . . yes, you might put it that way . . . hoping to fill a possible vacancy.'

'Wife number four?'

'No. Mistress number three.'

'An expensive hobby,' I mumbled.

'Hobby is not the word I would choose. That implies something is strictly recreational. In this case, it is more about re-creation. As for expensive . . . there too I would be cautious, Mr Doone, because expensive is a relative term. What might seem expensive to one person is a mere bagatelle to another.'

'What's a bagatelle?'

'Something that is not expensive,' he responded, as if I should have known that. 'Of course, where you Americans are concerned, you take the rather barbaric attitude of avoiding certain important expenses by simply walking away.'

'Huh?'

'The moment you divorce a woman, you also jettison your family. You toss the family out with the woman. I prefer the more civilized way. I always take care of my family.'

'That's what you call civilized,' I said, more as a statement than a question.

'Of course, it is,' he answered, thinking it had been a question. 'When it's over in America, it's over. You set up a family with someone, live there for a time, then move on and don't look back. Is that civilized? Hardly. Nor is it what I would call good manners.'

'Who moves on and doesn't look back?'

'You Americans. One reads from time to time about expensive divorce settlements, but that's the easy way out. Granted, it is often also the least expensive way out. But that is not, however, the way I conduct my life. If I establish a family with someone, I never leave them. I maintain the expenses of that family, at all costs.'

'In other words, you pay the bills but still move on.'

'It's not the moving on that matters . . . of course I may move on . . . and yes, of course I pay the bills. The most important thing is that the relationships are maintained. I'll have you know that I am on the best of terms with all of my wives and all of my mistresses, past and present.'

I thought of that woman on Park Avenue, but I never got her name and decided there was something wrong 'bout referring to her now, at least in this context, as that woman on Park Avenue. Instead I confessed, 'I still can't figure how can you juggle all those women . . . kinda like Indian clubs . . . you know, and never have one of them come crashing down on to your toes.'

'I suppose, one might say, it is much like the way I deal with several chauffeurs. They all have their own cars and they all have their own garages. It gets down to a workable separation of responsibilities.'

'You mean like my wife and me . . . I don't park in her space.'

He grinned. 'Or drive her car.'

'Ya'll mean, as long as everyone knows which car they're supposed to drive and where they're supposed to park it . . .' I nodded. 'Yeah, sounds like a plan.'

'It is a plan. A very workable plan.'

'But doesn't it sorta turn you into being the local corner gas station?'

'Turn me into what?'

'Fill 'er up.'

He thought about that, then started to laugh. 'Fill 'er up, indeed.' He nodded. 'I like that, Mr Doone.'

I told him sarcastically, 'Somehow I knew you'd be susceptible to flattery.'

We fell quiet again.

It was several more minutes before he turned to me. 'That wasn't flattery.'

And I found myself confessing, 'No, I reckon it wasn't.'

Chapter Six

It was my papa Joe's South Boston Irish whiskey blood that warmed me during those bitter cold Bean-town winter mornings of my childhood, and my mama Ruby's Tennessee moonshine-mash blood that flowed through my pores during those stifling, airless Great Smoky Mountain summer nights of my teenage years. It was my old man who tried to teach me to brawl and my mama's old man who tried to teach me to hunt squirrel. The only problem being that I wound up with my papa's brains and my mama's brawn. I was too chicken to pull the trigger, and too afraid to get punched, so I never amounted to much in my grandfather's eyes, 'cause I never killed a squirrel, and didn't amount to much in my papa's eyes, 'cause I was forever running away from getting the crapola kicked out of me.

It wasn't until I moved to New York that I discovered the best way I could manage basic survival skills was by winding Back Bay flat vowels 'round backwoods L'il Abner awe-shucks, 'cause it frequently confused men and often amused ladies. I even practised real good till I could turn it on and off like a spigot.

Academically, I might have had what it takes to do something meaningful with my life but I never got much of a chance to prove it. I started up north, got tossed out of Boston College in my sophomore year for running book on Celtics' games, headed south and, a year later, got tossed out of Tennessee State for shacking up with the daughter of a revivalist preacher who also happened to sit on the school's funding committee.

By the age of twenty I was resolved to the fact that all my serious options for ensured future success had scuttled out the door.

If I'd have had my druthers, I'd have opted to play pro-basketball but that was never gonna work out, not 'cause I was too short –

which at only five-eleven I was – but 'cause I don't have any real athletic ability. With hindsight, that's what also kept me from playing pro-baseball, pro-football, and pro-hockey, too.

Not having a clue what I was gonna do with the rest of my life, I turned down a job flogging real estate in Memphis – even without a future I still had higher ambitions than that – and wound up doing the only logical next thing that came along, which was getting myself a job in Boston flogging penny shares by phone to taxi drivers.

Hello, sir, my name is K.C. Doone and I was just wondering if, while you're stuck in traffic all day, going back and forth through the tunnel to Logan Airport or just trying to manoeuvre your way along Tremont Street, ya'll ever ask yourself, isn't it about time I secured my family's financial future with an investment in peanut oil?

I met my first wife Marylou at my papa's wake. He was twenty-nine years on the Boston Police Force, which means he should have known better than winding up getting killed trying to stop some teenage drug dealer from shooting another teenage drug dealer. I can only pray that it made some sort of sense to him at the time 'cause it has never, nor will it ever, make a helluva lot of sense to me. Anyway, Marylou, who was hustling mutual funds for State Street Bank, was the daughter of one of his cop friends. I don't know why she was there but she got as drunk as I did, spent an hour with me in the upstairs bathroom, and wound up saying yes to my marriage proposal somewhere between the cemetery and Las Vegas. That lasted exactly five months and three days. One month for non-stop sex. Four months for non-stop quibbling. And three days for a quickie divorce in Mexico. After it was over, she confessed that she could have managed it all in five months and one day but that the weather was good down there in Mexico and the hotel had a swimming pool, so she turned our quickie divorce into a long weekend.

I eventually admitted to her, what the hell, I'd have done the same thing.

'Cause Marylou made a living and I didn't, she got everything we had. All I got to keep was my Bill Russell autographed basketball, my collection of Elvis albums, the $200 pair of Nikes she bought me as a wedding present and the American flag they'd draped over my papa's coffin.

I stayed single for the next six years, during which time I moved to New York and, in a one-man attempt to get respectable, went from cold-calling on the phone to cold-banging on doors in office buildings within a four-block radius of Wall Street.

Then I met Carrie.

She worked as a weather girl on a New Jersey radio station and turned my head good. She was downright beautiful and spent most of her time practising yoga, which meant she was always running around in see-through leotards and coming up with weird positions to have sex. That suited me fine until the night I ended up writhing in pain, mostly naked, in the back of an ambulance on my way to the Emergency Room at Bellevue. Some young know-it-all in a white jacket, a snotty kid barely old enough to spell chiropractor, decided he could fix me up with a twist here and a snap there, which promptly sent me into wails of agony and three weeks' worth of traction. During that time Carrie started doing more than yoga with her yoga instructor and by the time I came home she'd moved out. The furniture was gone. So were my Nikes. So were my Elvis albums. I still had my basketball and my flag, but the thought of her yoga instructor wearing my sneakers galled me for months. At least till I discovered I had a minor dose of athlete's foot and that, given any real justice in life, he'd catch it. Then, 'cause feet were a regular part of her thing, I took genuine comfort in knowing that, eventually, she'd wind up with athlete's mouth.

After Carrie, I vowed to stay single for ever, or at least until I died, whichever came first. And I almost made it.

I bounced 'round a bunch of small firms, learning how to trade, till I got myself a job at GCB and started getting promoted up the dollar-sign dotted gold carpet. It was plainly evident early on that I was never gonna be part of Maynard and Cotton's masterplan for the universe. But as long as Old Man Garrison was still alive, and as long as I kept bringing him new business, no one had much choice but to keep promoting me. If nothing else, Old Man Garrison stuck by the regs. Before too long I was making what seemed to me to be some pretty good numbers, which led me to the understandable conclusion that I'd finally found my niche.

During those years I went through a string of ladies, at least that's the way I looked at it till one of those ladies suggested that what was really happening was that a string of them were going through me. I was still pondering that when I met Lorilee.

This time, I never stood a chance.

Here I was, closing in fast on forty, looking forward to several more years' worth of a mid-town bachelor's life which, 'cause much younger ladies were involved, had the added benefit of keeping my stomach flat. There she was, just twenty-two, all innocent-like, up from Nashville to hang out with her big-deal lawyer big brother till she could get herself a job as a model. Here I was, never giving much thought to what I was gonna do when I grew up – 'cause ducking and diving had worked okay so far – and there she was, with all that blond hair and that tiny store-bought nose, and those big blue doe-eyes and those neat, pointy breasts dancing around loose inside her silk blouse. Here I was, suddenly walking around all day with a semi-permanent erection 'cause I couldn't get my mind off her, even though deep down I guess I've always kinda known that when the blood rushes out of my head like that I wind up in trouble. And there she was, ready, willing and able to do something about it the moment I slipped a ring on her finger.

So that's what I did.

I slipped a ring on her finger, slipped her between the sheets, slipped myself into her and we stayed that way for much of the next three years.

At least, till yesterday.

'How's Lorilee?'

I opened my eyes to find my mama setting the breakfast table. 'Ah . . . well, she's been pretty busy,' I said, wondering what time it was.

'Did you tell her about the bank and my mortgage and everything?'

'Ah . . . she's been pretty busy . . . she's got other things on her . . . you know, kinda on her mind.'

''Cause maybe her brother . . . he being a lawyer and everything . . .'

I pulled myself off the couch, stepped into my pants, and moved to the sliding glass doors at the far end of the living room that led out to the terrace. 'Yeah, I gotta phone Duke later . . .'

She poured me a cup of coffee and asked if I wanted toast or something. 'How about some Puffed Rice?'

I smiled, 'Not this morning,' and thought to myself, *that's what mamas are supposed to be, someone who remembers to come up with the same breakfast cereal you ate when you were a kid.*

'I didn't want to send these by fax . . .' She reached over to the chair on the other side of the table and picked up a whole pile of papers. 'I didn't . . . actually, I couldn't 'cause it would have cost too much.'

'You mean there's more?' I needed two hands to take them all. 'Let me see.' Sorting through those papers, I determined that in order to win the fortune they promised her in this phoney sweepstakes game, she had to keep playing, and in order to keep playing, she had to send money. In all, she'd paid them $800.

That some con man had managed to bilk her out of her retirement money infuriated me.

That the scam didn't end there put me into a fighting rage.

She explained that a 'Sweepstakes Executive' showed up at her front door bearing a cheque made out to her for $42,500 but that before he could give it to her, he said she needed to open a 'fortune sweepstakes bonanza' account at a bank and also sign some standard 'winners' forms. Seeing him dangle the cheque was clearly more than she could cope with, so she signed. Yet, instead of handing her the cheque, he explained that, just like the way the Florida Lottery works, this prize too would be paid off over a period of several years. He then promised that her cheque would be safely deposited in a specially designated account with her name on it. But before he could do that, she had to fill out some signature cards. And before she realized what was going on, he was out the door with her $42,500 and paperwork effectively turning over her apartment.

A month later, a statement arrived from that operation called Padre Island Finance Management Services confirming that a $42,500 deposit had been made into her account with them but that the balance currently available to her was only $250. There was no mention of whether or not interest was being paid on this account, how or when the full balance would be made available or, for that matter, if she would ever get at any of the money.

A month after that, a second statement arrived from Padre Island Finance Management Services, this one noting a further $250 of available balance. The following month, a third $250 was made available to her. And attached to that statement was a 'winner's bonus check' made out to her for $50.

What they'd done was simply reimburse her the $800 she'd already paid them.

There were no more letters from Brownsville, Texas. The next batch was from Eton Island Finance Management and Trust Company saying that they were foreclosing on her mortgage and, as rightful owners of her property, advising her that she had ninety days to vacate.

I didn't understand how they could refuse her the right to pay off the mortgage till I went back to the sweepstakes paperwork to read the small print.

And was there ever a lot of small print!

Wrapped around a mountain of legalese, what I think it said was that they'd purchased my mama's apartment for $42,500 – about two-thirds of its real value – and that she'd be lucky to get anywhere near that much 'cause they had the right to withhold from that money any expenses entailed in taking possession of the apartment.

'What's it mean?' she wanted to know.

I couldn't bring myself to tell her the truth. 'No matter what this says, I say it's gonna be all right.'

She gave me one of her long looks, then said softly, 'I guess I've been had?'

'I don't know, mama.'

'Well, I know. You don't live with a policeman for twenty-nine years and not know something like that. I didn't want to tell you but they said I had to get out.'

'You're not going anywhere. Not now. Not in ninety days.'

'I knew I was in trouble,' she said, 'when Aggie next door told me she was a winner too.'

'Huh?'

'My friend Aggie. She won the sweepstakes too.'

I thought about that. 'Anybody else in the building win anything recently?'

'I don't know.' She admitted, 'I was too ashamed to ask.'

'How many apartments are here?'

'Twenty-two.'

I got up, walked out on to her balcony and studied as much of the tiny complex as I could see.

She followed me.

'Any of those apartments empty?'

She explained, 'My friend Betsy and her husband . . . they lived over there on the ground floor . . . they left about two weeks ago. Very sudden. Never even said good-bye. I knew he wasn't well so I just figured they moved back up north where their son lives. Somewhere outside Chicago. Then . . .' she pointed across the court '. . . I heard from Aggie that two apartments just came empty on the second floor. One belonged to a man from Pennsylvania. He lost his wife about a year ago but he kept to himself all the time. I didn't know him, 'cept to nod hello. And the other apartment . . . I don't know a single thing 'bout them, 'cept that they were from upstate New York, somewhere in the Finger Lake district, and their daughter works for an insurance company in Ohio. They have four grandchildren and the oldest one, a girl, just got accepted to Ohio State on a language scholarship. She speaks perfect Russian.'

'You say these are people ya'll don't know a single thing about?'

She assured me, 'Not a single thing.'

I stared at the empty apartments, then wondered, 'How often do you get a bill for service charges?'

'Every month.'

'How much is it?'

'Well, let me think . . . it was around $175 but it's gone up a lot over the past three or four months, what with those people gone . . . now it's almost double what it used to be.'

I said to the little voice, *someone's trying to empty this place.*

And the voice responded, *if only we were this smart when it came to marrying people.*

It wasn't yet 9 o'clock but Duke always got in early and the way Duke moved through the day, early was the best time to reach him. I was counting on him to help my mama. First, though, I needed to talk to him about his sister. So I told my mama that I had to make a private phone call and she left me alone for a few minutes. I dialled New York and, just like yesterday, wound up talking to Duke's secretary. She said she'd check to see if he was there and put me on hold. When she came back she said he hadn't come in yet. I didn't know if she was telling the truth or not. I said I'd call back.

I went into the bathroom, showered and shaved, put on the same stuff I'd worn on the plane, gathered up the papers I'd scattered over the table, shoved them all into a Publix Supermarket shopping bag, took another swig of coffee, told my mama that I'd be back later, got into the car and drove twenty-five minutes to Fort Lauderdale.

The United States Attorney's office is on East Broward, which is a pretty main road, so I had no trouble finding it. At the reception desk, clutching my shopping bag with both hands, I asked for Ira E. Babcock. The lady guard asked who I was, I told her, she dialled a number and announced my presence. A few minutes later, a tall young man with a round face and quickly thinning light blond hair appeared. We shook hands while he stared at my shopping bag.

'The paperwork,' I explained.

He nodded, signed me in, escorted me through a couple of doors that needed to be unlocked by swiping an ID card past an electronic eye, and offered me a seat in his office. But my visit with him didn't last more than a few minutes 'cause as soon as I told him that my mama lived in Lantana, he told me that I was in the wrong office.

'Sorry. But you need to speak with someone in the US Attorney's office in West Palm Beach.'

'It continues,' I sighed in desperation.

'What does?'

'Life on the wrong side of the tracks.'

'I am sorry, but if you'd have mentioned yesterday that this was about a matter in Lantana . . .' He motioned for me to wait while he reached for his phone, dialled a number and asked for Charlotte. When she got on the line, he told her that he had someone with him at the moment who needed to see her and asked if she'd be in the office all morning. He nodded, said thanks, hung up and wrote down on a slip of paper, 'Charlotte Meissen' then added the address. 'It's on Clematis.'

'I don't know where that is but I suspect I can find it.'

'You will,' he said, nodding towards the hallway. 'Straight down, past one door, then the first door on your left. Again, I'm sorry I couldn't be of more help. Good luck.'

'Thanks anyway.' I stood up, shook his hand and was about to leave when I decided to ask, 'Hey, just between us . . . South Florida Island Federal Finance? Eton Island Finance Management and Trust Company? Padre Island Finance Management Services? Alexander George? Any of them ring a bell?'

He paused, obviously to ponder his answer. 'Let me put it this way . . . I wouldn't be surprised if Charlotte has heard those names before.'

I said, 'Yeah, well, thanks,' left the office, climbed into the car and now drove forty minutes back up the coast to West Palm Beach. I found the US Attorney's office right where he said it would be, parked in a small lot down the block, carried my shopping bag inside and stopped at the front desk to tell the guard there, 'I'm here to see Charlotte Meissen.'

A huge man with a jowlly face, wearing a blue uniform and a big pistol, growled at me, 'What's that?' He pointed to my Publix bag. 'Food delivery?'

'No, it's not.'

'Open it.'

I did. 'Paperwork.'

He peeked inside, told me, 'Wait right there,' reached under his desk and produced one of those hand-held metal detectors that they use at the airport when your pocket change sets off the alarm. He swept it over and under the bag, until he was certain that there wasn't anything metal hidden inside. Then, pleased with himself for having managed that, he wanted to know, 'Do you have an appointment?'

'No. But she's expecting me.'

He tilted his head, the way a dog does when he hears a sound he doesn't recognize. 'Either you got an appointment or you don't?'

'I don't . . . but yes, she's expecting me. What I mean is, I didn't fix a time with her.'

'What you mean is, you don't got an appointment.'

'I kinda do 'cause she said that I should come to see her.'

He kept staring at me while he reached for the phone on his desk. 'Who do I say is expected without an appointment?'

'Doone. K.C.'

'Mr Casey?'

'No. Mr Doone. On the advice of Mr Babcock. She'll know.'

He dialled a number and while waiting for someone to answer, pushed a form across to me. 'Sign in. I'll need some form of identification.'

I put down my name and took out my driver's licence.

'It's a Mr Doone,' he said into the phone. 'For Miss Meissen. Says somebody called Mr Babcock sent him.'

I tried handing him my driver's licence but he seemed more interested in the way I'd signed the visitor's register.

He cupped the phone and pointed. 'It says right there, first name.'

'That's it,' I said.

'What's it? The letter K?'

I held up my licence so that he could see how my name was written.

'What's the K stand for?'

'Nothing. That's it, just two initials.'

'Oh yeah?' He didn't believe me. 'So what do your friends call you?'

'They call me K.C.'

'What . . . K period C period. Or Casey, like Casey Jones.'

'K period. C period.'

'Like Kansas City, huh?'

'Ah . . . right . . . like Kansas City.'

He went back to his call. 'Miss Meissen . . . fellow named Doone who doesn't have an appointment . . . says somebody called Mr Babcock sent him . . . okay?' Then he turned to me and grinned wide enough that I could see at least two of his front teeth were missing. 'You're in luck, Kansas City, she'll be right out.'

I said thanks and moved away from the desk, wondering if this guard was somehow related to the guard at the twin towers who'd chased us away from the entrance of the building 'cause crying was a fire hazard.

The clothes make the man, the little voice said.

Or is it the badge? I asked.

The voice reminded me, *papa had a badge.*

I answered, *then it must be the uniform.*

He had one of those too.

I told the voice, *screw you.*

And for a while, it went away.

'Mr Doone?' A small black woman in a dark red dress was standing at the far door.

'Oh . . . hiya.' I nodded, walked over to her and extended my hand. 'Miss Meissen?'

She said yes, shook my hand and asked that I follow her. 'Thanks, Wolf,' she said as the door swung closed behind us.

I asked, 'Wolf?'

'That's his name.'

'Charming fellow.'

'Yes, he is,' she said in a very businesslike manner.

'Struck me more like an acquired taste.'

She didn't answer.

I wrongly assumed she hadn't heard me. 'Kind of a walking ad for gun control.'

'Right in here,' she said, unlocking the second door, ignoring my remark, leaving me to think that she'd already acquired a taste for Wolf and perhaps didn't necessarily care to acquire one for me.

'Thank you.'

She motioned towards the first office on the left and on to a chair at the side of her desk. I kept the Publix bag on my lap.

'This is about South Florida Island Federal Finance,' she said, taking her place behind her desk.

'You know them.'

'Ira Babcock phoned me after you left. Yes, I know them.'

'They've scammed my mama out of her apartment.'

'That's what they do.'

'She's a cop's widow.'

'They're non-discriminatory.'

'All the paperwork is there. They've given her ninety days.' I started to take some of it out of the bag.

But she stopped me. 'I'm sorry to say that I've seen it all before.'

'So . . .' I looked at her. 'What do I do?'

She shook her head. 'I'm even sorrier to say that there isn't much you can do.'

'This is what my old man used to call bunko.'

'It's probably even fraud.' She shrugged, 'But saying it's probably fraud and proving it is fraud are two different things.'

'The sweepstakes came through the mail? How about mail fraud?'

'We've looked into it.'

'And?'

'We continue to look into it.'

'A swindle like this . . . there's nothing you can do to protect the people being conned?'

'Have you read the small print?'

'Miss Meissen, are you telling me that my mama is going to lose her apartment?'

'If there was something we could do, if there was something I could do, we would have done it . . . I would have done it . . . a long time ago.'

I wanted to know, 'How many people have they scammed?'

She thought about that for a few seconds. 'I think I could

safely say that this office has handled nearly a hundred complaints.'

'How many?'

She nodded. 'Mr Doone, South Florida Island Finance is a shell company owned by Padre Island Finance Management Services. In turn, they are, we believe, at least partially owned by Eton Island Finance Management and Trust Company. The operation here in South Florida is managed out of Texas and the operation in Texas is managed out of the Bahamas. It goes from there into a maze of companies around Europe. The company here is merely a contractor. An agent acting for other parties. In the case of South Florida and of Padre Island, the common link is a man named Alexander George. He's listed as a director of both companies. He is not, as far as we can discern, a director of the company in the Bahamas, but he is listed as a shareholder. All three companies use the same 1-800 telephone number. We believe that Mr George might reside in Antigua. If he does, that puts him beyond our jurisdiction. Furthermore, if one or any of these companies is acting as an agent for someone, and we can't get Mr George to tell us who, it means that there is little we can do to take any sort of action against the person or persons who hired him.'

'In other words, welcome to the wild goose chase.'

'Yes,' she said, hesitated, then added, 'and no. Yes, in the sense that even if we could somehow prove that Mr George is involved in fraud, there's little chance we could ever bring him to justice. On the other hand, if we could prove that fraud has taken place, or is taking place, and Mr George were to find himself in territory under the jurisdiction of the United States, at that point in time, we might be able to do something about it.'

I told her, 'Four or five apartments where my mama lives are already vacant. She and one of her neighbours have both been given eviction notices. I didn't have time to find out if anyone else in the complex has been thrown out, but as the place gets emptied out, service charges increase. My mama says they've doubled. We're not talking folk with Donald Trump bank accounts here. We're talking about a bunch of retired people on fixed incomes.'

'And as service charges go up,' she said, 'more people sell out.'

'So somebody winds up with twenty-two empty condos and a swimming pool.'

'That's right.'

I looked at her. 'And then what?'

'And then . . . maybe nothing.'

'So what's the point?'

'When I say maybe nothing, I mean, maybe nothing for a while.'

'Is it the old trick of clearing property waiting for an expressway to get built?'

She shook her head. 'No. I suspect it is the new trick of rebuilding the Garden of Eden. Except down here, we don't grow apples. We grow malls.'

'Just what Florida needs,' I mumbled, 'another mall.'

'I wish I could be more encouraging.'

'What do I do now?'

She leaned towards her office door, called out 'Maria?' and waited for an older Spanish woman to poke her head in. 'This is Mr Doone. Would you please help him fill out a formal complaint.' Then she turned to me. 'Are these photocopies?'

'Ah . . . no. Not all of them. My mama only photocopied some of them to fax me in New York yesterday.'

'Normally,' she said, 'we send people over to a photocopying place. But I think under the circumstances Maria can do it here.' She motioned that I should get up and follow the other woman out of her office.

'What happens when my mama's ninety days are up?'

'The usual procedure is that they serve papers which tends to scare most people. If you engage an attorney, he should know how to stall them for another three to six months. But that costs money and, at least in the few cases we know of where people have fought back, the small print beats them when they get into court.'

'How 'bout we just pay off the mortgage, or whatever this sweepstakes thing is?'

'That's entirely up to you, but I can tell you that in at least one case we're aware of, when someone tried to pay them off, they refused the repayment, which seems to be their right according to the small print, and only agreed to settle after slapping huge penalties on top of everything for early payment. That still leaves them the option of running up the service charges. Being the final tenant in a complex of condos can be a very expensive last stand.' She looked at me. 'I'm sure you recall, Mr Doone, Custer's last words?'

I said, 'You mean, where the hell did all them Indians come from?'

And for the first time, she allowed herself a tiny smile.

'Thanks for the free photocopies.' I stood up and offered to shake her hand.

'I wish I could do more,' she said, gripping my hand firmly.

'It's my mama,' I reminded her, 'whether you can or can't, I have to,' and followed Maria to the photocopying machine.

After promising my mama again that everything would be all right, and after phoning Duke who still didn't take my call, and after phoning Hussein at the bucket shop who arranged to get me on an early morning flight from Fort Lauderdale, I took my mama out to dinner. The next morning, I got up at the crack of dawn, drove all the way back to Lauderdale, returned the car and flew home.

I spent the whole plane ride trying to work out a plan.

I'll get Duke on the phone . . . eventually . . . or go down there and pull him out of one of those never ending meetings he's always in . . . and first thing, I'll tell him 'bout his sister and see what he has to say 'bout her . . . then I'll see if he can start the ball rolling on saving my mama's place . . . and even if that Miss Meissen can't do anything, he'll figure out a way for my mama and me to circle our wagons and fight off those sleazebags in Florida . . . then I'll sick 'em on Tweedle-Dee and Tweedle-Dum and get something out of them for wrongful dismissal, or whatever he decides to call it . . . and that should settle everything, with the exception of Lorilee and whether or not we're gonna get back together again.

Ten minutes after landing at LaGuardia I was climbing into a taxi on my way back to the city.

That's what I'll do, I kept telling myself all the way across the Triboro Bridge. *I'll sick Duke on 'em.*

The little voice agreed all the way down the FDR Drive. *Sounds like a plan.*

I'll let Duke worry about my mama and about getting me some money out of GCB, I said to the voice as I unlocked the front door to my apartment, *and maybe, just maybe I'll get 'round to phoning Lorilee and tell her that if she's real sorry I'm gonna give her one more chance . . .*

I stepped inside and stopped dead in my tracks.

Sunnuvabitch!

The place was empty.

Chapter Seven

It was hard to keep track of time but I reckon that maybe as much as fifteen minutes passed before Whitestone spoke again. And when he did, what he said was, 'I can't believe you just did that.'

'Just did what?'

'Insulted me.'

What could I tell him 'cept, 'I wasn't insulting you,' even though I kinda was.

'Well, it wasn't flattery. You said so yourself. So I have to assume it was an insult. How very rude of you.'

'I was . . . I don't know . . . look, why don't we just forget it?'

'Yes, you were insulting me,' he said, crossing his arms and legs and assuming a posture that was obvious brooding.

I left him to it, crossing my own arms and legs too. I tried to sit all the way back, to somehow get comfortable, but he took up a lot of room. So now I uncrossed my arms and legs and leaned forward.

My stomach rumbled.

Food, I thought, *what a good idea. Maybe we can phone out for a pizza. Hello, Dominos, do you deliver to people stuck in elevators? Good. Then we'll have one large pizza with . . .*

M & Ms. The voice inside my head chirped up with, *how about the bag that ripped in our pocket?*

I glanced down at my right-side raincoat pocket, realized it was easily in reach and thought to myself, *if I just go for it, there won't be any. But if I imagine there are some, not a lot, maybe only two or three, I'll bet there will be some.*

The voice assured me, *it won't work unless we pick the right number. If we just say three and there aren't three, then there*

*won't be any. But if we say two and there are two then there
will be two.*

Okay, I'll play, and continued to stare at the pocket until
I convinced myself that my X-ray vision could count how
many. *Three.*

What colours? The voice asked.

Screw you, I said and, moving very slowly so that he wouldn't
notice, slipped my hand in the pocket to find four. I took one,
glanced at him from the side of my eyes and slowly tried to sneak
it into my mouth.

'I can't believe you just did that,' he snapped.

'Just did what?'

'Ate something. I saw you. It is very difficult to fathom,' he
lectured, 'how someone in this situation can hoard food.'

'Hoard food?' I looked at him, then shrugged. 'Here.' I
reached into my pocket and handed one to him. 'Enjoy.'

He studied it. 'Hah. Smarties.'

'No,' I corrected, 'M&Ms.'

'Looks like Smarties to me.'

'Trust me, you're dealing with an expert.'

'You seem to be an expert in several areas, Mr Doone. Electrical engineering. My marital status. Now, Smarties.'

'M&Ms,' I said firmly.

He popped the candy into his mouth, smiled at me, pretended
to savour it, then swallowed it without chewing. 'Tastes like
Smarties to me.'

'I can't believe you just did that.'

'Just did what?'

'Didn't even chew it.'

'Oh, yes,' he nodded, 'you're the expert.' He shifted his body
away from me and re-crossed his arms.

I did the same.

No big deal, the voice said, *'cause he doesn't know that we know
there are more.*

Only two more, I reminded the voice.

*Only two's better than only one, 'specially 'cause we're
hungry.*

I wondered, *how do I get them without him spotting me?*

The voice advised, *we bide our time.*

Exactly, I agreed.

So that's what I did. I sat there, biding my time, waiting for the right moment when I could sneak the last two M&Ms out of my pocket and into my mouth.

Inside my head I began humming.

I started with 'Feelings' 'cause Marylou always liked that, then segued into 'At The Copa,' 'cause that was Carrie's favourite. But when I got to 'I Can't Get No Satisfaction' I stopped, 'cause that was Lorilee's favourite and I'd be damned if I was going to sit in here and hum anything she liked.

Instead, I started trying to remember the words to songs when I was a kid. I picked a year, tried to picture in my head what my homeroom looked like, who was sitting next to me, and how the songs went that year. But it wasn't as easy as I thought it would be and I kept drawing blanks. In fact, the only lyric I could come up with from High School was Carole King's 'You've Got A Friend', 'cept I couldn't remember exactly what year that was or who was sitting next to me.

In any case, I hummed that twice.

You just call out my name . . .

The voice wondered, *whatever happened to her?*

I answered, *she became the first rock star in history to appear on an album cover shoeless.*

The voice answered, *Shoeless Carole.*

I answered, *Shoeless Joe.*

The voice asked, *who?*

I answered, *friend of Carole King.*

The voice said, *we're going stir crazy.*

I said, *shoeless me.*

Which is when the voice shrieked, *shoeless him!*

I turned just in time to see Sir Tommy leaning forward, untying his laces, taking off both shoes, slipping off both his socks and cleaning in-between each of his toes.

'Huh?' I was aghast. 'I can't believe you're doing that.'

He looked at me. 'Doing what?'

I pointed to his feet. 'That.'

He shrugged. 'Don't you ever clean in-between your toes?'

'That's disgusting.'

He shrugged, 'One man's displeasure is another man's hygiene.'

'How would you like it if I did that?'

'Be my guest.'

'That's not the point.'

'Then what is?'

'The point is . . .' I tried to think of something. 'The point is we're stuck here together in a really confined space and . . . that's disgusting.'

'I don't think it's disgusting.'

'But I do.' I folded my arms, crossed my legs and turned as far away from him as I could. 'Please be kind enough to put your damn socks and shoes back on.'

'All right.' He did. Then he too folded his arms across his chest, crossed his legs and turned as far away from me as he could.

'It's going to be a long night,' I mumbled.

'It is only late afternoon,' he said.

And neither of us spoke again for a very long time.

Chapter Eight

Everything was gone.

There was nothing left in the kitchen, 'cept the fridge and the stove. No microwave. No butcher block table. No chairs. No pots. No pans. Not a plate, not a cup, not a saucer, not a knife, not a fork, not a spoon. No coffee machine. Not even the spare rolls of paper towels we kept under the sink. No Brillo, no chrome polisher, no E-Z Wrench. And when I popped open the fridge door to see if she'd gone so far as to take the butter, the only thing in there was my fax machine.

A little bit of Lorilee's nastiness, I said to the voice.

Not nastiness, the voice answered, *pragmaticness.*

Pragmaticness?

Sure. She didn't take the fax 'cause she's never been able to figure out how to change the paper, which is why we had to buy a plain paper fax machine for Connecticut.

I settled on, *pragmatic nastiness,* pulled it out of the fridge – it didn't seem any worse for wear – and carried it into the living room.

There was nothing left there either.

The couch was gone. The coffee table was gone. My television and my stereo were gone. So were my CDs, my phones, my phone books – in fact, all of my books – and the four little Persian prayer rugs we'd scattered over the parquet floors.

The answering machine was gone. So was my laptop computer. She'd even taken the can of soda and the pretzels. The only thing sitting in the middle of the floor was my still half-eaten turkey sandwich and the M&Ms bag.

It was empty.

There was nothing in the bedroom, 'cept the bed itself – it must have been too big to get out the door – and a handful of my clothes that were spilled on to the floor of my closet. One suit. Two sweaters. My raincoat. Two pairs of underpants. Seven socks, only two of which formed a pair. Three shirts. My beat-up pair of Gucci loafers.

The other closets were empty.

The dressers were gone. The phone and TV set that had been there were gone too. So were my ten pillows.

That's when I remembered my watch.

Aw shit!

I rushed into the bathroom.

Please be there.

The towels were gone. So was my toothbrush. So was my toothpaste. So was everything in the medicine cabinet. So was the shower curtain. So was the toilet paper.

So was my watch.

Sunnuvabitch!

The only thing she didn't take was the mostly-used bar of Dial soap lying in the bottom of the tub.

I reached down, picked it up, stared at it, then placed it carefully in the little slot on the edge of the sink where soap was supposed to go.

Look at it this way, the voice resolved, *we've got a bed to sleep in, a fax machine to fax on and soap to wash with. Now all we gotta do is buy some towels so we can stay clean, buy some sheets and pillows so we can sleep, buy a new phone so we can call some other lawyer to defend my mama and sue the Three Stooges, and while we're at it, sue Lorilee and maybe Duke, too.*

I didn't even have a piece of paper to make up a list.

What the hell does she think she's gonna do with the laptop? I moved back into the living room. *Unless Duke was here . . .* I stopped 'cause in that instant, I knew where it was.

Pragmatically nasty Lorilee.

She hated computers. Refused to figure them out. Never wanted them in the house. Hated it when I travelled with the laptop.

I walked back into the kitchen and opened the fridge's freezer door. The computer and the answering machine were both there, both understandably very cold.

'Cause I didn't know what the expected life-span of a frozen computer or answering machine would be, and didn't know who I could even call to ask – or could have called if I had a phone –

I decided the sensible thing would be to let them thaw out on the kitchen counter before turning them on to see if they still worked.

Waiting for that, I started pacing around the apartment. From the kitchen I went into the living room. From the living room I went into the bedroom. When I came out of there, I walked around the living room for a while till I headed into the kitchen to see how the computer and answering machine were thawing.

They were both still very cold.

Back to the living room. Then the bedroom. Then the living room again. Then, finally, I realized I did have a line to the outside world, so I plugged the fax machine into the phone socket and used that phone to ring Duke. His secretary took the call but I didn't say anything. I just hung up. Next, I dialled Lorilee. But when she picked up I didn't say anything to her either. I just slammed it down.

Instead of hanging up on anyone else, I headed out the door, trying to memorize my shopping list.

Plates to eat on. Silverware too. A kettle to make hot water and a real phone. Canned soups, instant coffee and enough M&Ms to get me through the rest of the week. Ten pillows – I wound up buying only four 'cause I couldn't carry any more – *some fitted sheets and a blanket.*

My arms full, I convinced myself I'd worry about whatever else I needed tomorrow. But once I got home with that stuff, I remembered I didn't have any pads or pencils, so I went out again, over to Office Max, to buy whatever I could think of that would turn the empty living room into an office. The only thing I didn't bother with was furniture. That would have to wait a few days.

Then I remembered I didn't have enough clothes, so I went out a third time, this time to pick up a couple of pairs of jeans, some shirts, socks, underwear, and a knock-off pair of track shoes that had Nykee written on the side in the familiar logo. They probably wouldn't last more than a month, but they only cost eight bucks and that was enough to get me between now and then. Eventually, I told myself, I'd go to Connecticut and reclaim my stuff.

How much we wanna bet, the voice asked, *she's donated everything we own to charity?*

I told the voice, *well, then, let's go up there and find out. I've got keys and we'll walk right in* . . .

The voice interrupted, *she's got keys too.*

Immediately, I plugged my new phone in the bedroom socket – at least in there I had the bed to sit on – asked Information for the number of the nearest locksmith and told him I needed someone to change my locks. He promised he was on his way. He arrived two hours later, installed new front-door locks, I handed him a credit card, and he deducted $175 for the visit.

The little voice pointed out, *a hundred and seventy-five bucks for twenty minutes work? We're in the wrong business.*

The computer and the answering machine were still pretty chilly, but both were less cold than they had been, and it struck me that by now they were either thawed or they weren't. So I opened the laptop, booted up and stood perfectly still, staring at it, hoping that something would happen.

The little voice said, *if we don't breathe it will work.*

I stood there holding my breath.

The screen blinked on – it was kind of a strange colour – but after a second's pause the disk booted and sure enough, eventually, I got a screen filled with icons.

I exhaled loudly.

Some of the icons were off colour and a couple of them looked garbled, so I took another deep breath, held it, re-booted – this time the screen looked more like its usual self – and exhaled even louder than the first time.

Carrying it carefully back into the living room, I left it on, telling myself that was the right thing to do, kinda like the way you run your car on winter mornings before you drive it.

While it was warming up, I tried the answering machine. The tape played a little off speed, then picked up speed and worked. I hooked it into the phone system, got on the fax line and called my own number. The machine answered.

Progress, the voice decided, *is sometimes as good as plain old getting even.*

Getting even? I started thinking about reporting a break-in, claiming the place had been vandalized. I had insurance, so I could get something back on that. And what better way to get 'pragmatically nasty' with Lorilee – and Duke, if he'd been here too – by sending the cops 'round to ask a lot of questions? But this was Lorilee's place too and I could picture Duke standing right behind his little sister, waving some clause in some marriage law somewhere to say that a wife had every right to trash her own husband's life.

Instead, I lay down on the floor with my computer and my M&Ms and my pads and my pencils spread out in front of me and tried to figure out how I was gonna put my life back together.

'Cept I didn't get very far.

It got too dark too quick 'cause I'd forgotten to buy lamps.

I don't usually sleep good regardless, but that night I slept real bad. It wasn't just 'cause I was pillow deficient, it was mainly 'cause I kept rehearsing what I was gonna say to Lorilee's face. And what I was gonna say to Duke's face. And what I was gonna do about my mama's place. And what I was gonna do about GCB. And how all those plans I'd made on the plane coming up from Florida had full-tilt headed south. When morning came, I was too weary to get up, so I lay there for a long time, drawing up another shopping list in my head.

One lamp for the living room.

One lamp for the bedroom.

A clock-radio.

And, a couple of glazed doughnuts.

I finally pushed myself out of bed – I didn't know what time it was but it looked lighter outside than it is when I usually get up – made a cup of coffee and took it with me into the shower. It always makes me feel good to just let the water run down the back of my neck and to do that while having breakfast – I learned the hard way – you gotta hold the cup right up against the wall otherwise you wind up with your coffee taking a shower, too. So I stood there, like that, drinking my coffee in the shower, till I decided I was hungry enough to go some place for a couple of eggs.

Dimi's place might have been my first choice, but he was clear across town. Anyway, there was a pretty good all-day-breakfast joint over on Third. So I towelled off, brushed my teeth – I couldn't be bothered to shave – got into some clothes, grabbed my new Lorilee-proof keys and headed downstairs. 'Cause I needed some money, my first stop was my friendly neighbourhood cash machine. I put my card in, punched up my code, told the display I wanted to withdraw a hundred bucks and stood there waiting patiently till the display answered my request with, 'Balance $0.'

Damn. Lorilee had beaten me to it.

I rushed back to the apartment to phone our other banks. The news at each was just as dismal. Now I called Duke and told his secretary, 'I gotta talk to him right now.'

'I'm sorry, but he's in a meeting . . .'

I cut in, 'What else is new?'

'However . . . I am at this very moment typing a fax to you that he dictated first thing.'

'What does it say?'

'I will send it to you in a few minutes.'

'Why not just tell me what it says?'

'I'm afraid I can't do that. You'll have it in a few minutes.' She checked my number and a few minutes after we hung up, a single page came rattling through the formerly fridged fax machine.

'Dear K.C. – Given the events of the past few days, I am afraid that, due to an obvious conflict of interest, I am no longer in a position to represent you. I would therefore suggest that you engage counsel, at your earliest convenience, to advise you on your dismissal from GCB and other matters that may arise relating to your marriage and assets. If you do not know anyone, my secretary will gladly furnish you with a list of attorneys whom, I am certain, will provide excellent counsel. With my many kindest regards, Duke.'

In a rage, I grabbed the fax, scribbled, 'Take your conflict of interests and your many kindest regards and shove them both up your damn butt,' and sent it straight back to him.

Then I rang Lorilee.

When she picked up the phone I demanded, 'What the hell is going on?'

'I can't talk to you,' she said. 'Duke won't let me.'

'Well, let me tell you something . . .'

Before I could, she slammed down the phone.

Now what the hell do we do?

Look at it this way, the voice answered, *we need a lawyer to protect us from Lorilee and Duke but we don't have any money. We need a lawyer to protect mama from those creeps who are trying to get her out of her apartment, but we don't have any money. And we need to start earning a living, but no one will hire us 'cause the Three Stooges have put out the word. All of which means the only sure thing left for us to do to earn a living is to start day trading. But we can't start day trading 'cause we don't have any money. So the answer is a no-brainer.*

I asked, *oh yeah?*

Yeah, the voice insisted, *get some money!*

It took some time before I could focus on how to do that 'cause I was so damned furious with Lorilee and Duke for leaving me to twist in the wind like this.

Get some money . . . get some money . . . I kept repeating it until the words of the legendary thief Willy Sutton popped into my head. *Why do I rob banks? 'Cause that's where the money is.*

I decided, *okay, time to rob a bank,* and began plotting my strategy.

It's not hard to do when you know how. The most important thing to remember is, never admit to a banker that you need his dough to survive. Truth turns out to make bankers nervous and the goosier they get, the tighter their vault door stays shut. The key to the vault is faith. Banks, after all, are in the business of handing out money to people who don't need it and will, whatever happens, almost always pay it back. Or, at least, make believe they will. So you start by telling the most junior banker you can find that you only want a little bit of money – a sum well within his discretionary limit – for something benign, and have decided to borrow it from him because your accountant has worked out a tax dodge which means the government will be paying the interest while your own money is on deposit earning a great return. To that you add, 'cause the government will only let me get away with this for a short period of time, I'll return the money to the bank in, say, six months.

As long as it sounds credible, the junior banker will go for it.

If you ask for too much, he's forced to bump you up to his supervisor, and the higher up you go in this food chain, the bigger the can of worms you've opened. Supervisors get to be supervisors by protecting their butt. They may pretend to be interested in your plight, but in reality they're only interested in making sure that nothing ever comes back to haunt them. In other words, their first reaction is to say no. For some warped reason, it turns out to be less hassle for a government like Brazil or Indonesia to get an unsecured loan for seven trillion bucks than it is for a normal person to get ten cents more than the junior guy's discretionary limit.

Knowing how they resent folk acting as greedy as them, I settled on the harmless sum of three grand. Anyway, in the back of my mind, I knew I could always make up any shortfall with a credit card cash advance, though their rates of interest bordered on usury . . .

Credit cards? The little voice started making sounds like alarm bells.

Oh shit! Duke and Lorilee would have thought about credit cards too. I flung open my wallet, grabbed the phone and told the operators at the end of the various credit card hotlines that all my cards had been lost. I said I wasn't paying for anything charged on them after, like, noon, yesterday. Then I remembered the one I'd used for the food and the stationery and my clothes and the locksmith, so I amended 'like noon yesterday' to 'like, this morning, right now, today'.

But they said, 'But you said . . .'

And I said, 'But what I really meant was . . .'

But they said, 'We see that the second name on this account is your wife so you'll have to check with her to see if she's made any purchases because if she has made purchases on this card those purchases will have to be honoured.'

And I said, 'Well . . . okay, but nothing on any of our cards from as of right this very minute, now. 'Cause mine's lost and I want her's stopped too.'

What I really wanted to say was that my credit cards had been stolen 'cause that's what was in the midst of happening, but I also knew that if I used the word stolen someone would want to see a police report. 'Yeah, they've all been lost,' I told each operator, 'and I'd appreciate it if you would please make sure that no new purchases get charged back to me.'

Some of them said, 'You're protected as of this phone call,' and others said, 'I have to remind you that there is a $100 liability on lost cards,' but all of them said, 'As of right now, your account is no longer valid.'

I glanced at my wrist to check the time, forgetting that my watch was gone, and 'cause I didn't know what time it was, I could merely pray that Lorilee hadn't gotten to Tiffany's yet.

I also told the various operators that I needed to change my address, asked them to send my new bills to the apartment and to forget Connecticut. 'And, oh yeah, please take my wife's name off the accounts as well.'

Each of them assured me they would and also promised I'd have my new cards within a week. It wasn't till I'd gone through the lot of them that I realized now I couldn't charge anything any more, or in the case of an emergency – the voice corrected, *yet another emergency* – couldn't wangle any cash advances, either.

First things first, I told the voice, *it's time to rob a bank.*

Never rob a bank, the voice warned, *unshaven.*

So I shaved.

First stop with my clean face was Chase Manhattan, where Lorilee had already emptied our account. As soon as I walked in, I recalled we also had a safe deposit box there, so I went downstairs to see if she'd recalled that too.

She hadn't.

Inside the box I found some paperwork which showed the apartment was free and clear, which started me thinking that maybe I could raise some cash by mortgaging the apartment or the house in Connecticut, or both. But they were in joint names, which meant she'd have to co-sign. On the other hand, I took it to mean that I could live here without her taking it away from me until a divorce was settled.

I had no doubt now that she'd be going that route. Course, she'd have to be fairly creative when it came to inventing grounds 'cause she could hardly sue me for her own adultery. She'd probably take the no-fault route, 'though I couldn't discount the idea that, just for good measure, Duke would come up with a whole slew of charges that made me out to be the bad guy.

My GCB contract was also there.

The woman who ran the safe deposit boxes was kind enough to make several photocopies for me, after which I emptied that box, closed it, rented another one – this time without her signature on it – and put all the originals there.

Next, I asked to speak with one of the junior managers – it turned out to be the same guy who'd originally opened our account a few years ago – and told him that I needed an unsecured $3000 loan to fix up my apartment.

Being a small enough sum, he approved it right then and there. I signed the papers, agreed to pay off the balance in six months, handed him back $1000 to open a new cheque account – in my name only – and told him he could automatically take the interest on the loan out of that account every month.

With two cashier's cheques for $1000 in my pocket, I walked across the street to Bankers' Trust, where I put $1000 on deposit, to be rolled over every thirty days. Based on my new banking relationship with them – meaning that they had enough on account to cover several months interest – I secured another personal loan with another junior manager to fix up the apartment for $3000.

Using that money, I bought three separate $1000 cashier's cheques and, together with the one left over from Chase, walked into four more banks. I put $1000 into a thirty-day rollover account in each and charmed the lowest person on the totem pole into four more $3000 unsecured loans.

By lunchtime I was $18,000 in debt to six different banks, with $5,000 on thirty-day deposit in five of them, plus $1000 in a cheque account at the first one. That left me with a dozen $1000 cashier's cheques, which I brought back to Chase and deposited in my new cheque account there.

That was gonna be my stake to save my mama's apartment, to buy whatever legal advice I could to even the score with GCB and Lorilee and, hopefully, to spend whatever was left to get on with the rest of my life.

But I still didn't have a credit card.

Of course, I could always take cash out of one of my new bank accounts and pay for everything with that, but I don't know anybody who uses cash these days, 'cept I guess, the Mafia. On the other hand, I could also write cheques for everything, but no one trusts cheques these days, and certainly not in New York. No, what I needed to do was find a bank manager who would trust me with just enough plastic to get through the week, until the rest of the plastic arrived.

The obvious candidate was my pal sitting behind his junior manager's desk over there in the corner – he looked up and smiled at me so I waved and nodded – but I didn't want to do anything that might awaken his curiosity. Guys who lend other people money, even if it isn't their own money, never see events as being mutually exclusive – and even if, in a way, my needing money and my needing a credit card wasn't mutually exclusive – there was no reason to let him worry about it.

Back on the street, I headed towards Lexington 'cause there were plenty of banks up and down Lexington, 'though I wound up going all the way down to 36th Street before I found one offering exactly what I needed.

God bless the New York Bank of Athens and all who sail on her.

I walked in, filled out the form, supplied my credit references – I listed Visa, Access, Diners Club and all my new bank accounts – and in the box labelled 'Personal References' I wrote down Dimi Ionides. Not only was he the only Greek guy I knew, but I also knew it didn't matter 'cause they wouldn't check. Next, this being one of those accounts where you can only spend up to the limit that you have on deposit with the bank, I wrote out a cheque for $500. That struck me as more than enough to get me from here to next week. But that meant I had to sit around for fifteen minutes waiting for the lady teller to phone Chase, who eventually confirmed that my cheque was good. Then again, it was worth the wait 'cause five minutes later, she handed me my very own New York Bank of Athens credit card.

Decorated in blue and white – same colours as the Greek flag, she pointed out – there was a dark outline of some statue in the background, the bank's name on top, my name with my card's number embossed in the middle, a photo in the corner of somebody who turned out to be Melina Mercouri and bold lettering across the bottom with the words 'Save The Elgin Marbles'.

'One penny of every dollar you spend on this card,' the lady teller explained, 'will go to the fund.'

'I'm very pleased that I have been given this opportunity to help,' I assured her, not having a clue what the fund was all about or why Melina Mercouri's picture was on my card. She thanked me. I thanked her. We shook hands. I pointed to the card and announced, '*Never On Sunday*.'

'Oh, no,' she assured me, 'our card will be accepted every-where seven days a week.'

On the way back up Lex, I celebrated, using my new card to purchase the lamps and a super-hi-tech, super-state-of-the-art digital clock-radio with all sorts of buttons and whistles. It was called a *Kyuukyoko* – the salesman said it was a Japanese word that meant 'ultimate' – and that this was the clock-radio version of a *tamagotchi*, one of those computerized toy animals that turns ten-year-old kids into manic depressives.

Maybe I should have known better.

But he convinced me that it would do everything I ever wanted a clock-radio to do, and more, including tell me the time of day, provide a way for me to find the time anywhere in the world, play AM radio, play FM radio and – the main thing I was looking for – give me the benefit of snooze control, so that when it went off in the morning I could go back to sleep.

And not just any sort of snooze control, he bragged, this would be the ultimate in snooze control. I could set it for fifteen minutes, or thirty minutes, or for any time from thirty to sixty minutes, or use the fifteen-day programmable alarm so that I could decide on Monday what time I wanted to wake up a week from Thursday.

I handed him my credit card, tucked my *Kyuukyoko* under my arm and headed for the doughnut shop.

They were out of glazed so I bought two French crullers.

They tasted almost as good.

Breach of fiduciary trust.

I read through my GCB contract three times. Read every word on every page. And even if I couldn't make a helluva lot of sense out of most of those fourteen pages, on just about every one of them I found those same four words.

Breach of fiduciary trust.

Lawyer speak, I assured myself. *Duke wrote it in such a way so that only other lawyers know what this is all about.*

That's right, the voice agreed, *lawyers do it on purpose to keep the rest of us from depriving them of making a living.*

The punch line of an old joke flew into my head, the one about the judge describing the plaintiff and the defendant as the screw-er and the screw-ee.

Not so funny, the little voice said. *'Cause this contract says we're the screw-ee.*

I tried to shove it all out of my head by telling myself that what I really needed right now was to get myself a trading account.

And for a while, it worked.

Normally getting a trading account wouldn't be too difficult to manage 'cause shops were setting up every day across the country to handle private, electronically traded business. But those places, at least the ones I was aware of, were stalking big-stake investors and long-term gamblers. They had no interest whatsoever in what I was looking to become – a little league day trader – which they referred to as a nickel-dime bandit.

At the same time, there were plenty of shops opening all over the country specifically to cater to day traders. But those places were either minimum-stakes-six-figure boutiques, or they were secretly in the real estate business. Those were shops that, for a couple of grand, would enroll you in their two-week training course, then rent you a work-station, a terminal and their custom-built software for around forty bucks a day, charge twenty-five in and twenty-five out on every trade – fifty bucks round trip is pretty standard for up to a thousand shares on the NASDAQ, where most of the action is – and for good measure, throw in a couple of young girls in short skirts to deliver free coffee whenever you raise your hand and giggle at your jokes when you're not trading.

No, that wasn't where I needed to be.

What I was hankering for was someone catering to independent traders who'd hook me into their system down the line, then waive the rules just enough to let me duck under the minimum-stake turnstile. I was planning to put up ten grand and hold on to the rest to spend on my mama, rent, the phone bill and a few minor necessities, like food. What I didn't know, and wouldn't know until I tried, was just how far into my pile of chips I'd have to dip before I started bringing home some bacon.

Before diving head first into the swimming hole, I reckoned to ask someone already swimming there if the water was deep enough. The problem was, judging from the reception I'd already gotten phoning around the Street looking for a friend, I couldn't count on a helluva lot of folk there. And, after thinking hard about who I could turn to for advice, I discovered I didn't know a single guy to call.

However, I reckoned that I did know somebody who might know somebody, so I phoned Dimi at his coffee shop. 'Ya'll got any customers day trading?'

'You know what time it is? You know what it's like in here?' He wanted to know. 'What happened to you?'

'What did you hear?'

'Nothing. Absolutely nothing. Except that you got your ass fired.' He called to someone nearby, 'He wants cold tomato soup, give him cold tomato soup.' He said to me, 'So now you're day trading?'

'It's either that or work behind your counter.'

'I could use a grill man.'

'I could use some names to call.'

'Maybe I know a couple of people . . . but how the hell can you call me at a time like this . . . hold on.' He put the phone down – I could hear someone shouting across the room, '*two burgers, fries and double-slaw*' – and came back a couple of seconds later to say, 'Mikey.'

'Mikey who?'

'How should I know Mikey who? No cheques. No credit cards. In God we trust, all others pay cash. Says so right on the door when you walk in. He's sometimes breakfast, occasionally lunch, dinner never. Just Mikey.'

'What do I do, ask Information for just Mikey?'

'Wise guy. The only thing personal I know about him is he puts ketchup on his eggs.' He screamed, 'Over there, knuckle-head, the three guys with the menus,' then said to me, 'But I also got his number. You want it or not?'

'You don't know his last name but ya'll got his number?'

'I'm in lunchtime-panic mode. The least you can do is pretend to be grateful.'

'Okay, I'm grateful.'

'Say "Thank you" and I'll say "You're welcome".'

'Thank you.' Then I remembered, 'By the way, I used your name as a character reference.'

'Why?'

''Cause it was a Greek bank and I didn't know how to spell Onassis.'

'Which Greek bank?'

'New York Bank of Athens.'

'Joke's on you, friend, they're Cypriots.'

'So why do they call it Athens?'

'Who'd bank with them if they called it Larnaka?'

'Oh.' What else could I say? 'Anyway, thanks for the reference.'

'Next time try O-N-A-S-S-I-S,' he said, then gave me Mikey's number. 'And maybe . . . I just thought of someone else . . . how about the guy with the weird name?'

'What weird name?'

'If I could remember what his weird name was I'd tell you his name, not that it's weird.'

'You mean to use as a reference?'

'No, I mean who used to put milk in his tea.'

'How would I know that?'

'I'll think.'

'Good. Think and let me know.'

'You're welcome again,' he prodded, then shouted, 'For Godsakes, don't put that many onions on the plate, I'm not the Red Cross.'

'Thanks,' I said.

He asked, 'You want the sheet?'

'How much?'

'Special price.'

'How much?'

'Stop in,' he said, 'we'll discuss it. Where are you?'

'On the East Side.'

'Fancy. You ever go to Herbie's Deli on Second?'

I paused just long enough to hear the little voice cut in with, *better be careful.* 'Herbie?'

'Yeah, Herbie. Second Avenue. Fancy place for fancy people. You go there?'

'Should I?'

'Either you do or you don't.'

'Never heard of him.'

'Good. I hate the bastard. What's the fax number wherever you are?'

I gave it to him.

'I'll fax the sheet . . .' He barked, 'Table six. Check,' then said to me, 'Stay outta Herbie's. You're welcome a third time.'

'Actually, I think it's the fourth. And thanks.' When I hung up with him, I rang Mikey. 'My name is K.C. Doone. Dimi at the coffee shop . . . you know, Cassandra . . . he suggested I call you.'

'Can't talk now,' Mikey said. 'Call me back tonight?'

'You still day trading?'

'Yeah. Call me tonight.'

I said I would.

That's when the fax machine clicked on. Two pages rolled off. The first was the latest issue of Cassandra. Nowhere on it was any mention of TransMare-Telco. I wasn't sure if that meant the sheet had come out before the company went bust or if Dimi simply had a convenient memory. The second was a scribbled message. 'Tea with milk. And, oh yeah, I forgot, too much sugar. Foreign guy. Something-weird Roe.'

I didn't have a clue what he was talking about.

Breach of fiduciary trust.

Those four words were starting to haunt me.

I tried to reassure myself, *even if I didn't understand everything I agreed to in that contract Duke must have put something in there that will save my butt.*

The little voice popped up with, *or save Duke's butt.*

Breach of fiduciary trust.

The more I stared at those words, the more they started to look like they were spelled wrong.

Breach of fiduciary trust.

The letters kept rearranging themselves.

Inside breach I found the word, *ache.* Inside trust I found the word *ruts.* Inside the word fiduciary I spotted the word *fraud.*

The little voice screamed, *time to get a lawyer.*

But that was gonna be easier said than done. I needed a lawyer who'd do two-fers – my case against GCB and my mama's case – two for the price of one. Duke was the only attorney I knew these days on a first-name basis, and there wasn't a snowball's chance in hell that I was gonna ask him for someone else's first name. Marylou had a lawyer, I guess, but he was in Mexico somewhere. And Carrie had a law-yer too, but thinking about him – and her – dredged up too many bad memories. I didn't have a lawyer for my first divorce and the guy I used the second time – some ambu-lance chaser in New Jersey – wound up costing me more for losing than Carrie's mouthpiece charged her for winning. No, this time I needed someone who would be on my side in both cases.

In all three cases, the little voice reminded me.

Oh yeah . . . Lorilee.

There was always the Yellow Pages. They were overflowing with lawyers. 'Cept that Lorilee had taken our phone books along with everything else, and anyway, that wasn't going to work 'cause any lawyer I cold-called would ask for money up front. I needed the kind of favour that was best kept in the family. The trick was gonna be to come up with someone whose family wouldn't mind.

The little voice suggested, *how about cousin Harry?*

I phoned GCB, lucked out again by getting Frannie and not Yolanda at the switchboard, and asked for Steven Pinkus. When Pinky answered I said, 'Call me back from outside. Ya'll know the number of the apartment.' Then I hung up.

It was ten minutes before he got back to me. 'I'm sorry, K.C., I really am, but the market's down and I was right in the middle of trying to dump some . . .'

'I was just phoning to ask, how's your cousin Harry?'

'My cousin Harry? You know him?'

'Not yet. But you told me he's a lawyer.'

'He's the best.'

'Yeah, well, I happen to be in the market for a lotta free advice and maybe a little help on the instalment plan.'

'If I tell you that my cousin Harry is the best, you can take that to the bank.'

'Can ya'll give me his number? And then, Pinky, do me another favour, call him first?'

'Sure,' he said right away. 'But I'll have to figure out what time it is there. He's probably gone home by now. Maybe I can catch him just after dinner.'

'What time it is where?'

'Tel Aviv.'

'Tel Aviv?'

'He lives in Tel Aviv.'

That stopped me. 'Pinky . . . when I told you about getting fired, you said your cousin Harry was a lawyer . . .'

'That's right, he is.'

'But he's a lawyer in Tel Aviv.'

'Built himself a lovely home there, too.'

'I need a lawyer in New York.'

'So . . . in that case . . . a lawyer in New York . . . how about my cousin Izzy?'

'Cousin Izzy?'

'Isidor Pinkus. My father's younger brother's second son. Cousin Harry is on my mother's side. Harry Kimmelman. But Izzy's name is Isidor Pinkus.'

'And Isidor Pinkus has a law degree?'

'From NYU.'

'And Isidor Pinkus also has a licence to practise in the State of New York?'

'In the State of New York, and maybe in the State of New Jersey too, but I don't know that for sure.'

'Where do I find him?'

'Brooklyn.' He gave me a phone number, then promised to phone cousin Izzy to say that I'd be calling.

'Thanks, Pinky. I'll be in touch.' I started to hang up.

'Oh . . . by the way . . .' he asked, 'you haven't forgotten, have you?'

'Forgotten what?'

'What you promised.'

'When?'

'You forgot.'

'I didn't forget,' I lied, 'it's just that . . . I'd like to confirm it with my memory.'

'About how when you get a new job you'll find jobs there for Debbie and me.'

'I didn't forget,' I assured him, even though I had no recollection at all of promising that. 'But for the time being, stay put at GCB.'

'They're talking about you all the time. All the time,' he repeated. 'Debbie heard them.'

'What did they say?'

'I don't know. She wouldn't tell me.'

'Okay, then do me another favour. After you call cousin Izzy, whisper in Debbie's ear that I want to talk to her and that she can call me here any time she wants. Just make sure she doesn't use any phones in the office.'

He said he would. 'Because I know that she wants to talk to you.'

I just assumed that meant she wanted to tell me what they were saying 'round the office.

'Who is it and what do you want?' Dimi was still in his lunchtime-panic mode.

'It's K.C. and I want to know, what does that mean, tea with milk, too much sugar, something-weird Roe?'

'You call me twice at a time like this to ask a question like that?' He shouted to someone, 'You want scrapple, go to Philadelphia,' then came back to me to say, 'Tea with milk. Too much sugar.' He shouted again, 'We need some clean glasses,' then said to me, 'Something-weird Roe. English guy.

But not just any English guy. You know, the English guy.' And with that, he hung up.

Not just any English guy. I asked the little voice, *the English guy?*

There was a very long pause before the response came. *Yeah, the English guy. We know. Lef-tenant.*

Bingo!

When I first started at GCB, there was a fellow who'd come over from Britain whose name was . . . well, yeah, something like something-weird Roe. He was a colonel who referred to everyone under him as a lef-tenant. We all thought that was funny. Lef-tenant. Ri-tenant. He quit a few months later to move to . . .

The little voice found it. *Chicago.*

He went there to work for a brokerage . . . I wasn't sure I'd ever heard the name of it before, or if I had, I couldn't remember it now. But it was definitely in Chicago 'cause I recalled him pontificating about how he was going to beat the Mercantile Exchange, and about how he expected that the weather there couldn't possibly be worse than the weather in England and how, given two years, he'd own the Windy City. I rang the Merc, but they didn't know him.

If he was still in the business, somewhere, anywhere – knowing nothing more than Roe and Chicago – I figured I could find him. So I reached for my laptop and dialled up my Internet provider. I'd been a long-time subscriber to a service called Re, named for the Egyptian God of the Sun. It was a lot more expensive than AOL and Compuserve, but being more expensive meant it was less crowded and less crowded meant it was faster. I also liked them because they offered access to a bunch of specialized stuff about stocks and a few pretty-fair on-line tip-sheets that the other providers didn't.

I started searching for the word Roe in news stories, in news groups – particularly those concerned with the markets – and through various e-mail directories. Several hundred Roes came up. I then narrowed my search with limiters like brokerage houses and trading companies and sorted my way through those results, finally feeding the word Chicago into the equation. But that brought up no results at all. So I expanded the limiter to Illinois, and that produced someone named Horatio, which sounded something-weird-Roe-enough for me.

He was listed as managing director of an operation called On-Time/Real-Time Trades with an address in Cicero, Illinois.

The voice reminded me, *the very same Cicero, Illinois where Al Capone used to hang out.*

I dialled his office and announced to the man who took the call, 'I'm looking for Horatio,'

'You got 'em,' he said, with no trace of an English accent.

I joked, 'Firm's that small, huh, that ya'll answer your own phone?'

He didn't laugh. 'Who's this?'

'Name's K.C. Doone.'

'Do I know you?'

'You do if you're the Horatio Roe who used to work for GCB?'

'GCB?' There was a long pause. 'Another life-time, pal.'

'Ya'll used to have an accent.'

'Ever been to Cicero? The only people with those sorts of accents here are poofters.'

'What's a poofter?'

'That's British for what you would refer to as a "fag", which actually happens to be British for "cigarette".'

'Don't sound British any more.'

'You from Immigration?'

'No, I'm from Boston.'

'With that accent?'

'Look who's talking.'

'Your thruppence, pal. How's that for speaking British?'

'Well, even if you don't remember me . . .'

'Can't say I do.'

'I'd only just started with GCB a few months before you . . .'

'Nope. Still can't say I do.'

'Okay, anyway, the thing is . . . the reason I'm phoning is 'cause I'm looking for someplace to day trade.'

He said right away, 'Minimum in is a hundred grand. But on days of the week that end with the letter Y we have a special and settle for fifty.'

'Ah . . . 'fraid that let's me out.'

'How much you got?'

'Ten?'

'You'll go bust. Put up twenty-five.'

'No got. Old lady's tied up the bank accounts.'

'Ten really the best you can do?'

'Really the only I can do.'

'You're severely under capitalized. I've seen it happen before. Even most guys with big bundles go belly up. You still at GCB?'

'I was until a day ago.'

'What the hell, you didn't ask for my advice and aren't going to follow it anyway. If you think you know how to trade, I'll take your money.'

'Trading might be the only thing I do know.'

'I'll still take your money. Start up is five hundred and fifty dollars for a password and the software. First month is included. After that, the service is three hundred and fifty dollars a month. Direct access to floor traders in all the big markets and some of the tiny ones too. We've got the fastest back office in the business. We use ZINGER-II, which they tell me is cutting-edge technology. It's like ZAP but with better colours. Make sense?'

'Nope.'

'Good. We wire up to your trading account, which unlike most of the other places, you don't have to keep with us. You can leave it in any bank that will let us wire in. Detailed trading reports faxed or e-mail while you sleep. Account settlement before you wake up.'

'Chase Manhattan any good?'

'Chase Manhattan is fine.'

I wondered, 'How about the New York Bank of Athens?'

'Georgia?'

'Greece.'

'You've got to be joking,' he said. 'First trades, thirty minutes before opening. Last trades, two hours after closing. Neither guaranteed, but we try our best, and just for good measure our best comes with a surcharge at one-sixth of a point. Most of our action is the S&P 500. Board of Trade is pretty good. So is the Merc.'

I told him, 'I don't know much about that stuff. Just the NYSE and NASDAQ. And I guess my kinda action is NASDAQ.'

'How much do you know about NASDAQ?'

'A lot.'

'You'll need to. NASDAQ round trip is sixty dollars. One way thirty-five. But then, why the bloody hell would you want to go one way? That's British again. I know, we're steeper than most but I've got two kids at university and you don't have the readies to open an account anywhere else.'

'Readies?'

'British for cash.'

'Sounds good enough,' I said. 'I'll Fedex a cheque.'

'I'll fax you the rules of the road and Fedex the software to you. When I clear your cheque, I'll e-mail your password, which some computer makes up but you can change it.'

Now I asked delicately, 'Do you really have to wait till it clears?'

'If I ring old man Garrison, will he vouch for you?'

'Such a healthy guy,' I said, 'he died.'

'I know.'

'So why did you ask?'

'How about Maynard?'

'Two days ago? Probably not. Today? Definitely not. He'll even tell you I'm the worst guy he ever met.'

'That's recommendation enough for me. But if your cheque doesn't clear, I'll have to agree with him.'

'You still drink tea with milk and too much sugar?' I asked.

He answered, 'Never did.'

I looked at my watch, was rudely reminded yet again of the fact that I didn't have a watch and was just about to go out to buy one when I remembered cousin Izzy. I dialled his number, hoping that Pinky would have got through to him by now.

It rang only once.

'This is Isidor Pinkus,' came the voice of a twelve-year-old, 'attorney at law, speaking. I can help you?'

'Mr Pinkus?' I had to ask, just in case it was his teenage kid. 'Is that you?'

'Yes, this is me, Isidor Pinkus, attorney at law, speaking. I can help you?'

I was totally thrown off by his voice. 'Mr Pinkus . . . ah, howdy, my name is K.C. Doone. Your cousin Steven suggested I call you.'

'Oh yes,' he said. 'My cousin Steven. He called me to say that you were going to call me. So tell me, are you a friend of his?'

'Yeah, I am . . . sure . . .'

'No, I mean . . . are you a friend of his sociably or a friend of his workably?'

'Workably?'

'As opposed to sociably.'

'Sociably?' It took me a few moments to understand what he was alluding to. 'Oh, you mean, do I . . . you mean, sociably sociably? No, the answer is workably. Yes. We used to work together.'

'Workably is good because sociably sociably . . . well, I'm sure I don't have to tell you that my cousin Steven means well, but it is difficult for us to accept certain things about him sociably . . . you understand.'

'Oh sure, I understand. Believe me, I know what you mean. And I agree, absolutely.' I only said that 'cause, after all, I was about to beg a favour. 'No problem. Workably, yes.' Then I changed the subject. 'Did he happen to tell you why I would be calling?'

'Something about not having to pay for free advice.'

'Ah . . . yeah, that's about right. Can we meet?'

'Meet? Yes. Let's meet.'

'Tell me where and when.'

'Where are you?'

'Midtown.'

'Okay, you tell me when and I'll tell you where.'

I asked, 'How about this afternoon?'

'It's almost three now. It should take you an hour from Midtown. Make it four-thirty. You know the F Train? Sit in the front part and take it all the way to King's Highway. But walk off the platform at the McDonald Avenue exit. I'm across the street. You can't miss it. Right under the sign that says, "Jesus Saves".'

Chapter Nine

We must have sat that way, kinda back to back, for an hour.

At least it seemed that long.

And even if it was only half that, it was still a long time to be sitting in such a small space, in the dark, listening to someone else breathe.

'Specially with him, every now and then, breathing real loud.

I figured he was doing it on purpose, so every time he did that, I clicked my teeth.

Every time I did that, he stopped breathing loud, till the next time.

Then I'd click my teeth again.

And he'd breathe softly for a while.

I needed him to remember that I was there too, that he couldn't always have his own way, that we were going to be stuck in this elevator together all night long.

And while we were on the subject, I rehearsed my speech inside my own head, *not only are you gonna have to deal with me right here right now in this elevator till we're saved, but you're gonna have to deal with me after we're saved too 'cause I'm not going home till you and I settle this business with my mama.*

He breathed heavy again.

I clicked my teeth.

He breathed.

I clicked.

He breathed.

I clicked one more time, then swung around towards him. 'Damn, but you gotta stop that.'

He turned very slowly to face me. 'Stop what, Mr Doone?'

'That breathing. It's driving me nuts.'

'You want me to stop breathing?'

'Just stop breathing loud.'

'And what about you? What about all those clicking noises you do. What about that, Mr Doone?'

I raised my hands in surrender. 'Okay. Tell you what. How about we call a truce?'

'A truce?' He was gloating 'cause he knew he'd gotten on my nerves. He'd held out longer. He'd won. 'Whatever for?'

'For however the hell much longer we're trapped in here together. I mean, if we don't set down some ground rules, we're either both gonna go nuts, ape-shit certifiable nuts, or one of us is gonna kill the other.'

'Ape-shit certifiable?' He made a face. 'Is that English?'

'Listen . . .' I tried to hold my temper. 'If you're doing it just to get my goat . . . I mean, come on, we're in this together.' I took several deep breaths . . . real loud deep breaths to show him I could do it too . . . then suggested, again, 'A truce. How about it? What do you say, we start being adults about this . . .'

He stared at me . . . 'Adults . . .' then sighed. 'All right, Mr Doone, adults it is. But that will require you to cease acting like a child.'

'No,' I snapped. 'You can't go getting on to my case or I'm gonna be getting on yours. That's my point. We drop the bullshit. You know, cooperate and graduate.'

'What does that mean?'

'It means we work it out together, you and me, hoeing in the same direction so that the green grass is gonna grow all around.'

'Mr Doone, what language are you speaking?'

'I'm speaking a language that says, we gotta get through this together.'

He studied my face, then slowly started to nod. 'No more bull-shit.' There was a pause, then a grin. 'No more ape-shit either.'

I didn't smile. 'And no more cleaning your damn toes.'

'Or clicking your teeth.'

'Or breathing so heavy.'

'I have to breathe,' he objected.

I looked at him and nodded, 'Yeah, sure, go ahead and breathe. But silently.'

'Ape-shit is out, silent breathing is in,' he smiled, then extended his hand. 'Is it a deal, Mr Doone?'

I hesitated, wondered if this was really his way of making peace, or just setting me up, but shook his hand anyway. 'Deal, Sir Tommy.'

He sat back, putting his hands on his knees, now turning so that we were facing each other. 'Shall we find something suitable to discuss?'

'Ah . . . yeah . . . sure.'

'Such as?'

'You choose.'

'No,' he insisted, 'you choose.'

'Ah . . . okay . . .' I knew about his interest in politics, so I suggested, 'That political party you tried to form.'

'But I did form it.'

'Okay, then how about that?'

'Do you really want to discuss politics?' He shook his head. 'All right. Shall we start from the premise, politics is fun?'

'Is it?'

'Indeed it is. In fact, politics is one of only two toys that are worth having. The other being media.'

'I don't get it.'

'Rich man's toys. Politics and media. Everything else is still a chore, no matter how much money one has, including making money. Oh, yes,' he added, 'and women.'

'Women? Do they fall into the chore or fun category?'

'Don't get me started on that subject or we'll be here even after someone lets us out. No, I suggest we discuss something neutral. Such as . . . children? I have a flock of them. Do you have any?'

'No.'

'Then it isn't fair. What about . . .' He thought for a while, 'automobiles?'

I told him, 'A friend of mine in Connecticut once bought an old London taxicab to use as a station car.'

'What's a station car?'

'You know, a car to drive from home to the station in the morning.'

'Why?'

'People who commute by train to New York every day have a car they can park at the station so that it's waiting for them when they come home at night.'

'No, I mean, why a London taxi?'

'Ah . . . I guess 'cause it's kinda neat . . . I don't know. Seemed like a good idea to him.'

'Rather working class, don't you think?'

'You wouldn't want to leave a Rolls-Royce in the station parking lot.'

'Why not?'

'Might not be there when you came home. Or, if it was, your hubcaps wouldn't.'

'How extraordinary. What on earth would someone do with Rolls-Royce hubcaps?'

'Sell 'em back to guys like you.'

He raised his finger. 'Truce, remember?'

'I wasn't being . . .'

'Yes, you were.'

I gave up 'cause this was going nowhere. 'Let's think of something else. How about . . . sir?'

'Sir?'

'Yeah, how come you get to be called sir?'

'I've been knighted.'

'Come with your very own round table?'

'No. These days all you get is the Queen tapping her sword on your shoulder and a piece of parchment that gives you the right to tell your friends they must call you sir. Oh, and you can also put little letters after your name on stationery.'

'What little letters?'

'Little letters that tell the world you're a knight.'

'How come she made you a knight?'

'She didn't. Well, I mean, she did, but only in name. It came from my politician friends. But that's the same for everyone. Politicians hand them out like sweets at a child's birthday party. The British version of *nomenklatura*. A way to cushion the political classes from the working classes.'

'So how did you get yours?'

'I'd like people to think it came for achievement and skills in business. But most people understand that it usually comes from remembering to drop suitable campaign contributions in the proper coffers.'

'You mean, you bought it?'

'Everyone does, in one way or another.'

'What does it get you, 'cept the right to call yourself sir?'

'A very good table at The Connaught.'

'Where?'

'The Connaught.'

'Is that sorta like the Buonorroti?'

'What's the Buonorroti?'

'That place where you made that speech in New York.'

'The Buonorroti? Is that what it was called? Hah.' He shook his head. 'Mr Doone, the Buonorroti struck me as an over-priced school dinner. The Connaught is . . . let's just say, it's not for people who confuse which spoon to use.'

'That's what you get for being called sir? You mean, if I phone up and say I'm Sir K.C. Doone, they'll give me a table when they wouldn't otherwise?'

'Not necessarily,' he explained. 'But if you were to ring up and say you were Sir Tommy Whitestone, there would be a table.'

'How about if I just said, Sir Tommy?'

He nodded proudly. 'That would work too.'

'And if I said, Sir K.C.?'

'Hmmm.' He thought about that. 'Most likely, they would very politely place your booking on the usual three months' waiting list.'

'Who waits three months for a meal?'

'No one who knows how not to,' he said. 'But that's not the point. The trick is to make certain people believe that they don't have to wait three months for a meal.'

'Huh?'

'It's their way of making people feel special, or guilty, or both so that they spend more.'

'Is the food really that good?'

'Good? Yes. But not extraordinarily good. Anyway, this isn't about food. It's about jumping the queue.'

'Oh.'

'Although perhaps . . .' He started to nod. 'Yes, perhaps Sir K.C. Doone is an odd enough name for them to think you were genuine and allow you to jump the queue. However, never forget that such a ploy would only work once. Your place in the queue on the next occasion would depend on the depth of your pockets during the previous visit.'

'You mean, how much I spend?'

'More how much you leave to show your appreciation.'

'Sounds like New York.'

A quizzical expression crossed his face. 'But what does it mean?'

'It means . . . you know, that money makes the world go round.'

'No, not that. Of course, I know that. I meant, what does it mean? The K? And the C?'

'Nothing.'

'Nothing?'

'Nope. Nothing.'

'Surely it must stand for something.' He poked my shoulder gently. 'Come on, Mr Doone. Kenneth Charles? Kevin Claude? Karen Caroline? You can tell me. After all, there's no one else here. And I promise not to repeat it to more than nine other people.'

'Really, they're just initials.'

'You've got to confess,' he said. 'It's part of the truce.'

I took a deep breath. 'My parents conceived me after a drunken 4th of July party at a Knights of Columbus lodge. Some of my dad's Italian cop friends had a shindig there and because he was forever grateful that they had in some small way contributed to the fact that the Doone name would live on at least one more generation, he insisted on naming me after them. Well, at least, naming me after their lodge. My mother put her foot down when he wanted to call me Knight Columbus Doone, so they agreed to a birth certificate compromise and just used the initials K.C.'

He pondered that. 'Yes, it probably would work. Sir K.C.' He nodded several times. 'See, you are sort of a knight too.'

'I hadn't thought of it like that.'

'Clearly, you have never tried to jump the queue at The Connaught.'

Chapter Ten

Horatio's fax arrived, the application was straightforward enough, I filled it out, wrote him a cheque, grabbed all the paperwork I needed for my new friend Isidor Pinkus and headed to my local neighbourhood Fedex store. I put the application form and the cheque into an overnight envelope and paid them to deliver it to Horatio before noon tomorrow, put my contract and my mama's paperwork into another overnight envelope – using theirs was cheaper than buying one of my own – stuck it under my arm and made my way down to 59th Street. On the way I stopped at a news-stand to buy myself a big packet of M&Ms and a copy of a magazine I spotted called *Day Trader*.

The Puerto Rican was right where I knew he would be 'cause that's where he's been hanging out for years – on the corner in front of Bloomingdale's. He was also dressed the way I knew he would be, easy to spot, 'cause that's the way he's been dressing for years – off-the-rack Tommy Hilfiger yacht-racing gear and a baseball cap, backwards, with the words, 'Lennie Bernstein Lives'.

I'd never bought anything from him before – every time we stopped at his table to see what he had, Lorilee made a point of saying, in a loud voice for everyone else on the sidewalk to hear, 'I only wear the real thing' – but when he spotted me, I gave him a hi sign, as if I was his best customer 'cause the first rule of haggling with street traders is make them think they've known you for a hundred years.

'Hey, my man, how's business?'

'Whatcha need, *hombre*?' He held out his hand, palm up, not to shake mine but so that I could slap his.

'A time-piece of distinction,' I slapped, doing my best imitation of a hip black guy.

His wooden fold-up table was covered with a bright red cloth, and the cloth was covered with watches. In the corner, there was a little handwritten sign that read, Bloomingdale's Annex.

'*Hombre* . . . for you or the *mujer*?'

I spotted the one I wanted right away – a red-face Cartier tank watch with a red leather strap – but I left it lying right where it was. 'For the *hombre*,' I said, adding, 'show me your wares, my man.'

He leaned forward to ask quietly, 'I can furnish you with Role-ex? Pia-jay? Bright-ling? Long-genes? But if you don't see it, that don't mean I don't got it. You know what I'm saying?' He winked.

I didn't know what he was saying, but I winked back, 'Right on,' and eyed all of his stock. 'How much for the Rolex?'

'My best watch, my man. High demand item. For you? Two big ones.'

Now I picked up a watch that had the words Baume and Mercier across the round white face and asked, 'How much?'

'Congratulations, *hombre*. That's my second-best watch. One twenty.'

I put it down. 'Too much.'

'But when I say, one twenty, that's the price for out-of-town tourists. For a *caballero* like you, hundred for the Role-ex, sixty-five for the B and M.'

'Hundred for the Rolex and sixty-five for the Baume and Mercier . . .' I pretended to think about it.

'Take a hundred for the two.'

'Or sixty-five for the Rolex?'

'You drive a tough deal, *hombre*.' He reached for the watch. 'Wrap it or wear it?'

'Not yet.' I reached for another, this time a round white face with three letters written on it. 'What does this stand for?'

'YSL?' He responded without hesitation, 'You Sure Late'.

'Gotcha.' I put it back and picked up a very attractive round black-face watch. 'How much for the Pia-jay?'

'*Hombre* . . .' He held it up to his own wrist. 'We are talking high high class. Tourist price two hundred. *Caballero* price . . . fifty bucks.'

'*Hombre* . . . how about medium-level class, *caballero* price? Like for that Bright-ling over there?'

'You're better off with the Pia-jay,' he said, showing me how it looked on him. 'What did I say, forty bucks? You're a very good customer, I know you . . . so I will sacrifice it to you . . . for thirty-five.'

'What's that one?' I pointed to a round gold watch with the words Patek Philippe on the face. 'Who's Philippe? And how much?'

'Now you talking high high again. Forget the out-of-town price. That's only for people from places like Ohio. For New York City *caballeros* . . . for the Pay-tek Felipe . . .'

'Who's Felipe?'

'Me.'

'Your name is Felipe?'

'No, it's Fidel. But that's close enough. Pay-Tek Fidel. Sixty five.'

'Gee,' I shrugged, 'I don't think so. Outta my league.'

'What did I say? Listen, did I say fifty bucks? I must be *loco de la cabezza*. For you, *hombre*, how is forty-five?'

'Can't do,' I said, held my hand out for him to slap and announced, 'Another time. *Manana* maybe.'

'*Hombre*, where you off to like that?' he said, grabbing my hand and not letting go. 'Now . . . *dos minutos*. How can a *caballero* like you walk away from a deal like this? Felipe. Fidel. What's in a name?' He tried to strap the watch on my wrist. 'Here I'm *loco*, I know it because I'm losing money.'

I wouldn't let him. '*Gracias. Manana. Manana.*'

'*Manana, manana?* I'm not Me-ji-cano. In Puerto Rico we don't say *manana*. We say, *hoy, hoy*. Today. Are you telling me there isn't a single watch here you don't want to own today?'

'Well . . . let's see . . . Fidel, my man . . .' I slowly reached for the Cartier.

'*Si, si, si.*' He started nodding furiously. 'I knew you were a *caballero* of class. That is my most expensive.' He took it out of my hand and this time I let him strap it on my wrist. 'This is exactly the one for a *caballero* like you.'

It fit pretty good. It also looked pretty good. '*Rojo.*' I shook my head and told him, 'My man no can do . . .' I started to take it off . . . 'Red just doesn't match my eyes.'

'Stay up late with a *senorita*,' he joked. 'Seventy-five. It is the best I can do.'

'My man . . .' I took it off and tried to hand it back to him. '*Manana. Gracias. Adios.*'

'Oh, *caballero* . . .' He refused to take the watch from me. 'You know how much this watch costs in there?' He pointed to Bloomingdale's. 'My partners in the main store would ask you hundreds of dollars, thousands of dollars, but here in the Annex . . . fifty is the best I can do. Fifty dollars for Cartier? *Hombre*, their ties cost more than that.'

'Difference is, my man, their ties weren't made in the Philippines.'

'*Filippinos?*' He acted insulted. 'No. This isn't junk from the *Filippinos*. This is genuine Thailand. Okay, maybe a little Vietnam thrown in. Who knows. But no *Filippinos*.' He carefully placed his hand on his heart. '*Mia madre* . . . my mother . . . no *Filippinos*.'

'Take ten?'

'*Caballero*, this is my best watch. Come on, I have a wife and six kids. Thirty.'

I inspected it again. 'Philippines,' I said. 'And not even Manila.'

'What Manila?'

I came up with the only other place I knew in the Philippines. 'In my expert opinion, my man . . . almost probably Corregidor.'

'Corregidor? *Hombre*, you have to do better than that. Corregidor is the island at the mouth of Manila Bay.' He shrugged. 'Call it twenty and with the other ten bucks you buy a book on geography.'

'Manila Bay, huh?' I handed him a twenty. '*Gracias*.'

'Don't go away,' he said, stuffing my money into his pocket. He reached under his counter and produced a Cartier box. 'The guarantee is inside.'

'Guarantee?' I left the box.

'*Hombre*.' He held out his palm, I slapped it, then gave him my coolest-black-guy secret handshake . . . the one where after you bang fists you intertwine fingers. 'You may not know no geography,' he said, 'but for a white guy, *hombre*, you sure talk funny.'

I winked and headed down Lexington, strutting with my brand-new fake Cartier strapped to my wrist almost as if it was real. I stopped at a cash machine to re-finance myself, and then at 53rd jumped on the F Train, riding in the very first car all the way to Brooklyn.

Being the middle of the afternoon like this, it wasn't crowded, though the New York City subway system never fails, at any hour of the day or night, to entertain. So I sat there munching on my M&Ms and flicking through the magazine, but mostly I kept watching the show.

There was one middle-aged lady with a large snake tattoo on her calf, a couple of old black ladies wearing hockey shirts, one guy in leather and chains with a ring in his nose, a couple-a-three teenagers doing a lot of whispering and giggling, and two fellows in smart business suits who were also wearing running shoes and cowboy hats.

And while I watched, the little voice inside my head kept singing that song about Charlie on the MTA.

He may ride for ever 'neath the streets of Boston . . .

When I was a kid growing up there, the Massachusetts Transit Authority had a strange custom of charging you to get on the subway and then, if it went from underground to overground, or vice versa, charging you again to get off. The song was all about some guy who was sentenced to a life of riding the subway 'cause he didn't have any money to pay to get off. I liked the part best about his wife waiting for the train to pull into a station and, as he passed by, handing him sandwiches.

The F Train heads west from Lex to Sixth, then downtown all the way to Washington Square where it cuts east, under Greenwich Village, to Delancey Street on the Lower East Side, and finally under the East River to Brooklyn. As the neighbourhoods change, so too the people getting on and off the train. There were businessmen along Sixth, and two kids with guitars at Washington Square. They played a couple of José Feliciano songs and then passed a hat. I like José Feliciano songs, so I tossed in a quarter. Two rabbis dressed in black and with white beards got in at Delancey, looked around the car, said something to each other and before the doors shut, got off. Squeezing past them, just in time to get on the train, were a couple of kids carrying spray cans. They sat at the end of the car, kind of suspicious like, as if they were waiting for the right moment to leave their graffitied signatures.

The little voice asked, *instead of a sandwich, why the hell didn't she just hand him some money so he could get off?*

At the first stop on the Brooklyn side, which I think was York Street, two women in Guardian Angels' costumes got on the train and automatically sat down facing the kids with the spray cans.

'Cause if she gave him some money instead of a baloney on rye, the song wouldn't rhyme.

At the next stop, which I guess was Fulton Mall, the kids with the spray cans got off. The Guardian Angels got off too. As soon as they did, the two little old black ladies in hockey shirts stood up, took magic markers and wrote on one of the walls 'Bird Lives'. They got off at the next stop and I sat staring at the message they'd left.

He may ride for ever 'neath the streets of Boston, he's the man who never returned.

In all, it took about an hour before the train pulled into King's Highway, and by then it had filled up with school kids. I took one last look at 'Bird Lives', and wondered if, maybe later, I should buy a magic marker and write somewhere on a subway train wall, 'Save Charlie From the MTA'.

Stepping off the train, I walked down to the street at the McDonald Avenue exit and spotted the sign immediately – JESUS SAVES – bright bold red letters on a poster covering the front of the second floor of a low brick building.

A small grocery store took up most of the ground floor. A door next to it bore a tiny plaque that read, 'Isidor Pinkus, Attorney at Law'. There was a bell to ring, so I pushed it, and when the door buzzed open, I found myself staring at a flight of stairs. There was no other choice, so I walked up the stairs to a landing where there was only one door. It was open. Inside it, sitting behind a plain metal desk was a very small and very young fellow with thinning blond hair.

He was staring at me, so I smiled at him. 'Mr Pinkus?'

'Mr Doone?' He motioned for me to come inside.

'Nice to meet you,' I said, as the little voice inside my head muttered, *the guy really is twelve years old.*

He extended his hand. 'Likewise.'

The office was sparse, to say the least. There was his desk, two metal chairs facing it, some law books on shelves, a framed diploma, a stand lamp, a fax machine, a telephone and a slightly sad ficus plant next to the room's one window which turned out to be almost half-covered by the Jesus Saves sign.

The little voice prompted, *let's ask how long he's been a lawyer and if it isn't yet a week, let's go somewhere else.* But

I overruled the suggestion. 'I appreciate you taking the time to see me.'

He gave me a good eyeing over, then nodded, 'Workably. Not that I ever doubted you.'

'Workably,' I reassured him. 'Did Steven tell you the nature of the problems I need advice on?'

'All he said was that you were looking for free advice.'

'Well . . . not really free . . . I mean, I wouldn't expect you to act for me for nothing.'

'Neither would I.'

'But among my problems is the fact that my wife has emptied our bank accounts.' I stared at him and shrugged.

He shrugged in return. 'You mean, it gets worse?'

''Fraid so.'

'So explain.'

But first ask how old he is, the little voice budged.

I blurted out, 'How long have you been a lawyer?'

'Since I graduated law school.' He pointed to his diploma. 'And passed my bar exams.'

From where I was sitting I couldn't see the date at the bottom of his diploma.

'Last year,' he volunteered.

'The bar exam?'

He hesitated. 'No, law school. This year the bar exam. But just because I'm only starting out . . .' He became very defensive. 'Even Alan Dershowitz had to start somewhere.'

The little voice chimed in with, *at least Alan Dershowitz is old enough to drink.*

'Please . . . I understand.' I suddenly felt guilty. 'Steven recommended you highly and I genuinely would welcome your advice.'

'Because he's my cousin, I understand and because it's free, I don't blame you. So explain.'

Over the next hour I told him about getting fired, about my problems with Lorilee and Duke and about the problems my mama was having in Florida. He listened attentively, took some notes, nodded whenever I paused to take a breath and when I was finished, stared at me for several seconds before asking, 'Is that all?'

'Isn't that enough?'

'You know what? You're right.'

'About what?'

'About having problems.' He took a deep breath. 'First things first. You said you've got a contract with your former employer.'

I handed it to him.

He read it, all the time mumbling to himself the same way dentists do when they've got your mouth stuffed with cotton. Hmmm . . . hah . . . tsk, tsk, tsk.

When I couldn't stand it any longer, I asked, 'How bad is it?'

He put the contract down on his desk and muttered, 'Breach of fiduciary trust.'

'What does that mean?'

'Politely, anything they want it to mean.'

'And not politely?'

'Not politely . . . think of Pinky sociably.'

'I get the picture.'

'Who wrote this contract for you? Or is it their standard contract?'

'My brother-in-law.'

'Whose side was he on?'

'What do you mean?'

He put the contract aside, then reached for the pile of papers concerning my mama's supposed mortgage. There was a lot more mumbling – hmmm . . . hah . . . tsk, tsk, tsk – as he thumbed through every page. When he finally tossed them on top of his desk, he confessed, 'I don't know.'

'Don't know what?'

'I don't know if they can do what they're doing, or not. I think these people . . .' He checked to find the names, 'South Florida Island Federal Finance . . . and Eton Island Finance Management and Trust Company . . . and Padre Island Finance Management Services and whoever Alexander George is . . . I think they've probably been smart enough to protect themselves so that even if there was something you could do, you wouldn't be able to do it in Miami or Texas, you'd have to do it somewhere like . . .' he looked again at the paperwork, '. . . like Freeport, Grand Bahama. And maybe even then that company would turn out to be nothing more than a shell for another company which would be a shell for another company . . .'

'You're telling me it's my turn in the barrel?'

'What barrel?'

'Think of Pinky,' I said.

He raised both hands quickly. 'I get the picture.'

'So GCB fires me and leaves me destitute 'cause they get to define breach of fiduciary trust anyway they want. These clowns take my mama's apartment 'cause no matter what, we gotta play by their rules. And I guess Lorilee gets to screw her brains out and then put the blame on me so she can keep our house and all our stuff and spend whatever's left in our bank accounts.'

He agreed, 'That's one way of looking at it.'

'Got any other way?'

He stood up and went to stare out the window. 'My little green plant is still little. Some people might say that's because it doesn't get enough light. Why doesn't it get enough light? Some people would say because of the sign out front that covers this much of my window. And why is there a sign out front? Some people would say because five years ago when there was a bank downstairs, someone decided to stick a sign on the building that made a bad joke. Some other people would say that because this is a Jewish neighbourhood, by putting a sign up here that says Jesus Saves, it's an affront, a very in-your-face way of being anti-Semitic. And there have been a lot of people in this neighbourhood who have fought very hard to get this sign taken down. If nothing else, maybe it would help my little green plant.' Now he turned to face me. 'What do you think?'

'Huh? Me? Well . . . I suppose . . . yeah, I guess it is a kind of a provocation.'

'Provocation? To some people, yes. What else?'

'What do you mean, what else?'

'There are always different ways of looking at things.'

'Such as?'

'Did you see my name plate on the door that says I'm an attorney at law? If I told you to get off at King's Highway and look for that name plate, you'd still be on the street trying to find me. Instead, all I have to do is say "Jesus Saves".'

I grinned. 'Okay. So how does Jesus save my mama? And get me a settlement from GCB. And stop Lorilee and Duke from leaving me penniless?'

'He helps you find me.'

That made me laugh. 'For some reason, acknowledging help from Jesus is just about the last thing I expected to hear . . . you know, from someone like you.'

'Why? I take referrals from anyone.'

'So just how do you and Jesus help me do all that?'

'First, by not worrying so much about what the sign says, and instead worrying about what really matters.'

'Which is?'

'How we can use the sign to our advantage.'

'Such as?'

'Such as, you do have a contract with your former employer and all we have to do is make them understand it will be cheaper to settle than to fight. It's a question of finding the right level. Such as, no matter how those people in Florida or Texas or the Bahamas think they've protected themselves with shell companies and offshore hocus-pocus, your mother's apartment is still in Florida and if they want it, they have to come to Florida. So we have to make sure that when they come to Florida, they meet us on our terms. Such as, the only thing your wife has going in her favour at the moment is a brother who's a lawyer. And no matter how good a lawyer he is, you have certain statutory rights that no amount of good lawyering, or even great lawyering, can exclude. I presume the incident with her personal trainer wasn't the first time.'

I didn't know.

'Then again, adultery is adultery. Quantity doesn't count. It isn't like baseball where you're only out on the third strike.'

'Okay.' I sat back. 'Now what?'

'Now you go home and I close my door and I spend some time thinking about all of this. And then I write a letter to your former employer and I write a letter to your wife . . .'

I cut in, 'About to be former wife . . .'

'About to be former wife,' he conceded. 'And then maybe I make some phone calls to see what I can find out about whoever is trying to take away your mother's apartment.'

I needed to know, 'And . . . what does all this cost me?'

He nodded several times, as if he was adding up figures in his head. 'It costs you a few letters and a few phone calls and a couple of hours of thinking time.'

'That all?'

'For the time being, that's enough.'

'Instalment plan?'

'Pinky said you'd be good for it.'

I stood up and shook his hand. 'Thanks.'

'Be patient.' He shook mine. 'Never forget what I told you.'

''Bout Jesus?'

'About Alan Dershowitz. Although, come to think of it, they both had to start somewhere.'

By the time I got back to the apartment my new watch said it was 7.00. I decided that was as good a time as any to phone Mikey. 'It's K.C. Doone, again. Friend of Dimi's.'

'Oh yeah,' he said. 'Sorry about before. You caught me in the middle of the market.'

'Dimi said you day trade?'

'Left Merrill Lynch two years, three months and six days ago. First year on my own was tough. Second year was break-even time. Last three months and six days have been . . . well, what can I tell you, I make out.'

'Can we meet?'

'Sure. You eat yet?' He didn't wait for an answer. 'How about we meet at Dimi's? I missed lunch there today and I hardly ever go there for dinner but I guess we owe him one. How about I see you there in half an hour?'

I arrived first.

Dimi had already left for the night.

There was a counter with stools running along one side of the place, four booths running along the far wall, and six tables in between. Always crowded during the day, it was pretty empty now, just two guys sitting together at the counter, the short-order cook at the grill, one guy behind the counter and a tired-looking red-headed waitress chewing gum. I'd never seen her before, but that was understandable, 'cause I'd never been in at night.

'Plenty of seating near the orchestra,' she announced, pointing to the counter. 'No credit cards. No cheques. Special tonight is corned beef hash. But I wouldn't if I were you.'

I said I was sort of a regular – 'The sometimes brunch set' – that I was meeting someone and wanted a booth. She said, 'Back two are closed. Take the one in front. Dimi says that's the best one because it makes the joint look busy.'

I slid into the side looking out to the street, and sat there reading through the menu until a very fat guy with a goatee – maybe in his late thirties – walked in, looked around, then stared at me through a pair of horn-rimmed glasses. 'You Doone?'

'Mikey?'

He sat down and immediately asked the waitress, 'How's the goulash?'

She answered, 'Same goulash you had yesterday for lunch.'

'How was it yesterday?'

'Same goulash you had the day before for lunch.'

'Okay, I'll try the goulash.'

I told her, 'Yeah . . . sounds fine to me, too.'

She called to the counterman, 'Two goos.'

He ordered iced tea, I did as well, she wrote our order down on her pad, ripped off the top copy, stuck it on the table under the sugar canister, and walked away. Now I confessed to Mikey, 'I've never been this brave here. I usually stick to bacon and eggs.'

'Best goulash on the West Side. I lunch here most days. Believe me, I've tried the others.' He pointed to himself, 'What I'm telling you is that I know a lot about goulash, pal. You're talking to an expert. I have probably eaten goulash in, like nine countries and twenty-four states. So if I tell you this is the best goulash on the West Side . . .'

'What about the East Side?' I asked.

'No contest,' he said immediately. 'Herbie's. Over on Second.'

I had to smile. 'No kidding?'

'Cook there used to work here. Turkish guy named Ahmed. He was the one who taught Dimi how to make goulash. Then Herbie hired him away.'

'Turkish goulash?'

'Turkish, Hungarian, what the hell, pal, I'll eat goulash even if it's made by a Chinaman. As long as it's great goulash.'

'Gee . . . you must like goulash,' I said, 'cause I couldn't think of anything else to say.

'I'm not the only one. Goulash is probably the biggest money spinner in the deli and diner business today. You don't make goulash, you don't make business.'

I confessed lamely, 'I didn't know that.'

'I'll tell you something else you probably didn't know. Any short-order cook in this town who can make just plain good goulash, well, the guy can write his own ticket.'

'And if he can make just plain great goulash?'

'Sky's the limit, pal. Great goulash . . . you're not talking delis and diners, you're talking restaurants. Linen tablecloth, linen napkins kinds of places.'

'I never knew this about New York.'

'New York? The single best goulash,' he insisted, 'this side of . . . I don't know, what's the capital of Hungary?'

'Budapest.'

'Yeah, that's it. Best goulash this side of Budapest.'

The waitress arrived with our iced teas.

Mikey stirred his, then took a sip. 'Anything you ever want to know about goulash, just ask me.'

'You must cook it a lot.'

'Cook it? What the hell would I want to cook it for when I can eat it already cooked? Who cooks?' He stared at me. 'You cook? When you can eat in places like this, why cook?'

'Places like this . . .' I nodded. 'I guess you're right.'

'Of course I'm right.' He sipped more iced tea. 'But enough about me. So what, you're looking to day trade, huh?'

'I was with GCB in the World Trade Center until a day or so ago . . .'

'Heard of them. But never heard anything very good. Those the guys who call everybody by some army rank?'

'That's it.'

'What happened? You get court-martialled?' He forced a chuckle. 'Good joke, huh?'

'Yeah.' I smiled politely. 'Let's just say I ran into a little disagreement with the management.'

'They fired you, huh?'

'Yeah. I found myself suddenly unemployed.'

'How good a trader are you?'

'It's maybe the only thing I can do.'

'That's a start,' he said, 'but it ain't enough. The thing you gotta remember is . . . when you're trading on the street, you're buying and selling investments for other people. When you're day trading, you're gambling. Pure and simple. Worse, this time it's your money.'

The waitress arrived carrying two bowls of steaming hot goulash and put one in front of each of us. Mikey now leaned forward, so that his nose was only a few inches over his bowl, then started waving his hands in front of him so that he could get the full aroma. His glasses fogged up but that didn't matter 'cause his eyes were closed, as if he was in ecstasy.

'So what's the secret?' I asked, watching him go through this ritual.

'There's only one secret,' he said, his eyes still closed, his nose still just above his plate. 'Two words. Red wine.'

'Huh?'

'Some people think it's all about paprika.' He peeked up at me. 'Granted, there is no doubt that paprika is important. It's undeniably important. Never let anybody tell you different. But the secret of good goulash is really rough red wine. Vintage Bordeaux won't work. Hungarian is good. Spanish is okay. Bulgarian is probably best . . .'

'No . . . I was talking about day trading. You know, asking if there are any secrets about day trading?'

He looked up at me through his fogged specs. 'You play poker?' Then moved his index fingers across the lenses, using them like windshield wipers to clear his view.

'Not really.'

'But you know how, right? Well . . . in a poker game . . .' He scooped up a huge spoonful of goulash. 'I'm talking about guys who know how to play . . . they sit at the table all night, staring at their cards, and mostly folding. They invest in five cards, take a good scrute, think about how much their five cards are worth, then get out because throwing good money after bad is a sure fire recipe for bankruptcy. They wait till they get five cards they can turn into a hand that's gonna win them back everything they've invested to that point, and more. Ask anyone who knows how to play. They'll tell you.' And now he shovelled the food into his mouth. 'If you get in on every hand, you lose. You only play the winning hands. Same thing with day trading.'

'Same thing,' I suggested, 'with investing.'

'Nope. Not at all,' he chewed. 'And this is where you can go wrong. You can't talk about investing and day trading in the same breath. Totally different mind sets.' He swallowed and gobbled another mouthful. 'By comparison, investing is always long term. Day trading . . . long term might be ninety minutes. And that's really long term. Short term, the more usual, is anything from one to fifteen minutes. More likely closer to three. Investing . . . that's where you want to make money tomorrow. Day trading . . . that's where you have to get in and out right now. Investing . . . you can afford to let the market dip. Day trading . . . the market dips you better be shorting it, and if you're not, you'd better be out. Investing . . . maybe you're thinking about capital gains and accruing income. Day trading . . . you're only thinking about making a few points real fast, then sitting around for however long it takes to get dealt another winning hand.'

'So the secret is, be a poker player.'

'Nah,' he said. 'The secret is, you gotta be patient.'

'Be patient. I told him, 'Funny, but you're the second person today who's used those words.'

'It's the truth.' He heaped another spoonful into his mouth. 'You fish?'

'No.'

'Well, it's exactly like fishing. Same thing but different. You sit there all day getting cold, getting your feet wet, pissing inside your own fishing gear, not moving around a lot, just waiting till they bite.'

I'd never seen anybody devour a bowl of anything with the same speed that he went through that goulash. 'How often do you trade?'

'Some days all day. Some days not for a week.' He finished his portion, wiped off what goulash had stuck to his goatee, took off his glasses, cleaned a few splashes off them, then looked at my plate. 'You sign up with anyone yet?'

I told him I was thinking about On-Time/Real-Time out of Illinois.

'Posh,' he said. 'Expensive. They've got their own guys on the floors, unlike some of the other operations who share guys. They also use that fancy new software.'

'ZINGER-II,' I told him, as if I knew what I was talking about. 'State of the art.'

'I'm still low-tech but I'm looking to upgrade.'

'Sounds like a tough way to eke out a living.'

'Be patient. Wait for the right cards. Always protect your downside. Never bet on whims or fancies. Never marry the market. Only bet on great cards. And specialize.'

'In what?'

'Anything that moves. Some guys like softs. Some guys like currencies. The only thing we all have in common is movement. That's it. But because everything is moving all the time, you can't try to deal in everything. So I watch. I dunno . . . I watch maybe twelve companies. Watch 'em like a hawk. And then wind up maybe playing two . . . three . . . four.'

'What do you watch?'

'Like everyone else, the hi-techs. Everybody plays Intel and Microsoft. I also watch a couple of bio-chems. Small. Volatile. All you need is to get one tip on a bio-chem that pays off and you're home free for the week.'

'Any in particular?'

'Whatever they're touting that morning on CNBC.' He shrugged. 'Some guys are tuned into Bloomberg. But I stick with CNBC because I got the hots for that little Italian chick. The one with the sexy mouth.' He shook his head. 'Not really a great mouth. But a good mouth.'

'Oh yeah, her,' I said, not knowing who he was talking about.

'Actually, it doesn't matter who you tune into as long as you've got your ears to the ground and can second-guess where the market is going the instant it starts to move.'

I mumbled, 'CNBC, huh?'

'Another thing . . . never be afraid to walk away and come back later. You don't marry the market. That's probably the best advice I can give you.' He sat back and stared at me. 'There are loads of other rules. Like . . . take the goulash when they pass the plate because you won't get everything handed to you on every trade. But you know what, pal? In the end, the best advice I can give you is don't take too much advice.'

'No?'

'Nah. You can get on the Net and check out all the day trading sites. There were dozens of them yesterday. There'll be hundreds of them by tomorrow. Everybody's got advice to hand out. But most of it's garbage. You know how to trade? That's a start. Spend whatever time it takes learning the software you're using because, no matter what, you can't let that get in the way. You've got to be able to get all the information you need in real time right away, and make the software do exactly what you need it to do at precisely the moment you want. After that, put your money on the wheel and watch it spin.' He pointed to my bowl. 'You gonna eat yours?'

'I've already eaten some of it.'

'What about the rest?'

There was little more than half a bowl left. 'If you want more, I'll get you another bowl.'

'If you're not gonna finish yours . . .'

I pushed my bowl towards him. 'Enjoy.'

'And disposition,' he said, now shovelling my goulash into his mouth. 'That gets back to being patient.' He took another spoonful. 'Did I mention CNBC?'

'The one with the sexy mouth,' I reminded him.

'No. I mean, did I mention the bump?'

'No, you only mentioned her mouth.'

'Well, you can't just stare at it, you gotta listen to it too. Her mouth tells you what's moving and sometimes even tells you why. That's why all the day traders on earth are watching. I don't fantasize about her when the market is happening, I'm listening to hear when something's headed north. Me and the rest of the world. When it is, everyone jumps in. There's an automatic bump of a few points. The price goes up. Then everyone gets out. If it stays up that's because real people have also gotten in. Or the mouth says it's heading south and everyone dumps shares. Dump and bump. The mouth gives the word and the herd of bandits moves. If you're fast enough, you can make a living just there.'

'The bump theory,' I mumbled.

'Without that you need real intelligence. And you should have real intelligence too. Look at everything you can get your hands on. Think electronic. The Net is filled with stuff, though, like I say, most of it garbage. I see all the usual trade stuff, all the newsletters and tip sheets, stuff like Cassandra, but by the time printed stuff gets to you, it's shelf worn. You know, when you see a bandwagon, it's too late.' He chewed, swallowed, then shovelled in more. 'Who said that?'

'Said what?'

'When you see a bandwagon, it's too late. Bet you don't know.'

I shrugged. 'Nope. Don't know.'

'One of the richest men in the world. Guy named Whitestone. Tommy Whitestone. Ever heard of him?'

'Whitestone?' The name rang a vague bell. 'Ah . . . I guess. Yeah, why?'

'Guy who raided Continental Tire and Rubber Company about . . . I don't know, maybe fifteen or twenty years ago. Went into Conti, bought options on a helluva lot of shares, then announced he was taking over the company and would fire half the workers and all of the management. He scared the shit out of so many people working for Conti that they had to buy the company back from him at like a three hundred per cent profit.'

'Corporate raider,' I nodded. 'Yeah, I know who you mean.'

'He was the guy who said it. And he should know. I always say, never argue with anyone worth a billion bucks. A mere millionaire, what the hell, they're a dime a dozen. Anybody can get lucky and make a million. Anybody who's gotten lucky and already made a million can stay lucky and turn it into ten million. But when you're talking a billion . . . sorry, pal, that's not luck any more. That's a guy who knows something the rest of us don't.'

'He's worth that much?'

'He must have made a couple hundred million just on Conti. And that was after he did some weirdo deal about paper or timber or lumber, remember that? He bought into a company in Washington State or Oregon or some place with a lot of woods. Took 'em for a fortune. Same scenario. Panicked the management, then stepped back just far enough to let them buy their way out. That's his act. Or at least it used to be. He doesn't do it much any more. But he used to do it all the time. Option in. Spook the board. Sit around counting all their money until the next time.'

'Sounds like he didn't win a lot of friends doing it.'

'Hey, life ain't a personality contest, pal. It might be nice being named Miss Congeniality but she ain't no Miss America. She's just another girl who lost.'

I mulled over the expression – *when you see a bandwagon, it's too late* – then started thinking 'bout all the times I'd traded into shares that were bandwagons. 'I'm not sure that's true.'

'Miss America? Only one girl wins. The others are also-rans.'

'No. The bandwagon. I've gotten into a couple of bandwagons that have paid off.'

'And brought home what? Fifty per cent? Maybe you even doubled your money? Big deal. Now factor in all the bandwagons that didn't pan out. What do you wind up with? Probably bubkus. What Whitestone is saying is that the real money is in owning the bandwagon, then selling it to clowns like us when we jump on. It gets right back to the Wall Street proverb, when everybody's buying, sell, and when everybody's selling, buy.'

'Your guy Whitestone said that?'

'Nah. Everybody's said that. But the bandwagon adage . . . come on, how many guys do you know who've come out of the market with a billion bucks?'

I had to admit, 'Not a lot.'

'So if a guy like Whitestone preaches it, I figure I can pray to it.'

'You're probably right.'

'I know I am, pal.' He raised his index finger again to signal another serious point. 'Never follow the crowd.'

'Whitestone again?'

'Mikey.' He bowed. 'And that's another thing about day trading. If you're following the crowd, you're gonna lose money because the crowd is sheep. You gotta predict where the shepherd is taking them. CNBC again. You gotta get in before the sheep and get out before the sheep. You do that and you're gonna make money. You don't do that and you're gonna wind up working in a joint like this, serving goulash to a couple guys like us.'

'A lot to think about,' I said. 'You want dessert?'

'What?' He looked at me like I was crazy. 'After a meal like this, I should gild the lily?'

We sat there for another ten minutes as he expounded on how New York had only managed to become the goulash capital of the world, 'By just edging out Istanbul.'

I took Mikey at his word. 'Istanbul. I'll remember that.'

He said thanks for the goulash, I said thanks for the advice, he said, 'Hey, pal, let's do it again real soon,' and I fibbed, 'Okay, pal, I'll look forward to it.'

There were still plenty of cabs around at that hour, but I decided to walk back to my place. The fresh air would help clear my head while I contemplated the bump theory. It took me forty-five minutes to get home. But that also gave me a chance to pass some gas.

By that time, I was convinced that if it was true – if day traders watched CNBC, heard a tip, got in, bumped the shares high enough to make a profit and then got out – then the bump theory deserved further research.

Yet if it was that easy, just another bandwagon, the bump theory could turn out to be a recipe for disaster. Being under capitalized, I didn't need the little voice to tell me that one disaster would be enough to sink me. So I stretched out on the living room floor, dialled up the computer and started looking for what the Internet's day trading gurus were saying. I went to the Infoseek search engine, entered the words 'bump theory' and got nothing back. I tried 'day trading', found 3532 references and bookmarked the list of results so I could see them again. I asked Hotbot the same questions. Nothing on bump theory but 3591 responses to day trading. I bookmarked those and tried AltaVista. The response there was two for bump theory – both turned out to be dance routines for strippers – and 4224 references to day trading.

After bookmarking that, I started hunting around the various newsgroups for the two terms, and found several instances where both were discussed, mostly in the Misc.Invest category. Checking bump theory first, I read the theories of a couple of guys arguing its merits – neither were convinced that it held water – then moved on to the day trading references, which were mostly people trying to sell stuff or bragging about big hits.

There was hardly a single comment that mentioned big losses.

It looked to me like the newsgroups were the electronic equivalent of the bar next to the fishing dock.

You should have seen the one that got away.

So I went back to the Web.

I didn't have any way to print out any of this – my printer was being held hostage in Connecticut – but I had a bunch of disks which meant I could put anything I downloaded on to them and print it out later. Even though my back was starting to hurt and my elbows were starting to ache – I was fast coming to the conclusion that I needed to get myself a desk and chair – I began making my way through the Infoseek list. Here too, most of the references were people trying to sell stuff. There must have been two dozen different brands of day trading software. But every now and then something looked like sound advice, and I downloaded it to read later.

After nearly three hours of lying on the floor like that – I'd only gotten through about 250 listings – my eyelids were doing some serious drooping. I shut down the computer and promised myself I'd spend the weekend learning as much as I could about day trading, 'cause come next week, I intended to start earning a living at it.

I got into bed and lay there thinking that it hadn't been too bad a day. I made some progress. I got myself a trading account. I found more reference materials than I know what to do with. I found a lawyer to call my own. And I learned a lot about goulash.

The next morning, I picked up some Alka Seltzer to undo dinner, arranged for a new cable box, bought a TV set so that I could watch CNBC, bought two wooden horses and a plank of wood so that I had a desk, and a fold-up canvas director's chair so that I had something to sit on in front of my desk.

I managed to schlep it all home and got there just in time to find an old guy in an ill-fitting greenish-brown suit standing in the lobby looking for K.C. Doone. 'You him?'

I asked what he wanted.

All he said was, 'You K.C. Doone?'

I said, 'Yeah, I am. Why?'

And all he did was hand me a court order from Duke preventing me from going anywhere near my own house in Connecticut.

My first reaction was to hit the old guy who delivered it. My second reaction was to crumple it up and throw it away. Instead, I phoned Lorilee. 'What the hell do you think you're doing?'

But she said the same thing to me this time that she said last time, 'I can't talk to you,' and hung up.

So I phoned Duke, got his secretary on the line and demanded, 'Ask him what the hell he thinks he's doing?'

But she said, 'He won't talk to you, though you are welcome to have your lawyer get in touch with him to discuss a settlement. In the meantime, he advises you that you disobey the court order at your peril.' Then she hung up.

Now I called Izzy. 'I just got a court order preventing me from going home.'

'Fax it to me,' he said.

'And then what do I do?'

'Don't go home.'

We both hung up.

I faxed it to him and he rang back a few minutes later. 'You're right. It's a court order preventing you from going to your own house in Connecticut.'

'I know what it is. But can Lorilee and Duke do that to me?'

'They already have.'

'I mean, can they stop me from going back to my own house?'

'They think they can.'

'What do you think?'

'I think they think they can too.'

'They want to play hardball? Okay. What do you say we play hardball too? Let's get us a court order keeping her away from the apartment here. And we'll call the police and report how she and her brother robbed my place of everything. And then let's sue her for divorce and put her personal trainer on the stand to testify about her personal training.'

He must have been thinking about that because he didn't answer for almost a minute.

'You still there?'

'That's it,' he finally said. 'That's it.'

'That's what?'

'That's what they're doing. They're waiting for you to hit back.'

'I don't get it.'

'It's like in chess when someone makes a move that tempts you into taking one of their pieces. It's a sacrifice. They take your piece and leave one vulnerable. You understand?'

'No.'

'Well, we won't fall for it.' He hung up.

'Huh? Izzy?'

The only response I got was the disconnected tone ringing in my ear.

I didn't have a clue what to do, or any M&Ms to fill my face, so I did what I usually do in situations like that – punt. This time it took the form of rearranging the furniture. The only problem was that, these days, I was pretty low on furniture. Still, I set up the horses in front of the window in my bedroom and put the board on top of them, put the canvas director's chair in front of the board and sat down.

The little voice wanted to know, *why are we doing this in the bedroom?*

I agreed, carried the chair into the living room, came back for the board and the horses, and set it all up in front of the window there. That made a little more sense, 'cept there was no electrical outlet handy and the phone wouldn't reach either. So now I walked over to Office Max to pick up an extension cord for the computer and a twenty-foot extension for the telephone.

Get fifty feet, the little voice said, *so it stretches into the bathroom.*

Sure enough I came home with the fifty-foot version.

I put the laptop in the middle of the desk, and my pads and pencils off to one side. I put the telephone on the other side, along with the answering machine and fax machine. I plugged everything in, turned it all on and, finally, sat down to see how it felt.

But it felt wrong.

My cable TV connection was in the bedroom and this way, if I was going to day trade to CNBC, I'd have to do it by running between rooms. So now I took it all down again and moved it all back to under the window in the bedroom. The thing was, as soon as I put the TV set at the end of the desk – turned just right so that I could also watch it in bed – there wasn't enough space left for the fax and the answering machine and anyway, the plug for the fax was in the living room.

There was nothing left to do but compromise. I left the computer and the TV set in the bedroom and told the little voice we were moving our communication centre back to the living room.

That's when the phone rang.

Convinced it was Izzy, I answered with, 'You figure it out yet?'

Instead it was Debbie, and she was in tears. 'I called you at home. I made a mistake. I got the numbers confused. I'm sorry. I didn't mean to do that. Your wife said you weren't living there any more. Maynard and Cotton fired you. Now she's fired you. Well, I'm quitting too. They can't fire you and talk about you the way they do. I won't stand for it.'

'Whoa . . . listen to me . . . hold your horses . . . are you on an office line?'

'No. And I can't hold my horses. I'm downstairs. I am quitting. You'll see. They fired you and your wife fired you . . .'

'Debbie . . . whoa . . . wait . . . just a minute . . . please . . . calm down.' It took a while before I could get her to listen. 'Ya'll gotta understand something. Quitting isn't going to help either one of us. It's just gonna play into their hands. Stay where you are. Keep your head down. Don't give them any excuse to get nasty with you. And you're right, they're horrible.'

'Is it true about your marriage?'

'Ah . . . let's just say . . . we're having some difficulties.'

'Your wife said she threw you out and wasn't going to take you back. Just like Maynard and Cotton. It's not right. I won't stand for it. You should hear what they're saying about you. What they're telling other people about you.'

'Who?'

'All of them. I mean, not your wife because I don't know what she's saying, except what she said to me. But Maynard and Cotton. I mean, breach of fiduciary trust to the tune of nine million dollars . . .'

'I know Maynard and Cotton would like to think that I'm in breach of . . . nine million dollars? Where did they come up with that figure?'

'The company in Hong Kong that got raided.'

'I didn't put GCB into anything for nine million.' The extent of their exposure was, tops, maybe half a million.

'Believe me, it's nine.'

Believing myself, I knew it was nowhere near nine. Couldn't have been. I wrote it off to Debbie having heard wrong. 'Listen. Everything's gonna work out okay.'

'Are you going to live through this?'

'Of course I am . . .'

'Because . . . I'm really worried, K.C., because I once saw a programme on Oprah where people lost loved ones to S-I-S.'

'To what?'

'S-I-S,' she said. 'Stress induced suicide. You know, where people get very upset and can't deal with the anxiety and then . . .' Her voice cracked. 'Please tell me you won't do anything rash.'

'Hey . . . hey, Debbie, trust me . . . everything's gonna be all right.'

'Poor you,' she said. 'Poor K.C.' And just like that, she hung up.

Straight away, I phoned Pinky. This time, my luck ran out 'cause Frannie took the call. 'GCB . . . Garrison, Cotton and Braddock, may I help you please?'

I put on my best Chinese accent. 'Ah . . . Ste-phen Pink-us, please.'

'Who may I tell him is calling, please?'

The only name I could think of was, 'My name . . . Charles Chan.'

She was too young to recognize the references and put me through. When Pinky answered I said in my own voice, 'It's me. Please phone me back.'

It took him nearly an hour. 'Cotton's been on my case. He thinks I'm talking to you. He thinks everyone is talking to you. Except Binterman. They figure Binterman's the only one definitely not talking to you.'

'Maybe you should tell him he's the only one who is,' I said, then decided, 'But I can't worry about Binterman just now, I've got other things happening that I need to take care of. Like Debbie.'

'I know. I know. She's in bad shape.'

'You gotta calm her down.'

'I can't. She's left.'

'She quit?'

'No . . . I mean, at least I don't think she quit. But she did walk out.'

'Can you find her? Where does she live? Get her home number and try there.' I hated to think she might do something foolish. 'Find her. Take care of her. Don't let her quit. Get back to me later.'

He said he'd try.

A few minutes after hanging up with him, my mama called, and she was in tears again. 'I got an official eviction notice. It's signed by a lawyer. I have to get out.'

'Fax it to me,' I said. 'Everything's gonna be all right, I promise. But you gotta fax it to me now.'

Through her hysteria she said she'd do it right away.

After waiting nearly an hour, when the fax didn't arrive, I phoned her. But there was no answer. Feeling kinda desperate, I dialled Izzy. 'My mama got some sort of eviction notice.'

'When?'

'A little while ago. She's supposed to be faxing it to me, but I haven't got it yet.'

'Who's it from?'

'I forgot to ask.'

'So when she faxes it to you, fax it to me.'

'Can they throw her out?'

'I don't know if they can throw her out, but I do know that they want her to think they can, which isn't the same thing as actually being able to.'

'Izzy, are you real sure . . .' I didn't know how to pose this question without hurting his feelings. 'What I mean is . . . Izzy, are you absolutely positive you can handle this?'

'Am I positive? Let me see. First, you want me to get some money from your employer who fired you. Second, you want me to arrange something with your wife so that you don't have to give her everything. Third, you want me to save your mother's apartment from these people who want to take it away from her.' He paused. 'Is that what they call a hat trick?'

I conceded, 'I reckon it is.'

'Well, then we'll just have to score a hat trick.'

'I'm counting on you.'

'You know what? So is your mother. And, frankly, so is mine.'

No sooner had I hung up with him than my mama's fax arrived. It was an official-looking document on letterhead from a lawyer in Miami named Juan Luis Gonzalez Ochoa. The way I read it, she had ninety days to vacate. I faxed it to Izzy and when he phoned back, he confirmed I'd read it right. 'She has ninety days to vacate.'

'That's bad.'

'No, that's good,' he said. 'Now we have to lure them into a courtroom.'

'You mean we fight it?'

'There's nothing to fight,' he said. 'From what this letter says, they're well within their rights. But that's only if you believe this letter.'

'So why are we taking them to court?'

'Discovery.'

My bell rang.

'What does that mean?'

The bell rang again.

'Hold on a second.'

'I can't,' he said. 'Call me next week. Just remember, the operative word is discovery.' He hung up.

I got to the bell just as it started ringing a third time. 'Who is it?'

'It's me,' a familiar voice said.

'Who's me?'

'Debbie.'

'Debbie?' I buzzed her in.

While she came up in the elevator, I started racing around the apartment to straighten up. 'Cept I didn't have much to straighten up. So I went to the door and opened it.

She was just walking down the hallway.

'Cept she was walking funny.

'You okay?'

She stared at me, saying nothing till she got to the door.

'K.C.?' There was a very strange look in her eyes. She handed me my Giants football helmet with some M&Ms still in it, then handed me my binoculars. 'K.C., I've come here today because . . .' Her speech was slurred. 'Because . . . the reason I've come here today . . .'

I had to ask again, 'You okay?'

'They fired you and your wife fired you . . .'

'Debbie . . .' I balanced the helmet and binoculars in one hand, then took her arm with the other and brought her into the apartment, closing the door behind her.

'K.C. . . . my darling poor sweet abandoned K.C. . . .' She looked up at me. 'I've come to be your woman.'

And promptly passed out.

Chapter Eleven

The longer Whitestone and I were trapped in that elevator, the slower time seemed to move. And yet I could feel my body getting tired faster and faster.

'I kinda wish ya'll hadn't mentioned food as I suppose we're not gonna eat again until tomorrow morning.'

'No more of those Smarties?'

'M&Ms.' I reached into my raincoat pocket and fumbled around till I found the other two. 'This time . . .' I opened my hand to let him pick the colour he wanted, 'please chew it.'

He leaned forward to look. 'Both?'

'One for you. One for me.'

'Can you tell which colour is which?'

'All cats are grey are in the dark.'

'So they are,' he agreed. 'This one could be red . . .' He popped it into his mouth and went through a whole exaggerated pantomime to show me how much he was chewing. 'Hmmmm.'

'Two or three crunches is all it takes,' I explained.

'I would assume that your philosophy dictates that the longer one makes it last, the better.'

'Right.' I crunched twice, then swirled what little chocolate there was around in my mouth, trying to melt it on my tongue so that I could savour it that much longer. 'I think mine was green.'

'Can't tell from the taste with these things.' Then he asked, 'Could you tell the difference between M&Ms and Smarties?'

I answered confidently, 'Sure could.'

'Bet you couldn't.'

I started to say, 'Could too . . . different shape . . .'

But he cut me off. 'I like to bet on things. Do you bet on things, Mr Doone?'

'I try to bet on stuff when I know I can win. Like the difference between M&Ms and Smarties.'

'Only betting when you know you're going to win? That's no fun.'

'Beats betting when you know you're going to lose.'

'That's not the point,' he corrected. 'Betting is not about winning or losing. It's about betting. Like when you see two statues and you bet which one the next pigeon will land on.'

'Or like spitting on the wall and betting on how long it will take the saliva to get to the bottom? We used to do that in high school.'

'We could do that here,' he said.

'Ah . . . you know, that might have been funny then, but lots of stuff that was funny then . . . thanks anyway.'

'Such as?'

'Such as what?'

'Such as what was funny then . . . that's what you were going to say, isn't it? Some things that were funny then aren't funny now? So, I said, such as?'

'I don't know . . . the kind of crazy stuff kids do.'

'How about crazy bets? What's the craziest bet you ever made?'

I couldn't think of anything. But that's not why he'd asked the question. He wasn't interested in my craziest bet, he wanted me to ask him about his. 'What was your craziest bet?'

'When my brother was at Oxford . . . I never got there, except to visit him . . . there was a girl who used to hang around his digs. I stayed in the flat with my brother. And she liked to parade around in a nightgown. Neither of us was sleeping with her, although we both tried to, mind you. She simply liked to come over and take off her clothes and put on her nightgown and walk around. When the novelty wore off, you know, when we stopped looking, she cut little holes in the top of the nightgown so that her nipples stuck out. Well, one day, my brother and I decided we should get her nipples hard by opening the window . . . you see, it was winter . . . and we bet on which nipple would get hard first.'

I stared at him in disbelief. 'Really?'

He nodded gleefully.

'Who won?'

'Actually . . . neither of us. We had to declare a draw.

We didn't realize that under the circumstances neither nipple would act independently. You see, when equal cold is applied equally . . . sounds like some sort of scientific formula . . . when equal cold is applied equally to both nipples, they both get hard at the same rate.'

'Great topic for a thesis,' I mumbled. 'More fun anyway than winning or losing a bet.'

'See? Some things that were fun in those days would probably still be fun today.'

'Ah . . . yeah, I guess so.'

'Anyway, as far as winning or losing a bet is concerned, I repeat, Mr Doone, that winning or losing doesn't really matter. In fact, it is inherently the same thing. They're both merely side-effects. Think of them as consequences. It's not about winning, losing or even nipples. It's about betting.'

'So ya'll don't mind losing, huh?'

'Of course I mind losing. I hate losing as much as I love winning. I suppose over my lifetime I have won huge fortunes. I suppose I have lost huge fortunes, as well. In truth, I know I have. But again, the end result . . .'

I wanted to find out, 'How huge is huge?'

'Winning or losing?'

'But it's the same thing.'

He grinned. 'Touché.'

'So how big was the biggest win?'

'I have always loved the gee-gees . . .' he started to explain.

'Gee-gees?'

'Horses.'

'Why "gee-gees"?'

'I honestly don't know. That's just . . . it's slang. I think children call horses gee-gees.'

'When I was a child I called them horses.'

'That's probably because you're not British.'

'What did you call them when you were a child?'

'*Chevaux.*'

'What's that mean?'

'It's French for horses.'

'How about if the horses were British?'

'Then we called them gee-gees,' he snapped. 'Do you want to hear about the bet or not?'

'Okay. Tell me about the bet.'

'I was still at Eton . . . you know, public school . . . this is before I quit school all together.'

'I've heard of it. 'Cept it's a private school.'

'Yes, Mr Doone, public school is private. In this case, very private.'

'Why did you quit?'

'Because if I hadn't, I would have been asked to leave. It amounted to the same thing, except this way I am forever able to say I did it to them before they did it to me. Now . . . to continue . . . I was still at Eton when . . .'

'So, you quit Eton and then what?'

'Then nothing.'

'How old were you?'

'Sixteen.'

'And that was the end of school for you? What about college?'

'You mean, university? Hah.' He pretended to shoo it away with his hands, 'Hotbeds of loony radicalism.'

'Loony radicalism?'

'Did you go to university?'

'A couple of them. I started but I didn't finish.'

'I won't even allow my children to start. I have a clause in my will that expressly forbids any of my children, and in the future, any of their children, from using any of my money to attend university.'

'That's in your will?'

'Indeed it is. Universities are hotbeds of loony radicalism and I will not have any of my children or grandchildren turned into loony radicals.'

'But your brother went to Oxford?'

'My brother is an exception.'

'Like the girl with the cut-out nightgown.'

'Not at all,' he said as if it should be evident. 'You wouldn't want your daughter doing that, would you?'

I reminded him, 'No kids.'

'I rest my case.' And just like that, he picked up where he'd left off several minutes before. 'So one afternoon I went to Lewes . . . it's a race course which you would probably call a track . . . and I bet a one-pound accumulator.'

'What?'

'My craziest bet.'

'Oh . . . oh yeah.'

'A one-pound accumulator. You would call that a parlay. I had it on three horses. And all three came in. I won eight thousand pounds. It was a lot of money in those days. Although I have at various times won and lost much greater sums. I once dropped more than a hundred thousand dollars in one evening of backgammon in Los Angeles. Although I won a quarter of a million dollars there the following night.'

'Now, that is a lot of money.'

'But it's not the same return. You could put a million quid on a roulette wheel, red or black, and if your colour hit, you'd win a million quid. You'd double your money but that's only a return of a rather measly one for one. And whether it's gambling or business, which is sometimes the same, mind you, what has always interested me is the return. So when my one pound returned eight thousand, well, I look on that as the biggest win of all.'

'So much for big bets,' I said, running my tongue over my teeth, still tasting that last M&M. 'So much too,' I said helplessly, 'for dinner.'

'In that case, how about dessert?'

'Yeah,' I said, 'I'll have the baked Alaska.'

'That's a dish I like.' He rubbed his hands together. 'Well done, Mr Doone. Now tell me, where was the best baked Alaska you ever had?'

I confessed, 'It was the first dessert that came to mind. I'm trying to think if I've ever even had baked Alaska.'

He said right away, 'The best baked Alaska I ever had was . . . Paris.' He nodded several times. 'My father's hotel. We had a chef.' He looked at me. 'You know that I was raised in a hotel in Paris, don't you? Le Relais Faubourg St Honoré. Right on the Faubourg itself, just down the block from the Elysées. You know, of course, that's the French White House. It's still there, the old hotel that is, although the name has been changed to . . .' Now he stopped. 'I mean, with all of your research I would have expected you . . .'

'Yeah, four rooms on the fourth floor.'

He nodded to show me he was impressed. 'Well, we had a chef named Monsieur Drapeau. Mr Flag. Everyone had to call him Monsieur Drapeau, or Monsieur Le Chef, because he was a tyrant and everyone was afraid of him. But he liked me and said I could call him Monsieur Flag. I suppose I was about nine years old at the time. I liked visiting him in his kitchen because he made the best desserts you could imagine. Including baked Alaska. Except, being French, he called it *Omelette Norvégienne*.'

'What does that mean?'

'Norwegian omelette.'

'Why would he call it that when it isn't Norwegian and it isn't an omelette?'

'But it is. It's an omelette of meringue and ice-cream.'

'Where I come from omelettes are made with eggs and bacon and green peppers and onions.'

'The egg is in the meringue. The bacon, green peppers and onions are,' he said snidely, 'optional.'

'Also, where I come from, you don't put ice-cream in an omelette.'

'You're not really going to begin defending the food where you come from, are you?'

'Yeah, I am. Which is why we don't call it an omelette from Norway, we call it baked Alaska.'

He shook his head and disregarded my comment. 'Sometimes, Monsieur Flag would add Grand Marnier to it. Then he'd let me have a little taste, on the promise, of course, that I never told my father. I also liked it when he would let me taste Cointreau. He used that whenever he was in the mood to serve it *flambée*.'

'Sounds delicious,' I said. 'But doesn't it melt the ice-cream?'

'You've never had baked Alaska served *flambée*?' He patted my shoulder. 'I'm truly sorry.'

'Me too,' I told him, because I couldn't think of anything else to say.

'Do you still want dessert?'

'I'll pass on the baked Alaska and just have coffee. Thanks.'

'How about some sugar and butter?'

'What for?'

'Dessert.' He leaned forward, reached into his blazer pocket and pulled out six sugar cubes, wrapped the way you find them in your coffee saucer in restaurants, and two small sealed plastic tubs of margarine, the kind that restaurants hand out when you don't want butter. 'You reminded me that I had this. May I offer you dessert?'

I stared at it. 'Do you always bring your own sugar and margarine to parties?'

'I picked it up at lunch.'

'Today?'

'Yes, of course. But I did it yesterday, too. They're upstairs in the flat.'

I didn't get it. 'You went to a restaurant for lunch today, and yesterday, and both days you stole sugar and margarine?'

He took offence. 'I don't steal it. It's free. I always take the sugar and, when they put these little plastic containers of margarine on my table, I take them too. And at breakfast in hotels, I take the tiny jars of marmalade. But I don't have any with me now. Sorry.'

'Sugar, margarine and marmalade . . . why not?'

'Sweet 'n Low, too. You know, for people who don't want real sugar in their coffee.' He smiled proudly. 'I don't think I've gone to a store to buy sugar or margarine in twenty years. We do buy marmalade though. But we never have to buy saccharin. He handed me three sugars and one of the tiny margarine tubs. 'Fifty-fifty,' he said, showing me that he was giving me half his cache. 'Now, I assume that if one dunks the sugar in the margarine . . .' He demonstrated by unwrapping one of the sugars, pulling the plastic top off the margarine, plunging a cube into the margarine, then popping it in his mouth. 'Hmmm . . . what a good dessert this is, Mr Doone.' He smacked his lips. 'Delicious.'

I was hungry, so I opened my sugar and opened my margarine and dipped one of the cubes into it and popped it into my mouth.

'It's awful.' I swallowed it anyway.

He suggested, 'But it's free.'

Chapter Twelve

I was too surprised to catch her.

She landed with a thud.

I put the helmet with the M&Ms down and the binoculars down too, then picked her up off the floor.

She reeked of gin.

I didn't have a helluva lot of places to unload her, so I carried her into my bedroom and put her down gently on Lorilee's side. That immediately looked wrong to me but I was afraid that if I moved her to my side I'd wake her. Instead, I propped some pillows under her head.

She was snoring loudly.

The thought crossed my mind that I probably should take off her shoes, but the little voice instantly proclaimed, *bad idea to take off her anything*, so I covered her with my blanket and left her there – still thinking I should have put her on my side – shoes on and all.

Back in the living room, I dialled GCB, only to be informed by Frannie – who referred to me as, *Oh yes, that Chinese gentleman* – that Mr Pinkus had already left the office for the night, it being Friday and him having special dispensation to get home before sundown for religious purposes. My next thought was to call him at home, but knowing the little I knew about his religion, I supposed he wouldn't answer the phone, or if he did, he'd never come out on a Friday evening, even to rescue little Debbie.

From us? the voice asked.

Or us from her? I said, *now what?*

When in doubt, the voice decided, *eat.*

I went into the kitchen, but the only thing in the fridge was a couple of eggs and half a loaf of raisin bread. There was no telling how hungry Debbie'd be when she woke up but there was no denying I was hungry enough already. I was also short on M&Ms, 'cause when I checked the Giants helmet, I could see that somebody had been at them. I figured I'd run out and get some stuff.

But the little voice figured different. *What happens if she wakes up, doesn't know where she is, starts screaming for the police, they show up, look at her, look at you, she's only a kid and you're twice her age . . .*

I surrendered without a fight.

Moving into the living room – *what the hell, there's plenty of things I can do, plenty of work I need to get done* – I was confronted with yet another what-if-Debbie dilemma 'cause the computer was on my desk and my desk was back in my bedroom. So I tiptoed inside, silently fetched my laptop, brought it into the living room, installed myself on the floor just under my lamp, booted up, dialled into Re and got on the Net.

For the next couple of real uncomfortable hours, I managed to get through another hundred references to day trading, plus a dozen newly discovered references to bump theory – a few of which I actually found helpful – before my back and my elbows couldn't take it any more and my stomach was nagging that if I didn't eat something now, I'd permanently regret it.

Standing up to stretch, I poked my head past my bedroom door. Debbie was calling geese now – honk, honk, honk – and the thought crossed my mind that if her own snoring didn't wake her, she might be out for the night.

Oh good, the voice said, *a sleep-over date*.

I went into the kitchen, took two pieces of raisin toast and two soft-boiled eggs, broke up the toast into tiny pieces, put them in a bowl, mixed the eggs in there, added a pinch of salt, contentedly chewed my way into the living room, sat down with my back against the wall, thought about what to do next, and couldn't come up with anything more interesting than calling my mama. 'Ya'll know what I'm eating?'

'What?'

''Member how you used to put soft-boiled eggs in a bowl with pieces of toast? Well, I only had raisin bread, so I had to use that, but I never woulda realized how good raisins drenched in soft-boiled egg yolk can taste.'

'The thought never crossed my mind, either,' a woman responded, 'cept she wasn't my mama.

'Honest, it's delicious. Who's this?'

'Patsy. Who's this?'

'K.C. Who's Patsy?'

'Me. Who's Casey?'

'Ruby's son.' I was a little confused why she was answering my mama's phone. 'Can I talk to her please? Is everything all right?'

'Ruby's son? Well, I'm Carrie's mother and Tyler's mother. But that's all of us. Sorry, no Ruby. I'm afraid you might have dialled the wrong number.'

'Oh. What number is this?'

'Nope. You have to show me yours before I show you mine.'

'What?'

'Perhaps I should phrase that differently. What I meant was, you'll have to tell me what number you're calling before I tell you what number you've got.'

I did.

'Alas,' she said, 'close but no Almond Joy.'

'Shouldn't that be cigar?'

'We're a no-smoking house. You've got the same number, except that you've dialled area code 516 and not area code 561.'

'Oh . . .' That surprised me. 'I'm sorry. You see, I don't usually dial her number, which is why . . .'

'That's not nice. A boy should make a habit of ringing his mother often.'

'I do call her real regular, but I use one of those pre-programmed speed-diallers . . . I mean, I used to . . . I kinda replaced my phones and this one doesn't have that button.' I stopped when the little voice demanded, *what the hell are you going into explanations for?* 'Anyway, listen, I'm sorry to have bothered you . . .'

'Not at all,' she said, 'but do tell . . . this raisin bread and soft-boiled egg dish of yours. Did you get that out of a cook book?'

'No. Truth is, I never did it before with raisin bread. But my mama always used to make it for me and I was hungry and I didn't have any white toast in the fridge.'

'Hmmm,' she paused for a moment. 'It strikes me that with some milk, butter, sugar and eggs and, well, yes, even raisin bread, you could make *pain perdu*.'

'What's that?'

'Bread and butter pudding.'

'Bread and butter what?'

'Pudding.'

'Something tells me that's not a country boy's kinda thing.'

'What country?'

'Boston.'

'That explains everything,' she said. 'On the other hand, now that you're visiting New York . . .'

'How do you know I'm visiting New York?'

'I can see from my caller ID. You don't think I'd carry on a conversation with a total stranger about something as important as bread and butter pudding without being sure that it wasn't a crank call.'

'How do you know it's not a crank call?'

'Because crank callers make certain their crank calls can't be traced back to them.' She read out my phone number. 'I therefore presume you don't qualify. Although,' she said, 'anyone who puts raisin toast in soft-boiled eggs might fall into the category of crank cook.'

I explained, 'Where I come from cooking is merely the art of adding heat to food, 'cept if you're my mama and can make stuff like fried peanut butter and banana sandwiches.'

'Sounds absolutely horrible.' She wondered, 'Do country boys from Boston eat that before, after or with their shad roe?'

'Home of the bean and the cod,' I told her, not recalling how the entire poem went. 'Obviously, you never spent time in the south.'

'South Boston? Or south Florida? I've been to both places but no one there ever made us eat anything like that.'

'South south, like Tennessee,' I said. 'You don't know what you're missing. My mama makes the best fried peanut butter and banana sandwiches on earth. And country boys from Boston eat that instead of shad roe.'

'You present a good case for culinary synergy.' She cupped the phone and I could hear her say to someone, *you will be back by eleven and that does not mean eleven fifteen*, before she said to me, 'I can only wish you *bon appetit*, Mr country boy Casey.'

'Oh . . . it's not Mr Casey. It's Doone. K period C period Doone.'

'Mr Doone.'

'Nope, Mr Doone was my father, I'm just K.C.'

'Only two letters? Do you capitalize them or leave them small the way e.e. cummings did?'

'Who?'

'I'm sorry. I'm teasing.'

'Oh.' I didn't know who she was talking about and that made me feel kinda silly. 'Well, Miss Patsy, I hope whoever's supposed to be back by eleven makes it on time. Ya'll have a nice evening.'

'Oh, yes, she will be back on time. I guarantee that. Because if she's not, she's going to find herself grounded for a month. Good night, K period C period Doone.'

'Good night,' I said, and was just about to hang up when she insisted, 'One more thing . . .'

'What's that?'

'Now phone Ruby.'

I laughed, hung up and did just that. 'What's happening with you?'

'I can't sleep. I can't eat. I'm worried sick about that lawyer's letter. What am I going to do? I don't want to have to move north and live with you and Lorilee, that wouldn't be fair.'

'Believe me,' I said without any hesitation, 'that's not gonna happen. You're gonna live right where you live now. I've hired a lawyer and he's looking into everything. There's nothing to worry about.'

'You hired a lawyer? Is he in New York or in Florida?'

'New York?'

'Is he someone famous?'

'No. He's not exactly famous.'

'Does he ever appear on Court TV?'

'Gee, I doubt it . . .'

She sounded disappointed. 'Oh.'

I reassured her, 'But only 'cause he's probably much too busy for that.'

'Does he have any famous clients?'

'Mama . . . let me put it this way, I didn't see OJ Simpson in his waiting room. But, ya'll believe me, he's gonna do whatever needs to be done. There's no need to worry 'bout anything. It's all gonna work out. Trust me. I'm taking care of it.' I promised to call her over the weekend. She asked what Lorilee and I were going to do this weekend. I answered truthfully, 'Nothing at all', reminded her that I loved her and hung up.

As soon as I did the little voice wanted to know, *what the hell is culinary synergy?*

It wasn't all that late but my back hurt so I shut down the computer, stood up, took a real good stretch, then went to peek in on Debbie. There was no longer any doubt left in my mind that she was out for the night and 'cause I was still hungry, I decided to run out to get some stuff.

At my local all-night Korean joint, I stocked up on milk and coffee, butter, eggs and white bread. I picked up some sugar too in case Debbie took sugar in her coffee. Then, 'cause the little voice reminded me, she's only a kid, I took another stroll around the entire store – it's only one aisle up and another aisle back – and wound up buying a box of Cheerios. Finally, I succumbed to withdrawal and bought myself a jumbo bag of M&Ms, half of which I ate before I even got home.

Back at my place, Debbie was still snoring away.

I stood in the bedroom doorway, staring at her, finishing the M&Ms, and wondering where I was gonna sleep.

The little voice pointed out, *the only option a jury will accept as being beyond a reasonable doubt is the floor.*

I wasn't going to sleep on the floor just like that, so I snuck three pillows from under her head, took the blanket, covered her by doubling the top sheet back in half over her – I made certain to leave just enough room for her shoes to stick out at the bottom – and carried my own bedding into the living room.

Normally I sleep in my underwear.

This time I decided I really needed to keep my pants on, though I compromised by taking off my shoes, socks and shirt.

It took a long while after I shut off the lights to settle down – damn but the floor was hard – and even though I managed to get some sleep, it was a pretty bad sleep 'cause I kept tossing and turning and cursing Lorilee for leaving the hardwood floors there and not letting me put down thick carpeting the way I'd originally wanted.

I want some of that really deep pile stuff.

I'm telling you that's so out. Just you thumb through all those interior decorating magazines and you'll see nobody buys deep pile stuff, 'cept maybe people who can't afford real fine hardwood.

'Cept ya'll can't do on hardwood floors what ya'll can do on deep pile fluffy carpet.

Someone rang the door bell twice.

'Cept all that fluffy stuff gets everywhere and anyway, who says I wanna do stuff on the floor.

Ya'll used to.

Yeah, used to . . . and afterwards all you ever used to do was complain 'bout your damn knees . . .

The door bell rang again.

I assured myself that it was still the middle of the night.

My eyes stayed shut.

Then again, I supposed, it could be morning.

Morning?

I jumped up and barked into the speaker phone, 'Who is it?'

The answer came back, 'Fedex.'

'Fedex? At this hour?' I buzzed him in.

Almost as tired as I'd been when I went to sleep, I opened the door and stood there waiting for him. When he stepped out of the elevator, I motioned to him 'Right here' and only then realized I was wearing nothing but my pants.

He didn't so much as blink 'cause, I suspect, Fedex delivery guys have seen it all, the least of which being other guys with no shirts on.

'Mr Doone?'

'You start early.'

'Guaranteed before ten-thirty.' He handed me an envelope, a receipt and a pen.

'What time is it?' I signed and handed the receipt back to him.

'7.46.'

I mumbled, 'Cutting it kinda close to ten-thirty,' just as Debbie screamed, 'Oh, my God!'

The Fedex guy and I both looked to see her rushing out of my bedroom. 'Oh my God . . . oh my God . . . what have we done . . .' She hurried for the bathroom. 'Oh my God . . .'

Now the Fedex guy raised his eyebrows at me. 'See, we're always around when you need us most.'

I started to explain, 'She's just a friend,' but stopped, said, 'Yeah, well, thanks,' shut the door in his face, and turned towards the bathroom. 'Debbie?'

She answered, 'I'm going to be sick,' and slammed the door.

There wasn't much I could do for her, besides give her enough space to be sick all alone in private, so I retreated to the living room, put down the Fedex envelope, put on my shirt, socks and shoes and paced the floor, worrying 'bout her, till she came out, which she did ten minutes later.

'How ya'll doing?'

She was looking very small, very pale and very dishevelled. 'This is like . . . so-oooo embarrassing . . .'

I wanted to be comforting. 'No problem. Believe me, I understand.'

'You couldn't . . .' She started shaking her head. 'I mean . . . here like this . . . spending the night . . . being sick and . . .' She looked up at me with utter dread. 'What happened last night?'

'I guess ya'll kinda had one too many.'

She shook her head. 'That was before I got here. I meant . . . you know . . . after I got here?'

'After you got here?' I told her, 'You slept it off.'

'And?' She paused, as if she didn't know how to say what she wanted to say. 'And . . . what? You know, before I slept it off?'

'You mean, in between?'

She nodded anxiously.

I shrugged. 'Nothing. Ya'll passed out.'

'Passed out? Like . . . I didn't know what was happening?'

'Instant replay,' I announced. 'You knocked on the door, said hello . . .' That was a lie but I reckoned she needed to know the edited version . . . 'handed me my helmet with the M&Ms, handed me my binoculars, then passed out. Right there at the door. So I picked you up, carried you inside and . . . nothing. You slept there. And I slept . . .' I pointed to the three pillows and the blanket . . . 'there.'

She thought about that for several seconds, then begged, 'Please, K.C., please, never tell anyone that I . . . you know . . . almost . . .' Her eyes opened wide. 'Oh God . . .' She rushed back into the bathroom and slammed the door again.

I picked up my pillows, tossed them on my bed, then went into the kitchen to make some coffee. When she reappeared a few minutes later, her clothes were slightly straighter and her face had a little more colour. 'I have to leave.'

'Breakfast is included.' I felt bad that she was having such a rough time. 'I just made coffee and last night I went out and bought you Cheerios.'

'No. No coffee. No breakfast. I . . . really, I have to go.'

'What about the Cheerios?'

'No Cheerios . . . please . . . you'll never tell anyone?'

I raised my fingers in the Boy Scout pledge. 'Promise.'

'Because . . . this wasn't supposed to . . .' She moved towards the door. 'So-oooo embarrassing.'

'Listen . . . Debbie . . .' I was also embarrassed 'bout the state of my apartment. 'I'm sorry I couldn't have made you more . . . you know, more comfortable and all . . . it's just that I'm not yet set up to receive . . .'

The voice cut in, *sleep-over dates.*

'Guests,' I said.

'Really . . . I have to leave.' She hurried towards the door, stopped, turned to me and begged again, 'You promise?'

'Honest Injun. But, hey, if you don't want my Cheerios, we can go to a place down the block for breakfast.'

'No, really . . .'

'Well, then . . . if I can't buy ya'll breakfast, the least I can do is treat you to a taxi cab home. How about that?'

When she didn't object, I grabbed my wallet and headed out the door with her.

'So-oooo embarrassing,' she kept mumbling.

I figured she needed to think of other things. 'I bought the Cheerios 'cause I didn't know what else to buy. I figure everyone loves Cheerios. Though, when I was a kid and didn't feel good, my mama used to give me tea and cinnamon toast.'

'No . . . really . . . thanks.'

We headed downstairs. 'To this day she still says that when you have an upset tummy, the thing that settles it real fast is cinnamon.'

'Really, K.C., it's okay . . .'

I babbled away as we walked through the lobby. 'She swears by cinnamon. And, you know what? I once read somewhere that cinnamon does have magical qualities. The Inca Indians discovered it . . .' I didn't know if that was true or not but it sounded good enough for small talk. 'They found that by drinking cinnamon tea . . .'

'It comes from India,' she corrected as we got to the door. 'And the only thing that I can think of right now that the Incas invented was sacrificing virgins.'

'We'll get a taxi on the corner,' I said as fast as I could, 'there are always plenty of cabs there at this hour . . .' and took her elbow to help her through the door.

But just as we stepped outside she screamed, 'Oh, my God.'

I thought she was going to be sick again so I turned to grab her.

'God . . . no!' She shoved me away.

'What's going on?' someone demanded.

'It's not what you think,' Debbie blurted out.

'It's eight-fifteen in the morning.'

Pinky was hovering over us.

I said, 'Hey.'

He demanded, 'Hey, what? How could you do this to her?'

'Do what?' I asked.

She protested, 'He didn't.'

He insisted, 'It's eight-fifteen in the morning. Debbie, I'm ashamed of you. And as for you, K.C. . . .'

'As for me . . . what?' I still didn't get it. 'Wanna come for breakfast?'

'I have never been so mortified,' he went on, 'in my entire life.'

'It's not what you think,' Debbie said.

'Did he force you?'

'Force you?' That's when I got it. 'Pinky, you crazy? What the hell are you talking about?'

'About her spending the night with you.'

'She didn't,' I lied 'cause I'd promised her I would.

'Yes, I did,' Debbie contradicted.

I said, 'No, she didn't', realized that wasn't gonna play and tried, 'I mean . . . she did, but not the way you think.'

An elderly couple coming along the sidewalk slowed as they got to us.

'Everyone knows your wife left you,' Pinky screamed, then turned to Debbie. 'Are you the other woman?'

I blurted out, 'She's not some other woman, she's a teenage girl.'

'I am too a woman,' Debbie objected.

The couple stopped to stare.

Good one, the voice said, *why not insult the old folks as well.*

'I know you are.' I tried to retrace my steps.

'You know she is?' Pinky shouted at me, then turned to her. 'So, you are the other woman.'

'What other woman?' I asked.

'Shame on you,' the lady half of the old couple pointed at me. 'At your age!'

I wanted to know, 'Pinky, what are you doing here?'

'You mean at her age.' Pinky pointed to Debbie.

'Are you her husband?' the lady asked Pinky.

He answered her with a very swish, 'Hardly.'

I tried again, 'Pinky, what are you doing here?'

Pinky had obviously freaked-out the old guy 'cause he began tugging at the lady's arm. 'Let's go, dear.'

'Take her home immediately,' the lady ordered. 'Get her away from . . .' She glared at me. 'This reprobate.'

'Reprobate,' Pinky confirmed and announced to Debbie, 'I'm taking you home right now.'

I asked her, 'Reprobate?' Then tried for the third time, 'Pinky, what are you doing here?'

The lady chastised me, 'Shame on you,' linked her arm inside Debbie's arm and tried to comfort her. 'Don't be afraid of him, dear, everything will be all right. You need to speak to your mother . . .'

Pinky took Debbie's other arm. 'If I hadn't seen this with my own eyes, I never would have believed it.'

'Reprobate,' the lady confirmed, and with Debbie, Pinky and the old guy in tow, she headed down the block.

'This is not what you think it is,' I called after them. 'Debbie, tell them.'

But Debbie was outmanoeuvred and too soon, too far down the block.

I wondered, *how did I manage to lose control of the morning so early?*

The voice answered, *if only it was just this morning.*

As long as I had my wallet with me, and as long as I was downstairs anyway, I walked over to the news-stand on the corner, bought *The Times*, the *Wall Street Journal*, *USA Today* and two bags of M&Ms – the sleazy guy who owns the place only stocks the small bags so you wind up paying more than if he had the big bags – and then, just 'cause I figured it couldn't hurt, I put a buck on the lottery.

The little voice suggested, *go for Lorilee's birthday and that way if we win tonight, we can hold it over her for ever.*

I played the numbers five and one for the first of May. Then, on a whim, I played Marylou's birthday and Carrie's birthday, too.

Back upstairs, I ripped open the Fedex envelope to find a

form letter of introduction from On-Time/Real-Time Trades, a CD-Rom that contained the ZINGER-II I'd need to trade on-line, an instruction manual that looked much too thin to be useful and several subscription forms for on-line news-letters.

After grabbing a few handfuls of dry Cheerios and a fresh cup of coffee, I sat down at my desk and opened the much-too-thin instruction manual to chapter one which was titled, 'Installing Your Software'.

The little voice reminded me, *we've got forty-eight hours to get our act in shape.*

I munched, *plenty of time.*

But the little voice wasn't so sure. *Wanna bet?*

When it comes to making a brand-new software program work the first time – even when it's state of the art, which I could see that ZINGER-II was 'cause it said so right there on the CD-ROM – the trick is not to get trapped into doing anything that the instruction manual says you should.

There are two reasons.

The first is, 'cause the instructions were written by someone who speaks a language known only to six other people on the planet. The second is, 'cause that same person buckles his pants just under his armpits and never gets dates.

Combining the two, you understand that the instructions are really nothing but a weapon to settle scores with the rest of us who speak English, wear our pants at belly-button height and do get dates.

Believe you me, if Sigmund Freud were alive and well and practising his brand of sorcery today, he'd never bother so much over people who dream sexy stuff 'bout their mamas, but instead scrutinize the dangerous sexual inadequacies of folk who write software manuals.

I mean, come on. There is no way that anyone who preaches stuff like – *the default for extended memory system alternate maps is 32 but can be changed with the .nnn perimeter, allowing that the range must be 0-255, although conflicts might arise while trading in multi-screen mode if the script installer hasn't been moved into extended memory which should not be done unless real-time trading limitators are resident and stacks=9,256 appears in the Config.Sys after the line DOS=UMB* – can get it up.

What's more, 'cause they know that we know, they've booby-trapped Automatic Install and Express Install so that no matter what you do, you're guaranteed to wind up facing a screen filled with messages like, *fatal exception at 2f2:00345.* The way to beat them is to choose Custom Install, which makes them think that you're gonna screw it up on your own, and then fool 'em by clicking yes at every option.

Which is exactly what I did with the ZINGER-II CD-ROM.

A little icon of a stock graph appeared on my desktop, the program booted and the voice announced with justified cockiness, *Peckers 1, Nerds 0.*

My screen was now divided into lots of little boxes, with room for specific information to come up in each one on a real-time basis. Four rectangles framed the main screen. The one running down the left side was for confirming buy orders. The one running down the right side was for confirming sell orders. Whatever real-time wires I wanted would run through the box at the bottom of the screen from right to left, while the rectangular box along the top would keep a running calculation of my stake.

Inside the perimeter formed by those four rectangles, the screen could be divided into as many as nine small squares, kinda like a tic-tac-toe game, with each box programmable to keep an eye on specific shares. It would display the bid and asked prices of up to a dozen market makers, showing the volume and prices of shares they were looking to trade in and highlight the 'touch', which was the best bid and offer spread available on the market at any given time.

It took me a couple of hours to set it up in such a way that I knew I'd be comfortable – to make it look something like the screen I'd gotten used to at GCB – and another couple of hours to run through the practice trading sessions that were included on the CD-Rom.

That turned out to be a game where you traded in and out of shares as fast as you could to beat the machine to a hundred grand profit. The first time I played I lost $72,450. The second time I played I lost $58,580. The third time I played I only lost $53,710.

Convincing myself that I was making some progress – *with only a few more hours practice,* the voice suggested, *we won't go broke till Monday noon* – I closed it all down, climbed on top of my bed, got all my pillows arranged just right, shut my eyes to take a nap and was almost there when my mama's comment flew inside my head.

Has he got any famous clients?

The voice scoffed, *famous clients? How about, any clients?*

Now I wanted to know, *how about other lawyers and their clients?*

The voice asked, *Izzy?*

I answered, *nope, the Spanish guy*, pulled myself off the bed, went back to my desk, found my copy of the lawyer's letter to my mama and got on to the Internet to see what I could find out about Juan Luis Gonzalez Ochoa.

There were a couple of thousand references to people named Ochoa – a whole bunch of them turned out to be Colombian drug dealers, which didn't please me a helluva lot – but after whittling down the search to the bare bones, I came up empty-handed. There were no references at all to any Ochoa with the combination of first names Juan Luis Gonzalez. I checked a few of the on-line phone books but couldn't find him there either. Not a phone number. Not an address.

And that worried me.

There was an address and phone number printed on his letterhead, so now I did a reverse search, checking to see who worked there and also checking to see who that phone number belonged to.

Again, nothing.

Funny, the little voice said, *you'd think that legitimate lawyers would want to be found.*

That got me thinking that maybe I should start checking the companies that were trying to take away my mama's apartment. So I ran a search on South Florida Island Federal Finance Company, Padre Island Finance Management Services, Eton Island Finance Management and Trust Company and, for good measure, threw in Alexander George.

This time I found a wad of goodies, including more than I wanted to know about Alexander A. George, Orthodontist, Alex G. George, dance instructor, Professor Alex Q. George, University of Wichita, and twenty-nine different guys just named Alexander George – no middle initial – including one who had a Ferrari for sale, one who came in sixth in the Vancouver to Victoria Island bathtub race, one who after his sex change was calling himself Alexia George and one who was mentioned in a brief article headlined 'Sweepstakes Warning to Seniors' in Jacksonville's *Florida Times Union* newspaper.

My guy!

The paper named him in conjunction with South Florida Island Federal, noting that some readers had expressed concern about the same sweepstakes which had stung my mama, and urging senior citizens to be wary of any company offering any form of sweepstakes winnings.

That led me to another article, this one in the *Miami Herald*, which explained how certain firms – among them, South Florida Island Federal – were alleged to be preying on senior citizens.

According to this, some thirty-two states plus the District of Columbia – but not Florida – were in the midst of passing laws which would set strict standards for terms such as 'winners' and 'finalists', the main gimmick these companies used to seduce folks into buying whatever it is they're actually selling. Law-makers across the country – but not in Florida – said they wanted to ban these companies from announcing that someone was a winner if they hadn't actually won something.

The article went on to point out how, in turn, many of these companies were insisting that they needed to retain the right to say someone was a winner, even if that didn't necessarily mean the person holding the sweepstakes ticket had truly won something – especially the ersatz cheque that was attached, made out with their name on it, to the tune of ten million dollars.

The biggest of these companies, the story continued, markets magazine subscriptions by sending sweepstakes promotions each year to something wild like two-thirds of the entire country.

By my count, that's a whopping 200 million people.

But big or small, the *Herald*'s journalist explained, all these sweepstakes gimmicks seem to work off the same basic theory – that the average guy on the street can be convinced to spend a little bit of dough if, by spending that, he thinks he's got a shot at winning real big bucks.

The thing is, however, that in some states – namely, those thirty-two plus the District of Columbia, but not Florida – there are lawyers who have filed suits alleging deceptive advertising practices. Their claim is, these mailings imply someone is just a step away from winning and that all they have to do in order to grab a bag of untold riches is buy a year's worth of *TV Guide*, a set of dishes, term life insurance, five radial snow tyres, a 36-volume set of encyclopedias, whatever.

Or, in my mama's case, give up her home.

The main bone of contention of those lawyers working for states which were objecting to this sort of stuff is that the too-tiny print at the bottom, which says you don't have to do anything of the kind to remain eligible for a prize, is just that – too tiny.

I downloaded the article for future reference.

A third item that I found, this one in the *Tallahassee Democrat*, quoted State Senator Thornton Roamers saying that some of these sweepstakes were out and out fraudulent and that men like Alexander George were a menace to the elderly population. Dated only two days later was a letter to the editor wondering why the state would not act to protect its senior population from sweepstakes in general and Mr George in particular. That was immediately followed by a note from the editor saying that Senator Roamers was, on the advice of his attorneys, withdrawing his previous statement and apologizing to Mr George for any insinuation of illegal activities.

Now I jotted down the senator's name.

From there I headed into the Internet's newsgroups, searching for any and all references to the three companies, to sweepstakes, to George, to Ochoa and also to Senator Roamers.

Here too the response came back good and plenty.

The problem with gleaning so much stuff off the Net is that if you're not careful, you can wind up getting lost, just like hiking through the woods. You find a path and start following it, come to a bunch of other paths, take one and head down there till you come across even more paths, needing to decide for yourself which one to follow. Unless you're dropping bread crumbs every few steps, you never find your way out.

So, fearing that it was much too easy to get lost, instead of poring over any of the stuff that popped up then and there, I downloaded it all on to my computer for reading and sorting later. 'Though I did spot an official public notice from the City of Gainsville, Florida that a company called Tower Benahavis Properties was granted the right to develop a huge shopping complex, which I probably never would have found 'cept it was Alexander George who'd filed documents supporting the company's application.

Particularly intrigued by that, I added Tower Benahavis Properties to my search, went back on to the Net and found a bunch of references to them. Namely that they seemed to be a subsidiary of Tower Benahavis Developments, a company based in the Bahamas. I couldn't find anything in those references to Mr Tower or Mr Benahavis, but the company's address, which I assumed was some sort of mail drop of convenience, turned out to be the same as George's.

The two men listed as directors were Herbert I. Werner and Carlos Bianco-Sanchez. The other name that appeared on the document was the company secretary's, none other than Juan Luis Gonzalez Ochoa.

Not a bad day's trek, the voice proclaimed as I downloaded all of that and headed out of the woods, making sure to leave lots of crumbs right where they were so that I could find my way back tomorrow.

I disconnected and announced, *nap time*.

But the little voice had other ideas. *Phone time*.

I knew not to argue 'cause it would only keep me awake to prove its point, so I took the phone, asked information for the number of the *Tallahassee Democrat* and called down there. But it was Saturday and no one was around and the operator couldn't tell me where to get in touch with Senator Roamers. I went back to information, got the number of the State Senate and tried again. 'Cept it was still Saturday and the security guard who answered said I'd have to ring back on Monday. I put the phone down and figured I could worry about it on Monday.

The voice refused to give up. *How 'bout if the Florida State Senate has its own website?*

I got back on the Net, found that it did, located Senator Roamers' address, disconnected, grabbed the phone and called him at his constituency office in St Petersburg.

An answering machine explained that the office was closed for the weekend but offered up another number in case of emergency. I told myself that this was sort of an emergency 'cause I needed to do it before I could take a nap, dialled that number and heard a woman with a very gentle voice answer, 'House of Funerals.'

That stopped me. 'Whose funeral?'

'House of Funerals. May I be of assistance?'

'Funerals?' I didn't understand. 'I was calling Senator Roamers' office and there was a message on his answering machine . . .'

'Yes, sir. This is Roamers' House of Funerals. If you want the Senator's office, you'll have to phone back there on Monday morning . . .'

'Senator Roamers lives in a funeral house?'

'Senator Roamers is in the mortuary business.'

'He's an undertaker?'

'Yes, sir, this is Senator Roamers' family business.'

I asked, 'I don't suppose that he's there now, is he?'

'Well, sir, actually he is but the Senator prefers not to mix politics and funerals and unless it's an emergency . . .'

'Well . . . you see . . . yes, ma'am, it's my mama. She's getting on in years . . . I'm calling from New York but she lives in Florida . . . and, well, I didn't know who else to turn to for advice.'

'I understand, sir. Is her death imminent?'

'Imminent? No, I don't think I could rightly say that. I mean, I don't expect it to happen this week.'

'Please know, sir, that I can sympathize with your circum-stances. When the time comes, would this be a denominational service? We have advisers for most denominations, including Catholic . . .'

'No . . . it's definitely non-denominational.'

'Then perhaps I should put you on to our Mr Grayson who handles non-denominational services.'

'Well, ma'am . . . I'm sorry, but I don't think that Mr Grayson . . . I mean, if Senator Roamers had a minute, I'd be very grateful.'

'Certainly, sir, but I believe that the Senator would appreciate your speaking to our Mr Grayson first. I'll connect you now. May I have your name please?'

I acquiesced, 'Doone.'

There were a few clicks, and then a man with a deep voice came on the line. 'This is Grayson Roamers,' he said, 'how may I be of assistance to you in this darkest hour of need?'

'Grayson Roamers? Are you related to the Senator?'

'I am, indeed, sir. I'm his eldest son. Let me begin by saying that our primary concern is your family's peace of mind in the hours leading up to this inevitable moment, your mother's dignity after she passes and, of course, the comfort we can provide in the days, weeks and months following this saddest of all moments. It is our sincerest wish that at every stage, we can stand by you and reassure you that you have done the right thing for her and for yourselves.'

'I appreciate that,' I said, trying to think of a way to get from here to Alexander George. 'The thing is, my mama is a very independent woman and she always told us . . . I'm referring here to the whole family . . . that she wanted to make all of her own arrangements . . .'

'This is not as out of the ordinary as you might expect.'

'But I'm not certain that she should be doing that, you know, not now . . . what with things kinda pending . . .'

'If I may take a moment, let me explain to you the various programmes we might be able to provide.' He launched into a well-rehearsed list of services on offer, eventually suggesting that the most suitable might be the one he referred to as 'The Final-48'. When that saddest of all moments came, he said, a simple telephone call to a freephone number from anywhere in the country would alert them to the situation. They would then arrange to fetch the body, transport it back to their funeral home and provide a suitable burial plot in the St Petersburg area, all within forty-eight hours of that phone call. The casket, flowers, limousines and catering were all extra, depending on a wide array of choices, and there were various supplements to be considered, such as in the case of cemeteries with scenic views of the Gulf of Mexico.

'But we have time to discuss all of that,' he explained. 'The important thing to consider now is obtaining a subscription from us which will secure our forty-eight-hour response. You can do that by filling in our very detailed form, at your leisure and in the comfort of your own home. Once that form is returned to us, we put the information we need on to our database and when . . . as I said, that saddest of all sadnesses finally arrives . . . we do everything for you, as per your pre-arranged wishes.'

'That sounds really terrific,' I said.

'I can assure you that this is first class all the way. Now . . . because I know this can be a difficult moment, I want you to understand there is no need at this time to speak about such mundane things as money.'

I didn't know what else to say. 'Oh, that's good.'

'Of course,' he added, sounding just like a used-car salesman, 'the initial subscription is only a hundred dollars. But, again, that's not the most important thing. Considering that your own peace of mind is at stake, as well as that of your loved ones, why don't I get all the necessary forms to you, complete with several booklets which I would like to send you so that you and your family can face up to this event with courage. There is also a booklet I would be very pleased to send your mother, if you thought it would be helpful. It's a small offering that my father wrote, based on all his experience in this business, entitled, Packing For the Next Voyage.'

I couldn't believe it. 'Packing For the Next Voyage?'

'Please be kind enough to allow me to enclose a copy, of course, with my compliments, when I send you our other brochures and forms. Then, after you read it, if you feel that your mother will be comfortable reading it . . . and I can assure you, it is designed for just such occasions . . .'

'Well . . . yeah, sure . . . that would be very kind.' I gave him my name and address.

'Mr Doone, I'm on my way to the post office right now. So what I will do is personally send everything to you by express mail. I expect you will have it in New York City on Monday morning.'

'Mr Roamers . . .'

'Please call me Grayson.'

'Grayson . . . what can I say . . . thank you very much.'

'And thank you, Mr Doone, for putting your trust in my family.'

What he really means, the voice said, *is thank you for not kicking the tyres and looking too close under the hood.*

'You've been very helpful. I much appreciate your thoughtfulness. I don't think I could have contemplated any of this without you.'

'That's very satisfying to hear.'

'You know what I'd like to do, Grayson. Just before you go to the post office, if you'd fax me a copy of the form to sign up for the Final-48 programme, I'd like to sign up right now, today. Do ya'll take credit cards?'

'I can assure you that there is no need to rush into anything,' he said, 'and yes, of course we take credit cards. Visa. Mastercard. American Express. And Diners Club.'

'Well, that's good. What time will you be back from the post office?'

'I'll put a package together for you right away, fax you the forms, take everything to the post office . . . it's just sort of down the block near the mall . . . and I expect to be back by, say, an hour?'

'You fax me that form just before you leave and I'll phone you back an hour later.'

He agreed that sounded like a good idea, I gave him my fax number and said I looked forward to speaking with him later. Then I hung up and waited for his fax to arrive. When it did, I read through it. Seems that once you pay the initial $100 subscription, the fees for the Final-48 plan come to $3,500. And again, that's not including all the really important stuff, like a comfortable box, an air-conditioned hearse, flowers your friends can take home and fresh seafood platters which include lobster.

The voice observed, *that's why they take Diners Club.*

It also said, right there in black and white, that cemeteries with a Gulf view were subject to a twenty-five per cent premium.

I read it all a second time, then walked over to my watch and stared at that for a couple more minutes. Finally I reckoned, *time's up*, phoned back to Roamers and asked for my new friend Grayson.

'Is that Mr Doone again?' the woman said. 'I'm terribly sorry, but our Mr Grayson has just left for a few minutes. May I have him phone you upon his return?'

'Darn . . . I just missed him?'

'I'm afraid, sir, that you have.'

'Ah . . . well . . . you see, he sent me this fax and I needed to fill out a form and I wanted to get it straight back to him . . .'

'He shouldn't be very long, sir. Perhaps only be an hour. Certainly not more.'

'An hour? Gee . . . I'm just on my way out and . . . you see, I won't be able to get this form to him otherwise . . . it's only one or two small questions I have . . . and I really would like to fax it to him as soon as I can . . . you know, for my own peace of mind . . .'

'Well, sir, perhaps if you would leave blank anything that . . .'

'After all, it's my mama. Perhaps if there was someone else . . . Mr Grayson did mention that if he wasn't there, you know, if I had any questions, his father could help . . . it won't take long.'

She said right away, 'I'll see, sir, if the Senator can be of assistance.'

There was a click on the phone, some soft music, and finally a very deep voice saying with practised pathos, 'Mr Doone, this is Thornton Roamers. I understand you've been speaking to my son about the imminent passing of your mother.'

'Yes, sir . . . although,' I told him the truth, 'imminent is not quite the term. At least, I expect not. But I am interested in the Final-48 plan and I did have some questions.'

'Well, then, sir, may I be of assistance in answering those questions?'

Getting him on the phone was only the first step. 'It's so sad,' I said. 'A woman of her years . . . and her dignity . . .'

'The passing of a loved one is, perhaps, among the most difficult of tasks that we are asked to face in life . . .'

'Never quite prepared for it.'

'Indeed not,' he agreed. 'Is she *compos mentis?*'

'*Compos mentis?* Well . . . she was in full control of all her facilities till that phoney sweepstakes robbed her of her will to live . . . but as for being . . .'

'Sweepstakes?' He fell for it. 'What sweepstakes?'

'It's a real long story and I don't want to bore you with my mama's troubles.'

'That's all right. Tell me.'

'Well . . . she's a cop's widow and she's been living down there on my papa's pension. You see, my papa was killed in the line of duty and the force has provided for her, not lavish you understand . . . but I could help out a little and she was okay . . . 'cept now she's going to lose her home and the only thing she's got left is that medal they gave her for Papa's courage . . .'

And the American flag that draped his coffin, the voice reminded me, *which is in Connecticut and we'll be damned if Lorilee thinks she's gonna keep that.*

'If only,' I added, 'she could summon up the same kind of courage . . .'

'Which sweepstakes in particular are you referring to, sir?'

'Something from a company named South Florida Island Federal Finance Company.'

'Ah yes, I know them well.'

'I've been to see the US Attorney . . .' I stopped, hoping he wouldn't ask me which US Attorney because I'd have to say the one in Palm Beach and he'd wonder why, if my mama is on the east coast of Florida, I wanted to sign her up for a funeral a couple of hundred miles away on the west coast, 'specially since my dad is buried in Boston. 'It's not easy doing all this by remote control . . . you know, being up here so far away. I've tried everything. I even thought of appealing to the sense of right and wrong of the man who got her into all this trouble . . .'

'Do you recall his name?'

'Alexander George. I rang the phone number on his letterhead and as there are some other companies involved that always seem to lead back to him, I phoned them all too. Several times. But I never could get hold of him.'

'I'm not surprised. Mr George is the agent for some very powerful property developers. You know, of course, that I'm a State Senator?'

'Yes, sir, I heard that.'

'Well, I took a personal interest in Mr George a long time ago and keep trying to do something about these various sweepstakes, but every time I attempt anything, I get my fingers burnt. I spoke out just recently and wound up getting severely warned by some powerful legal beagles that I'd better back off.'

'So you backed off?'

'Not by choice. But they made it perfectly plain that I do have to be careful what I say.'

'I understand. 'Cept I can't back off 'cause this is my mama.'

'Well, son, my personal advice to you is to proceed very carefully. These are very determined people. They're playing for big stakes and playing rough. Your mother got in the way and I'm sorry to say, they've dealt with her the way they've dealt with hundreds of folk all over the state just like her. If you get in their way, they'll do whatever they have to do to get you out of their way.'

'I don't much like the sound of that. What do ya'll mean, whatever they have to?'

'Just what I said.'

'Talking about physical violence?'

He roared with laughter. 'Mr Doone, maybe that's the way it is up there in New York City, but you sound like a good old southern boy to me and down here no one with money has to break legs. They break bank accounts instead. We're talking about fellas with more money than Jesus Christ, our Lord, himself. They hire the best lawyers and tie you up in litigation until you're penniless. That's worse than breaking legs. Unless you're a racehorse, legs heal. With these fellas, poverty is terminal.'

'So how come, if you know so much about them, ya'll can't do anything to stop them?'

'Because so far, they're perfectly legal. Which makes them perfectly unstoppable. I try to do what I can in Tallahassee, but they've been pretty damned effective at keeping me on the sidelines. So just you be careful. Real careful. All the more so because behind them is one helluva multimillionaire.'

That didn't sound good. 'Ya'll mean rich multimillionaire or real rich multimillionaire?'

'I'm talking one of the richest. Probably even billionaire. Ever hear of a fella called Thomas Whitestone?'

'Whitestone?' The name rang a bell. 'It sounds kinda familiar . . .

'Thomas Whitestone. An Englishman. Some sort of big deal over there, too, because they call him Sir. Son of a bitch if there ever was one.'

The voice found it. *Goulash.*

'Oh yeah . . . him. Yeah. Funny, but his name came up last night. He's the guy who said, when you see a bandwagon, it's too late.'

'That's the fella.'

'And he's behind these sweepstakes?'

'Ultimately.'

'But why? What does he want that he can't already buy?'

'Him, personally? Probably nothing. Might not even know that the sweepstakes exist. But George is an agent for a company developing land throughout the state and that company is owned by another company which is owned by yet another company, and so on, all the way over to London, England, till you come to Whitestone.'

'So is this Whitestone guy breaking the law?'

'Who said anybody is breaking the law?'

'Well, I just assumed . . .'

'You don't assume that someone as rich as him ever breaks any laws because that might be slander or libel. And also because he's got expensive mouthpieces to keep you from voicing assumptions like that. Another reason is because his mouthpieces wouldn't hesitate one fraction of a second to shut you up right fast if you didn't take the hint the first time. Anyway, even if he is breaking the law, and remember that I'm not saying he is, he's got those same mouthpieces to keep you from proving he knows anything about it.'

I thought about that. 'So it all gets back to Mr George?'

'If you can find him, it might. But you won't.'

'The letter says he's in the Bahamas.'

'Is that what it says? Mr Doone, the letter also says his name is Alexander George.'

I paused. 'You mean, that's not his name?'

'Mr Doone . . . I have to be real careful here because they get real upset with me whenever I speak out . . . and I don't know you or anything about you. But let me say this . . . whether you're dealing with property in Florida, with property developers in Florida, with any get-rich-quick scheme like those sweepstakes, or with one of the richest men in the world . . . and in this case, you may be dealing with all four . . . just you remember that what you see is not what you get.'

'It isn't?'

'It surely isn't.'

'So who do I go to complain to? Who do I talk to if I want to save my mama's apartment?'

'You referring to the good guys in the white hats or the bad guys in the black hats?'

'Start with the good guys.'

'You already did when you went to the US Attorney's office. How far did that get you?'

'Then how about the bad guys with the black hats?'

'I have to assume that any guy you can find wearing a black hat is a step in the right direction.'

'How will I know if he's the right guy?'

'Most likely, unless he's an English Sir, he won't be.'

I had to admit, 'Sounds like pretty good advice.'

'It's the only advice,' he said. 'Now what's that information you need on the form for your mother?'

'Ah . . . yeah, my mama.' I thought fast. 'This deposit to guarantee a place in the Final-48 plan . . .'

'That's a hundred-dollar fee, which is fully refundable when you sign up, our guarantee that there will always be a place for your mother should the sad time arrive before we've had a chance to make all the necessary arrangements. It's kind of like insurance which is designed to give you additional peace of mind. It's effective within seventy-two hours of payment, regardless of whether or not all the paperwork is signed, sealed and delivered.'

'So the Final-48 is valid after the initial seventy-two?'

'That's just so that no folk can phone us from a loved one's deathbed and come straight to the front of the line.'

'Folk do that?'

'Mr Doone, my people have been in the mortuary business for three generations. My sons will make it four. You'd be surprised what folk do when death comes knocking on their porch door. Now . . . if you wished to sign up . . . I could take all your credit card details . . .'

'Well . . . if I do that . . .' After all my shopping, I could only hope there was still at least $100 left on my credit card.

'You go ahead and do whatever you think you need to do, and any time you need any more information about any old thing, you just tell Grayson to put you through to me.'

That being the case, I gave him my credit card number.

'Your address, card expiry date and bank name?'

I gave him my address and the expiry date, then confessed, 'New York Bank of Athens.'

'Georgia? You don't sound like a good old boy from Georgia.'

'Athens, Georgia? No, more like Tennessee.'

'Never heard of Athens, Tennessee,' he said. 'But I sure do look forward to hearing from you again. Call me any time.'

'Sure will,' I told him, then rationalized to the voice, *see that, for a hundred bucks I get to phone him again.*

The voice added, *and we get to bury Mama in the wrong state.*

Chapter Thirteen

'Did ya'll really say, when you see a bandwagon it's too late?'

'I shall have you know,' he announced with distinct pride, 'that that particular quote appears in the *Oxford Dictionary of Quotations* bearing my name on the bottom of it.'

'It's a real good quote.'

'I thought so too when I heard it.'

'When you heard it? I thought you said it.'

'I did say it.'

'Well, what do you mean . . . when you heard it?'

'Are you asking, did I coin the expression? That's hardly of any importance. The fact is, I am credited with it. That quote will forever be acknowledged as mine.'

'You didn't make it up?'

'What's the difference?'

'Pretty big, if you ask me.'

'Why? Do you really think that Winston Churchill made up the term iron curtain? Or your Abe Lincoln made up four score and seven years ago?' He scoffed, 'It's not the inventor or the discoverer who goes down in history, it's the person who understands how to take the credit.'

As tired as I was, I couldn't let him get away with that. 'Abe Lincoln did make up four score and seven years ago. Course he did. He wrote it down on the back of an envelope.'

'What does that prove? Maybe the person sitting next to him made it up. Or the person who lent him the envelope. The point is, he knew what really counts, which is taking the credit.'

'That can't be right . . . come on, if it's not your quote, if you didn't make it up, then you shouldn't take the credit for having made it up.'

'How about your President Kennedy and his famous I am a chocolate doughnut speech?'

'His what?'

'*Ich bin ein Berliner.*'

'What about it?'

'Only that he didn't say, I am a Berliner. That would have been, *ich bin Berliner*. What he said was, *ich bin ein Berliner*. That *ein* changes the meaning totally. When you put the *ein* in there it means, I am a chocolate doughnut.'

'Huh?' I didn't know whether or not to believe him. 'Anyway, what does that have to do with you taking credit for a remark you didn't make.'

'But I did make it.'

'But you didn't make it up.'

He paused to take a loud, deep breath, kinda the way you do when you're losing your patience with a child. 'Did Columbus really discover America?'

'Course he did.'

'Course he didn't. It was some Viking. Eric the Red. Or Hagaar the Purple. Who knows? Who cares? But Christopher Columbus understood how to take the credit. Consequently, he is the one who made it into the history books.'

'It's not the same.'

'Not only is it precisely the same, Mr Doone, but if you truly want to be donnish about it, which I assume you do, Columbus really rates only half the credit.'

'What's donnish mean? And who gets the other half?'

'It means pedantic. And there happens to be someone who, while he obviously did not arrive in the New World before the Vikings or Columbus, still today revels in the splendor of being the one who named it. Do you know who I'm referring to?'

'No.'

He made it sound like a school quiz. 'The country's not called Colombia, is it?'

'You mean, the one where the capital is Bogotá?'

'No, the one where the capital is Washington.' He sneered, 'Another chap who knew how to take credit for things he never did or never said. Hah. Chopping down a tree and then claiming, I cannot tell a lie. The entire story was a lie.'

'Time out,' I signalled by making the 'T' sign with my two hands, the way they do in basketball games. 'Time . . . out! First of all, George Washington most definitely did chop down the cherry tree. And second of all, he definitely did say, I cannot tell a lie. Every kid in America knows that.'

'Every kid in America may know that story, but do they know if it's the truth?'

I came back with, 'Maybe kids today don't know if it's the truth, but the people who knew him in those days obviously knew it was the truth 'cause they named the city after him as an honour.'

He countered, 'Hardly a sound argument, Mr Doone. Still, tell me this. Why didn't they name the country Colombia?'

'If you mean the one where the capital is Washington, it's 'cause the name was already taken by the one where the capital is Bogotá.'

'No. That country only gained independence from Spain in . . .' He thought for a moment, '. . . I'd say, 1819 . . . when Simon Bolivar liberated it. And here you have a perfect example of just the opposite, of someone who did not understand how to take proper credit. Otherwise the country would have been called Bolivia.'

'Isn't there already one of those?'

'Indeed there is. But is there one called Vespucci? Mr Doone,' he said with some finality, 'I rest my case.'

'Why on earth should there be a country called Vespucci?'

'But there is. Indeed. Yours. The United States Of Vespucci.'

'Huh . . . Oh . . . yeah . . .' I hated it when he won these little games. 'Him.'

'Hardly just any him,' he said with great authority. 'Him explored Brazil and found the mouth of the Amazon. Him got to the West Indies, too, admittedly some years after Columbus. That not withstanding, Him gave the world a system for computing longitude and made the observation, eventually widely accepted, that South America was a separate continent. Note that I said South America and not South Columbus. Which, I suspect, you would remind me is in Ohio.'

'It is,' I agreed. 'But as for Vespucci . . .' After thinking 'bout it, I didn't have much choice 'cept to concede . . . 'so, okay, you're right, Vespucci got his name into Rand McNally even though Columbus discovered the place.'

'Or didn't,' he corrected.

'Or didn't,' I acknowledged. 'But still, none of that explains how come you feel entitled to take credit for a quote that you didn't say.'

'May I remind you, once again, that I did say it.'

'But not first.'

'It explains the matter entirely.'

'Does not,' I persisted.

He remained silent.

I waited for him to go on. When it became evident that he had no intention of doing any such thing, I asked, 'So who really said it first?'

'Said what?'

'Your quote.'

'Not that it actually matters, Mr Doone, but if you must know, the man's name was Reuben Abramowsky.'

'Who's he?'

'The chap who first said, when you see a bandwagon it's too late.'

'Yeah, but I mean, why did he say it?'

'Because it's true.'

To show my exasperation, I mumbled, 'How come I get the impression I'm going nowhere fast?'

'Rather appropriate,' he observed, 'for someone stuck in a lift.'

'I'll try again. Why did Reuben whoever say whatever he said, even if it is true, which, the more I think about it . . . well, it may or may not be?'

He answered, in a very patronizing way, 'A rather fine tailor. He happens to be my tailor. He happens to be the man who said, a stitch in time saves nine.'

'Whoa? Hold on. Just a second. That's not your tailor, that's Benjamin Franklin.'

He scoffed, 'Another man who was evidently quite expert at claiming credit for saying things he almost certainly did not say.'

'Where do you get this crap from? Franklin published all his wise sayings in his almanac. It's all there in black and white . . .'

'Mr Abramowsky may not have published his own almanac, but his wise sayings are all part of the patter that comes along with each fitting.'

'You're comparing your tailor to Ben Franklin?'

'Is there something wrong with that?'

'You mean, ya'll buy a suit and instead of two pairs of pants, you get a wise saying to call your own?' I thought that was funny, which, judging by his silence, I could tell he didn't. 'I suppose that means you wouldn't be in the least embarrassed to find your name under a few of Franklin's wise sayings?'

He looked at me. 'Even if you honestly believe that Benjamin Franklin said everything you believe he said, I would be willing to wager that you can't quote six of his wise sayings.'

'No bet,' I answered. 'But I can.'

'Go ahead then.'

At least I thought I could. 'Okay . . . let's see . . . besides a stitch in time saves nine . . .'

'Abramowsky,' he said.

'Franklin,' I insisted. 'How about . . . this will be number two . . . early to bed, early to rise . . .'

He finished it . . . 'Makes a man happy, healthy . . . but decidedly dull.'

'How about . . . time is money.'

'Surely not.'

'Surely so,' I said, trying to think of another, 'Something about, there is no such thing as a good war or a bad peace.'

'Although I remain unconvinced about quote number three, I will concede to your erudition in these matters and allow, that's four.'

'Okay . . . that's four. Now . . . ah, you know, the one about three people can keep a secret if two of them are dead.'

'If I didn't know better, Mr Doone, I'd think you were miscrediting some of these quotes.'

'Look who's talking.'

'Still . . . if you say that's five . . . then there remains one more.'

'How about . . .' I didn't know one more. 'Ah . . .'

'You're stumped,' he cheered.

'No . . . wait . . .'

'Time's up. Hah. Only five. See, I usually know a good bet when I see one.'

'Yeah, well, do you know any?'

'My particular favourite.' He recited, 'Having made a young

girl miserable may give you frequent bitter reflection . . . none
of which can attend the making of an old woman happy.' He
grinned. 'There, that's six,' then added smugly, 'between us.'

'I never heard that quote. What does it mean?'

'Franklin often used to talk about older women. Ah, splendid . . .
I just thought of another. It goes something along the lines of,
in all your amorous adventures, always favour an older woman
because . . .' He listed them by counting on his fingers, 'they
don't tell, they don't swell and . . . they are grateful as hell.'

'No. Sorry.' I refused to believe it. 'Benjamin Franklin did
not say that.'

'I assure you that he most certainly did. Or at least that he
took credit for it, which as we both know, is the same thing.'

'It is not.'

'Tell me this, Mr Doone . . .' he gloated, 'how should it be
that a half French, half British Eton drop-out knows more about
Mr Franklin than someone born and bred in the United States
of Vespucci?'

'This,' I commented, 'coming from the same man who is not
in the least embarrassed about taking credit for quotes he didn't
invent.'

'Such as, never invest in anything that eats or needs repainting?'

I'd heard that one before. 'You didn't say that!'

'Oh yes, I said it. And yes, again, I'd be happy to take
credit for it. Actually, I sometimes do. But did I coin it?' He
shrugged. 'How about the variation on that one, never invest in
anything that flies, floats or does anything else beginning with
the letter F?'

'Sorry,' I said flatly, 'there's absolutely no way you invented
that one either.'

'Why not?' He seemed insulted. 'As a matter of fact, I
didn't. But why would you automatically assume such?'

'Because you invest in planes, boats, a lot of wives and how
many mistresses?'

'Who better, then, to know?' He shook his head several times.
'I'm surprised at you. I thought you were more astute than that.
I've invested in all sorts of things that have proven profitable,
even when I knew better, such as when they flew, floated or
anything else that begins with F, such as fought, fantasized or
fornicated. Hah.'

'Or fibbed.' I glared at him.

'Or fatigued.' He glared back at me. 'Simply because one takes credit for saying something, that doesn't mean one necessarily believes it or, worse still, follows one's own advice.'

'In other words, you don't believe what you say, don't follow your own advice, and yet happily take credit for making up stuff that you didn't make up.'

'I'll ask you again, Mr Doone, who better to know whose advice to follow? And, for the tenth time, what difference does it make if I made it up as long as I get credit for saying it, which I do because I did.'

'But your friend Abramowsky said it first. So shouldn't his name be in *Bartlett's*.'

'What's *Bartlett's*?'

'The book of quotations.'

'For all I know, it may be. But, surely, the only book of quotations that truly matters is the *Oxford Dictionary of Quotations*. And my name is in there.'

I blurted out, 'Here's another F word . . . furiating!'

'Ah, what you do to my language,' he complained. 'But then, Americans are so predictable. As soon as someone challenges your superiority about anything, from gunships to dictionaries of quotations, you become riled.'

'Oh yeah?'

'Oh yeah,' he mimicked, then sighed. 'Alas, Mr Doone, 'tis a pity. If it wasn't mere child's play to get an American's goat, this would be such a good game.'

Chapter Fourteen

*N*aptime, I declared.

Not so fast, the voice protested.

Ever spineless, I got back on the World Wide Web, put through a search for Thomas Whitestone and found more than I think I ever wanted to know about any single human being, with the possible exception of Miss O'Toole, who was the hottest eighth-grade English teacher since Gutenberg invented homework. Tiny and slim with long brown hair and a very particular look in her eyes that I suspected meant something neat – even if I didn't learn for a very long time just how neat – she caught a whole bunch of us guys naked in the locker room one afternoon. We were taking showers after track and she just happened to walk in, sorta accidental on purpose. We covered up pretty fast but when she didn't run away all that fast, the other guys dared me to invite her to take a shower with us. Which I did, 'cause she was real hot. Which got me suspended for a week, 'cause she didn't think it was as good an idea as us guys did, even if I'd like to think maybe she did consider it for a fraction of a second. Anyway, I spent the rest of junior high fantasizing about her, and most of high school too, 'specially when I heard that she used to meet the basketball coach in the locker room every Wednesday afternoon and take showers with him.

Oh, Miss O'Toole, what I wanted to know about you.

Instead, I found out about the man who was supposed to be behind the companies trying to take away my mama's apartment.

Thomas d'Aquin Whitestone was born in Paris, France in 1933, 'cause his mama was French and his papa, Major Alastair Thomas Whitestone, was chairman of the Anglo-French Pierreblanche Hotel group.

Originally, the family was German Jewish. According to one of several dozen biographical sketches I found on him, his great-grandfather was Israel Weisstein who, like the Rothschilds and Goldschmidts, had the foresight to get the family the hell out of Germany long before the Nazis came to power. It meant that, unlike the Jews who waited too long, this crowd got to bring their money with them.

Israel Weisstein begat Eugene Weisstein who took some of that money and went into the hotel business in London. Eugene Weisstein begat Alastair Thomas Weisstein, who quickly translated his name to the decidedly less Jewish, and by inference more acceptable, Whitestone. After spending a few years in the Army polishing his WASPish shine, he came into the family business, got himself elected for eight years as a Conservative Member of Parliament, saw opportunity across the Channel, abandoned politics – he didn't need it any more because, by this time, most of his friends were willing to pretend they'd forgotten he was born Jewish – and expanded the hotel chain to France.

Having deliberately set out to be more English than any of his chums who hadn't changed their names, Alastair lived the life of a wealthy bachelor officer and gentleman, eventually marrying a French Catholic girl twenty-five years his junior. Her name was Espérance de Saint-Benoit. Together, they begat Alastair II and Thomas.

The boys grew up in a fourth-floor, four-room suite in Papa's chic-est hotel, though as soon as he could, their old man shipped them both back to England to school, buying their way into Eton.

Alastair Junior, a.k.a. Ally, followed the script, went from Eton to Oxford and got himself a degree in something that would assure him a good paying job once he'd blown his inheritance.

But Thomas d'Aquin, always called Tommy, had ideas of his own.

He dropped out of Eton – most accounts noted that he got kicked out for gambling and cavorting – and returned to France, where he used what money he won gambling to buy American manufactured antacid tablets which he then flogged to the French at a huge mark-up. As a result, years later, he would be constantly referred to in the British gossip columns as Sir Tums.

Though much of the money he made on heartburn got ploughed back into gambling, by the time he turned twenty he'd already made his first fortune.

His second fortune happened along when he married it.

Within a year, Tommy had fallen for an eighteen-year-old Bolivian tin heiress named Constanza Alvarado. Nicknamed Gypsy, she was the daughter of Jorge-Emilio Alvarado, the richest man in Bolivia, then worth around $180 million. Tommy might have loved her and undoubtedly she loved Tommy, but her old man didn't seem right pleased. When Tommy and Gypsy tried to elope to Casablanca – shades of Rick and Ilse – Papa Alvarado followed them and dragged his daughter kicking and screaming back to Paris. His excuse was that his family didn't usually marry Jews. Tommy hardly won any points when he answered that his family didn't usually marry Red Indians.

No sooner was everyone back in Paris when Tommy and Gypsy eloped again. This time they flew off to Scotland in the dead of night, with Don Jorge-Emilio in hot pursuit. What the old man didn't know, however, was that his little girl was already three months' pregnant.

The race to Edinburgh was a dead heat. Still, Tommy and Gypsy gave Don Jorge-Emilio the slip some time on the second day and made it to city hall. The instant Tommy became Mr Gypsy, he also became half-owner of Mrs Tommy's considerable boodle. And maybe, like any good fairy tale, the couple would have lived happily ever after, punching out a whole tribe of Jewish Red Indians, 'cept that whcn Gypsy was in her seventh month, she suffered a brain haemorrhage. The child was delivered premature by Caesarean section and Gypsy died that night, leaving Tommy with a baby daughter.

Not to mention the second half of Gypsy's dowry.

What followed was a huge court battle over custody of the child and signature authority on the Alvarado account. Tommy eventually won and used that money to launch himself into selling snake oil. Well, not literally snake oil, but companies which flogged stuff like liquid diet concoctions. His timing was perfect and he managed to parlay that into his third fortune.

Life being a roller-coaster ride, he almost went broke a few years later. On the verge of bankruptcy, luck triumphed when French bank employees went on a wildcat strike, coincidentally stalling his creditors just long enough for him to raise enough money to stave them off. His empire reconstructed, before too long the Pierreblanche Group was one of the world's largest food conglomerates, selling everything from soup to nuts, and not just one but an entire range of American manufactured, over-priced antacid tablets.

By that time, he'd married a French girl named Giselle DuTronc – her nickname was Kiki – and they had two kids. Next, he married a British gal called Lady Jacintha Portman, and had a couple of kids with her too. Nicknamed Flower, the fact that when she married Tommy she was still married to one of Sir Tommy's best friends didn't appear to bother anybody because, as it turned out, when Tommy married her he was still married to Kiki.

As if that wasn't enough, a few years later he hooked up with another French woman – Letitia Giradot, who was called Lou – with whom he had two more kids. For whatever reason, it seems he never got around to marrying her. Instead, he moved her into a big house in Paris, which she wound up sharing with Kiki and all the various little Whitestones.

With each acquired family, his fortune seemed to double. He bought himself into the British newspaper business and asset-stripped companies the way jackals prey on wounded buffalo. Then, only a few days before the stock-market crash of 1987, he sold every share he owned in everything – at all-time highs – took the money and ran.

Having more cash in the bank than most banks, he bought himself his very own Boeing 757 – it said right here that he outfitted the plane with a double bed specially designed to withstand turbulence, though it didn't explain if the turbulence was outside the plane or inside the double bed – plus his very own political party, which he personally financed in a one-man effort to keep Britain from becoming too European. At the same time, he got himself elected as a Member of the European Parliament – campaigning as a Brit who didn't want to appear too European – but representing France.

While all this was going on, he was also buying up houses around the world. Besides the place in Paris, he owned a huge estate just outside London, a house in Spain – the story said that was where he intended to die because that was where he kept the bed in which he was born – a château in Bordeaux, a penthouse on Park Avenue, and a monster property in Mexico that was supposedly almost the size of Rhode Island.

Paris. London. Spain. Bordeaux. New York. Mexico . . .

I went back to Spain because something caught my eye.

The story described his house there, hidden in a forest of olive trees in a tiny village just outside Marbella. The place was called Torre de Benahavis.

Sunnuvabitch, I said out loud.

I didn't need to look any further for Mr Tower or Mr Benahavis 'cause I'd just connected Thomas d'Aquin Whitestone with the sweepstakes.

What the hell, the voice suggested, *if this is the guy behind all those companies trying to separate Mama from her apartment, it's pretty pathetic 'cause he's about the last guy on earth who needs a tiny one-bedroom apartment in Lantana.*

My interest clicked into second gear, I trucked on through another few hundred web pages with stuff about him, including the singular fact that on Tuesday night – this very coming Tuesday night – this very same Sir Thomas d'Aquin Whitestone was booked as the guest speaker at the annual dinner of the 200 Club.

I didn't have a clue what the 200 Club was, but if it was going to save my mama's apartment, I was sure as hell gonna find out.

The phone book used to be a pretty good invention, at least it was in the days before folk started moving around so much – meaning that even when you get the latest edition you can bet that maybe half the numbers are wrong – or found out the hard way that when you're listed, anyone in the world can figure out how to get in touch. That's why I much prefer the on-line variety you can find these days on the Internet. Not only are they always being updated, but if you know how to look, you can locate just about anybody, including folk with so much money that they don't think they're locatable.

Including – Whitestone, T. D., 1060 Park Avenue, New York, N. Y. 10028.

And right there under his address was his home phone number.

After jotting that down, I went in search of the 200 Club. But this time there was nothing. Off-line, I phoned Information. They had nothing for the 200 Club either.

Shutting down the computer, I announced *nap time*, threw myself on my bed – one of the pillows smelled a little like Debbie and her booze – snuggled up to it, tossed the blanket on top of myself and shut my eyes.

Nap time, I repeated.

Dream time, too, the voice answered.

Dream time . . . yeah . . . sure . . . how about Miss O'Toole?

All that hair coming down off her English teacher's head and those big eyes that always had a strange look in them and the smell of gin on Debbie and the picture branded on my brain of Miss O'Toole just sort of strolling real casual like into the locker room and seeing us all naked . . .

Oh, Miss O'Toole.

Was she the same age then as Debbie is now?

Hey, Miss O'Toole, why not step inside this shower with us . . . Oh Miss O'Toole . . .

That's all, the voice screamed, *end of dream time.*

I agreed, opting for a cold shower. I yanked off my clothes and ran for the bathroom. The water did the trick. It also woke me up.

I towelled off, got back into my clothes and thought about making my bed, 'cept I've never understood why I should bother making my bed when all I'm ever gonna do is get back in it before too long, unless some girl's coming 'round. Then, the only reason to make it is so that she doesn't think another girl just left. Which happened a lot when I was single, which is why I used to make my bed a lot in those days. But it wasn't going to happen today, or any time soon that I could foresee, so I left it. Though I took the pillow case that Debbie used, carried it into the bathroom, filled the sink with water and dropped it in there to soak.

Your mission, if you choose to accept it, the voice proclaimed, *is to find the smallest bottle of liquid Woollite in the City of New York.*

Stepping into my shoes, I headed out the door, temporarily convinced that I was now a man with a purpose.

Woollite is my purpose, I mumbled.

Naw, the voice said, *your purpose is never to confuse little Debbie with Miss O'Toole.*

Out on the street, I instinctively glanced down the block, half thinking that Debbie and Pinky would still be there.

They weren't.

I even looked both ways.

Sadly, neither was Miss O'Toole.

When I first came to New York, and discovered that some uptown girls could be real downmarket, I hooked up with one named Rhea. She told me she was a hat model but I never saw any pictures of her anywhere – not that I read hat magazines – nor ever saw any hats for that matter, 'cept the Cubby's baseball cap she always wore 'cause she was from Chicago.

She had a neat trick she used to pull on Saturdays and 'cause we hung out together for near on a month, I got to do it with her on a couple-a-Saturdays. She lived in a walk-up on 89th, just off Third, and what she'd do is head down to the River on her street, then back to Park on 88th, then down to the River again on 87th, and so on, till she got to the corner of 80th and Second. Or, till she couldn't carry anything more and had to give up. Whichever came first.

What she was carrying was whatever she found along her route that looked good enough to sell.

New Yorkers, she always said, *throw out better garbage than most people in Chicago-land ever buy.*

The reason she always quit at 80th and Second was 'cause of her fence – that's what she called him 'cept he wasn't really a fence – Hiram of Hiram$ What'$ Old For You$ I$ New For U$ – We Pay Ca$h.

It was fun doing that with her and I reckoned I could use some fun now. A walk would also help get me thinking clear. So I aimed myself towards the River, then one block uptown and all the way back to Lexington, at which time I turned north for another block and east to the river again.

A bird cage sitting on top of some black garbage bags on 71st off Third caught my eye, but it was in pretty bad shape so I left it there. I also passed up a sofa on 72nd 'cause it was much too big to carry, a flower stand coming back on 73rd 'cause it was pretty ugly, and a couple of old wooden skis down towards Lex 'cause what the hell was anybody gonna do with a couple of old wooden skis in the City of New York? But on 74th, just off First, I found a carton filled with paperback books.

Now, there's absolutely nothing illegal 'bout helping yourself to someone else's garbage. Fact is, it's exactly like claiming a ship deserted on the high seas. But it's one thing to do it, another thing to get caught doing it. So I looked up and down the block real good before I took the carton and then waited till I got a block away before I sat down on someone's stoops to check it out.

Three dozen tawdry romance novels. They weren't my kinda thing but I was hoping that Hiram could love 'em. And from the back of my head I could imagine Rhea approving too, with her usual, 'Go Cubs' which amused me when she'd call it out on the street after finding great garbage but which was decidedly less amusing when she used to shout it out during sex.

Tucking the carton under my arm, I continued down the street.

I rejected a bathtub on 76th for obvious reasons, but on 77th helped myself to a small, flaking, green-painted three-legged milking stool.

Nothing much more came up till I'd worked my way to 82nd where, kinda weary from schlepping all this stuff and slightly embarrassed 'bout the strange looks I was sometimes attracting – more than one guy I passed went 'Moo' – I found a giant deflated inflatable ice-cream cone. The kind of thing that guys selling ice-cream at the beach usually have flying out front filled with helium. I studied it for quite a while – three scoops sitting on top of a sugar cone – finally deciding, *tutti frutti*.

The carton of books under my left arm, the green milking stool dangling from my left hand and the deflated ice-cream cone in my right hand, I made my way back to 80th and Second, where the junk shop was.

'Cept it wasn't.

I walked up the block, then down it again, and even stopped to ask someone. No one knew. I could only conclude that either Hiram had gone belly up – which mighta made sense considering the junk he sold – or Hiram had moved somewhere, or I was dead on the wrong block and would never find him.

All dressed up and no place to go, the voice admonished.

The way the game worked, Rhea would present whatever she picked up to Hiram, he'd say what's all this junk, and she'd make up some real elaborate story about whatever it was and how she acquired it. The better the story, the higher the price he'd have to pay for it. Kind of a garbage man's version of Scheherazade.

Not that we're talking 'bout a lot of money. If she wanted a buck for something, and could embellish the story real good, he'd give her a buck and a quarter. Otherwise, he'd say no, and never offer more than fifty cents.

Whatever cash she got out of him she'd spend on breakfast.

Well, I could still afford to pay for my own breakfast, which at this hour would be more like late lunch, but without Hiram, I wasn't sure what to do with all the spoils.

Thinking it might be worth trying to find another Hiram, I headed down Second. But junk shops turned out to be like cops. Never around when you need one. I got all the way down into the mid-60s before deciding *the hell with it, I'm outta energy, outta stories, outta the junk business.* I decided to dump everything in the first garbage can I found.

The voice came back with, *lots of garbage cans just across the street. But I vote for keeping it. We can always sit on the stool while reading the books and the ice-cream cone is our kinda thing, anyway.*

I stared at four garbage cans all neatly lined up along the sidewalk on the other side of the street.

It's not as if we've got an apartment already filled with too much junk.

Looking past the garbage cans to the storefront behind them, I read the words on the big window – Herbie's Deli.

Hah.

I don't know how many times I must have walked up and down this block, but it was the first time ever that I noticed the place. And if Dimi hadn't mentioned it, I probably wouldn't have noticed this time either. Then again, if Dimi hadn't warned me not to go there, I wouldn't have stepped inside.

'Lunch?' asked a very paunchy guy, much shorter than me but 'bout my age.

'Yeah, sure,' I said.

The place was almost empty.

'What's all this stuff?' He led me to a booth at the back, waited till I sat down, then joined me. 'You some sort of artist?'

'No,' I said, a little startled that I suddenly had company. 'Just picking up some things for a friend.'

'I like that.' He pointed to the stool, then extended his hand to shake mine. 'I'm Herbie.'

'K.C.' I announced, thinking to myself, *Go Cubs*. 'But it's not the right one.'

'What's not the right one?'

'The stool.'

'Not the right one for what?'

I came up with, 'Her monkey.'

'What monkey?'

'The one who owns the stool. Or, in the case of this stool, doesn't.'

'It's a monkey stool? I thought it was a milking stool.'

'You see . . . this girl I know . . . the one who has the monkey . . . mistakenly left her stool at . . . the ice-cream place . . .' I motioned to the deflated cone. 'She used to work there. Well, I came in one night and insisted on *tutti frutti* . . .' I pointed to the deflated cone again, ''cause that's what they said they had. 'Cept they didn't. So I said they should have had *tutti frutti* 'cause that's what they were advertising. Well, the manager decided if I wanted *tutti frutti* I had to go someplace else for it. I told him he couldn't throw me out 'cause I was Rhea's boyfriend . . . that's her name, Rhea . . . but he threw me out anyway, and fired her at the same time. So now she reckons that it's my fault she forgot to take the monkey's stool with her. I said I'd get it for her, which I did, but they must have switched stools 'cause when I showed up with this one, she threw me out. So now I don't have Rhea and her monkey doesn't have a stool. I kinda figured the monkey would never notice . . .' I stopped. 'Sorry . . . I didn't mean to bore you with my sad story.'

He shut one eye, to stare at me with the other. 'You putting me on?'

'Hey. How many guys you know walk around New York on a Saturday afternoon carrying a monkey stool? 'Course, as far as I'm concerned, it's just another stool. But then, I guess, not all stools look alike if you're a monkey.'

Finally he asked, 'So what are you going to do with it?'

'Why? You got a monkey?'

'No, but I like the stool.'

I shrugged, 'Ya'll want to buy the stool?'

'How much?'

'Gee . . . I hadn't planned on selling it . . . but Rhea doesn't want it and I . . . well, how much is breakfast? You know, couple of scrambled with bacon and toast?'

'All day special? Deal.' He stood up, promised, 'Be right back', shouted my order to the counter man, and disappeared into the back room with my stool.

The waitress – a woman in her mid-twenties who wasn't any skinnier than Herbie – had just delivered my eggs and bacon when he reappeared. 'So what did you say your name was? You live around here?' He sat down again. 'How come I never saw you in here before?'

I told him I didn't live too far away but I'd never been in before 'cause ... 'I don't know ... just never found myself hungry when I was walking by.'

'So what do you do?'

'Little of this. Little of that.'

He nodded. 'Unemployed, huh?'

'Self-employed,' I corrected.

'Get a lot of self-employed guys in here,' he said. 'Used to get actors. About ten years ago everybody wanted to be in show business. A couple of them started coming in here. This was before we started getting lawyers. A lot of lawyers in the neighbourhood. Anyway, the actors brought their friends and this kind of became an actors' hangout. So I figured I'd encourage them and started putting out Herbie's Variety. You know, a promotional thing where I'd put all the actors' names on a mailing list and mail them the latest gossip, which I picked up listening to the other actors. Then the lawyers showed up. So after a while the actors stopped coming in and I changed the newsletter to Herbie's Law Review. That was pretty good. No more mail. Strictly fax. It ran for almost two years. Now ...'

The voice cut in, *Now we know why Dimi hates Herbie.*

I took a stab at, 'Herbie's Wall Street Journal?'

'Herbie's Day Trader Newsletter,' he said. 'I mean, once upon a time, every unemployed guy in the world wanted to be in show business. Now every unemployed guy in the world is a day trader.'

I told him, 'It's supposed to be a good way to earn a living?'

'Day trading or publishing a newsletter?'

'Day trading.'

'Naw, most people lose their shirts. Newsletters? That's better. But it's not a living. I mean, I haven't got it yet to the point where I can give up goulash and do it full-time. You know, we're famous for our goulash here. That's Ahmed.' He pointed to the counter man, who heard his name and waved. 'Best in the business. I mean, they even wrote him up in *New York Magazine*. Want to see a copy?'

'Yeah. Sure. But tell me, what's this newsletter of yours look like?'

'I thought so,' he nodded emphatically. 'I can always spot a day trader.'

'I admit to dabbling.'

'You want to subscribe?'

'Like to see it first.'

'Totally electronic. Not like some of those other sheets. None of that faxed-shmaxed nonsense. E-mailed from me to you, guaranteed by seven every morning.'

'I could be interested.'

He stood up. 'Be right back.'

I got a few forkfuls down before he was back, this time with a photocopied article from *New York Magazine* which proclaimed Ahmed of Herbie's Deli as one of the six best goulash chefs in the city – Dimi's was not listed – a computer print-out of his newsletter and a very skinny teenage kid with long hair and a bad complexion.

'This is Kevin,' Herbie said, shoving him into the booth, then sitting down next to him. 'And this is Herbie's Day Trader Newsletter.' He pushed the single page across the table to me, then called out to the waitress, 'Doll, two coffees. And the usual for Kevin.'

The newsletter was only a series of one-line tips – little more than a mix of voodoo and clairvoyance – hinting at what to buy, what to sell, what price range to look for in certain shares and a box at the bottom called Gossip over Goulash, being the latest day trader chatter overheard the day before at Herbie's Deli.

Under that was the You Trade – We Deliver daily special.

Kevin, who couldn't have been more than seventeen, was editor-in-chief and, according to Herbie, the best rumour-monger in New York. 'Kid's really good. And he's born here. Right here in New York. Pure American. Not like some other guys I could name in the newsletter business.'

I pretended not to understand who he was referring to. 'So?' I turned to Kevin. 'Who do you like at the bell on Monday morning?'

He shrugged, 'I'm not so good on Mondays.'

'Okay. Who do you think you'll like at the bell on Tuesday morning?'

He shrugged again, 'I'll have to wait until Monday to decide.'

'What sort of things do you look for?'

He shrugged a third time, 'It's hard to say.'

'That's my boy,' Herbie hugged him, making Kevin decidedly uncomfortable. 'Never give a thing away.'

Now Kevin said meekly, 'Excuse me,' waited for Herbie to stand up so that he could slide out of the booth, and walked away. 'Nice meeting you.'

'My brother's kid,' Herbie explained. 'Took a journalism course in high school. Needed a job. Figured I'd give him his first break. But I meant it when I said he's really good. So? You want the newsletter?'

'Gee . . .' I hated to tell him that tip-sheets like his were a dime a dozen and Kevin hadn't exactly inspired me to put my money on his sense of the market. 'I'll give it a think and call you.'

'The kid threw you off, huh?' Herbie shook his head. 'A comer, but not much in the way of a salesman.'

The waitress arrived with two coffees and a slice of apple pie with a ball of vanilla ice-cream on top. 'Where's Kevin?' She put a coffee in front of each of us but held on to the pie.

Herbie offered it to me. 'Give it to him. Home made. On the house.'

She put it in front of me before I could say thanks anyway.

'So what's in the carton?' she asked.

'Books,' I told her.

'What kind of books?'

The voice in my head yelled, *Go Cubs*.

'Terrific books,' I said. 'Used books, yes. But the plots . . . they read like new. What kind of books do you like?'

'Books?' she asked. 'Me? What can I tell you . . . I read a lot of Plato.'

'Plato?'

'Yeah. And when I'm not working here I'm studying for a Ph.D. at Harvard.'

Herbie explained, 'Actress.'

'An authentic future Lady Macbeth,' she said, made a face then added, 'at this rate.'

'Tell you what,' I said to Herbie, 'how much is the news-letter?'

He understood. 'Let's see the books first.'

I put my hand on the top of the box. 'Sight unseen.'

'How many are there?'

'I counted thirty-six. Let's call it, give or take two.'

'Paperback or hardcover?'

'Paperback.'

'Covers all in good shape?'

I shrugged, 'Yeah, I guess so.'

'First editions?'

I stared at him. 'First editions? Yeah sure, and all signed by Hemingway himself.'

'Thirty-six books . . . give or take two . . .' He calculated. 'Sight unseen . . . eighteen days.'

'That's what . . . just over three weeks?' I thought about that. 'A month is twenty and a couple . . . so make it a month.'

He nodded to the waitress. 'Okay, Doll, they're yours.'

'Hey, thanks.' She grabbed the carton, opened it and sorted through the titles. 'Oh good . . . romance stuff . . . not Plato but it will do. Thanks, Herbie.' She took the carton back to the counter and showed the books to Ahmed.

'Made her happy,' Herbie said.

Now Ahmed shouted to me, 'Got any books about basketball?'

I held up both my hands. 'The way the Knicks are playing, it would have to be science fiction. Sorry.'

Herbie handed me a paper napkin and a pen. 'Put your e-mail address down here. You're on for a month.'

I jotted it down, then asked. 'After that, if I want to subscribe, how much is it?'

'Five bucks a month.'

'You mean . . . I just sold you thirty-six perfectly good books for five bucks?'

He nodded. 'Hey, pal, you were the one who wanted to play sight unseen.'

So that was my Saturday walk and my introduction to Herbie's. I got some exercise, a free breakfast, a month's subscription to his Day Trader Newsletter, and one souvenir deflated inflatable ice-cream cone.

I also got a few hours outside in the fresh air to clear my head.

Finally, the voice declared as I walked into the lobby of my building, *it is nap time*.

Except it wasn't.

'K.C.?'

I turned to find Pinky standing there.

'You?' I had to know, 'What the hell was all that about this morning?'

'She told me everything,' he said, rushing up to me and throwing his arms around me. 'I'm sorry that I ever doubted you. Really I am.'

I wasn't going to let him off the hook that easily. 'You come up to us on the street this morning, and start shouting at me and accusing poor little Debbie of all sorts of crap . . .'

'I'm sorry. I'm sorry . . .' I thought he was going to cry. 'K.C., please . . .'

'Just tell me why you wouldn't listen to the way it really was.'

'I'm sorry,' he kept saying over and over again. 'I'm sorry.'

I looked at him – the voice decided, *enough* – put my arm around him, announced, 'All's forgiven,' and brought him upstairs. 'Pull up a floor,' I said, directing him into my empty living room.

'What happened?'

'She took everything.'

He gave me one of his doleful looks. 'It was just that this morning when I saw you two together . . .'

'But Debbie told you everything, right?'

He nodded.

'Okay. So let's just forget it. 'Cept, I still want to know what you were doing here at that hour?'

'Looking for her. I snuck out to call her on the phone Friday night . . .' He put a finger to his lips, so that I'd know it was a secret 'cause he wasn't supposed to make phone calls on his Sabbath. 'But she wasn't home. And then, this morning . . . I snuck out again and when she didn't answer . . . because I knew she was upset about you . . . I walked all the way here.'

'All the way from where?'

'My mother's apartment on the West Side. I cut through the Park. I told her I was going to synagogue. I made two sneaky phone calls on the *shabbus* and also lied to my mother. But I didn't take a bus. I didn't ride. I walked. I was waiting downstairs for nearly two hours because I didn't want to wake you.'

I smiled. 'Thanks. Believe me, I appreciate it.'

He looked at me and smiled. 'You're welcome.'

There was a long pause.

'Ah . . . I don't have much in the fridge,' I said, still clinging to my deflated ice-cream cone. 'Though I guess I can do coffee.'

'I've got to go.' But he didn't move.

'Well . . . hey . . . thanks for stopping by. Where are you off to now?'

'Back to my mother's.'

'It's a long walk.'

'About an hour.' He still hadn't budged.

'Can you sneak a taxi?'

'From my mother, yes. From me, no.'

'Well . . . then remember look both ways before crossing the street.'

All of a sudden he blurted out, 'She's in love with you.'

'Huh?'

'Debbie confessed everything. She told me she's in love with you.'

'What are ya'll talking 'bout?'

'That's what she said.'

'Debbie said that? She told you . . . listen, Pinky, Debbie doesn't know what she's talking about. She got a little drunk last night and showed up here . . .' I didn't know how much of the story she'd told him so I stopped short of quoting her last words before passing out. 'And she was pretty embarrassed about it this morning. Especially with you coming along the way you did and finding her here.'

'She's in love with you.'

'No, she's not. She's just . . .' I didn't know what she was doing. 'Fantasizing,' I suggested. 'She's just feeling sorry for me 'cause I got fired.'

Pinky started shaking his head. 'No, no, no, no. She's in love with you. She told me.'

'Come on, man, I'm old enough to be her father. She's a kid. Pinky, I'm also a married man . . . several times.'

He was still shaking his head as he slowly made his way to my door. 'She's in love with you. She told me.' And just like that, he walked out.

Terrific, I said to the voice, *some guys get Michele Pfeiffer, we get little Debbie.*

Not only that, the voice added, *but we forgot the Woollite.*

My nap simply wasn't to be.

The voice kept insisting, *we need to remind Debbie that this isn't our first rodeo.*

But worrying 'bout Debbie was not what I needed to be worrying 'bout, which really annoyed me 'cause that's exactly what I was worrying 'bout.

Deep down, I was telling myself, *if Debbie is really thinking like that, I need to find a way to help her make a soft landing.*

At the same time, the little voice was telling me, *nothing to do 'bout that now.*

The fastest way I could think of pushing Debbie outta my mind was by phoning my mama to reassure her that everything was gonna work out fine.

She asked how Lorilee was.

I answered, 'Nothing's changed.'

I don't know what I really meant by that, but Mama accepted it and I told her I'd phone her again tomorrow.

The next thing I did to push Debbie outta my mind was to remind myself that practice makes perfect and went back to playing the day trading software game a few more times.

Each time I went through the routine, I found myself feeling a little bit more comfortable.

'Cept each time I played, I still lost upwards of $45,000.

After a while I contemplated maybe going to a movie but I couldn't think of anything I wanted to see, so I curled up with that *Day Trader* magazine and started reading until my eyes started closing.

When I woke up, it was the middle of the night. I turned on the television, not really to watch but to have a little noise in the place, talked myself into being hungry and made another one of those raisin bread and soft-boiled egg concoctions.

Culinary synergy, the voice reminded me.

I thought about that Patsy person but there was no question of phoning her, not at this hour, even if I was curious to know what she meant by culinary synergy. Anyway, I wasn't sure I should be phoning her again. She said she had a couple of kids and from that I could rightly deduce she also had a husband somewhere and I knew from experience that most husbands don't take to guys who start phoning their wives.

If she has a husband, the voice theorized, *he didn't mind her carrying on a conversation with some guy who dialled the wrong number.*

Yeah, well, probably 'cause he wasn't there.

Or isn't there.

No matter, I told the voice, checking my brand-new clock-radio to see that it was 3.40 a.m., *he's likely to be there now.*

How about we try again in twelve hours?

How about we go back to sleep?

I put my bowl and spoon in the sink, fiddled with the TV dials – still couldn't find anything, not even on the porn channels, which is what Lorilee and I sometimes watched when we woke up in the middle of the night – tuned to the wrestling and stared at that while a bunch of heavyweight baboons knocked each other silly. Finally, out of total desperation, I switched over to Court TV.

That was another of our little tricks. If the porn channels didn't put us in the mood to fool around, or we really just wanted to go back to sleep, there was always good old Court TV.

Lawyers, I'd remind her, can cure insomnia.

'Cept Duke, she'd protest.

'Cept Duke, I'd agree.

When I finally got back to sleep I dreamt that I'd hired Alan Dershowitz to be my lawyer and there he was on Court TV, dressed up like a heavyweight wrestler, with Izzy as his tag-team partner, and there they were, the two of them yanking Duke to the ground and stomping on his head.

It was the best dream I'd had all week.

The next morning I walked over to the Korean joint, stocked up some on food – mainly pasta 'cause that was easy enough to cook – bought enough M&Ms to refill my Giants helmet and also picked up a copy of the *Sunday Times.* I made my way leisurely through the paper while munching on a bowl of bow-tie pasta, then went back to the day trading software and spent another few hours, popping M&Ms, trying to get ready for Monday morning which, the way they used to say it in the sixties, was gonna be the first day of the rest of my life.

I was in the middle of the third game of the afternoon, now only losing $32,750, when the phone rang.

'Why did he phone me on a Sunday afternoon to wake me up?' It was Lorilee. 'How dare you hire someone to harass me?'

'Who?'

'Calls here on a Sunday and wakes me up. Wasn't even two in the afternoon yet. Starts telling me that he can't get in touch with Duke and wants me to relay a message to him . . .'

I tried again, 'Who?'

'The guy you hired to harass me.'

'What on earth are you babbling about?'

'Ya'll just listen to me, K.C. Doone, I am not going to stand for it. Bet your sweet ass, neither is Duke.'

She slammed down the phone.

I stared at it, shook my head 'cause I didn't understand a thing, hung up and went back to my day trading game.

Problem was, she'd broken my concentration and my losses quickly climbed to $62,500.

I bailed out and started again.

Not ten minutes into game four, Duke called. 'Ya'll listen to me, K.C. I'm going to warn you and warn you only once.'

'Howdy, Duke. How ya'll doing?'

'Don't give me any of your howdy Duke shit. Ya'll just better understand that I don't take lightly to threats. *Comprendo, amigo?*'

'Ya'll have a nice day now,' I said, just as he hung up. '*Adios* . . .' The phone went dead. '. . . *amigo.*'

Determined to conquer the software program before the software program conquered me, I rebooted and tried again. But then the phone rang for the third time that afternoon.

'I've got news,' came a twelve-year-old's voice.

That's when the other boot dropped. 'Izzy, ya'll been threatening Lorilee and Duke?'

'Not me. One of the things they taught us in law school is that a good lawyer never threatens . . . all he has to do is stay calm, speak very quietly and be a good lawyer.'

'They both just phoned me, furious.'

'Serves them right.'

'What did you tell them?'

'I didn't threaten. I merely phoned them both today . . .'

'On a Sunday?'

'I never phone people on Saturdays. I sometimes phone people on Sundays.'

'And what did you tell them?'

'I very politely asked your wife to make sure that her brother explained to her how we'd drag her sexual history through the courts . . .'

'Sounds exactly like a threat to me.'

'. . . and when I got her brother on the phone I . . . no, I didn't threaten, I informed. That's right. I informed him that we were seriously considering filing criminal charges for breaking and entering and that we would ask the courts to look into his behaviour in this matter . . .'

'You did what?' I couldn't believe it. 'Izzy, Duke is not someone who takes to . . . being informed . . .'

'Informed? Well, maybe it's better to say, I good-lawyered.'

'Izzy . . . ya'll gotta understand something here. Duke is a particularly nasty guy. You don't fool around with him like that. I mean, threatening Duke with criminal prosecution . . . he'll come straight at you . . .'

Izzy said cheerfully, 'He promised he would.'

'I wouldn't want to be you if he does.'

'You mean, when he does.'

I had to ask, 'Are ya'll listening to me when I say you're messing with a guy you shouldn't be messing with?'

'I hear you.'

''Cept from the tone of your voice I'm not convinced you're convinced. They both just phoned me hopping mad . . .'

'I'm just good-lawyering to him the way he tried to good-lawyer to my client. Remember the writ he served on you? What do you think that was? It's not called a threat, it's called a court order.'

'So . . . I don't know . . . serve him a court order back. But don't threaten the guy.'

'That's for tomorrow.'

'What is?'

'The court order.'

'What for?'

'To show him we won't stand for his kind of good-lawyering.'

'Stand for it?' I didn't have the heart to tell him that some-where early on in the first round, Duke would make sure Izzy wasn't standing at all. 'Look, Izzy, maybe we oughta have a talk about all this . . .'

'You hired me so you have to trust me.'

'I trust you. I just want you to know that . . .' How could I tell him he wasn't merely out of his league, he wasn't even in the same solar system. 'Izzy, Duke is a very . . . protective brother. That's kinda the politest thing I can say 'bout him. He's gonna do whatever he has to in order to make sure she comes out of this real sweet. Now, if that means coming down on you and me, he's not gonna hesitate one iota.'

'You have to trust me,' he repeated. 'Anyway, I've already taken advice on the matter.'

'Advice? From who?'

'Another lawyer. The best. Harry Kimmelman. Remember when I said even Alan Dershowitz had to start somewhere? Well, when Alan Dershowitz was just starting, he used to say that even Harry Kimmelman had to start somewhere.'

'Alan Dershowitz said what?'

He hesitated. 'Not really. But maybe. If he'd ever heard of Harry Kimmelman, I'm sure he would have said it.'

'Izzy, who the hell is Harry Kimmelman?'

'My cousin Harry.'

'The guy in Tel Aviv?'

'See that. Even you've heard about him. I called cousin Harry this morning because it's Sunday in Tel Aviv and of course he goes to the office on Sunday. I told him everything I knew about your case and we plotted a strategy. So you have to trust me because I trust Cousin Harry.'

I didn't want to ask point-blank, *Are you sure you know what you're doing*, so I tried, 'Are you sure that this isn't going to backfire on us somehow?'

'Cousin Harry says it works most of the time.'

'Most of the time?'

'I've got all the paperwork drawn up. I'll get it into a court early tomorrow morning and see that both your wife and her brother are served at the same time. In the meantime, you've managed to ruin their Sunday afternoon.'

'Me?'

'I'm only acting for my client. That's you.'

'And just what does this writ say?'

'In layman's terms?'

'No, in English that I can understand.'

'It says, neither one of them can do what they've already done, nor can they do what they think they can do.'

I waited for him to go on. 'Huh?'

'That's what it says. Cousin Harry assures me that's enough.'

I sat all the way back and took a deep breath.

'You still there?' he asked.

'I'm still here,' I answered.

'So, do you want to know the news on the other two fronts?'

'Other two fronts? You mean, my mama's apartment and my getting fired from GCB?'

'Yes. You want to know the news?'

'Tell me.'

'Nothing. There is no news. Cousin Harry had to go so I didn't get a chance to ask him for his advice. I promised to phone him tomorrow. So I'll phone you tomorrow too. As soon as the writs are served. You'll be hearing from me.'

I knew I'd be hearing from Lorilee and Duke as well and told Izzy, without any hesitation, 'Yeah, we'll talk tomorrow.'

Hanging up with him, I didn't feel like going back to the software – even though I knew damn well that I had to get the better of it real fast – 'cause Izzy's voice was still ringing in my ears.

So I shut down the computer and tuned into some of the late afternoon talk shows. I didn't actually listen to any of them, but sat in front of the set, kinda zombie like, as journalists and politicians paraded themselves on their weekly outing to pontificate, satisfying the American public's thirst for inside knowledge about the foibles of journalists and politicians who pontificate.

When that was done I thought about getting back on the Internet to see if I could find something on the 200 Club. But the little voice decided, *hey, if Thomas Whitestone is supposed to be in New York on Tuesday night, maybe he's here already.*

Figuring I had nothing to lose, I dialled his number on Park Avenue and let it ring a bunch of times. A woman finally answered but she was speaking out-of-breath Spanish and 'cause I can't even speak in-breath Spanish, I hung up.

Now the voice reckoned, *Go on, what the hell, why not, it's more than twelve hours later.* And as long as I was within arm's reach of the phone anyway, I took a shot and dialled Patsy.

When she answered, I said straight away, 'I've got two questions to ask you, and the first is, what's culinary synergy?'

She answered straight away, 'Culinary means of or used in cooking. Or having to do with the kitchen. I suppose that's right because it comes from the Latin *culina* which means kitchen. And synergy, well that I know comes from the Greek *sunergos* which I think means something like working together. The idea is that when you combine certain elements, the result is something that neither of those elements could achieve on their own. You know, the result is greater than the sum of the parts. So when you combine those words, culinary and synergy, you wind up with someone honestly believing that raisin toast mixed in egg yolk tastes great. Next question?'

I was near-on speechless. Eventually, I managed a wavering, 'Are you some sort of schoolteacher?'

She said, 'Well . . . some sort of.'

I asked with real hope, 'Eighth grade English?'

'Sorry. High school principal.'

'Huh?'

'Does that frighten you?'

'If you're anything like Mr Wilson it does.'

'I'm sure I am.'

'He used to wear combat boots. Had a moustache. Looked like what Hitler would have looked like if he stood six three and weighed two hundred and fifty pounds. Always carried a wooden yardstick that he'd snap on the lockers in the hallway whenever he spotted anyone there without a hall pass.'

'Hmmm . . . well . . . yes, I'd say that fits my description to a tee.'

'Yardstick and all?'

'Not quite. Metric ruler.'

I laughed. 'So . . . did whoever it was get home by eleven the other night?'

'My daughter. And wouldn't you if Mr Wilson was your mom?'

'Are you her principal?'

'I am. My son's too.'

'How old are they?'

'My goodness, for a fellow who started by saying he had two questions to ask, that's almost six or seven? The answer is, he's seventeen and she's fifteen.'

'How do they like having you as their principal?'

'They tell me they love it. However, I know them both well enough to say they're lying through their teeth. The truth is, they're very embarrassed by it. They get teased all the time. Not in front of me. But you don't get to be Mr Wilson unless you have ears that pick up high-frequency teasing. But that's all right. The thing I like best about being their principal is that they're both too chicken not to get very good grades.'

'I don't know what I would have done if my mama had been my high school principal. Probably got tossed out even before I did.'

'Ruby would do that?'

'Mr Wilson did.'

'Threw you out of high school?'

'Not permanent . . . just a week at a time.'

'Whatever for?'

'Well . . . once I turned all the clocks ahead. I found the master clock in his office. Worked off a kinda ticker tape. I pulled it, all the clocks in the school jumped forward and we got out 'bout fifteen minutes early. That was the first time. Half an hour early the second time. Unfortunately, the third time I tried it, I broke the damn tape and wound up sitting home for a week.'

'I would have made you work it off. Productive rehabilitation not punishment.'

'Yeah, well, we didn't have big words like that where I went to high school. Anyway, it wasn't my first offence.'

'What was?'

'Ah . . . gee . . .' I worried 'bout telling her, what with not having any idea who she was and whether or not Mr Patsy was going to interrupt at any moment, threatening to neuter me for talking like this to his wife. 'Cept I told her anyway. 'You see . . . all us guys had to take shop class. And the shop was right next to the gym. And they had these big power drills in shop. And the back of the shower in the boys' gym was the same tiled wall as the back of the shower . . .'

She broke up laughing. 'You didn't.'

''Fraid so.'

'You got caught looking?'

'If only. The girls' gym teacher got kinda suspicious when she heard all the drilling noise and saw tile dust falling into their shower and then this drill bit came through the wall.'

'I can see how that might have piqued her curiosity.'

'I thought it was a good idea at the time.'

'If I were Ruby I wouldn't have agreed.'

'I can honestly say that no one else agreed. Not Ruby. Not the girls' gym teacher. Certainly not Mr Wilson. 'Though I heard later that some of the girls discovered how the hole in the shower worked both ways and . . . oh well, never mind.'

'Any other major achievements in high school?'

'Not that I could expound on to a total stranger.'

Now she said, 'Not exactly total.'

I smiled. 'Ah . . . I guess not total. But almost. After all, I didn't know you were a high school principal.'

'All you had to do was ask.'

'Ask . . . yeah . . . and that actually brings me to the second question that I started to ask, now 'bout eight or nine questions ago.' I stopped.

'Go ahead.'

'Well . . . you were kinda fun to talk to on the phone the other evening and so I got to wondering . . . which is really why I phoned back tonight . . . are lady high school principals married to guy high school football coaches or something?'

'Some of them are, I suppose.'

I dared, 'How about you?'

'No . . . no football coach.'

'Ah . . .' I didn't like the way she said that. 'Oh well . . .'

'You sound disappointed.'

'Not disappointed that you're not married to a football coach . . . but, I mean, the way you said it . . . I guess there is a Mr Patsy, huh?'

'Yes,' she said. 'Mr Patsy is an aeronautical engineer. He designs airplanes.'

'Oh . . . well . . .' This time I didn't hide my disappointment. 'Listen, Miss Patsy, high school principal, ya'll tell him he's a lucky guy to have such a pleasant wife. I'm sorry to have bothered you . . .'

'You haven't bothered me.'

'Thing is,' I said honestly, 'if I were him, this kind of thing would be bothering me.'

'Would it? Why?'

'Why? Come on, some strange guy phoning my wife . . .'

'Yes,' she agreed, 'you do have a point. But I really don't

think he'll be bothered unless you do start phoning his wife . . . in Westchester. Would you like her number?'

'Oh?' Now my tone changed, 'Oh. Ah . . . well . . . in that case can I phone you again sometime?'

'You mean, next time you're in port, sailor?'

'No, I mean, next time I want to find out something, like what culinary synergy means.'

'Why don't you dial and see if I answer?'

I said, 'Okay, I will,' hung up, waited a few seconds and dialled her again.

'Guess what?' she said as soon as she picked up the phone.

'What?'

'I answered.'

Chapter Fifteen

My eyes began to close.

I heard someone say, 'Maybe we should get some sleep,' and wondered who it was, until Sir Tommy answered, 'That's probably a good idea,' and I realized it was me.

I folded my arms across my chest, leaned as far as I could to my right, propping my shoulder up against the side of the elevator, and mumbled, 'Night.'

He answered, 'Good night.'

And for the longest time, there was only quiet.

My eyes stayed shut but if sleep was in the neighbourhood, it hadn't yet come to my street. I whispered, 'This could be a long night.'

He squirmed. 'We shall just have to be patient.'

I said quietly, 'I guess.'

And he said just as quietly, 'One of the greatest virtues . . . patience.'

I said again, 'I guess.'

Now he turned to me and asked in a normal voice, 'Do you remember a singing group called Patience and Prudence?'

'Huh? Called what?'

'Patience and Prudence.'

'No.' I purposely kept my eyes closed.

'I haven't thought of them in years.'

'That's nice,' I said. 'Good night.'

'I always liked their music,' he explained. 'Are you sure you never heard of them?'

'I'm sure.'

'It was very good music. One of their biggest hits was a song entitled, "Tonight You Belong To Me".'

Now I opened my eyes to look at him, but he was leaning back with his eyes closed. 'Julio Iglesias kinda music?'

'There's nothing wrong with Julio Iglesias. I know him. We're not exactly neighbours in Spain, but I've met him socially on several occasions.' He opened his eyes, realized I was staring at him and grinned at me. 'Let me tell you about Julio Iglesias . . .'

I didn't think I could bear it so I interrupted, 'Before you do, what time is it?' I pulled up my sleeve but couldn't tell because my knock-off Cartier didn't have a dial that glowed in the dark. 'I'm trying to figure out how long we've been here and how much longer we have to go.'

He strained to see the face of his Rolex Oyster. 'It appears to be around half-ten.'

'Half-ten? What time is that?'

'Ten-thirty.'

'Christ . . . we've been in here for . . . over eight hours.'

'Seven and a bit,' he corrected.

'Okay, almost eight hours.'

'No, not almost eight hours, only seven and a bit.'

'Well,' I told him, 'it seems like eight hours.'

'You're doing it just to annoy me, aren't you?' He raised his hands in surrender. 'But, you know what, Mr Doone, patience and prudence. I am not going to allow you to annoy me. I am going to be patient and I am going to be prudent. If we have to be here throughout the night, I am resigned to either carrying on a civil relationship with you, accepting the fact that this is all your fault, or completely disregarding you by pretending you're not here. I shall go away to somewhere else.'

'Go away to somewhere else? Like where? And how could you possibly pretend I'm not here?'

'That would be simple. I would leave here by exercising my mind, sleeping for some hours, playing various word games and mathematical games in my head, sleeping for several more hours and eventually it will be morning. I would return in time to be rescued.'

'You can completely tune out to the fact that I'm trapped in here with you, even if . . .' I decided to drive home this point '. . . even if it is clearly your fault that we're here?'

'I have given you fair warning,' he announced. 'Good-bye, Mr Doone.'

'Good-bye, Mr Doone?' I had to laugh. 'Hey, ya'll know

what? If that's the game you want to play . . . all right, good-bye, Sir Tommy. Have a good trip. And when you get bored going to wherever it is you think you're going, there'll always be room for you in my elevator. You're always welcome to come back. You can even bring your pal Julio with you. You see? I refuse to be as childish about this as you.'

'Oh, you think I'm the one who's being childish?'

'Of course not,' I said sarcastically, 'I am.'

'Not half.' He turned his back, folded his arms and stared up at the ceiling of the lift, as if he was concentrating deeply on something important.

I had to find out, 'What does that mean, not half?'

'You're not here,' he said.

I reminded him, 'I'm still here. You're the one who's decided not to be here.'

'Whatever.'

I waited for him to say something else. 'So?' But he didn't answer and after what struck me as being a very long silence, I asked again, 'So . . . what does not half mean? Half-ten? What half? What language are you talking?'

He continued to pretend like he was thinking.

'A quarter is not half. But then, neither is a whole. I said to you, I refuse to be as childish about this as you. And you asked me if I thought you were the one being childish. And I said, of course not, I am. And then you said, not half. It doesn't make any sense.'

'Perhaps,' he conceded, still not looking at me, 'the language that you speak and the English that I speak are indeed very different.'

'Okay, so how about if I say to that, not half.'

'That would be quite correct. But, of course, you wouldn't know why. To begin with, you don't know what it means. Furthermore, if I hadn't used the expression first, you never would have heard it at all.'

'It still doesn't make any sense.'

'It makes perfect sense.'

'So I'm gonna say, not half, 'cause as far as I'm concerned, it doesn't make even half sense.'

'It doesn't make any sense at all,' he said, 'seeing as how I'm not here.'

I shook my head, leaned back and shut my eyes. 'Right.'

And neither us spoke again for what seemed to be an eternity.

Then he broke the silence. 'Patience and prudence.'

'And Julio Iglesias makes three.'

'I'm referring to the virtues,' he said. 'I suppose I have been a patient man most of my life, though . . . I will admit that I have little or no patience at all for most people. As for prudent . . .'

'Wait a second.' I had to know, 'How can you call yourself a patient man if you have little or no patience for most people?'

'I'm patient with myself.'

'That doesn't make any sense.'

'Now you are the one displaying both a lack of patience and no notion whatsoever of prudence. I, however, am losing patience with you, Mr Doone.'

Shaking my head, I sat back and shut my eyes. 'For a guy who isn't here, it sure sounds like you're here.'

'I shall be both patient and prudent, and in so doing, set an example for you.'

There was another very long silence.

I felt myself just beginning to fall asleep when I heard him say, 'Soap, too.'

'Huh?' I snapped back to the moment. 'Soap what?'

'Too.'

'What?'

'Soap, too. That's what I said.'

'What's that supposed to mean?'

'It means exactly . . . soap, too.'

'One for each of us?'

'Not t-w-o. Not the number. T-o-o. Also.'

'What also?'

'Soap also.'

'What about soap also?'

'I don't buy that either.'

'You don't buy soap?' I looked at him. 'Does that mean ya'll don't bathe?'

'Of course I bathe. And sitting this close, you should be the first to be grateful. But I never buy soap. They give it away in hotels. I simply collect soap from hotels and stock all of my bathrooms in all my homes with it.'

'Sugar. Butter. Soap. Anything else?'

'Postcards.'

'What postcards?'

'Postcards.' He leaned forward, reached into his jacket pocket and pulled out several. 'See.'

In the darkness I could just barely tell that they were scenes of London hotels. 'I thought you weren't here.'

'I was there,' he pointed to the postcards. 'Of course I was. That's where I got them.'

'That's not what I meant. However long ago it was, you told me you were leaving, going someplace else, and that you wouldn't come back till someone showed up to rescue us.'

'That's right.'

'Well, it kinda looks to me like ya'll just came back.'

He turned towards me and flashed on one of his big smiles. 'As a matter of fact, I have returned. And look, Mr Doone, I've brought you some souvenir postcards.'

Chapter Sixteen

We stayed on the line for a long time.

I wanted to know if she always spoke to strangers. 'After all, I'd hate to be just another pretty voice.'

She wanted to know if I was currently married. 'After all . . . force of habit.'

I told her the truth, that I'd been married almost as many times as I'd been kicked out of high school and that my current wife and I were living apart.

She told me that she'd never spoken to a wrong number before more than twice. 'The first time to say, you've got the wrong number. The second time to say, you've still got the wrong number.' Then she asked, 'Will you stay apart?'

I answered without any hesitation, 'Oh yeah.'

'That's too bad. It's never happy when a marriage breaks up.'

'Practice makes perfect,' I mumbled, then changed the subject, asking her where she went to school and how she got to be a principal.

'Alas, that, I am sorry to say, will have to be saved for the sequel. I fear that my kids are getting a little too curious about who I'm talking to, and have cottoned on to the idea that it might be a gentleman. If I don't put a stop to it immediately, my life will be misery until I confess to everything.'

'First of all, tell them it's no gentleman, it's only me. Second of all, it's dangerous confessing stuff. My advice is that, in this case, honesty is not the best policy.'

'It isn't?'

'Not at all. Come on, if you were your kids, would you believe that Mama just spent . . .' I checked the time . . . 'how about sixty-four minutes on the line with a wrong number?'

'Now that you mention it, that is worrying.'

'The wrong number?'

'No. That you're counting.'

I laughed, then hesitated . . . 'Can I give you my number?'

'I already know your number. Remember my caller ID?'

'Oh . . . well . . . should I call you or will you call me?'

She said right away, 'You should phone me.'

'Standing on ceremony, are we?'

'Not at all. I'm certainly old enough to phone a man if I choose to. But I also have a fifteen-year-old daughter for whom I am trying to set a good example.'

I admitted, 'I know exactly what you're talking 'bout 'cause I was once a fifteen-year-old boy.'

'And you,' she insisted, 'were clearly the sort of fifteen-year-old boy I would not want my daughter phoning. Good night, Mr K.C. Doone.'

'Good night, Miss High School Principal.'

'Mrs High School Principal, to you,' she said. 'Good night.' And hung up.

Handled that pretty good, I announced to the voice.

Not bad, the voice responded.

Guess I've still got the touch.

Hey, this is a grown-up lady, so let's hope not.

My brand-new ultimate clock-radio suddenly went off at 5.55 on Monday morning – just like that – which startled me 'cause I'd forgotten that I'd set it. Then I realized I hadn't set it. So I lay in bed for fifteen minutes, fiddling with it, trying to figure out how come it just snapped on like that. I pushed all sorts of buttons but nothing happened. Considering how long it had taken me to program my VCR, I worried that I was destined to be up at 5.55 every morning for the rest of my life.

Eventually I crawled out of bed, not because I wanted to get up yet but because I needed to find the directions so that I could snooze for another half-hour. That's why I'd bought the damn thing. But when I finally located those directions sitting in a pile of stuff under my desk – 'cause I'd forgotten to buy a wastepaper basket – they turned out to be in Japanese.

Even the little diagrams kinda looked like they were in Japanese too 'cause they didn't make one bit of sense. Then again, it didn't make any sense to me how come it hadn't turned itself on before now.

I put the damn thing back on the side of my desk, turned down the sound – 'cause nothing would turn it off – traipsed into the kitchen, made coffee and toast, and decided there was still time for one more run through the day trading software before I started playing it for real.

By 8.15 I was losing $87,000.

Tuning into CNBC, I took out a fresh pad, a stack of sharp pencils, filled up my coffee cup, sat down in front of my laptop and signed on-line.

A little flashing icon indicated that there was a whole stack of stuff waiting in my mailbox. Most of it was junk e-mail – *Talk XXX To Hot Girls, How To Pay No Car Insurance, Subliminally Seduce Your Wife's Best Friend, Boyz Will Be Boyz, Live Lesbian Video Sexxx* and *Hidden Camera XXX Videos* – all of which I deleted. Then there was Herbie's Day Trader Newsletter, four letters from people I'd worked with at GCB and a note from Debbie.

Kevin's Monday morning *Tout de Jour* was a small biotech outfit called TapTech Corporation. But then, everyone else's tout of the day these days were small biotech outfits called something like TapTech Corp.

The GCB crowd mostly expressed condolences on my having gotten fired, 'though one of them – that idiot Binterman – wrote that after having displayed my true talent by nearly sinking 'his' company with TransMare-Telco, would I please be kind enough to remove his name from my list of professional references.

To delete or undelete, the voice asked, *that is the question.*

If it had been anyone else, I might have simply forgotten his little jibe and gotten on with my life. But I'm not built like that. So I told the voice, *undelete*, went back into the Recycle Bin on my desktop – where deleted files live until you erase them for ever from your machine – resurrected the porno e-mails and subscribed to everything offered in every one of them, using Binterman's return e-mail address. I also made certain to push the little 'cc' button – the electronic version of carbon copies – so that every time Binterman received a response, so would Messrs. Maynard, Cotton and Braddock.

Then I re-deleted all of that stuff, and for good measure,

emptied the recycle bin, sending the evidence of my vengeance off into the oblivion of cyberspace.

Debbie's note simply said, 'So-ooo embarrassed. So-ooo sorry.'

I filed hers and Kevin's, figuring this way I could check later on how accurate Kevin was – or wasn't – and had plenty of time to think of something to say to Debbie besides, *so-ooo this ain't gonna work out.*

The important message was a very long and detailed Welcome to On-Time/Real-Time Trades, which ran to a couple of dozen pages. I downloaded it, logged off and read it all with my coffee. The bulk of the missive was rules and regulations. There was a section on trading tips – *shares are ripe for day trading when volume is rising and remains high for a quantifiable amount of time in relation to its average* – and how to customize my password. I liked that, so I jumped back on line, signing on with their pre-assigned password – six random letters, two numbers and one more letter – and elected to change it. Then I realized I hadn't yet come up with anything to change it to.

Thinking real hard, I needed something I could easily remember. I ruled out Lorilee, Carrie and Marylou. I ruled out KC, Ruby and, even though the little voice was just about to suggest it, I decided it was seriously premature to even consider Patsy.

I ruled out *kyuukyoko*, ruled out Binterman, ruled out IBM Thinkpad, ruled out CNBC, ruled out the name of the Italian gal with the mouth that Mikey liked – maybe 'cause she wasn't on yet and I didn't know who she was – ruled out Mikey, ruled out Dimi, ruled out deli and settled on goulash.

The software accepted it and now I had my password.

On-Time/Real-Time was up and running, even though Chicago is an hour earlier than New York. I typed in my trading name, which was K-C, used my new password for the first time, and watched as the software took over and my screen came alive. The NASDAQ wire didn't have prices yet, just symbols, but it was running full steam ahead at the bottom of my screen.

Configuring boxes for shares to watch, I chose Microsoft and Intel – 'cause they're always in the top ten active dollar volume – then added a few companies I'd always liked at GCB. I put up a chart on TucsonBancorp, which was just getting ready to break out of the Southwest and move into California. And a chart on Atwater Marquette Micro Systems which was the only manufacturer in the country that made whatever it was they made which, I'd been told, every modem in the world needs.

Thinking the screen still looked empty, I added Church Centre Med Life, Scotsel Cellular and AptApplied Syscorp, three small companies that had been very actively traded over the past few weeks. Then I keyed in to the trading floor to make sure the connection was up and running. A little note scrawled across my screen that read, *Hi K-C, ready when you are.*

Finally, I was ready.

But the market was still closed.

I checked to make sure that my trading account had $10,000 available, only to see that it was a few hundred dollars short. So I rang On-Time/Real-Time to find out what they'd deducted. Turned out to be next month's fees in advance and a few bucks in hidden charges that they said I would have known about had I read their e-mailed rules and regulations.

Then I simply sat back and waited – one eye on CNBC, one eye on my computer – for something to happen.

And for the longest time, nothing did.

Hong Kong, Singapore and Tokyo were all up on the day and I briefly toyed with maybe taking a punt on some dragon bank shares. Yet being, as I was, only a week away from the TransMare-Telco fiasco, I didn't need the little voice to remind me that I'd best leave the Far East alone for a while.

No one at CNBC seemed to have any real idea where the market would be going, though at the opening bell Intel jumped a half, Microsoft dropped seven-eighths, and none of the other companies I had on my screen did anything.

'Bout ten minutes into the session, someone came on the tube and started talking about TrakMark Security, which was in the hi-tech home and office burglar alarm business. The guy on television said that an announcement would be forthcoming from the company to confirm their much rumoured merger with Auto Guardshield Group, a company that made guaranteed thief-proof car alarms that were somehow rigged to satellites which, if the thief hadn't read the guarantee before stealing the car, would track him until the police caught up. He said it was a 'Perfect match' which caused me to wonder if the satellites were going to track someone's house if that got robbed.

The little voice in the back of my head responded, *bump*

theory, so I put TrakMark on my screen, saw that the best offer of any market maker was $6\frac{3}{8}$ for a block of 1000 shares, told the voice, *time to get our feet wet*, and put in an order.

The box that displayed my trading account balance turned bright red, within thirty-two seconds the floor guy confirmed the buy, and within a minute my screen showed best offer was now $6\frac{1}{2}$. I punched in a stop at $6\frac{1}{8}$ – meaning that if the shares dropped to that price, the floor guy would automatically try to sell them, which if he could, would protect my downside – and started hunting around for something else to buy.

I noticed that Scotsel Cellular had dropped a half point, from $9\frac{7}{8}$ to $9\frac{3}{8}$, watched for ten minutes, saw the market makers now bidding at $9\frac{1}{4}$ and punched in an order to sell 1000 shares. I didn't own the shares I was selling, but the idea was that I'd let the price keep dropping, find a level I was comfortable with, then buy back those I'd sold and the difference would be my profit.

That's when I heard someone on CNBC talking about TexCanMex Off-Shore, a bunch of modern-day wildcatters based in Guadalajara who'd just landed a big oil-drilling contract in the Pacific off the Mexican shoreline. The shares had opened at $7\frac{3}{16}$, were already up to $7\frac{3}{4}$ and still climbing. I managed to spot a block of 1000 shares at $7\frac{15}{16}$, and at the same time got my stop in at $7\frac{1}{2}$.

Within twenty minutes of the market opening, I was holding on to shares worth almost $24,000. All this, based on my ten grand stake.

My screen confirmed what CNBC was saying – that the NASDAQ was up a little, but not much – and so I sat there staring at both for another five minutes, waiting for some action. The trick was always gonna be to choose just the right moment to sell what I'd bought and buy what I'd sold and come out of it with a profit.

At the same time, the trick was also always gonna be to keep myself protected so that if everything headed south, I wouldn't blow too big a chunk of my original stake.

Nothing at all was happening with Scotsel Cellular, which began to worry me. The slide had stopped dead in its tracks, I didn't like the volume that was being traded and very quickly got cold feet. I convinced myself that terrible things were about to happen, bought back the shares and swallowed a one-eighth loss.

Abruptly spooked into believing the entire market had flattened out – there's no short-term money in a flat market – I began thinking 'bout closing out my other two positions. That's when CNBC beat me to it, divulging that the company was now saying the merger was off. The shares sank like rocks in a stream. My stop clicked in – I got lucky, 'cause they don't always – and a message appeared in the sell box on my screen that my stake had been unloaded.

Turning to TexCanMex, they were up to $8^{3}/_{16}$. But I hesitated just one beat too long, 'cause a fraction of a second before I sold, the shares slipped back. I closed out at 8.

My account balance box went from bright red back to dark blue, but after all that – in little more than forty-five minutes – I'd managed to lose $480.

Well played, K.C., I congratulated myself, *by this time next week we'll be eating in soup kitchens.*

Gun-shy, I stayed out of the market for the rest of the morning.

By noon, everything was ground down to a snail's crawl. I had no trouble convincing myself, 'nough for one day, signed off, jumped into the shower, got dressed, turned on the answering machine and headed to the Korean's place to drown my misery in a jumbo bag of M&Ms.

From there, I munched my way over to the bank, took $500 in cash and kept on eating candy all the way to 36th and Lex where I deposited the cash into my Greek credit card account. I asked the lady at the counter what charges had come in and was relieved to see that there'd been just enough to clear the hundred bucks to Roamers' House of Funerals.

That got me thinking again 'bout my mama's place and from there I started wondering 'bout Sir Tommy Whitestone's place. If his address in New York was 1060 Park, I calculated, that would put him up in the high 80s. Even though the weather was good, it was too far to walk. Anyway, I was out of M&Ms and didn't feel like buying any more. So I strolled back to Grand Central, jumped on the subway, rode it straight up Lexington to 86th, walked one block west to Park and one block north to 1060.

A huge black doorman in a uniform that was much too tight 'cause of all his pumped-up muscles, intercepted me as soon as I stepped under the sidewalk canopy and asked who I wanted.

I told him, 'Whitestone apartment,' thinking that way I'd get to whoever was home.

'Who do I say is calling?'

'Name's Doone.'

He ordered me to wait, ducked inside to the house phone, spoke to someone, shook his head, then poked his head out the door to ask, 'Got an appointment?'

I motioned towards my twenty-buck Cartier. 'I'm early.'

He accepted that, went back inside, spoke to whoever it was on the phone again, then came out to ask me, 'Who you got an appointment with?'

I said, 'Tell him it's concerning tomorrow night. Sir Thomas Whitestone and the 200 Club.'

'Just a minute.' He left me standing there for another few minutes, then came out to shrug, 'No one knows anything about it but go on up. South penthouse.'

I said thanks, walked through the dark lobby, stepped into the elevator and rode it all the way up to the top floor. When the door opened – directly into the foyer with a real plush living room just behind that – a woman was standing right there wearing a shocking pink designer jogging suit.

She was in her mid-fifties, slim, blond – the colour might have come out of a bottle but if it did, that was one damned expensive bottle – and with a definite trace of the real beauty she must have been thirty years ago.

'Did you say you were looking for Tommy?' Her voice was low and gravelly, the kind that women of a certain age acquire through years of drinking and smoking.

'That's right, ma'am.'

'Did you say you have an appointment with him, here?'

I smiled and extended my hand. 'My name is Doone, and I'm terribly sorry to bother you. But I could have sworn my office said to meet him here. It's about tomorrow night. The 200 Club?'

'What club?'

'200 Club? He's our guest speaker.'

'He is?'

'You mean . . . he didn't mention it?'

'Mention it? When? And why? I haven't heard from him for fifteen years.'

'Huh? Are we talking 'bout the same Whitestone? Sir Thomas Whitestone from London, England? Doesn't he live here?'

'And in Paris and in Spain and in Mexico.'

'And 1060 Park Avenue, New York City? This is the south penthouse, isn't it?'

She pointed towards the living room, 'South,' stared at me for a very long time, then asked, 'Want a drink?'

'No,' I said, 'thank you anyway. No, I was looking for . . .'

'Come on in,' she motioned.

The instant I stepped away from the elevator, the door snapped shut behind me.

'Maria?' she shouted over her shoulder. 'Maria?' She motioned for me to follow her into the living room. 'South. See, south.'

The view from beyond the bay window, past her shrub-lined balcony, was spectacular. You could see all the way down to the Battery, and along both sides of Manhattan.

'South,' she continued saying, almost as if she needed to convince herself. 'Sure you don't want a drink?'

I turned to say no thanks again, only to find a tiny little woman in a maid's outfit standing next to her, panting.

The woman said to out-of-breath Maria, 'Get him something. Coke? Yes, get him a Coke. And I'll have a Bloody Mary.'

Maria nodded, '*Bueno, bueno,*' and rushed off.

'It's that time of the morning,' the woman explained.

I didn't point out that it was now nearly 1.30 in the afternoon. 'Yeah, sure, Coke will be fine, thanks.'

'That's south. The other way is north. On a clear day I can see Venezuela. On a clear day they . . .' she pointed north . . . 'can see Yonkers.' Now she motioned towards one of several couches. 'What did you say you do? And, what's your name? Doone? Doone what?'

'No . . . Doone is my last name. First name is K.C.' I sat down on one of the couches with lots of cushions.

'Casey . . . is that like Casey the locomotive driver?' She sat down much too close to me.

'Locomotive?' I didn't know who she was referring to, but it was easier to just say, 'Exactly.'

'So, Mr Casey the locomotive driver . . . when you're not driving your train . . . what is it you do?'

'I'm the unofficial coordinator of speeches for the 200 Club.'

'Is this some sort of porno club?'

'Ah . . . no, not at all.'

'Surprising,' she mumbled.

'It's for . . .' I came up with, 'Investors. And Mr Whitestone is
our guest speaker tomorrow night. My office said that he needed
to talk to me about . . . you know, the microphones and whether
or not he'd need . . .' I forgot what those things were called, so
I told her, 'a *kyuukyoko.*'

'What the hell is a . . . kay-u--whatever?'

'Special kind of lectern . . . with a built-in teleprompter. You
know, those little windows that come off the side of a podium,
so that someone can read a speech and still maintain eye-contact
with the audience . . .'

'Oh.' She seemed greatly relieved when Maria showed up
with a Coke for me but especially with a Bloody Mary for her.

'Here's to Sir Tommy.' She raised her glass.

'To Sir Tommy,' I repeated.

Then she said only just under her breath, 'That son of
a bitch.'

'Huh?'

'Well, what would you think,' she slurped, getting tomato
juice on her upper lip, making it look like she had a red
moustache. 'What would you think if he left you waiting here
for fifteen years?'

'You haven't seen him for fifteen years?'

'Have you? Send him my regards.'

'Isn't this his place?'

'I don't know.' She shrugged. 'All I do is live here.'

'But not with him.'

'Listen, Mr Locomotive, you seem like a nice young man . . .'
She finished her drink in two gulps and called for Maria who
automatically arrived with a second Bloody Mary. 'And one slice
of toast,' she told Maria, then asked me, 'You want some toast
with your Coke?'

'No thanks.'

'I don't know how anyone can drink Coke for breakfast,' she
said, taking a long pull on her fresh drink. 'I shouldn't really call
him a son of a bitch because he did, after all, set me up here.
Except that he is a son of a bitch.'

I asked gently, 'You mean, he set you up here fifteen years
ago and never came back?'

'Naw,' she scoffed, to show me I'd gotten it completely wrong.
'He set me up here sixteen years ago and hasn't been back in
fifteen.'

By the time she finished her second Bloody Mary, lit a cigarette, started eating her toast and downing Bloody Mary number three, her story was flowing smoothly. She'd met Whitestone on a trip to London while she was working as fashion editor at some magazine I'd never heard of. They had a six-month fling, during which he wined, dined and flew her around the world, brought her home to New York and moved in here with her. He convinced her to quit her job, promised to take care of her and then disappeared.

'Ya'll mean he just walked out one day, and never came back?' I'd heard stories of folk saying they were just going out for a pack of cigarettes and then disappearing for ever, but I'd never actually met anyone that had happened to. 'Did you call him? I mean . . . what did you do?'

'Did I call him? What did I do? Of course I called him. What I did was call him every hour on the hour for the next five years.'

'And?'

'Does it look to you like he's ever returned my calls?' She shrugged. 'So after a while I got smart and just gave up.'

I was astonished. 'And he left this place to you?'

'One of his henchmen showed up one day and assured me that I would be looked after for the rest of my life. And every month all my bills get taken care of.'

'All of them?'

She nodded as if that was obvious. 'Somebody's got to pay for that view. It's south.'

Sipping my Coke to give myself a chance to think, the best I could come up with was, 'Never showed up again. How strange.'

'How original,' she said as if that was somehow ironic. 'Except that he does this to everybody. Struts into a girl's life. Is the most charming and romantic and wonderful lover on earth. Then, struts out.'

'Does he leave every woman with a place like this?'

'Probably.'

'You gotta admit that's pretty original.'

'Not that I don't appreciate my good fortune . . .' She shrugged. 'But he has proven very difficult to replace.' She forced a grin.

'Oh yeah,' I agreed. 'I can understand how you might have found him uncommonly unique.'

She wanted to know, 'Doesn't that mean the same thing?'

I conceded, 'Most of the time. But not in his case,' then stood up, 'cause it seemed like it was time to go.

'Must you?' she asked. 'Do you want to stay for dinner? I know we've just had breakfast. But I can ask Maria to make us a few more Bloody Marys and then . . . she's a wonderful cook. Or, even better, I can send her home and make my special lasagna . . .'

'Gee, that would be nice . . .' I said, eyeing the foyer, 'but unfortunately . . . what, with this dinner planned for tomorrow night . . .'

'If you're watching your waistline, Mr Locomotive . . . well then, perhaps I could watch it with you.'

'You're very kind.' I edged my way towards the elevator, all too aware of the fact that I was being especially clumsy. 'Thank you . . . really . . . very much for your time. And ah . . . as for Sir Tommy . . . if you'd like, perhaps I shall tell him that we've spoken and maybe he'll give you a call . . .'

'What for?'

'I just thought that as long as he was in New York . . .'

'I know where to find him in New York, but why would I bother?'

'Oh?' I stopped. 'You know where to find him?' I dared, 'You mean, his office in New York?'

'Naw. Where he lives New York.' She made a face to suggest that it was something everybody knew. 'He keeps a suite at the Waldorf Towers.'

'Ma'am . . . I have to tell you that this has been a real pleasure . . . thank you so much.'

'Just remember one thing.'

'What's that?'

'Never let the son of a bitch out of your sight.'

I gave her a little wave and a smile as I pushed the button for the elevator, 'Thank you for everything,' waved again when the elevator arrived and stepped inside.

By this time, she couldn't give a hoot. Yet another man had turned down her special lasagna.

The Waldorf Towers is the upmarket hotel inside the old Waldorf Astoria Hotel, with a separate entrance on East 50th Street off Lexington. But that's the entrance for the general public. The private entrance is through the garage next door, which leads you into an elevator that takes you straight upstairs to the Towers.

The story I once heard was that they opened that entrance and installed that elevator 'specially for General MacArthur who lived in the Towers after the Korean War, in the days when the place was fancy apartments. These days, the garage is still the entrance of choice for folk who know.

So I came back down Lex, got off the subway at 51st, walked over to 50th and went through the garage to the elevator where I promptly got stopped by a guy in a concierge's uniform.

'Help you?'

'I'm here for Mr Whitestone.'

'Mr Whitestone?'

'Sir Tommy.' I winked, so that he'd understand that I knew him.

'Sir Thomas Whitestone? I don't believe he's in yet.' He went to a little desk to check. 'Not yet. Have you got an appointment?'

The voice warned me that I had to be more careful here than I'd been at his apartment. 'He's talking at a dinner tomorrow night and I thought I'd surprise him here. Try to mooch an invitation.'

The concierge must have believed me because now he revealed, 'Not expected in until tomorrow.'

'Damn. Tough work getting a free meal out of old pals,' I said, 'thanks anyway,' and turned to leave.

The voice suggested, *ask him where*.

So I stopped to ask the concierge, 'Oh . . . by the way . . . do ya'll know what time that dinner is tomorrow night?'

He apologized that he didn't.

I took a punt, 'It wasn't too clear from his message . . . I didn't understand, is that dinner being held here?'

He wasn't giving anything away. 'What dinner is that, sir?'

'200 Club.'

He motioned for me to wait, picked up a phone, turned his back so that I couldn't eavesdrop on his call, spoke to someone, hung up and turned back to me to announce, 'No, sir. No function here tomorrow night for that organization. Sorry.'

I said thanks anyway, and walked away.

Okay. Now I knew where he was. And about when he was.

Problem was, I didn't know where or when I could catch up to him. My intention was to get back on the Internet and somehow locate the 200 Club, but it turned out I didn't get much of a chance 'cause my answering machine noted there were eight messages waiting for me and right from the first one I knew that all hell had broken loose.

Beep. 'Listen to me, K.C. . . .' It was Duke . . . 'What the hell kinda half-assed stunt do you think you're pulling? I consider this an all-out declaration of war and ya'll better believe me that this is no longer about Lorilee and you . . . now it's all about you and me.' He slammed down the phone.

Beep. 'K.C. . . .' It was Lorilee. 'How dare you treat me this way? I'm phoning Duke right now.'

Beep. Lorilee again. 'You really are a bastard, K.C. Doone, and I'm sure gonna take you for everything you own.'

Beep. Her for the third time. 'I just spoke to Duke and he's even madder than me.'

Beep. 'In all my years of practice . . .' It was Duke. 'Do you know what you're doing to your own wife? I mean . . . I have never seen a dumber jack-ass stunt than this one.'

Beep. Lorilee yet again. 'Duke told me not to call you but I'm calling you anyway to say that he thinks you're an absolute shit and so do I.'

Beep. 'I just phoned you at the office.' It was my mama. 'They said you don't work there any more. Then I called you in Connecticut. Lorilee said you don't live there any more.' She started to cry. 'What's going on? Please call me. I'm still your mama.'

Beep. 'Hello, K.C. Doone? Are you there? This is Isidor Pinkus calling. Your attorney. I've been phoning you for some time but your number has been busy. And now there's a machine. Are you there? Hello? Are you not picking up? Well okay. This is Isidor Pinkus, your attorney, and I am now back in my office after getting some writs processed on your behalf. I believe they will be served momentarily and that you might be hearing soon from your wife and or her brother. My advice is not to speak with them. Please refer them to me. Good-bye.'

The machine stopped.

Just as it did, the phone rang. I switched the machine back from play to answer, just in case it was Duke or Lorilee.

Beep. 'K.C., this is Pinky. We have to talk . . .'

I grabbed the phone . . . 'Pinky?' . . . The machine blasted me with feedback, I shut it off and said again, 'Pinky? I'm here . . .'

'What was that noise?'

'Nothing. What's going on?'

'What did you do to Binterman?'

'Me? Why?'

'I know it's you. And he knows it's you. It's got your hand-writing all over it.'

I wasn't going to admit to anything. 'What are you talking about? And where are you? Are you calling from the office?'

'No. I'm downstairs. But I've got to hurry back. Debbie will phone you in a little while. She's the one who found it.'

'Found what?'

'All because of what you did to Binterman,' he said. 'I've got to go. Good-bye.'

'What are you . . .' He hung up. 'Pinky?' I wasn't going to phone him at the office, and I didn't want to phone Debbie, so I rang Izzy. 'It's K.C., what's going on?'

'You haven't heard from your wife or brother-in-law, have you?'

'Yeah, I have. They've left messages. All sorts of messages. Hopping mad messages. I've been out. I mean, they're both real pissed. What did you do?'

'I got a court order which instructs her that she cannot sell, give away, hide or otherwise dispel any assets that you brought to your marriage or acquired during your marriage, and that she must provide the court with a full and complete inventory of all assets currently in her possession, including any and all assets that you brought to the marriage, that you acquired jointly dur-ing the marriage and that she brought to the marriage. What's more, anything she might have already dispersed of must be accounted for and returned. She gets it all back or she buys new ones. That includes everything in Connecticut and everything in New York. Plus everything in any location not named.'

'She has to make up an inventory of everything we own?'

'She's got a week to submit it . . .'

'Takes her that long to do a grocery list.'

'That's not our problem.'

'It is if it takes her six months. What are we supposed to do in the meantime?'

'It might take her six months if she was going to do it at all. But she won't. She'll get her brother to fight it.'

'So what's the point?'

'It will take him a couple of days to try to get it overturned, it won't be because it's reasonable, and then it will take him several weeks before any court will even entertain a hearing. Which they may not be willing to do very quickly, seeing as how I joined the writ against her with the writ against him. He may even have to get his own lawyer.'

I didn't understand. 'He is a lawyer.'

'They taught us in law school that a lawyer who defends himself has a fool for a client.'

'Defends himself? You've accused Duke of something?'

'Not accused. Named.'

'Named what?'

'Named him as a co-conspirator.'

'Jeezus. Izzy . . . I told you how nasty Duke can be . . .'

'Did you tell him how nasty I can be?'

'What did you accuse him of?'

'Named him. I didn't accuse. I named.'

'Named him what?'

'I told you. As a co-conspirator.'

'A co-conspirator of what?' That didn't sound right. 'In what?'

'Of or in the theft of your apartment. Well . . . not really the theft but the slightly illegal . . . or maybe totally illegal . . . or at least I think it should be illegal removal of all your worldly goods and possessions.'

I sat back, took a deep breath and wondered how deep Izzy had just buried us in legal manure. 'Are you really sure 'bout all this stuff, 'cause Duke doesn't play softball.'

'I'm not sure but Cousin Harry is.'

'Yeah, but Cousin Harry doesn't have to stand around staring at the walls when the shit hits the fan.'

'Don't worry. We just needed to tell your brother-in-law that he can't get away with what he's trying to get away with.'

The little voice said, *knowing Duke, he probably can.*

I settled on, 'Izzy . . . I'm really not sure I understand what you're doing.'

'What I'm doing is not allowing them to define terms.'

'Yeah . . . well . . . if you say so.'

'It's not me who says so. It's Cousin Harry who says so. He also says, just like I've said, don't talk to your wife or her brother. Refer them both to me.'

'Okay,' I promised. 'Now what?'

'Now the ball is on their side of the field.'

I corrected, 'Don't you mean in their court?'

'No. It's our court. And because the ball is on their side of the field, it's our ball.' He said, 'Remember, don't talk to either of them. I've got to go. Good-bye.'

'Good-bye,' I said, hung up and told the voice, *poor kid, he's about to become Duke's lunch.*

Problem is, the voice pointed out, *we're on the menu for dessert.*

Just in case, I turned the answering machine on again.

I went into the bedroom to call my mama from the second line in there, the one I'd been using for the modem so that if someone did phone, they wouldn't get a busy tone and think I was home.

'I got your message,' I told her when she picked up. 'Now, don't ya'll worry 'bout anything. Everything's gonna be okay.' I explained that Lorilee and I had split, but didn't go into any specifics, such as why. 'It was all kinda sudden but it's for the best.' Then I explained that I'd left GCB. 'I kinda was looking for a career change and, it just sorta happened at the same time.' I didn't go into specifics here either. 'Trust me, Mama, everything's gonna work out fine.'

'But if you don't have a job . . . what about my apartment?'

'Two different things, Mama. I'm working on it. I got us a real good lead and I'm gonna see someone here in New York tomorrow 'bout it. I figure I can straighten it all out in a day or two.'

There was a long pause before she said, 'K.C., if ya'll don't manage it, I've got no place to go.'

'I'm gonna manage it.' She was crying again. 'Mama, I'm gonna make it right.'

No sooner had I hung up with her, than the other line rang, the machine clicked on and I heard Debbie's voice. 'K.C., I really really need to talk to you. Wait till you hear what I heard. Are you there? K.C., if you're there please pick up.'

I grabbed it just in time. 'I'm here. It's me. What phone are you calling from?'

'Downstairs. And I can't talk long because I think Binterman knows that I know. But Cotton doesn't know that I know. And maybe Binterman only suspects. I can't be sure because he gave me a real weird look just now when I walked out of the War Room to come downstairs to phone you. Pinky says Binterman gives everybody real weird looks. But I know a real weird look when I see one and he knows . . .'

'Debbie . . . Binterman knows what?'

'Knows that I know.About TransMare-Telco.'

'What about it?'

'Cotton and Braddock have been telling everyone that because of you they have to write off nine million.'

'I know. And it's not true.'

'But that's what they're planning to write off. That's what I heard. Binterman got all this dirty e-mail stuff coming through his computer and he started screaming that you'd sabotaged him, so he went complaining to Cotton and Braddock and they knew all about it because they had all this dirty stuff in their computer too, but with his name on it. He accused you of doing it and they told him that he shouldn't worry about you because you were already in enough trouble. They said they were taking care of you in their own way.'

'You heard them say that?'

'Well . . .' She stopped. 'Not exactly. I mean, not exactly me. You know that guy Alex, he's a sergeant? He told me that the fellow who sits next to him . . . his name is Stewart . . . well, he said that Stewart had been talking to that girl Brenda . . .'

'Hold it. Debbie? Ya'll got this stuff third or fourth hand? It's not that I don't appreciate your telling me this . . . but I already know that they're talking nine million and the total of the exposure . . . I mean, grand total, everything added together, wasn't never gonna be any more than . . .'

She cut in, 'Five twelve and change.'

'What?'

'Five hundred and twelve thousand dollars and a handful of pennies.'

'How'd you come up with that?'

'It's what I've been trying to tell you. That guy Alex . . . I'm not talking fourth hand. That's what Cotton has been working on all week. That guy Alex . . . he's the guy who's forever changing the colours on his computer screen and coming up with those fancy screensavers. He's always tampering with his computer, and when he heard about all that porno stuff in Binterman's e-mail, he went looking for it and somehow found his way into Cotton's personal files.'

'He hacked his way into Cotton's computer?'

'No, just Cotton's personal database. Then he got scared because he figured he could get arrested or something, but not before he saw the second set of books.'

'What second set of books?'

'The one Cotton keeps. The one that shows what really happened with TransMare-Telco.'

'What really happened?'

'Well . . . ah . . . that's sort of the problem. He got scared and got out and now he doesn't know how to get back in. But, don't worry, K.C. because his work station is down there opposite Cotton's and he says that without even looking real hard, he can see everything. So when Stewart told him what Brenda said . . . he knows that you and I are real good friends, so he told me that after Binterman went to see Cotton . . . Alex says that the company is writing off nine million on TransMare-Telco, blaming you for that, when Cotton has a file somewhere that proves it isn't true.'

'Debbie, if this is true . . .'

'It is true. They're cooking the books.'

I wouldn't have put it past the Three Stooges to pull a stunt like that. But not putting it past them and proving it were two very distinct things. 'Listen, Debbie . . . if you hear anything else . . .'

'I'll let you know. I promise.'

'But ya'll gotta protect yourself. Gotta be real careful that no one cottons on to you knowing anything 'bout this.'

'That Cotton doesn't cotton?' she said. 'Pinky says to tell you that we'll be careful. Really careful. No one will ever know what we're up to. I've got to go.'

'Up to what?'

'I'll call you soon. Bye.' She hung up.

'Up to what?' But she was gone.

Up to finding out who killed cock-robin, the voice said.

And I said, out loud, '*Oh shit!*'

Even if I'd wanted to, which I didn't, there was no way I was gonna get back into the market today. My head wasn't there.

Still, I figured it was worth a check to see what was going on, so I logged on and took a look at the NASDAQ wire.

TexCanMex and TrakMark were both up on what they'd been when I sold. Scotsel Cellular was down lower than it had been when I bought back those shares.

Scribbling numbers on the pad next to my laptop, I realized at these prices I would have been up two and a half grand.

The voice insisted *and the fish that got away had two heads and was fourteen feet long.*

Chapter Seventeen

I was fading fast.

I didn't want to be here.

I didn't want to be here with him.

But mostly I didn't want to be here with him and still be awake.

'I gotta sleep,' I announced.

Whitestone turned to me. 'Wouldn't you like to play another game?'

'What are you talking about?'

'I asked,' he repeated very slowly and with an odd tone to his voice, 'wouldn't you like to play another game?'

'And I answered, What are you talking about?'

He snapped, 'Why do you do that?'

'Huh?' I couldn't keep my eyes open. 'Do what?'

'You do it deliberately, don't you?'

I didn't understand. 'Do what?'

'Why do you always answer questions with another question?'

'What question?'

'Such as the one I just asked. What kind of an answer is that?'

'My answer?'

'Yes,' he said, not hiding his anger, 'your answer. That answer. All your answers.'

'I don't see anything wrong with that answer or any of my answers. Maybe there's something wrong with that question or all of your questions.'

'My questions have been very straightforward. Such as when I asked you, wouldn't you like to play another game?'

'And my answers to your straightforward questions have been just as straightforward. Such as when I answered, what are you talking about?'

'What I'm talking about, right now, is that you answer questions with another question.' He insisted, 'You have to answer a question with an answer.'

'Ya'll mean there are rules for this too?'

'There are rules for everything. There have to be rules, otherwise everyone will break them. Don't you understand anything about life?'

I was tired, but not so tired that I couldn't ask, 'How can you break a rule if there are no rules?'

'You've done it again.'

'And by everyone,' I pointed out, 'course you mean, everyone 'cept you.'

'Breaking rules when there are no rules,' he lectured, 'is called anarchy. As for my own breaking of rules . . . yes, of course, I do. But that's the difference between a successful man and a failure. Success might even be defined by one's ability to get away with breaking the rules.'

'Huh? That's not the difference between a successful man and a failure.' I thought about it for a moment and decided that in some warped way he might be right. 'No,' I contradicted myself 'cause I was too tired and wouldn't otherwise give him the satisfaction of agreeing. 'That's the difference between . . .' I needed to come up with something and decided on, '. . . an honest man and an anarchist.'

'Why can't an anarchist be honest?'

I didn't have a clue. 'I get it. This is the game you were asking me if I played?'

He grinned. 'Mr Doone, you are beginning to understand.'

I nodded, 'Terrific,' sat back, shut my eyes and stayed that way until I felt myself falling asleep.

'What other games do you play?'

'Huh?' He woke me. 'Huh? Is this the same game or a new one?'

'No,' he corrected, 'this is a straightforward question and yet again, you have answered it with a question.'

'We've already played this one.'

'Mr Doone,' he spoke softly, 'perhaps I should rephrase my question in order to prod you into a specific answer. Instead of asking, what games do you play, I shall list some. Do you play backgammon?'

'Not really.'

'Oh.' He sounded disappointed. 'Too bad. I should have enjoyed talking about backgammon.'

I mumbled, 'I should have enjoyed sleeping in a bed tonight.'

'I could teach you,' he said enthusiastically. 'I could teach you right here. The basics are very simple . . .'

'Thanks anyway,' I said. 'But I think the fact that we don't have a backgammon board might just . . .'

'One doesn't need a backgammon board.'

'How can you still be awake?'

'Second wind,' he said.

'Yeah, well, mine has long since blown away. Anyway, I already know how to move the pieces. I mean, I know how to play. It's just that . . .' I thought back to Lorilee and that trip to the Bahamas when we played strip-backgammon one night on the beach and every time one of us lost a piece of clothing we burned it in the little fire we'd lit and she had to walk back to the hotel stark naked . . . 'Maybe another time. Next time. In daylight. Now it's bedtime. Good night.'

'Well, if you do know how to move the pieces . . .'

'Huh?'

'We shall play in our minds. You know, the way some people play chess. After all, if one knows chess well, one doesn't need a chess board. One simply visualizes everything. Go ahead. I'll even allow you to choose your own opening dice.'

'No. No. Thanks. I really don't think so . . .'

'Here.' He pretended to hand me some dice. 'Go ahead. Your roll. Do you want to open with 3-1? Or 6-1? They're both very good opening moves. You choose which one and then I'll let you choose which opening moves you want . . .'

'Really . . .' I raised my hands, not to take his dice but to signal defeat. 'Maybe another time. I'm too tired now.'

'All right,' he gave in. 'Perhaps, instead, you would like to know about my variation for the end game?'

'Huh?'

'My variation for the end game.' He launched straight into it. 'Consider the fact that the luck to skill ratio in backgammon is anything from 70-30 to 90-10. Therefore, it behoves better players to find amendments to the rules which will favour them. After giving this principle considerable thought, I have come up with one small amendment which diminishes the luck factor, benefiting the more skilful player with a slight edge where he needs it most, which is in a running game.'

'Sounds . . . fascinating,' I mumbled, hoping that his rambling might finally put me to sleep.

'The idea is simple.' He rubbed his hands excitedly. 'Accepting the fact that the less skilful player will rely more heavily on higher numbers with which to run, once either player has removed one of his fifteen pieces from the board, doubles will no longer count as four times the number rolled, but merely two. Do you see the beauty of this? The weaker player who is running is automatically slowed down, while the better player, who has perhaps been forced into a back-game, may still count doubles as four times the value of the dice, giving him the privilege of staying a roll or two longer inside the weaker player's home board and, at the same time, of catching up by running faster, always accepting the fact that he still has fifteen pieces on the board. In other words, it slows down the runner and gives the strategist a little more leverage. I've studied this in depth and have calculated that my rule, which I've dubbed the Whitestone Amendment, could reduce the luck factor by as much as ten to fifteen per cent over all, and more in certain situations, which you would have to admit, is considerable.' He stopped. 'Yes or no?'

'Huh?'

'Yes or no?'

'Ah . . . sure . . .' I needed to say something if he was ever going to let me fall asleep. 'Absolutely.'

'Absolutely what?'

'Yes . . . it's . . . absolutely . . . I don't know . . . absolutely adorable.'

'Absolutely adorable?' His tone changed. 'What a terribly condescending attitude you have, Mr Doone.'

'Huh?'

'Is that all you can say? Absolutely adorable?'

I had to know, 'What are you getting on my case for?'

'Do you see anyone else in this lift on whose case I can get?'

I needed him to understand. 'Hey, this ain't my first choice either, pal. So how 'bout we go back to our truce?'

'Our truce?' He agreed, 'Yes. All right. Fine. We'll go back to our truce.'

'And stick to it.'

'And stick to it,' he agreed. 'Fine.'

'Fine.' I tried to find a more comfortable position. 'Thank you and good night.'

He sat back and folded his arms across his chest. 'It's a pleasure and good night.'

My eyes shut tight.

There was another very long silence.

I was finally on my way.

'This is not a good game,' he said. 'No, I don't care for it at all. Don't you know any others?'

'Huh?'

'This is not a good game.'

'What?' I managed to ask. 'What isn't a good game?'

'Dammit, Doone, you've done it again. You're doing it on purpose because you think that's a better game than any of the games I propose.'

I somehow forced my eyes open. 'What the hell are you talking about?'

'Answering questions with questions. I said, this is not a good game, referring to our renewed truce, and you said, what isn't a very good game?'

'Hey . . . I gotta ask you something.' I leaned towards him. 'I mean, you and I are stuck here until tomorrow morning, so I kinda figure I've got a right to know.'

'Ah. Finally. You're no longer answering my question with a question.'

'Yeah . . . right. You see, what I would like to know is . . . are ya'll playing with a full deck?'

His head tilted. 'Do you know that there are literally dozens of card games that aren't played with the full deck?'

'Huh?'

He started to cackle with laughter. 'There. See? I've finally done it to you. I've answered your question with my question.' He folded his arms again and leaned all the way back. 'What a good game.' He was obviously content with himself. 'Good night, Mr Doone. Renewed truce.'

I mumbled, 'Yeah, sure, good night, Sir Tommy. Renewed truce.'

Several minutes later he added quietly, 'You play well Mr Doone. Unfairly. And well.'

Chapter Eighteen

Two and a half grand.

I ripped the page from the pad, crumpled it up and tossed it angrily across the room.

Sunnuvabitch!

I had no one else to blame but myself.

And for the longest time, I did just that.

Intellectually, I know you can't let it get to you that prices change after you bail out 'cause prices always change. And from all my years as a trader I know, too, you can't sit around worrying about what might have been 'cause that's the surest way to wind up missing what's about to be. But I'd lost my nerve and in this game, nerve was just as important as patience. I was annoyed 'cause I didn't think I'd need to work too hard at finding the right combination of nerve and patience. I was annoyed, 'cause I thought I kinda just knew it.

'Cept I didn't.

Now I was worried too.

I had to figure it out real fast or I was gonna go bust. If that happened, my mama was gonna be out on the street.

I was staring down the throat of two very real possibilities.

And both were unacceptable.

As long as I was on-line anyway, I went back into the woods, following my trail of bread crumbs, looking for more stuff about Tommy Whitestone. If nothing else, trying to find more links between him and the Florida sweepstakes would keep my mind off the fact that I'd blown a chunk of my bankroll.

While I was hunting around in there – discovering that Whitestone's world was a huge web of companies, one only just interrelated with the other, all of them criss-crossing back and forth between Spain, France, England, the Caribbean and the United States – I stumbled across an article called, 'The Laws of Libel versus Freedom of the Press' published in a Canadian law journal.

In it, Whitestone was cited by the author – a professor at McGill University in Montreal named Rae – as a flagrant example of how a rich man could deliberately misuse the law to strangle the free flow of information. It seemed that over a nine-year period, Whitestone had filed no fewer than fifty-eight different suits against some magazine in England called *Private Eye*.

Every time they wrote about him, he sued, which worked out to better than one law suit every other month.

The article suggested that Whitestone didn't care whether or not he won his suits, his real message was in notoriously suing anyone who ever wrote about him. By doing that, he successfully kept a lot of legitimate reporting from being published.

I'd never heard of *Private Eye*, but the footnotes in the article referenced all fifty-eight stories about Whitestone and most of them, I noticed, featured the words 'golden goolies' in the title. It didn't make any sense to me, though I kind of assumed that was some sort of derogatory term.

It didn't take long before the thought dawned on me that whoever wrote those articles might know some interesting stuff about Whitestone, so I got *Private Eye*'s number and dialled it. It rang about eight times, till I realized it was near ten at night in London. I made a note to give them a shout first thing in the morning.

Not being ten at night in Montreal, I got the main number for McGill University and asked for Professor Rae. He turned out to be a nice enough old codger, more than happy to talk to me about Whitestone. Though he was fast to say, 'Never met him. Don't know much about him, neither. Just what I wrote in my article. Heard a lot about him. Never spoke to him. Don't care about him. Never answered his letter.'

'His letter?'

'Letter written on his behalf. Not by him. By some corporate counsel. Wrote me after the article appeared. Felt I'd been nasty to him. Didn't say I'd been libellous. Wouldn't dare. One thing being a bully in Great Britain. Court system works in a rich man's favour there. Won't work here. Not in Canada. His New

York mouthpiece must have understood that. Never went any further.'

'New York mouthpiece?'

'Corporate guy. In house. Struck me as being funny he'd use a fellow already on his shareholders' payroll. Could afford to hire his own lawyer with his own money. How cheap rich men can be, eh?'

'You wouldn't recall off-hand, would you, the name of the company?'

'Ten years ago now. But just like all his other companies. Nothing memorable. Had I-N-C after the name instead of L-T-D.'

I said, 'Thanks very much for your time,' and was about to hang up when a question popped into my head. 'By the way, professor . . . all those articles about him in *Private Eye*. The titles kept using the term golden goolies. Is that some sort of derogatory way of referring to him?'

'He thought so. I wouldn't have. Goolies. Means *balls*.'

'Balls? Oh . . . *balls*. Oh. Well, thank you again.' I got back on the Internet to run a search, spelling goolies the way *Private Eye* had, then in as many different ways as I could think of. Goullies. Goullees. Ghoolies.

Nothing.

So now I made my way back into the woods, found a company called Surrey County Nutrition Inc. which, it said here, was a subsidiary of Surrey County Nutrition UK Ltd. and phoned the New York office. 'It's about Sir Tommy Whitestone . . . I'm an old friend . . .'

The operator cut me off, 'One moment, please . . .' played some music in my ear, then connected me with another woman who announced, 'Press and public relations.'

'Oh . . . hello . . . press and public relations?' That made sense. 'Sorry to bother you with this . . . the reason I'm phoning is because I think your company's a subsidiary of Surrey County in England and that's owned by my old pal Sir Tommy Whitestone. I heard he's speaking in New York tomorrow night and as I'm only in town for a few nights, I thought that would be a real good chance to say hello . . .'

'Mr Whitestone is no longer involved in the day to day running of this company and therefore we have nothing at all to do with whatever personal appearances he might be making.'

'Oh? He's no longer involved with the company?'

'That's correct.'

'But he owns it, right?'

'Not really. Although he maintains a holding . . .'

'Sorry, I don't mean to interrupt,' I said deliberately interrupting, 'cause if he didn't own the company I was wasting my time. 'But, would ya'll happen to know off-hand about this dinner tomorrow night? It's at someplace called the 200 Club.'

'No, sir. I don't.'

Thanking her, I hung up, wondered for a moment what other companies he owned or didn't own, then heard the voice in my head ask, *press and public relations?*

I phoned the *Wall Street Journal* and asked to speak with whoever it was who'd be covering Sir Tommy Whitestone's speech tomorrow night at the 200 Club. Nobody there knew what I was talking about.

I tried the *New York Times*. No one there knew anything about it either.

I called the *Daily News* and *Cranes*. Two more nothings.

But when I dialled *Bloomberg*, mentioned Sir Tommy Whitestone and the 200 Club, I got passed around to a bunch of folk until some guy got on the line, apologized that they weren't planning on doing anything, but said he appreciated the tip. 'Thanks for thinking of us and I hope you will again when news breaks next time.'

'No problem,' I said, ''cept I'm not selling, I'm buying. I phoned to ask if ya'll knew anything about the 200 Club, like where they're meeting? I'm trying to get in touch with Whitestone. He's an old pal and I thought maybe you could point me in the right direction.'

'Oh,' the fellow said. 'Sorry. Got the wrong message.'

'Ya'll ever hear of the 200 Club?'

'Group of guys who claim to be the richest men in America?'

'Could be,' I said. 'I don't know.'

'Sounds like them. Two hundred. One hundred. Something like that. They want people to think that's who they are, but they aren't. You won't find Bill Gates or George Soros or Warren Buffett or any of that crowd attending. We did something on them a year or two ago. As I recall, they're just a bunch of reasonably successful guys from the greater New York area having dinner every six months and paying someone who really is one of the richest guys in America . . . in this case, I guess, the world . . . paying him a hundred grand to tell them how he got so rich.'

'A hundred grand just for having dinner?'

'That's what our story was on. Big bucks for shaking hands, explaining away their own success for half an hour, shaking more hands and going home.'

'If they pay him a hundred grand, what's the price of admission?'

'Apparently a lot more than the food's worth. I think when they started these shindigs, about eight or ten years ago, dinner was two grand. They had to raise it when it turned out too many people could pay that much for dinner, meaning they couldn't pretend to be so ultra-rich and exclusive any more.'

'A lot of money for rubber chicken.'

'What did you say your interest is?'

'Old friend,' I lied. 'Trying to get in touch. But I can't find out where the 200 Club is. Not listed any place.'

'Wouldn't be,' he answered. 'It's not as if they have a tree house or anything. They used to meet at Buonorroti. I don't know if they still do.'

'A spaghetti house.'

'Not quite. Private dining club over on 56th. Operative word is private. Need a mortgage to get past the front door.'

I thanked him, got a number for Buonorroti – *how ultra rich and exclusive can they be if they're listed?* – and dialled it.

'I'm phoning 'bout the dinner tomorrow evening,' I said, putting on my poshest voice 'cause I figured that's what was expected. 'The 200 Club meeting with Sir Tommy Whitestone?'

'Yes, sir,' the gentleman on the other end of the line responded in his poshest voice. 'Have you reserved?'

'Ah . . . no . . . unfortunately I kinda misplaced my invitation . . .'

'Terribly sorry, sir, but I'm afraid there have been no cancellations. You might try again tomorrow at noon, in case a place comes free.'

As long as he mentioned free, I wondered, 'How much is it?'

'The usual, sir.'

'Well, you see, I'm a new member . . .'

'Four thousand dollars, sir.'

I managed to stifle my gasp. 'One other question please . . . what time is dinner?'

'The programme calls for cocktails from 7.30, dinner promptly at 8.30, carriages at midnight.'

'Carriages?'

That's correct, sir.'

'What's that mean?'

'It's polite talk for when we throw everyone out.'

There was no way I was gonna join Whitestone and friends for dinner at Buonorroti. Not at that price. Not even, these days, at ten cents on the dollar. But I could get into the Waldorf Towers' garage for free. And if carriages were at midnight, I was gonna be there by 11.30.

Sounds like a plan, the voice agreed.

It was too early for dinner – anyway I wasn't all that hungry – and deep down inside I reckoned it was much too soon to phone Patsy the Principal again. I didn't feel like going through the trading software right now – or ever – and I'd already spoken to my mama today. If Izzy had anything to say, he would have phoned me. And I wasn't going to phone Pinky or Debbie to ask either of them what they were up to 'cause I wasn't sure I was ready to deal with any of that just now.

Growing increasingly desperate, I thought maybe I'd give Mikey a holler – just to have someone to talk to 'bout day trading and the market – but I wasn't desperate enough to suffer Dimi's cooking again. Or, for that matter, witness Mike eating it.

There was nothing on the news of any interest. Nothing on any of the cable stations of any interest. And it was too early for the ball games to start.

I figured maybe what I'd do is go out, take a walk, stock up on M&Ms, buy a couple of magazines – I recalled I still hadn't gone through that day trading magazine – eventually find some place for a bite to eat and wander home in time to watch the Knicks get stomped.

Moving into the living room, I took a good stretch and wondered if, maybe, as long as I was going out, I'd check on what was playing at that multiplex over on First Avenue, just in case there was an early movie.

That's when the bell rang, startling me, 'cause I sure wasn't expecting anyone.

Don't be Debbie, I said, thinking maybe I shouldn't answer it. It rang again.

I stared at the intercom, then figured, *why the hell shouldn't I answer my own door*, so I picked it up and asked, 'Who is it?'

A voice came back, 'Doone residence?'

I had visions of another process server with a retaliatory writ from Duke. 'Who ya'll looking for?'

'Doone.'

'Who wants him?'

'Five Boroughs.'

'Who?'

'Five Boroughs.'

'Don't know anybody by that name. What's it about?'

'It's a delivery.'

I wasn't expecting anything. 'Who's it from?'

'Hey Mister, if your name is Doone, I've got this truck outside with stuff in it for you. I'm on overtime, so I've got all night. But if you're not Doone, would you please tell me where I can find him because any minute now some over-anxious cop is going to show up and give me a ticket.'

'Yeah, I'm Doone.' I buzzed him in, then moved to my front door, put my eye up to the spyhole and waited there for what seemed to be a real long time, at the end of which, nothing happened. No one came up in the elevator. No one appeared in the hall.

Now I got worried.

The residents' committee sends letters around every few months asking us all to be careful about letting people into the building who didn't belong.

I cracked open my front door to check the hallway, couldn't hear the elevator coming up, shut the door and for good measure, chained it too.

Whoever it is, the voice decided, *couldn't have gotten our name from the mailboxes 'cause they're inside.*

I moved back into the living room, thinking to myself that maybe I should phone the super – an old drunk, retired plumber, who had a place on the ground floor – and tell him that there's this guy coming into the building.

The voice suggested, *maybe they're coming to murder us.*

Yeah right, I said, wondering why that didn't sound as funny as I thought it should.

Bang.

I jumped.

Bang.

Someone was banging on my door.

I demanded, 'Who's there?'

'Five Boroughs,' the man said. 'You Doone?'

I raced to the spyhole and saw three guys standing there in overalls that looked like New York Yankees' uniforms with the words 'Five Boroughs' written across the top. Two of them were carrying stuff. The other was standing there with some paperwork, in front of a pile of cartons and crates and a couch.

'What the hell . . .' I opened the door, forgot for a second that it was chained, had to shut it to unchain in, then opened it wide. 'What's all this?'

'Yours,' the Five Boroughs Man said, handing me a form to sign. 'Print Doone in the box and sign under it.'

Before I could do anything, the two guys carrying stuff moved past me.

One asked, 'Where do you want it?'

The other answered, 'It's empty here,' and dumped the load in the living room.

When the hallway was empty, the three left for a few minutes, came back with a second load which they deposited in the living room, left again, came back a third time, left a fourth time and came back two more times.

It took nearly an hour but by that time, my living room was chock fulla cartons and crates, and my couch was in the middle of it, tipped over on its side.

I printed and signed where the guy with the paperwork told me to, he initialled a pink page, ripped it away from the green page underneath, handed it to me, said, 'Have a nice evening,' and walked out. The other two followed. I closed the door behind them, then turned to see that there was now no way I could get from there, through the living room, back to my bedroom.

'What the hell . . .' I pushed my way past crates and my couch, and moved other cartons out of the way until I was in the middle of the room. Then, shaking my head, I said out loud, 'God dammit, Duke . . . you miserable sunnuvabitch.'

Long after midnight I was still fighting my way through the mess, trying to get organized, trying to find places to put all this stuff.

Eventually I crawled into bed, all the time cursing Duke and Lorilee. I was still cursing them in my dreams when my ultimate clock-radio did it to me again.

5.55 a.m.

It was too early to phone Izzy to find out what he knew 'bout all of this. And by the time I was in any shape to even start thinking about going back to arranging my stuff, it was nearly eight and I had to start getting my head around some trading in the market.

I booted up the computer, dialled on-line, checked my e-mail – mostly junk but also a short note from Debbie saying, 'We're making progress, fingers crossed' – and Herbie's news-letter.

Today, Kevin was touting Scotsel Cellular.

Knowing that I needed to find better intelligence than that, I surfed around for a while, looking at tipsters' pages, trying to hang on something – anything – that could put me back into the game and keep me ahead.

Just as Mikey had promised, the Net was filled with guys selling tips, exactly like the way newspapers are filled with guys picking horses. And probably with the same results. Everybody knows everything till the gates fly open and the race begins, and then all the handicapping and voodoo in the world doesn't mean a damn thing if the horse doesn't run the fastest.

Still, with nothing much else to go on, I bookmarked about a dozen pages that kinda made some sense and decided to make them part of my morning routine.

If one guy comes up with one tip that works, the voice said, *it's more than we've got now.*

By the time the market opened at 9.30, CNBC was reporting that Microsoft was having problems – yet again – with the Department of Justice and those shares were down thirteen bucks.

Now, every trader knows the theory that says buy dips and sell rallies. In a funny way, it's the opposite of the bump theory. But making that work inside a ten or fifteen minute time frame isn't just hard, it's near-impossible. Even if it wasn't, there still didn't seem much sense in running after Microsoft 'cause, the way I saw it, this was one particular bandwagon that had long since left town.

Some of the other hi-techs had reacted to the news at

Microsoft and also taken dives. Everything else seemed to be going sideways.

The more I stared at the screen, the less I liked the whole feel of the market.

So by 9.40 I was spooked enough to say, *to hell with it*, and logged off.

The voice had no trouble convincing me, *this time we've got plenty of furniture to rearrange*. It was the soundest excuse I could muster to avoid falling on my ass two days in a row.

I'd only just righted the couch when Izzy phoned. 'This is Isidor Pinkus, your attorney, calling to tell you there's no news.'

'Oh yes, there is,' I contradicted. 'My furniture's back.'

'It is?' He groaned. 'Ech . . . I lost my bet.'

'What bet?'

'Ten dollars.'

'Not how much, what?'

'I made a bet with Cousin Harry that they wouldn't return it. He said they would. I said they wouldn't. I bet him ten dollars that they wouldn't, and they did. But don't worry, bets do not get charged to expenses.'

I wanted to know, 'Why did you make a bet with Cousin Harry?'

'Because Cousin Harry told me what to put on the writ and said, if you do it right, I bet you ten dollars they return his stuff.'

'You did it right 'cause the moving guys showed up last night.'

'With everything?'

'Yeah . . .' I said right away, then realized I hadn't checked. 'I mean, it looks like everything.'

'Her clothes too?'

'Her clothes?' Come to think of it, I hadn't seen any of Lorilee's clothes. 'Ah . . . no, in fact, I don't think so.'

'Ech . . .' he groaned again. 'I just lost another ten dollars.'

'Why?'

'Because I made another bet with Cousin Harry.'

'You bet that my wife . . . I mean, Lorilee, wouldn't return her own clothes?'

'No, I bet your brother-in-law would. But he didn't. So I lost.'

'Why would he return her clothes?'

'I was sure he would but Cousin Harry said he'd be so angry about having gotten a writ of his own, that he wouldn't have been thinking clearly enough to remember Brocklebank v Hurst.'

'Who?'

'Not who, them. A couple. But not a couple like you and your wife. A couple like my cousin Pinky, if you know what I mean. Mr Brocklebank versus his wife Mr Hurst.'

'Izzy, what does this have to do with the wholesale price of manure?'

'With manure?'

'Just an expression,' I explained. 'Why should Duke have remembered Mr and Mrs Brockle-whatever.'

'Bank. And if he didn't, which he clearly didn't, he will. I'll even bet you ten dollars he will. I've got to go. Good-bye.'

How come every time we hang up with him, the voice wanted to know, *we're more confused than when we answered?*

I went back to my furniture.

Two minutes later, Izzy was on the line again. 'See that? I forget Brocklebank v Hurst too. Happens all the time.'

'Izzy, you just told me 'bout that.'

'No, I only mentioned. I didn't tell.' He launched into a longwinded story about the case a man named Brocklebank had filed against his former lover, a man named Hurst, and how it related to Lorilee's court order keeping me away from Connecticut. 'Remember I told you it was like a chess match? Someone makes a move that tempts you into taking one of their pieces, and when you do you realize that you've left a more valuable piece open to attack?'

'Yeah.'

'You don't remember,' he said. 'But never mind. The writ preventing you from going to your own house in Connecticut was your brother-in-law's ploy to get you to say, okay, if I can't come to Connecticut, then you can't come to New York.'

'But I never said that.'

'But if you had, you would have. It defines the grounds for settlement. When she says the house is hers and you say the apartment is yours . . . you see what I'm getting at?'

'No.'

'If I said, Flemons v Flemons or Jennerette v Jennerette or Dickenson v Hudson, would you understand?'

'No.'

'So it doesn't matter, because I understand. Those were cases where the court decided one person had relinquished a property in exchange for another and that, having done that, they could no longer claim the first property. In these cases, oral agreements were worth the paper they were printed on.'

'I still don't understand.'

'But your brother-in-law does. Which is why Cousin Harry told me to issue writs against both of them. Requiring them to return everything, and naming him as a co-conspirator, which he would have found infuriating, meant that as soon as they removed all your wife's property from the apartment they were relinquishing your wife's claim to the apartment, surrendering it to you, while you still maintained your right to the house in Connecticut.'

'Huh?'

'Enter here, Brocklebank v Hurst,' he went on, as if he was oblivious to the fact that I'd lost him ages ago. 'By returning everything, your brother-in-law is saying that his sister maintains a claim on the apartment. But your wife doesn't know that. She kept her own stuff. And he's too angry to remember Brocklebank. Only natural. But in doing so, she has shown her clear intention to abandon the apartment in New York. Get it?'

'Truly? No.'

'Then again, why should you because you don't have to. Cousin Harry did and I do too. Suffice it to say that your wife has been satisfactorily Brocklebanked.'

'I still don't . . .'

'I'll try again. Listen. When Mr Hurst walked out on Mr Brocklebank he took his clothes with him. The court ruled such action showed his intention of never returning. Even though your wife has returned the furniture, by keeping her clothes she hasn't established her intention to return, even if she thinks she has. Your brother-in-law should have known it all gets down to socks and underwear. But he had other things on his mind. Cousin Harry knew that. Even I did. Now you do too. Good-bye.'

'Good-bye,' I said, but it was too late 'cause he'd already hung up.

After moving so much stuff from one room to the other, then

moving some of it back 'cause I figured now I could put it where I wanted to and not where Lorilee used to put it, I just had to get outta there. So I went down the block for a couple of slices of pizza, picked up the newspapers, stocked up on M&Ms and returned in time to find the mailman delivering my new credit cards.

Hoping maybe my luck was coming home, I peeked in on the market and sat around for a few hours waiting for something to happen. But I still didn't have the feel for it and even when Microsoft started clawing back a few points, I couldn't step off the diving board. Instead, I went back to unpacking and straightening up, and probably would have stayed there for the rest of the day, 'cept the door bell rang and it was Five Boroughs again.

I asked down the intercom, 'What is it this time?'

The guy said, 'Ladies' clothes.'

The voice screamed, *Brocklebank's revenge.*

'Take 'em back,' I ordered. 'Sorry. No one's home.'

He rang the buzzer several more times but I refused to answer. When it stopped, I phoned Izzy to tell him, but his machine was on so I left a message.

I eventually got all my clothes hung up and arranged in the closets – without Lorilee's stuff there was plenty of room – but now my eyes were starting to close and I couldn't keep from yawning.

The clock said it was only just 8.15.

If it took me this long to get everything back in, I asked the voice, *how the hell did they get it out of here so fast?*

Cause getting everything in is uphill and getting everything out is downhill, the voice answered.

Which is where I'm going fast.

Nothing that a night's sleep couldn't cure.

I agreed, got out of my clothes, climbed into bed with the papers and lay there reading, at least till the voice added, *or a big win on the lottery.*

Lottery?

I remembered my ticket for Saturday, jumped out of bed and found it on the bottom of a pile of papers I'd put on the floor under my desk, the same papers I was intending to throw out as soon as I bought a wastepaper basket, which I no longer needed 'cause my regular old wastepaper basket was back. Anyway, there's a phonc number you can dial in New York that gives you the winning numbers, so clinging to the ticket with my right hand, I dialled the number with my left hand, then held my breath while a recording went through the numbers. I did it that way 'cause the voice assured me, *hold the ticket in your right hand and hold your breath real hard while checking the numbers and we can't lose.*

I'd played Marylou's birthday, Carrie's birthday and Lorilee's birthday.

And just like each of those marriages, not a single one hit.

So much for holding your breath, I said, ripping up the ticket and tossing it into the pile of papers under my desk.

I crawled back into bed.

The voice suggested, *maybe we should have held it in our left hand and breathed heavy.*

I argued, *maybe we should figure out how to make a living day trading and then we won't need the lottery to solve our problems.*

I snuggled into all my pillows, now having more than enough to bury myself under them.

Wouldn't it have been ironic, the voice suggested as I faded into sleep, *if a jackpot lottery had been the same amount we're gonna need to save Mama's apartment from a jackpot sweepstakes.*

I dreamt I was smiling. And 'bout all that money. Twenty-nine million bucks worth of money. And what I'd do with it and how maybe I'd get my mama a bigger, better place and then she wouldn't have to worry 'bout winning sweepstakes and losing sweepstakes 'cause I'd have won.

Sweepstakes.

My eyes shot open.

Sweepstakes?

It was dark and I wasn't immediately sure where I was, till I spotted my ultimate clock-radio and saw that it was 11.30.

I screamed, *Jesus Christ,* and jumped out of bed.

Grabbing my clothes, I threw some cold water on to my face to help wake up and raced out of the apartment. Luckily I found a cab right away. But we hit some traffic. I told him to go down Lex and across on 49th. He did and of course that's where we got stuck behind a truck with a flat tyre. I threw some money on the front seat, bailed out and ran the rest of the way.

Somehow, I made it to the garage entrance by five to twelve.

'My pal Sir Tommy back yet?'

The concierge glared at me. 'Mr Whitestone?'

'Yeah.' I needed to catch my breath. 'He back yet?'

'He expecting you?'

'Yeah. Sort of.'

'Not yet,' he said.

'Good.' I smiled reassuringly to him at the same time.

But he wasn't smiling at me and seemed a little concerned 'bout how hard I was still breathing. 'What do you mean, sort of expecting you?'

'Sorta . . . kinda,' I said. 'I told him I might be in New York but I don't think he really believed me and I couldn't make it to the dinner tonight . . .'

He gave me a very steely-eyed look. 'Yeah?'

'Yeah,' I assured him. 'It's okay.'

'Yeah, well . . . you want to step out of the way, please. If you wait just over there. Cars keep arriving . . .'

One was pulling into the garage as he said it. I stared at the man in the back seat, then realized I didn't actually know what Thomas Whitestone looked like, beside the fact that he was tall.

The concierge grabbed the back door and said good evening as a couple got out. They were both short. I smiled at them as they walked past me to the elevator and went upstairs.

A taxi arrived. A woman got out. Then another taxi arrived. This time a man got out. I was almost about to ask 'Sir Tommy?' when I heard him tell the concierge, 'Ya'll pay for it, wouldya kindly, and put it on my tab.'

I smiled at him too, as much to be polite as thinking to myself, *no way Sir Tommy talks like that.*

More cars pulled into the garage – my breathing was back to normal now – and more people got out, and as they did I started to notice that the concierge was regularly looking at me before he looked at the people getting out of the cars.

He was worried about me hanging around like that.

Mark David Chapman, the voice called out.

I stared at the concierge and forced a smile.

He turned away.

He's thinking we're like the guy who shot John Lennon and that we're here to plug Whitestone.

Just then a white stretch-limo pulled into the garage.

The concierge stepped off the kerb, glanced back at me,

moved to the rear door, gave the man in the back seat just enough room to step out, then positioned himself between me and the man.

That's him, the voice knew.

A very tall, fine-looking man dressed in a tuxedo – he had a balding head, round baby face and clear blue eyes – walked with a slight stoop towards the elevator.

All alone, the voice pointed out, *just like John Lennon*.

'Sir Tommy? Hi.' I waved and moved towards him. 'K.C. Doone.' The concierge kept me in his sights. 'Sorry I missed the speech this evening.' I extended my hand. 'Hope it went well.'

'Very well, thank you.' Whitestone gave me one of his huge smiles and shook my hand. 'Very nice to see you.'

'Sir Tommy . . . I know this is an awkward time,' I said, 'and I hate to bother you about this . . . I hope ya'll don't mind, but there's a company of yours that operates out of Miami . . . doing real estate deals . . . company called South Florida Island Federal Finance.'

'Oh yes,' he said in such a way that I couldn't tell if he knew what I was talking 'bout or just being Britishly polite.

I nodded reassuringly to the concierge who finally backed away.

'The thing is . . . this company of yours runs a sweepstakes operation . . . I'm sure you're not involved in this, and maybe you don't even know the kinds of methods they use . . . but this sweepstakes of theirs . . . it's all pretty shady. And the way I know what's going on is 'cause my mama, who lives down there, fell for it and 'cause of this sweepstakes, it looks like she's gonna lose her apartment . . .'

'I see . . .' He patted my shoulder consolingly.

'I couldn't get in touch with the fella running that company, whose name is Alexander George . . . and another fella whose name is Herbert Werner . . . and there are two guys with Spanish names, one being a lawyer . . .'

He held up his hands to stop me. 'Mr Doone? It has been a very long day for me. I just flew in from London this afternoon which makes it now some time after five in the morning in my life. Would you mind terribly if we scheduled a more convenient time to discuss this?'

'Ah . . . yeah, sure,' I said, thinking to myself, *I got to the man and he's gonna make it right.* 'Ya'll tell me what time is good for you. Tomorrow? Morning? Afternoon?'

'Yes. Certainly. Tomorrow morning. I hope you will excuse me tonight.'

'What time?'

'How would nine be for you?'

'That would be fine.' I asked, 'Here?'

'Indeed,' he said. 'Here.'

I extended my hand. 'Mr Whitestone . . . Sir Tommy, thank you.'

He gave me another big smile, shook my hand and said, 'Good night.'

I said 'Good night' and watched him walk to the elevator.

He went upstairs and I went home.

Got to the man, I kept telling the voice. *Got to the man and he's gonna make it right.*

This time when my ultimate clock-radio went off at 5.55, I was glad that it did. I made coffee and toast, felt good when I jumped into the shower and felt even better as I got dressed.

I arrived at the Waldorf Towers by 8.40, strolled into the garage entrance and announced to the concierge at the desk that I was there to see Sir Thomas Whitestone.

It wasn't the same concierge I'd seen there a couple of days ago, or even the same fella from last night. So it made sense to me that he asked, 'Do you have an appointment?'

I confidently answered, 'Sure do. Nine on the dot. Name is Doone. K.C. Doone.'

'Doone?' He gave me a quizzical look. 'And he told you to meet him here this morning?'

'At nine. Am I too early?'

'Hardly,' he said. 'Mr Whitestone left for London at six-thirty.'

Chapter Nineteen

I dreamt I won the lottery.

I was holding my ticket – this time grasping it tightly in my left hand and taking long deep breaths – dialling the lottery phoneline with my right hand.

The recorded message answered, *is that you, K.C.?*

I said, *yeah it is.*

All right, K.C., here are the winning numbers for this week's New York State lottery. The first is . . . Marylou's birthday.

That's May First, I said. *That's five and one. I got it.*

Next is Carrie's birthday.

April twenty-first. That's four and twenty-one. Got it, I said again. *Hey, that's four out of six.*

Well then, we'll move on to the last two numbers. Are you ready?

I played Lorilee's birthday. September twenty-third. That would be nine and twenty-three, wouldn't it? That's what I played.

The recorded message wanted to know, *and if those are the two remaining numbers, then what?*

What do you mean, then what? Then I win twenty-nine million bucks.

Well, sort of. After all, you didn't do it alone. You needed Lorilee's help.

Huh? She didn't do anything.

It's her birthday.

Hey, I bought the ticket and I played those numbers. All she did was get born that day, which if you think 'bout it, had nothing to do with her.

What do you mean? If you think about it, without her birthday you wouldn't win the jackpot.

So what?

You know, so what.

Are you trying to tell me I have to cut her in?

What do you think?

I think you're a recorded message and you're only supposed to tell me what numbers came up, not what I have to do.

All right, if that's the way you want to be . . .

Yeah, that's the way I want to be.

So, if I tell you that the last two numbers are ten and nineteen . . .

Wait a minute. Don't tell me that. Don't tell me just any old numbers. Tell me Lorilee's birthday.

Why should I?

Cause then I win twenty-nine million dollars and that solves all my problems.

Does it?

Yeah, it does.

How?

Kinda obvious, isn't it? I win all that money to get even with the creeps who are trying to steal my mama's apartment and get even with GCB and get even with Lorilee . . .

That's what you call solving all your problems?

That's exactly what I call solving all my problems.

Getting even?

Precisely.

Why wouldn't you just walk away?

Walk away? What are you talking 'bout, walk away? And let them win? Why would I do that?

Do you really think that if you walk away, they win?

That bunch at GCB fired my ass and Lorilee was cheating on me.

So? If you walk away, who really wins and who really loses?

For a recorded message, ya'll sure are annoying.

You haven't answered the question?

Why can't I do whatever I damn please with my twenty-nine million bucks?

Like what?

Like . . . getting even.

Why bother?

Cause getting even feels good.

Maybe walking away feels even better.

Why should I reward them for what they did to me?

Reward them or reward you?

Hey, if you'd just do what you're supposed to do, which is tell me that the last two numbers are Lorilee's birthday, I'll worry about who's won and who's lost and who gets rewarded.

You'll see, the voice warned.

Yeah, yeah. Now go on, tell me the last two numbers are Lorilee's birthday.

All right, K.C., the last two numbers are . . . Lorilee's birthday.

I won. I won. I jumped up and down, holding on to my ticket so tight that my knuckles were getting white. *I won. I won. Twenty-nine million bucks. I won. I won.*

I was jumping up and down.

I won . . . I won . . . I won . . .

I was holding on to a cage door and every time I jumped up and down I banged it against the side of a wall.

Then someone was shaking my shoulder.

'Please help me.'

I won. I won. My knuckles were white and the side of my head hurt. *I won. I won.*

'Please . . . help me . . .'

'Huh?' My eyes opened.

'Mr Doone . . . please help me . . .'

I looked around but it was too dark to see anything.

'Please help me.'

'What?' I was trapped in an elevator. 'Huh?'

'I think I am going to be ill.'

Chapter Twenty

'What do ya'll mean he left here at six-thirty?'

'I mean, Mr Whitestone checked out of the Towers at six-thirty this morning to fly back to London.' The concierge shrugged. 'I don't know what else I could mean.'

And I didn't know what else to do, 'cept mumble 'Sunnuvabitch', and walk away.

Sunnuvabitch, the voice couldn't believe it either. *He tells us to meet him here at nine . . .*

I suggested to the voice, *maybe he got called away suddenly.*

Yeah, the voice retorted, *like suddenly at six this morning to avoid us.*

Something came up, I tried to rationalize.

Find somebody who believes that, the voice said, *and we can sell them a bridge in Brooklyn.*

I went straight back home, noticed the time, realized the markets were just opening, but didn't have the stomach for it.

Flew back to London, huh? I told the voice, *how 'bout we see for ourselves?* I picked up the phone and called American Airlines. 'What time is your first morning flight from New York to London?'

The woman checked. 'We have one flight, American 142 departing at 8.30 and a second . . . let's see, American 106 . . . which is just leaving now, at 9.30.'

'I'm not sure which one my friend Mr Whitestone caught this morning . . .'

'I'm sorry, sir, but we can't give out any sort of passenger information . . .'

I thanked her and hung up.

To catch the 8.30 it made sense that he would have left the hotel two hours before. 'Cept if he was on that flight,

or even if he was on the 9.30, then he needed a reservation.

Unless, the voice argued, *he bought his ticket at the last minute.*

How 'bout we find out when he booked his ticket? I phoned
Hussein of bucket shop fame and explained that I needed
a favour.

'Don't tell me, mister . . . a really cheap seat to Florida on a
flight leaving in the next half-hour?'

'Not this time. How much pull you got with American Airlines? A friend of mine flew to London this morning and I'm
curious 'bout when he booked his seat.'

'The airline computers are very difficult to access, mister.
They don't give out information about their customers to just
anybody.'

'But you got a friend, right?'

'I have many friends,' he said. 'I also have a very large family
and sometimes that's even better than having many friends. If
you get my drift, mister.'

'Fella's name is Whitestone. Thomas Whitestone. Or maybe
just booked as Sir T. Whitestone. Flew in yesterday. Left this
morning.'

'May I phone you back?'

I said sure.

Ten minutes later he did. 'This friend of yours . . . mister, are
you sure he travelled with American Airlines?'

That stopped me. 'No.'

'Because he didn't. Not under that name. Not on this morning's flights to London. Or anywhere else with that airline.
Not today.'

'Oh . . . well . . . who else flies there? I guess British Airways.
Never even thought 'bout them.'

'Mister, I did, but he didn't. Not on their regular service. Not
on the Concorde. And just so that you know I am a very thorough
man, mister, I also checked with United. Your friend did not fly
back to London this morning with them either.'

'Huh.' I sat back and listened to the little voice say, *maybe the
concierge got it wrong and he didn't go to London. Maybe he went
to California. Or Paris. Or Spain. Or Mexico. He's got a house in
Mexico. That's where he went.* 'Thanks anyway,' I said to Hussein.

'Mister . . . you will remember my number when it comes
time to buying your next ticket?'

'Of course I will.' I hung up, shrugged and told the voice, *so he got called away, or just went away, or took a trip to Mexico, what difference does it make?*

A lot, the voice said. *Called away is one thing. Gone away, when he knew he was going, is another.*

The words of Whitestone's old girlfriend, that woman who lived on Park Avenue, came back to me.

Never let the son of a bitch out of your sight.

Then another thought popped into my head. Something I'd seen in one of those stories about him on the Internet. I booted up my computer, went into the files where I'd downloaded all that stuff and ran a search for one word – airplane.

Sure enough, the reference appeared.

His very own Boeing 757.

I phoned Hussein again. 'If a guy has a private plane, how can I find out when he left?'

'Where did he leave from?'

'New York.'

'Kennedy? Mister, I doubt it. They don't like private planes coming and going out of there. But he might have used Teeterboro.'

'New Jersey?'

'That's where many of the private planes go.'

Now I got on to the flight operations office at Teeterboro and told the fella who answered the phone that I needed to check on a departure of a private plane.

He asked, 'Tail number?'

'No idea.'

'Call sign?'

'Gee . . . I don't know.'

'So if you don't know, buddy, how am I supposed to know?'

'Well . . . it's my friend who flew in yesterday from London and flew out this morning . . . I just wanted to make sure they got out okay.'

'Listen, buddy, I'm more than happy to keep track of everybody's friends flying to everywhere. In fact, I'm really thrilled to be doing this job. But in my merry world everybody's friends either have a tail number or call sign.'

'His name is Whitestone.'

'Like the bridge?'

'Exactly.'

'Means nothing. No bridges flew out of here that I saw.'

'If he was flying in his own plane back to London . . . I mean, he'd fly out of your airport, wouldn't he?'

'We get a lot that do, I have no idea about the ones that don't.'

'How about the ones with their own seven-five-seven?'

'Seven-fives? Your friend's got a seven-five? Why didn't you say so. Hold on.' I waited several minutes before he came back on the line. 'I know the plane. It's the only seven-five we ever see. Not even the Arabs fly seven-fives. Let's see . . . yep . . . computer says a seven-five got out of here, wheels in the well, at seven-forty-one bound for . . . flight plan says . . . LGW . . . that's Gatwick, England.'

'Flight plan?' I wondered, 'When did they file that flight plan?'

'When? Why?'

'Just curious . . .' I needed to think of something so I said, 'Ya'll gotta understand that this friend of mine is a stickler for details. One of those fellas who dots all his I's and crosses all his T's, and never leaves anything to the last minute.'

It didn't make any sense to me, but it must have to him 'cause he answered, 'Says here they filed the inbound same time they filed the outbound which was . . . yesterday from LGW . . . at thirteen forty-five GMT.'

'Yesterday? Huh. Thanks.' I hung up with him, then told the voice, *He knew yesterday that he was leaving the hotel at six-thirty this morning.*

And the voice responded, *sunnuvabitch.*

'This is Isidor Pinkus, your attorney, calling.'

'Hey.' I was still fuming about having been stood up by Whitestone.

'There is good news and there is bad news.'

'When it rains it pours,' I mumbled. 'Hit me with the good news first.'

'The good news is that there is no news from either your wife, or perhaps I should presume soon-to-be ex-wife, or your brother-in-law, hereinafter known as your soon-to-be ex-brother-in-law since you refused to take your soon-to-be ex-wife's clothes back, hereinafter referred to as a smart move.'

'That's the good news?'

'Compared with the bad news, yes, that's good. The bad news is that I have just received a letter from lawyers representing Garrison-Cotton-Braddock Incorporated, World Trade Center . . .'

'I know their address,' I snapped, and instantly felt bad that I had. 'What I mean is, what did they say?'

'They said . . . at least this is what their lawyers say . . . that their clients, Garrison-Cotton-Braddock Incorporated, feel they are under no obligation whatsoever to respond favourably to my request.'

'What request?'

'The request that I made on your behalf.'

'I didn't know you made any request on my behalf.'

'You forgot? I wrote them a letter. I told them they wrongfully dismissed you and that if they did not pay you ten million dollars, we would sue.'

'Ten million dollars?'

'It's a nice round figure.'

'Izzy, you never mentioned anything to me about ten million dollars.'

'I didn't? I must have forgotten. Like you forget that I was making a request to them on your behalf.'

'I'm not surprised they didn't just enclose a cheque.'

'Funny, that's what Cousin Harry said too.'

'This was his idea?'

'No, this was my idea. And I'll tell you something, it's a shame that it was because when I told him about it he called me a cheapskate for not demanding twice as much.'

'Izzy . . . did you honestly believe that they were gonna say okay to a letter like that?'

'It only cost a stamp.'

'I didn't go to law school like you. Fact is, I didn't go to very much school at all. But, Izzy, if I'm reading right, breach of fiduciary trust is a polite way of saying, fuck off!'

'Of course it is,' he agreed, ever cheerful. 'Just like my asking for ten million dollars is my way of saying I want ten million dollars. But you know what? In between breach of fiduciary trust and ten million dollars, there's room for a shopping mall and a parking lot.'

'Don't hold your breath till they start installing neon signs.'

'If they do, I'll take thirty per cent. If they don't, I'll still take thirty per cent. So why would you worry when I'm the one who really has to worry because thirty per cent of a shopping mall and parking lot is a lot, and thirty per cent of nothing is nothing. See what I mean?'

'Yeah . . . Izzy . . . I definitely do see what you mean.'

'Anyway,' he said, 'it's not as if I've been over-priced so far.'

That made me laugh. 'You're a one-off, Isidor Pinkus, attorney-at-law.'

'My mother thinks so.'

'Tell your mama I said she's right.'

'If only you were a Jewish girl, I'd have you tell her.'

'Seems to me law school should have been filled with them, no?'

'And all of them wanted to marry doctors.'

'Then how about hanging out at your local neighbourhood medical school?'

'All of them want to marry doctors too.'

'And your mama's on your case, huh?'

'My mother's on my case but I'm on your case which I think balances everything out.'

'I wish I could help,' I told him, 'but the only single girl I know these days is an about-to-be-divorced *shicksa* in Connecticut.'

'At least the Connecticut part I could deal with,' he said. 'So how come you know the word *shiksa*?'

I laughed again. 'Cause the Jewish girls I knew in Boston were all too smart to have anything to do with me. They were looking for you.'

'You've got my number,' he said, 'if any of them are still looking.'

'You'll be the first person I call.'

'And if there is news, you too will be the first person I call.'

The thing is, the voice said as soon as I put the phone down, *if we sit around waiting for news, no one is ever gonna call. So how 'bout we make some of our own? Let's turn stool-pigeon.*

I found the number I needed, dialled it and asked for 'Charlotte Meissen, please.'

A man wanted to know, 'Who do I tell her is calling?'

'Name is Doone. K.C. Doone. I was in to see her last week.'

'Oh yeah, guy with the just initials name.'

'Howdy, Wolf, how's it going?'

'So we're already on a first name basis, huh? Hold on Kansas City, I'll put you through.'

There were a few clicks, then there was a pause, then she came on the line. 'Mr Doone? This is Charlotte Meissen.'

'Hi again,' I said. 'Remember me from last week?'

'Yes, I do. What can I do for you, Mr Doone?'

'Well, that matter we discussed . . . all those companies trying to separate little old ladies like my mama from her apartment . . . I've done some research and I've found the power behind the throne.'

'The power behind the throne?'

'If you follow the trail, all those companies lead back to a fella in England named Whitestone. Sir Thomas d'Aquin Whitestone. Ever heard of him?'

'Should I have heard of him?'

'One of the richest men in the world.'

'And how do you know he's behind these sweepstakes?'

''Cause I followed the trail back to him.'

'Which means?'

'Which means . . . all right. Here goes.' I explained to her how I'd gotten on the Internet, run a whole bunch of searches on the three companies involved with the sweepstakes, added searches on Alexander George, Juan Luis Gonzalez Ochoa, Herbert I. Werner, Carlos Bianco-Sanchez, told her who those guys were, and explained how those leads got me to Tower Benahavis Properties, Tower Benahavis Developments and Torre de Benahavis. 'That's the name of Whitestone's house in Spain.'

There was a long silence. 'You say that the sweepstakes is run by one of the richest men in the world and you know all this because you know the name of the house he owns in Spain?'

'That's right.'

'Mr Doone, if there is something we can do in this matter, it will have to come about through hard facts and evidence.'

'I know. But you don't seem to be coming up with any hard facts and evidence, so I'm trying to. I gotta save my mama's apartment. And I know this guy Whitestone is behind those sweepstakes. Fact is, I met him last night. I mentioned the sweepstakes and he knew . . .' That wasn't quite true but it sounded better than saying maybe I think he knew. 'When I went to see him this morning to confront him, he'd already skipped.'

'I see,' she said, merely being polite.

'He left town. Back to England. He knew what time I was coming to see him and he got out before I got there.'

'Back to England?' She paused for a moment. 'Mr Doone, last week you were telling me about a company in the Bahamas. Today you're talking about Spain and England. Do you recall that at one point I used the word jurisdiction?'

'I also recall at one point you said you'd received something like a hundred complaints about these sweepstakes.'

'We have.'

'In any of those hundred complaints, anyone ever mention the name Whitestone?'

She admitted, 'No, they haven't, Mr Doone.'

'Well then, you and I are making progress.'

'Even if this Mr Whitestone is somehow involved . . .'

'He is,' I assured her. 'Trust me. He is.'

'That remains to be proven. Not only does the matter of jurisdiction arise, but proof does come into it. Without both, not one but both, I'm afraid, Mr Doone, there isn't much else I can do.'

'Well,' I told her, 'seems to me that you and I are pretty consistent folk.'

'How so, Mr Doone?'

'Last week you said ya'll can't do anything. This week you're saying the same thing. Last week I said I gotta do something 'cause it's my mama. This week I'm saying the same thing. How 'bout we sign a pact?'

'A pact?'

'Yeah, Miss Meissen. I find you the proof, you find the jurisdiction.'

She paused, then answered, 'Mr Doone . . . if it's Great Britain, we've got treaties.'

Back on the Internet, I strolled on through the woods following my bread crumbs, going down the path that got me from South Florida to a house in Spain, then looking for another one to take me from there to Sir Tommy Whitestone's front door in England.

Along the way, I found several companies I hadn't known about – again, all somehow interrelated with London and Paris, and one in particular that was in Mexico that looked to me like it led back to the Caribbean. Reason I couldn't tell for sure was 'cause all the stuff was written in Spanish. The only thing I could figure out was that it had something to do with Juan Luis Gonzalez Ochoa and Carlos Bianco-Sanchez.

No matter, I downloaded anything and everything that might make sense, and kept on going till I finally couldn't see straight. That's when I realized I'd been sitting in front of the computer for more than seven hours.

Not only were my eyes beginning to cross, but my stomach was rumbling. I knew I had to eat something. So I shoved all the Spanish stuff I'd downloaded on to a floppy disk, stuck it in my pocket, and headed out to buy a slice of pizza at a joint I didn't much like over on Third Avenue.

I didn't much like the place 'cause their crust was wrong and their cheese wasn't stringy enough and if you're gonna eat New York pizza, the crust has gotta be right and the cheese has gotta be real stringy. But I went there 'cause right next door is one of those photocopying and fax places, where they also print out from computer disks. So while I was suffering with the pizza, my Spanish downloads were getting printed. After washing it all down with a root beer, I grabbed the fifteen sheets of print-out, and headed for Bloomingdale's.

'*Amigo* . . .' I called out as soon as I got into range of the Puerto Rican who'd sold me the twenty-buck Cartier. 'Fidel . . . *que pasa?*'

'Hey *hombre* . . .' He gave me one of those very complicated handshakes that I messed up 'cause I never know when you're supposed to bump fists and when you're supposed to lock thumbs. 'You buying the Pia-jay this time?'

'Nope. I'm buying some time, but not that kinda time.' I showed him the papers. 'This kinda time.'

He pointed to the watches. 'Hey, *gringo*, I sell this kinda time. What is that kinda time?'

'It's ten bucks for fifteen minutes.'

He didn't understand. 'To do what?'

'Read through this stuff real fast and tell me what it says.'

He looked at me like I was crazy. 'How many pages you got here? And you want to pay me what?'

'Fifteen pages . . . okay, fifteen bucks. It's gonna take you fifteen minutes.'

'*Hombre*, my man, you know how many watches I can sell in

fifteen minutes? I'm talking Role-ex. Patek-Felippe. Pia-jay.' He shook his head. 'No, man, I'll stick to watches and let the United Nations stick to consecutive translation.'

'Okay, twenty and I'll buy a watch for . . . ten more.'

'For how much? I don't take less than fifty bucks for any of these watches.'

I didn't remind him what I'd paid for the Cartier. 'Come on, Fidel . . . it won't even take you fifteen minutes. Be a bro.'

'A bro?' He gave me a very strange look. '*Hombre*, what colour are you?'

'I'm talking 'bout being a brother at arms,' I said, not having any idea what I was talking 'bout. 'Please, Fidel . . . from one *caballero* to another.'

As I was trying to hand him the pages, a very well-dressed man in his early seventies stopped at the table and started looking at one of the rip-off Rolex Oysters.

Instantly, I shoved the print-outs into Fidel's hands, leaned forward and said to the gentleman 'Howdy, sir', pointed to the Rolex and told him, 'That's my best watch.' I picked it up and reached for his wrist. 'Here, sir, why don't you let me help you put it on?'

'How much is it?' he asked.

Fidel announced, 'Hundred and twenty-five dollars.'

'Hey, this man's a personal friend,' I said to Fidel, then winked at my customer. 'Ya'll bought watches from me before, haven't you, sir? I recognize you.'

The man hesitated. 'Me . . . well, I ah . . .'

'Sure you have. My partner here was thinking that ya'll are new to Bloomingdale's Annex. He's talking a hundred and twenty-five plus tax. I'm saying that the price for you is an even hundred. And that's tax included.'

'What . . . you mean sales tax . . .'

'Yes, sir, the governor is covered.'

He didn't seem sure. 'Gee, I don't know . . .'

'Look how nice that sits.' I turned his wrist up and down so he could see. 'Genuine leather strap. And the watch . . . sir, we're not talking 'bout Filipino merchandise here. Ya'll gotta know that if you went into our parent company . . .' I pointed to Bloomingdale's . . . 'they'd charge you twenty times as much.'

He studied the watch, nodded, took out his wallet, handed me $100 and confirmed, 'Tax included, right?'

I said, 'Right' and told Fidel, 'How 'bout a box for my customer?'

He looked at me, handed the gentleman a box and one of those suspect guarantees, then announced, 'You're a lucky *hombre* because I wouldn't have known you're a regular customer. I would have had to charge you the first-time customer price.' Then he added, 'Including tax,' all the time glaring at me.

The gentleman waved, nodded and strolled away.

Fidel ripped the hundred-dollar bill out of my hand and shoved it into his pocket. 'That was a two-hundred-dollar watch.'

'Which ya'll were gonna to sell to me last week for six-ty-five.'

'Last week it was on sale.'

'And this week we sold it.'

'We?'

'Me.' I pointed to the papers. 'What do they say?'

He mumbled, 'Not bad for a *gringo*,' half sat on the table with his back to the sidewalk, told me, 'Keep an eye on the store,' and started reading.

It only took him ten minutes before he handed the papers back to me. 'These are bad dudes.'

'Why? What have they done?'

'Says here this *caballero* named Carlos Bianco-Sanchez was a director of some *Mejicano* company but that the *Mejicanos* didn't like the way he did business so they made him resign.'

'Forced him out?'

'*Hombre*, this is complicated. I don't understand a lot of it.' He shrugged. 'I don't even understand a little of it. But I can tell you this for sure, the *Mejicanos* will let anyone do anything as long as they pay the right people. If this *caballero* got into trouble in *Mejico*, there must be something very wrong.'

'That's what it says there?'

He nodded. 'On every page.'

I reached into my pocket for some money, thinking now that I'd have to get this properly translated.

'Hey *gringo*,' Fidel stopped me. 'No charge. After all, we used to be in business together.'

'*Gracias*, dude.' I held up my hand to hi-five him.

He slowly began shaking his head. 'Some white guys just never get it.'

*   *   *

I pushed the print-out into an envelope and addressed it to Izzy, adding a note. 'I think there's something in this that might be interesting but I don't talk Spanish. Do you know anyone who can translate it for us on the cheap?'

Then I sat back and tried to psych myself up. *If the sunnuvabitch wouldn't meet me this morning, he's got something to hide. And if he's hiding something, then I want to find out what.*

The voice chimed in with, *so let's go find out.*

Yeah, I answered, *just like that, we'll get on a plane and go to London and bang on his door and find out why he's trying to steal my mama's apartment.*

The voice agreed, *sounds like a plan.*

But I wasn't convinced. Running off to some foreign country was gonna cost me a lot of money . . .

Maybe not, the voice said.

On a whim, I phoned Hussein again. 'How much does it cost to go to London?'

'Hello, mister . . . when do you want to leave?'

'I'm not even sure I do. Just wanna know how much it would cost.'

'Advertised fares? Maybe four hundred dollars. Unpublished . . . how would half that be?'

'Two hundred bucks to London? You talking one way . . .'

'Mister . . . I'm talking one ninety-nine, round trip.'

'How much?'

'Including tax.'

'And for that you get a plane that has a pilot who went to flying school?'

He wanted me to know, 'A pilot, a co-pilot and a first-run movie.'

'How 'bout a maintenance man who makes sure every day that all four engines are screwed on tight?'

'Scheduled service, mister.'

Taking that to mean it would be an airline I'd actually heard of, I said, 'I'll phone you back.'

I was willing to concede, at least that part was do-able, but I needed more encouragement. So later that evening I called Patsy. As soon as she answered, I said, 'I'm phoning for some free advice.'

I liked the fact that she knew who it was right away, 'cause she answered, 'I'm very good at free advice. That's what I do

all day. Such as, why don't you drop Calculus and Chemistry
and take Home-Ec instead?'

'Ya'll let your students get away with that?'

'Do I sound as if I let them get away with that?'

I grinned. 'I liked Home-Ec.'

'No, K.C. Doone, you didn't like Home-Ec. Believe me, I
know the difference. I've got half a high school filled with
teenage boys. You liked the girls you could meet in Home-Ec.'

'Same thing, no?'

'For sixteen year-old-boys it appears to be.'

'How 'bout free advice on another subject?' I told her about
my mama's apartment and about the sweepstakes and about
Whitestone and how he'd skipped on me. I said, 'I need you
to play devil's advocate. A little voice inside my head says I
should go to London and find out what the hell is happening.
I need you to talk me out of it.'

'Why?'

''Cause maybe it's a bad idea.'

'Do you think it's a bad idea?'

'I think it may be a crazy idea.'

'You know about Mohammed and the mountain.'

'Made the trains run on time?'

'That's the one.'

'So?'

'So if you think you need to find out from him what's going
on, and he wouldn't talk to you in New York, maybe he'll talk
to you in London.'

'You're not playing the devil's advocate, you're saying I
should go halfway around the world to chase after him?'

'It's not halfway around the world. And you're the one who
keeps saying you have to do whatever you can for Ruby.'

'I do . . . but . . . London's way over there.'

'Have you ever been to Europe?'

'No. We . . . my wife . . . former wife . . . well, we used to
go to the islands. She liked the sun and I liked . . .' I stopped,
'cause I nearly said I liked what Lorilee didn't wear while she
was sunbathing, but that seemed pretty tacky. 'I liked just doing
nothing.'

'London is only overnight and they speak English. To some
degree anyway.' She asked, 'Will you send me a postcard?'

'Sure I will. You been there?'

'Actually, yes I have. I . . . we . . . had our honeymoon there.'

'You and the guy who designs aeroplanes?'

'The only honeymoon I've ever had.'

'So I guess you liked it.'

'At the time? Or with hindsight?'

'Both.'

'At the time the trip was magic. With hindsight, it was London that had the magic.'

That's when I suddenly blurted out, 'Okay, so if you're so big on me going there, why don't ya'll come with me?'

'What?'

'Yeah, sure, come on along.'

'To London?'

'Why not?'

'How many why-nots do you want?'

'How many you got?'

'How about if I start with the why-not that you and I have never even met? Another why-not is because I've got two people who live with me who not only need me to be here for them, just as I need them to be here for me, but who would never, ever, in a million years, understand how their mom could run off to London with some stranger.'

'I thought you said you had your honeymoon there.'

She laughed. 'Stop interrupting because I have plenty more why-nots, and anyway, he and I weren't strangers.'

'Okay. Tell me more why-nots.'

'How about the why-not that I have a high school to run?'

'Just think how every kid in that school would love it if they knew their principal had run off to London with a stranger.'

'Just think of the abuse my children would then have to suffer.'

'You counted your kids once already. No fair. Only one why-not for every two teenagers.'

'Instead of London, how about if we just meet for an ice-cream soda?'

'Ice-cream soda? I haven't met a girl for an ice-cream soda since . . .'

She said it, 'High school?'

'Wow, time warp. Next you'll be inviting me to one of those Friday night dances in the smelly gym.'

'They're fun.'

'All that cheap crêpe paper hanging off the walls with Scotch tape?'

'I still get to go. And as long as you mentioned it, even though I won't go to London with you, if you want, I will invite you to a Friday night high school dance.'

'Can I wear my white socks?'

'Sure. The kids will laugh at you, but I'll understand.'

I remembered back to those days. 'It really would be fun to do it all over again, wouldn't it?'

'The dances?'

'High school. The dances. All that stuff.'

'Do you mean it would be fun to do it this time as an adult or all over again as a teenager?'

'All over again as a teenager.'

'No, there you're wrong. I see them every day and I can tell you that this generation of teenagers isn't having a lot of fun. It's not like it was when we were sixteen.'

'Well . . . no, I don't think I'd want to be sixteen again.'

'How old, then?'

'Nineteen,' I said right away. 'Yeah. I'd be nineteen, in a heartbeat.'

'Why?'

''Cause it was the spring of my life. Cause I was full of myself and full of life and hopelessly in love with a girl who was only ever gonna wind up shattering my heart.'

'And if you had it to do all over again,' she asked, 'would you?'

'Sure would. 'Cept this time I'd want to know then what I know now.'

'That's what everyone says.'

'Not quite. The difference being that everyone who says it means that by knowing then what they know now they wouldn't make the same mistakes.'

'Don't you?'

'Nope. I'd want to know then what I know now so that when I made the exact same mistakes, I'd be able to enjoy them this time around.'

She asked, 'This about that girl you were in love with?'

'Among other things.'

'What about her?'

'Maybe this time 'round I'd know how to keep her.'

'Then it wouldn't have been the same mistake.'

'In that case . . .' I shrugged, 'maybe I'd know how to make it hurt a lot less.' I changed the subject. 'So, ya'll coming to London or not?'

'My children would never allow me to run off to Europe with a man I've never met. My mother would object too. So would Ruby. Instead, shall we say sunset at the top of the Empire State Building?'

'Empire State Building?' I didn't get it. 'Sunset's fine but . . . they serve ice-cream there?'

'Bad sign,' she said. 'You don't like old movies, huh?'

'Old movies?'

She prodded, 'Couple meets at the top of the Empire State Building?'

'How old?'

'Real old.'

'Ah . . . yeah . . . kind of rings a bell . . . something about Seattle?'

'*Sleepless in Seattle?*'

'That's it.'

'Too bad, K.C. Doone, wrong generation.'

'Who, you and me?'

'No. Tom Hanks and Meg Ryan.'

'I woulda thought they were kind of our age, aren't they? Aren't we?'

'I'm referring to romantic generation.'

'What's romantic generation? That anything like culinary synergy?'

'No, it's more like Cary Grant and Deborah Kerr.'

'Cary Grant?' That funny Alan Sherman song flew into my mind. 'All day, all night, Cary Grant. What can he do, that I can't . . .'

'What's that?' she laughed.

'Old song. Real old. Goes with old movie, real old. Actually I know a lot about a few old movies. Saw *Gone With the Wind* three times. My mama's favourite.' Then I added, 'And *Casablanca*. Did you know that he never actually says, Play it again, Sam?'

'Yes, I do know that. Every old film buff does. What about *An Affair to Remember?*'

'He doesn't say that either.'

'Ever see it?'

'Is that the one . . .' I took a guess, 'about the *Titanic* sinking?'

'No, that's *A Night to Remember*.'

'Oh. So we're not talking 'bout one night, we're talking 'bout a whole affair.'

'I don't know what you're talking about, K.C. Doone. I'm referring to a movie with Cary Grant and Deborah Kerr where they meet at the top of the Empire State Building.'

I finished the song. '. . . big star, big deal, Cary Grant.'

'I am impressed with your choice of music. Though, I must admit, I might have considered running off to Europe with you had you said, oh yes, *An Affair to Remember*, wasn't that a remake of a film starring Charles Boyer and Irene Dunne?'

'Really? You would have?'

'Really, I wouldn't have. But you would have impressed me.'

'I would have impressed me too,' I told her. 'Never heard of any of those folk.'

'Ever heard of a movie called *Love Affair*?'

'That the one 'bout Lou Gehrig?'

'Who? The baseball player?'

'Yeah, seems to me I saw that one. But it wasn't starring either of those people you mentioned.'

'This is the original one where they meet at the top of the Empire State Building?'

'Nope. This one's where they hit home runs at Yankee Stadium.'

'Made in nineteen thirty-nine?'

'Must be a different Lou Gehrig.' I could hear her chuckling, so I tried again. 'Wanna come to London?'

'Nope. But I'll meet you at the top of the Empire State Building.'

'Sounds like a plan.'

'You promise?'

'It's a promise,' I said.

'That's two promises today.'

'Two? What was the first?'

'Not very inspiring, a man who forgets his promises.'

'No, I remember, precisely. Just remind me.'

'You said you'd send me a postcard from London.'

'That's right. Just testing.'

'Does that mean you're going?'

I heard myself saying, 'Guess it does' then telling her, 'Yeah, I think so.' And by that time, I was almost convinced. 'You didn't talk me out of it.'

'Maybe that's what a good devil's advocate should do, but it's not necessarily what a friend should do.'

'No?'

'No. The biggest favour a friend can do is always let the other person decide for himself. *Bon voyage.*'

I said, 'I will send you that postcard.' And when we hung up, I phoned Hussein and asked, 'Ya'll told me you can get me to London and back.'

He said, 'Mister, when do you want to fly?'

With my mind still not totally made up, I answered, 'Today. Tomorrow. How about . . . in the next half-hour?'

Chapter Twenty-one

'I think I am going to be ill,' Whitestone said.

'What's wrong?'

'I'm feeling very nauseous.'

'Maybe . . . ah . . .' My brain was still filled with cobwebs as I tried to think of something helpful. 'Maybe you should take off your shoes . . . and loosen your collar.'

'My collar is loose.' He spoke slowly and deliberately. 'What's more, the last time I took off my shoes, you objected.'

'This is different.' I helped him yank off his shoes. 'Now take some deep breaths. Lean back . . . very deep breaths.'

He tilted his head back, opened his mouth and started breathing very loudly. 'My medication.'

'Where is it?' Instinctively I reached for his jacket. 'Have you got it with you?'

'No. It's upstairs.'

'Oh.' I left his jacket hanging where it was, looked up at the ceiling and thought to myself, *maybe I should try to climb out.*

Don't you dare mention it, the little voice cautioned.

I argued, *but if he gets sick in here . . .*

Yeah, the voice retorted, *and if we get zapped up there . . .*

'I wish we had some water or something . . .'

'I wish . . . frankly . . . Mr Doone . . . I wish we weren't trapped in here.'

'Look . . . maybe . . .' *What the hell,* I told the voice, *I can't spend my entire life punting.* 'Maybe if you boost me up high enough I can get out past whatever it is that's sparking up there and get some help . . .'

'I shall need my medication soon. I'm being treated . . .' He stopped, then shook his head to say never mind. 'I don't think I can lift you . . . I feel very weak. Anyway, it does neither of us any good if you climb up there and get electrocuted or start a fire . . .'

'But if you're going to get sick in here . . .'

'I'm very sorry . . .' He leaned forward, putting his head in his hands. 'I don't believe I have the strength . . .'

The only thing I knew about medical emergencies I'd learned from watching *ER* with Lorilee – she had the hots for George Clooney – and that's how I knew he shouldn't be sitting all slumped over like that. 'Maybe if you sat up. Maybe . . . I know, maybe we should take a walk.'

'A walk?'

'Yeah.' I stood up. 'Come on. We can even make it real interesting by walking somewhere nice.'

'In here?'

'That's right,' I said, 'Watch,' and showed him how we could walk in place. 'Come on. It's like exercise. To get our hearts beating. Wake us up. Get us breathing better.' I offered my hand to help him stand up. 'I'm sure this will make you feel better. It will be good for both of us.'

'Mr Doone . . .' He sat where he was. 'I am very weary of this lift . . .'

Still walking in place, I said, 'So here we are in Central Park on a Sunday morning and it's spring and we're checking out all the girl joggers.'

'. . . and, indeed, wearier still, of you.'

'Trust me,' I said, reaching again for his hands.

'Mr Doone . . . please . . .' He stared at me.

I kept my hand extended, offering it to him. 'Come on.'

And then, very slowly, he stood up.

'That's good. Let's take a walk.'

Reluctantly, he began shuffling his feet.

'How about that chick over there in the day-glo tank-top?'

He stopped. 'This is ridiculous.'

'Come on, keep walking, once around the reservoir.'

'Mr Doone . . . I don't think you understand . . .'

'I love day-glo tank-tops.'

'. . . that I am a sick man . . .'

'Well, a little fresh air . . .' I took a deep breath. 'Smell the spring?' But the elevator just smelled of us. 'Spring always smells real nice.'

He shut his eyes, sighed out loud, shook his head several

times, then, as if he'd resigned himself to humouring me, started moving his feet again.

'Good . . . breathe deep . . . Think tank-tops . . . but . . .' I was the one who stopped walking. 'Ah . . . gee . . . there's just one thing.'

He stopped too. 'What is it?'

'You see . . . facing each other this way . . . we're walking towards each other. If we're gonna pretend we're walking together we've gotta do it side by side . . .'

'That's all, Mr Doone. That's enough.' He grabbed at the cage door and shook it violently. 'I must get out of here. Enough. I have had enough of being trapped in this place and more than I can stand of you.' He started screaming, 'Help! Help! Help!'

'Sir Tommy, please . . .' I took him by his shoulders. 'Okay, all right, I'll try to climb out. I'll do it. I'm sure that if I go slowly I can . . .'

He spun around, his face only a few inches above mine. 'You don't understand, Mr Doone. I am going to die.'

'No, you're not. We're gonna be fine. We're gonna make it. I'll get us out of here. Right now.'

He stared at me, then repeated, this time in a whisper, 'I am going to die.'

I thought he meant then and there.

Chapter Twenty-two

I needed to get to Newark, New Jersey, which normally isn't too difficult, 'cept at that time of the afternoon it seemed like everybody on earth was going to Newark, New Jersey, and all of us were trying to fit through the Holland Tunnel together.

Then, when my taxi pulled up to the airport, I had to walk clear across to the other terminal 'cause the driver let me out at the wrong place.

Then, I had to stand in line for half an hour at the check-in 'cause Tri-State Airways only had one person at one counter handling the entire flight.

Then, when it was my turn, that one guy behind that one counter chastised me for not checking in at least two hours before the flight. As it was a mere forty-five minutes before the flight, he said the only seat I could have was in the middle of a middle row at the rear of the plane and that my carry-on – just my usual sports bag – was too big and therefore had to be checked.

I made the mistake of arguing that it fit under the seat. He retorted, not only wouldn't it fit under the seat, but if I didn't check it in the way he was telling me to, it would be too late to check in any luggage and I'd have to go without it. I asked for his supervisor. He said he was the supervisor.

Putting on my most polite tone, I tried, 'Ya'll sure this won't fit under the seat or in the overhead locker?'

'I'm all sure. And not only am I all sure, I'll prove it to you.' He grabbed the bag, motioned for me to follow – despite the growling of the fifteen or twenty people behind me still waiting on line – and marched all the way down to the other end of the hall. He pointed to a metal contraption that, he insisted, every carry-on bag needed to fit into. Dropping my bag on top of it, he noted it didn't fit. 'See?'

I asked, 'Can I try?'

He snapped, 'You can try all you want but that bag of yours isn't going to fit.'

'Maybe it will.' I opened it, took out a sweater, put it on, took out my raincoat – which I had 'cause when Hussein sold me this ticket he promised me it always rained in London – put it on, took out the envelope with the print-outs, squeezed them into the inside pocket of the raincoat so he didn't count the envelope as another carry-on, then easily slipped my bag inside the slot. I grinned. 'Okay?'

'Not at all.' He pointed at my laptop computer bag. 'Only one carry-on. You'll still have to check the bag.'

'How 'bout . . .' I took my sports bag out of the contraption, laid the computer inside it sideways so it wouldn't be too wide, rearranged my clothes 'round the computer bag, stuffed my socks and underwear into my raincoat pocket, and again got the bag to fit through the slots. 'How's that?'

He made a face, turned on his heels and marched back to the check-in. I grabbed my bag and hurried after him. He handed me my boarding pass and an 'Okay For Carry On – Tri-State Airways With A Smile At Your Service' tag for my bag, looked over my shoulder and shouted, 'Next?'

I mumbled, 'Ya'll have a nice day,' walked to the end of the check-in area, took the computer out of my sports bag, put my socks, underwear and the print-outs back into it, took off my raincoat and sweater, put them back in the bag, threw both bags over the same shoulder and went to the gate.

The flight was totally full, which I might not have minded so much had I not been stuck in such a terrible seat. The computer fit under the seat but the sports bag didn't, and the overhead lockers were already full. The stewardess, reminding me that she was just doing her job, put my sports bag in the toilet for take-off, then returned it to me where it sat under my feet for the rest of the flight. The food was horrible. The movie sound didn't work. And we were totally on the other side of the ocean before I managed to get a little sleep. A couple of hours later I woke up at some airport I'd never heard of called Luton in England.

For a one ninety-nine round trip ticket, which in the end actually wound up costing two twenty-four, the little voice in the back of my head decided, *we can't rightly expect a gourmet meal or a movie with sound.*

Or, I added, *a real airport.*

Getting off the plane exhausted, I was slightly amused that everybody suddenly talked funny. That the cars drove on the wrong side of the street. That Hussein had lied, 'cause it wasn't raining. Sure, I'd heard British accents before, and been in cars on the wrong side of the street before – it works like that in a bunch of the islands – but the fact that it was a real sunny morning prompted the voice to suggest, *this is a good sign.*

I gave a woman at a bank a handful of money. She gave me back only a few colourful bills with funny pictures on them, plus couple of tiny coins. I bought myself a ticket on a crowded train from the airport into town, then a ride in one of those London taxis.

Just like my friend's station car, I decided, 'cept better 'cause it was cleaner and newer. Cleaner and newer than taxis in New York, too. And more comfortable. Besides the fact that my knees weren't banging on the seat in front of me, the way they always do in New York cabs, the thing didn't bounce around like New York cabs.

The driver was polite, he didn't cheat me on the fare – at least it seemed reasonable enough, until I remembered he was talking pounds, not dollars – and when I walked into my tiny hotel in some place called South Kensington, where Hussein had booked me a room, the woman was actually pleasant and expecting me.

For the first time in twenty-four hours, things had gone mostly right.

I'd gotten up the morning before at my usual ultimate clock-radio crack-a-dawn time, stumbled around thinking maybe I should go, talking myself out of it – *what the hell am I gonna do when I get there* – then trying to convince myself, *I gotta go 'cause it's for my mama.*

Reckoning that if I was going, I'd need to pay for it, I checked Kevin's pick of the day – he liked Intel and Cisco Systems – wondered if he knew something I didn't, and got into the market before the opening bell. I bought Intel and Cisco Systems, then also bought TexMexCan 'cause I was hoping it would stay lucky for me.

Within a few minutes of the NASDAQ opening, I also took a position on a technology company CNBC was touting called Mainframe Mann. The bump theory worked and I sold a few minutes later with a $3/16$ths profit. But Intel and Cisco headed south and although TexMexCan was lucky again, by the time I cashed out, just before ten, I was down $430.

The phone started ringing.

My mama wanted me to know, 'I've gotten another letter from those people. And Mrs Hutchinson from the other side of the court moved out this morning and someone put a note through my door saying that the service charges would have to be raised.'

That was enough to convince me to tell Hussein, 'Get me on a plane tonight.'

Next, just as I was reaching for the phone to dial Izzy, Debbie called. 'Maynard and Cotton know that we're looking for something, that's why I can't talk to you right now. But they don't know what we're looking for. Don't call me at the office. I'll be in touch.'

Then Hussein was back on the line. 'Okay, mister, yes, I can get you on a flight tonight to London. I've got the airline on the other line and they need to know now, otherwise they'll sell the seat to the next person who phones.'

'I'll take it.' I hung up with him and dialled Izzy. 'I don't know what's going on at GCB, but Pinky and a girl there named Debbie are trying to find something and they may be getting into trouble. I can't call there. Can you? Or, maybe better, get a hold of Pinky tonight and find out what's happening. I don't want them doing what I fear they're doing, which is getting in way over their heads.' I also told him 'bout my mama's call, and how I was going to London to find Whitestone.

He warned, 'Don't forget the time difference. Five hours. So you won't always find me here if you need me. When it's nine in the morning in London, it's four in the morning in New York. If you phone me at nine in the morning London time, I won't be awake yet. So write this down.' He gave me a Brooklyn number. 'It's my apartment. That way, if I'm not yet awake, you'll reach me there.'

That out of the way, I tried to think 'bout what I needed to take with me but I couldn't focus on anything 'cept having blown more money on the market. So I got back on line and spent the rest of the morning trading in and out of anything that CNBC said looked good. For a while I was actually ahead. But by lunchtime the market had flattened out and I slipped back into the red. Still, I'd advanced on the morning losses and was only down a couple a hundred bucks for the day.

Just before I started to pack, I remembered I needed access numbers from Re in order to get on line from London. A woman at their help desk told me, 'All of our overseas access numbers are on the Re website.'

'So from London,' I wanted to know, 'how do I get on to your website if I don't have an access number to get on line in the first place?'

'How about,' she said, as if I should have thought of it first, 'you look up the numbers before you leave?'

Hanging up with her, I did just that.

Then Debbie phoned again. 'They are on to us. I can't talk now. But we're on to them too. It's now a race to see who figures out who's the fastest.'

Then someone from Five Boroughs phoned, to ask when they could deliver Lorilee's stuff. I said I wouldn't accept it.

Not five minutes later, Lorilee phoned to threaten me. 'Ya'll take back that stuff or else.'

'Or else what?'

'Or else Duke is gonna personally show up and ram it down your throat.'

'How 'bout,' I suggested, 'he brings it over tomorrow, 'round noon?'

'He'll be there.'

I grinned, hung up, then decided Izzy had to know. 'Lorilee and Duke just threatened me.'

'Great,' he said. 'At least we've frightened one out of three. You understand, I'm counting them as one.'

'What do you mean, at least?'

'Ah . . .' he said. 'Funny you should mention it. I was going to phone you. I got a fax just now from my friend Pauly.'

'Who's Pauly?'

'My friend.'

'Besides being your friend?'

'In Miami,' he said. 'I told you about Pauly.'

'Never heard of Pauly.'

'You forgot. This forgetting things all the time,' he said, 'is very worrying. Especially for someone your age . . .'

I disregarded that. 'Tell me again, who's Pauly?'

'He's that fellow I went to law school with who now lives in Miami. You know, Pauly whose sister married that basketball player. I told you.'

'Oh,' I said, shaking my head 'cause it seemed easier than repeating that I'd never heard of him.

'Well, I brought him into the case as a consultant. He's been looking into that sweepstakes company. He says it doesn't look like we can do anything. Unless of course, we can prove that they've been deliberately deceptive. You know, set out to defraud people . . . which, I'm afraid, could mean that your mother may lose her apartment.'

'Not a chance,' I snapped. 'If I have to wring the bastard's neck with my own two hands.'

'Don't do that in London,' he warned, 'because I can't defend you over there. You have to do that here. And don't worry about the law suit. That I can handle from here. Although I haven't yet managed to get in touch with Cousin Harry because he's playing golf.'

'Law suit? You mean we're not just threatening GCB, you've filed a suit against them?'

'Not quite,' he said. 'But I told you already.'

'You told me you threatened to sue them for ten million bucks.'

'I also told you that they were suing you for twelve million.'

'Doing what? Izzy, you never told me . . .'

'That's right. They've filed against you for twelve million. Actually, twelve point four, to be exact, but it sounds a little better when you round it down . . .'

'You never mentioned . . . twelve million?'

'Breach of fiduciary trust. They're now saying that when you resigned . . .'

'I never resigned.'

'They're saying that you told them, you can't fire me because I quit.'

'No way. Not true,' I insisted, trying to remember what I actually said which, I had to admit to myself, might have sounded something like that. 'Anyway, Izzy, you never mentioned anything at all about a law suit.'

'Don't get so upset. It's nonsense. It's to balance out our claim against them. So you know what I'm going to do? Instead of threatening to sue for ten million, we'll do what Cousin Harry said I should have done in the first place and we'll sue them for twenty million. We'll settle for half. They'll settle for half. We'll split the difference and you still come out ahead.'

'When did all this happen?'

'I got the papers this morning.'

'Terrific,' I mumbled. 'What the hell happens if they come out ahead?'

'They're not going to. You don't understand lawyers. It's all nonsense. We make a living creating paperwork. That's where the real money is. No one actually wants to sue anybody because going to court takes away from creating more paperwork. Believe me, the money is in the paperwork.'

As soon as I hung up with him, Hussein phoned back. 'Mister, you're booked out of Newark tonight for London. The flight is scheduled to leave at eight. You've got to be there two hours ahead which means six. You'll get into London at something like about nine tomorrow morning. I'll send your tickets to you by messenger right now. The price is one ninety-nine, including tax, just like I said it would be, except for the ten bucks I have to charge for the messenger and the fifteen bucks that I have to add on because I needed to bribe somebody to get you on the flight tonight because it's full. Do you need a hotel? I can highly recommend the Thurloe Court, where I am certain you will find the accommodation to your satisfaction.'

'Whoa,' I stopped him. 'Just a second. Now it's two twenty-four.'

'Mister, the flight is totally booked. The only way to make a reservation with them on a totally booked plane is to take care of the person who handles the booking.'

I had to know, 'What's the airline?'

'Tri-State.'

'Who?'

'Mister, believe me, I send many people to England with them and no one ever complains.'

I told myself, *don't ask why no one ever complains in case the answer is, 'cause no one ever returns.* 'An airline I never heard of . . . and you say this is a scheduled service?'

'Absolutely mister. They fly to London every Thursday night.'

'Once a week?'

'In each direction.'

'Wait a minute. When am I booked to come home?'

'Next week.'

'I don't want to stay a week. I want to go for two or three days. You never said anything about staying a week?'

'Who says you have to stay a week?'

'The fella flying the plane 'cause he only does it in that direction on Fridays.'

'Mister, when you are ready to come home, you can phone me. Like last time with Florida.'

'And what happens if it's not a Friday?'

'There are many airlines flying between London and New York,' he assured me. 'Some of them are even direct. Now, what about that hotel? And have you packed a raincoat?'

I phoned my mama to tell her I was gonna be out of town for a few days – I thought maybe I should tell her where I was going and why, then ruled it out 'cause I didn't want her believing the situation was as desperate as I reckoned it was. I found my passport, stuffed all the clothes I needed into my sports bag, took that copy of *Day Trader* magazine I still hadn't finished reading and added that to the bag. Then I took my laptop, put all the files I'd downloaded on to a disk and left it to charge while I ran over to that place where they print out stuff. On the way back, carrying a big folder of print-outs, I stopped at the bank to fill up with cash.

By five, I was on the street hailing a taxi.

Here we go, the voice said, as I climbed in.

Here we go, I agreed.

How come we're so nervous? the voice asked.

Who's nervous? I answered the voice and told the driver, 'London, England, please.'

My room at the Thurloe Court was tiny but clean. There was a television set – I turned it on and found CNN but couldn't find CNBC – and a telephone on a little table next to the bed. I checked the plug, only to discover that my modem wouldn't fit 'cause British phone plugs were the wrong size. That got me thinking 'bout electricity, and sure enough British electrical plugs were the wrong size too. Not to mention real weird looking.

Time to buy some adaptors, the voice announced.

First things first. I eyed the bed and had no trouble convincing myself, *nap time.*

It was just after eleven in the morning and the thought did cross my mind that I should probably phone down to the front desk and ask the woman there for a wake-up call at, like around two. That would be enough. Then I decided, why bother, I'll wake up anyway in a couple of hours. I got undressed and climbed between the sheets.

The next thing I knew it was five.

It took me a while to get oriented, then to take a fast shower, then to remember that it was Friday and to realize that if I was gonna find Whitestone in the next couple of days, I'd need his address. So I opened the phone book, found a number for that magazine *Private Eye,* phoned over there and asked for the editor.

He wouldn't get on the phone.

I asked for his secretary.

She wouldn't get on the phone either.

I told the person who'd answered the phone what I wanted. 'It's about Sir Tommy Whitestone.'

Magically, a fella came on the line to find out, 'What about him?'

I said I was doing some investigative journalism.

He asked, 'Who for?'

I said, 'Magazine in the States . . .' looked at the one on the dresser and announced, *'Day Trader.'*

That must have been good enough for him, 'cause now he said, the person I really needed to speak to was a Fleet Street hack named Tel Wright.'

'Who?'

'Too Right Tel.'

'What's that mean?'

'That's his name.'

'Too Right Tel?'

'Tel Wright.'

I still didn't get it. 'And what's a Fleet Street hack?'

'A journo.'

'What's a journo?'

'A journalist.'

'Oh. And how do I find this fella?'

He gave me a number. While it was still ringing the first time, a man answered, 'Wright.'

I told him my name, said that *Private Eye* had given me his and explained that I was looking into some matters involving Sir Tommy Whitestone.

He said, 'What for?'

I said, 'I'm an investigative journo.'

He said, 'Bully for you.'

I said 'Oh' thinking to myself that maybe investigative and journo were words that don't work together. 'I'm trying to get to him.'

'He'll talk to you,' Too Right Tel volunteered. 'You can get to him easily enough as long as you avoid all of the hangers-on around him, especially Mary Beth DeSantis. She's his front-line protection. His secretary. Might as well be a bodyguard because she's got a black belt temper. Been in love with him for years. Her and every other woman working for him. They all protect him. You must also stay away from Noel Zachary. He's the PA, you know, personal assistant. All around henchman. Christ only knows, he might be in love with Whitestone too. Not that he's ginger, but he'd take a bullet for his boss. They all would. If you can avoid them, Whitestone will talk to you. But after he does, he'll sue you. What else do you want to know?'

'What's ginger?'

'Ginger beer.'

'What's ginger beer?'

'Queer.'

It took a moment before I figured it out. 'Oh.' Then I asked, 'So where do I find Whitestone?'

'Exactly where you wouldn't expect to. When he's in London, he works out of his home. Never goes to the office during the week. But he always goes there at weekends. Without the Rottweilers. He tries to be unconventional and winds up ticking like a clock. Just stand outside his office on a Saturday or Sunday and eventually he'll show up.'

'That simple?'

'What else?'

'Addresses?'

He gave me the address of Whitestone's house in a London

suburb called Richmond, plus the address of his office on a small
dead-end street off St James's, right in downtown London.

I asked, 'How 'bout some phone numbers?'

He gave me a whole bunch of them for both addresses, then
cautioned, 'Ringing is the surest way to wind up being told,
bugger off.'

'What's that mean?'

'How long you been in England?'

'Got here today.'

He promised, 'You'll figure it out. Good luck.' And just as
fast as he'd answered the phone, that's how fast he hung up.

Now I called down to the woman at the front desk, 'How far
is Richmond, please?'

But she was intent on telling me, 'You know that I am
Hussein's mother's schoolhood friend, don't you? Did he tell
you that? I know he is a very good personal friend of yours . . .'

'Absolutely,' I said, 'a very good personal friend. Which is
why he recommended your hotel so highly. Now, what I'd like
to know is how far Richmond is?'

'He always sends me his best customers,' she said. 'I haven't
seen him in several years now . . .'

'Yeah, well, he told me to make sure I brought you his very
best regards. And to tell you he'll be over to see you one of these
days . . . Now, 'bout getting to Richmond?'

'Did he happen to say when he planned on coming over? I
would like to reserve a room for him . . .'

'No, but next time I speak to him, I'll be sure to ask. Now,
can ya'll please tell me how to get to Richmond?'

'By tube? Maybe twenty minutes. Thirty tops.'

'Tube?'

'Underground.'

I took that to mean Subway, heard the voice say *no time like
the present*, got into my clothes, got a Subway map in the lobby,
followed her directions to South Kensington Station – which
turned out to be only down the block – got on a District Line
train to some place called Earls Court, got off there, asked a
gentleman on the platform for the next train to Richmond –
he pointed to the train I'd just gotten off – I jumped back on
and fourteen minutes later wound up in Richmond.

There was a taxi stand at the station, I showed the first driver
in line the address I wanted, he said, 'Know it,' motioned for me

to jump in the back, and just as the meter clicked over to three pounds, announced, 'Here we are.'

He deposited me at a set of gates that guarded a large, three-storey red-brick house with vines crawling up the front. I waited till the cab pulled away, found a bell to push on the wall next to the gate, took a deep breath and pushed it.

Nothing happened.

So I pushed it again.

This time a woman's voice asked, 'Yes, please?'

'Ah . . . hello . . . I'm here for Sir Tommy Whitestone.'

'Who is calling, please?'

'My name is Doone. K.C. Doone.' I almost added, *the guy he ran away from in New York,* but I knew that wouldn't be helpful.

'Have you got an appointment?'

'Ya'll might say that. Though I suppose I'm a little late.'

She asked me to wait there for a moment. I did. Then a man's voice came over the speaker. 'Hello, may I help you?'

'I'm looking for Sir Tommy Whitestone.'

'This is him. May I help you?'

'K.C. Doone. From New York.'

'Doone?' He paused. 'Mr Doone? From New York?'

'We met in the garage at the Waldorf Towers.'

'Mr Doone?' He said, 'Indeed, what a pleasant surprise. Just a moment.'

The front door of the house opened and out he came, lumbering down the steps and along the driveway, waving at me like we were old friends. 'What on earth . . . how nice to see you again.' He was wearing a white shirt and tie but no jacket. 'Mr Doone . . .' Coming right up to the gate, he gave me one of those big smiles, reached through and shook my hand.

I gave him my biggest smile in return. 'I thought we were gonna have a chat at nine the other morning.'

'Mr Doone, I am so sorry. I didn't have a number where I could reach you. And I needed to return to London. But what on earth are you doing here?'

'Came to see you,' I said. 'Like I tried to explain in New York, it's concerning my mama's apartment in Florida and a couple of your companies . . .'

'Oh yes,' he said. 'You did indeed mention that.'

He still wasn't giving me any sign that he knew anything 'bout those companies.

'See, they're running this sweepstakes thing . . .'

'Mr Doone.' He held up his hand. 'I know this is going to sound very rude of me, but I am in the middle of something . . . it's rather important . . . how long will you be in London?'

I lied, 'Couple of days.'

'Well, then, how would tomorrow be? Here, tomorrow, say, end of the morning?'

'Ya'll want me to come back? And this time you're gonna be here?'

He gave me another big smile. 'Tomorrow. End of the morning. And please excuse me for this evening.' He extended his hand. 'What a surprise.'

I shook it. 'Here. Tomorrow. End of the morning. That's what, 'round eleven?'

'Indeed. Let's call it eleven.' He nodded, 'Tomorrow, then?'

'Right. Tomorrow, then. Here. At eleven.' I stepped back from the rail. 'Okay. Thanks.' He waved one more time and walked back into the house. I started down the street, only to discover that I was now a real long walk from wherever it was I wanted to be.

He'll be there this time, I kept reassuring the voice. *He's out of excuses.*

The voice simply responded, *'member that bridge in Brooklyn?*

By the time I got back to South Kensington, all the stores were shut so I couldn't get any adaptors for the phone or the electricity. But there were plenty of restaurants that were open and I wound up having a meal. I couldn't get to sleep – 'cause even though I was tired, midnight was still only seven in New York – and by two in the morning I was thinking 'bout phoning Patsy, to say Hi from London. But I couldn't figure out how to dial the States and when I phoned down to the front desk, no one answered. I guess I eventually drifted off by four. It must have been that late, 'cause when I woke up it was 10.15.

I lay there for a few minutes, telling myself *I'm in London, England,* then recalling that I was supposed to be in Richmond, England by eleven.

Christ.

I jumped out of bed, washed, dressed, raced out of the hotel and on to the subway. This time the train seemed to take longer than it had last night. So did the taxi ride. Still, I was ringing the bell at Whitestone's gate by 11.20.

The same woman who'd answered it yesterday answered it this morning. 'Sir Tommy please.'

'Who is it?'

'K.C. Doone. He's expecting me.'

'He is?'

'Yeah, he is.'

'Are you sure?'

'I'm sure. He told me to be here at eleven. Sorry that I'm a little late . . .'

'He told you that?'

'Yeah . . . why?' Where is he?'

'Sir Tommy? He went to Paris.'

Sunnuvabitch! the little voice screamed.

I demanded, 'What do ya'll mean he went to Paris?'

But all she knew was, 'He said he was going to Paris.'

'Where is he in Paris?'

'I don't know . . . but maybe at his house.'

'When's he coming back?'

'I don't know . . . but maybe not for a week.'

I stormed back to South Kensington, found out that there was a train I could take to Paris, just like that checked out of the hotel and climbed back on the Subway, this time aiming for Waterloo Station.

'Paris,' I said to the woman at the Eurostar ticket counter, when I'd finally snaked my way through the long line of people wanting to do the same thing. 'Paris, France.'

'When will you be travelling?' she asked in an obviously disinterested way.

'Right now? When's the next train? How long does it take?'

'It takes three hours. The next train is in fifteen minutes. Do you have a reservation?'

'Nope. I need to buy a ticket.'

'No reservation?'

'Nope.'

'Sorry. The train is fully booked.' She looked over my shoulder. 'Next?'

'Wait a minute. Fully booked? I only need one seat.'

'Sorry. Next?'

'No. Not sorry. Not next. How can I get to Paris today?'

'There's an information booth just outside . . . this queue is for ticket purchases . . .'

'Okay, so I wanna purchase a ticket. Now, when have ya'll got a train with a seat for Paris?'

She showed her annoyance with me by sighing, 'When do you want to travel?'

'Today. Right now if I could.'

'I've already told you sir, the next train is fully booked.'

'How 'bout the train after that?'

She pretended to check her computer. 'When will you be coming back?'

I wasn't planning on coming back, 'cause in my mind I was thinking that I'd get to Whitestone, resolve the problem once and for all, and then either ask Hussein to finagle me on to a flight from Paris or just buy myself a damn ticket and get home that way. 'How 'bout if I only want to go one way?'

'Then you won't be permitted to take advantage of a special round-trip fare.'

'Okay, if a round trip is cheaper, then I'll take a round trip.'

'Sir, if you want to purchase a round-trip ticket, I will need to know when you want to return.'

'Monday at noon,' I said, 'cause it was the first thing that popped into my head.

'I'm sorry, sir, there is no train at that time.'

'Any time, it doesn't matter 'cause I probably won't be on it anyway.'

'If you're only travelling one way, sir, then you can't buy a round-trip ticket.'

'Ya'll know what? I just decided I'm travelling two ways. So what's the closest train to noon Monday?'

'There is a train leaving Paris at eleven forty-three . . .'

'That's fine.'

'It's fully booked.'

'What's the first train after twelve noon?'

'That would be the twelve-nineteen . . .'

'That's fine. How about the twelve-nineteen?'

'If you were to purchase your ticket seven days in advance . . .'

'I just said this Monday . . .' I was getting nowhere. 'Ya'll got a supervisor?'

'He's not available,' she said.

'How 'bout I wait right here until he is?'

She shook her head in disdain, pulled herself up from her seat, went into the back room and came out with a very thin, mangy-looking man in his early twenties, whose voice actually trembled when he spoke. 'Can I help you, please? I understand you're trying to book a seat on trains that are either full or don't exist.'

I forced a smile. 'What say you and I start all over again? I need to get to Paris today. I don't know when I'm coming back. Now what can you do to help me?'

He looked over my shoulder at the long line of people still waiting, suggested, 'Would you please step down to the end of the counter, sir, so that this person can help the next customer.' There he leaned up real close to a computer screen and stared at it. 'When do you want to leave?'

'Now?'

'The next available train would be the fifteen twenty-three, arriving in Paris at nineteen twenty-three. One way or round trip?'

I said, 'Round trip.'

He said, 'When would you be coming back to London?'

I said, 'First train after twelve on Monday.'

He said, 'That would be the twelve nineteen. Now, if you were to book seven days in advance . . .'

'I can't book seven days in advance 'cause I need to get there today.'

'I'm only trying to be helpful, sir.'

'Appreciate it.' I took a deep breath. 'Tell you what, how about one seat on the next train to Paris, and one seat coming back any time Monday afternoon? Doesn't matter when. I'm flexible. Can you help me with that?'

'I'll try,' he said in a way to suggest that I shouldn't hold out much hope. He leaned up close to the computer screen again, this time punched a few keys on the keyboard, then announced, 'All our trains are very very crowded. But I have managed to find one seat for you on the fifteen twenty-three, arriving in Paris today at nineteen twenty-three, and one seat returning on Monday on the twelve nineteen, arriving in London at fourteen thirty. That will be one hundred and forty-nine pounds, please.'

I stared at him. 'How come that lady said the trains were fully booked?'

'They are, sir.'

'So how come you found seats?'

'At a different fare, sir.'

'What's the difference?'

'Sir,' he didn't disguise how weary he was of helping me, 'there are no seats available on these trains at any of our lower fares. However, there are seats available on these trains at one hundred and forty-nine pounds. Do you want it or not?'

I handed him a credit card. He handed me my tickets.

I wound up sitting in a near empty train for three hours, bored out of my skull, uncomfortable, munching on a real bad sandwich and drinking watery tea, crawling at a snail's pace through the English countryside – now Hussein was right 'cause it was pouring outside – trying to see what the Chunnel looked like, 'cept it was too dark. Eventually, I worked it out that for the same price I could sit on a plane for five and a half hours, eating bad food, being uncomfortable but at least get all the way from New York to Los Angeles.

When we pulled into some place called Gare du Nord, I got out, walked into the middle of the station and reminded myself, *I'm in Paris, France.*

A woman at the tourist booth in the station spoke English, was helpful enough to recommend a small hotel on the Left Bank, gave me a subway map – here they called it the Métro – phoned to make sure they had a room, and told me how to get there. By the time I checked in it was near on nine.

I walked around the neighbourhood, found a place to eat, went back to the hotel and tried to get to sleep. When I couldn't, I found out how to call the States and dialled my mama. 'Everything all right?'

She was crying again. 'Everything is not all right. I'm telling you, K.C., they're gonna throw me outta here.'

I promised, 'No, they're not, Mama,' calmed her down, then called Patsy. Her son answered and said that she wasn't home. I checked my watch. It was now midnight Paris time, which was six New York time. I didn't ask where she was and didn't leave a message.

The next morning I was up real early, telling myself that now all I had to do was find out where Whitestone hung out in Paris and hope that he was there. Only problem was, I didn't have a clue where to begin.

He wasn't listed in the Paris phone book – I hadn't really expected him to be – and the man who ran the hotel couldn't help me, even if he wanted to, 'cause he didn't speak any English. I tried calling Too Right Tel, but his number didn't answer. Then I remembered all those print-outs and thought maybe there'd be some clue in them. And while I did find one reference to his house in Paris – 'in a plush, right bank quartier' – there was nothing more precise than that.

I wondered 'bout those two families of his, with two different women sharing the same house – *Kiki and Lou*, the voice recalled – found their maiden names in the print-outs and started thumbing through the phone book looking for them. And while there were plenty of listings for folk named DuTronc and Giradot, none of them appeared to be called Giselle, Kiki, Letitia or Lou. Even reading through all the addresses, I had no idea which were plush and which weren't.

Still in a quandary by noon, I tried Too Right Tel again but there was still no answer.

No one goes to an office on a Sunday, the voice pointed out.

'Cept some people, I said, *like folks working on Monday's newspaper.*

I got a number for a paper called *Le Figaro*, looked for help there but couldn't find anybody who'd listen long enough.

I tried *Le Monde* and ran into the same problem.

Nobody wants to know, the voice said.

I thought, *more like nobody wants to understand.*

The voice came back with, *so let's find someone who speaks English.*

The phone book had a listing for Associated Press. I guessed that they spoke English and that they worked Sundays, and was right both times. 'Cept no one seemed to know where Whitestone lived. One guy thought it was on the Avenue Foch. Another said it was probably somewhere in someplace called 'New-ee'. I had him spell that for me and it turned out to be N-E-U-I-L-L-Y, which struck me as crazy having all those l's and not using them.

Anyway, the last person I spoke with at Associated Press had the best suggestion. She said, 'Call Sam at the *Herald Tribune*, he knows everything.' Unfortunately, she hung up before I could find out Sam who?

So I found a number for the *International Herald Tribune* –

oddly enough, they also turned out to be located in Neuilly –
but when I asked for Sam, the operator also wanted to know
'Sam who?'

I said 'He's an old friend of an old friend but our old friend
never told me his last name.'

The operator suggested, 'Sam Abt?'

I said, 'Sounds good to me.'

She said, 'Sorry, no one comes in on a Sunday till about
four.'

So I had to wait a whole bunch of hours before I could get
that Sam on the phone to find out if he was the right Sam.

Turned out he was.

I told Sam that some woman at Associated Press had suggested he knows everything and that I was looking for Sir
Tommy Whitestone, and Sam answered, 'Hold on a minute . . .'
When he came back on the line, he gave me Sir Tommy's
address.

'About as plush as anyone can get in Paris. Just off the Avenue
Foch on a tiny street called the Rue –' Sam was even kind
enough to spell it for me – 'M-A-R-C-E-A-U.'

I commented, 'No l's?' But he didn't get the joke. So I thanked
him, looked on my subway map, found out how to get there, and
headed off yet again to find Tommy Whitestone.

This house wasn't as wide as the one in Richmond but it was
taller – five storeys instead of three – and even if it didn't seem
as big, it was still a big house right smack in the middle of the
city. It was stone, obviously old, and this time instead of vines
growing up the front, it had wooden shutters on the outside of
every window. Each of the shutters was painted green and after
stepping back to take a good look, I decided I kinda liked that.

Town house this big, the voice decided, *on the east side of New
York . . . easily in the twenty-five-mil category.*

I thought to myself, *twenty-five million bucks is a lot of bread
even for such neat green shutters*, and rang the bell.

An older woman opened the door – she didn't look like a maid
but then she didn't look like she was someone's mistress, wife or
otherwise owner of such a place – and asked, '*Monsieur?*'

I said, 'Do ya'll speak English?'

She shook her head no, and shrugged as if to apologize.

I tried, 'Mr Whitestone? Sir Tommy? Here?' I pointed. 'At
home?'

'*Monsieur Vite-ston?*'

'Yeah,' I nodded. 'That's the one. Is he here?'

She motioned, '*Attendez une minute*,' which I took to mean *don't budge*, and shut the door.

I didn't budge, facing the door for several minutes, then stepped back to look again at the green shutters. I noticed that there were other houses on the street that also had shutters like that, before wondering if maybe what she'd said to me was the French equivalent of Too Right Tel's expression, *bugger off.*

Thinking that this was now taking too long, I was just about to ring the bell again, when the door opened and he was standing right there.

'Howdy. Remember me?'

'Mr Doone?' This time he was wearing what used to be called a smoking jacket – a paisley silk thing over a coloured shirt, with a pair of slacks and what I spotted to be very expensive loafers. 'Mr Doone . . .' He laid on yet another of those big smiles. '. . . you seem to be in Paris.'

'Only 'cause you are. Didn't ya'll say we were gonna meet yesterday? I think your exact words were, end of the morning? 'Round eleven?'

'Mr Doone . . .' He clasped both of his hands together as if he was praying. 'I did indeed. And yet again, I didn't have any way of getting in touch with you when my plans suddenly changed.'

'If I didn't know better, I'd think ya'll were avoiding me.'

'Mr Doone . . . I assure you that is not the case.'

'Thing is, I keep trying to tell you that there are these companies of yours in Florida . . .' I pointed to the hallway I could see behind him. 'Ya'll got a few minutes so I can explain this to you? I've come a real long way and I'd be grateful.'

'As a matter of fact, Mr Doone . . .' he pointed behind me, 'under any other circumstances . . .' Then he started talking perfect French. I spun around to find a well-dressed couple coming up the sidewalk, talking back to him in French. 'I'm afraid that your timing leaves a great deal to be desired, Mr Doone. Please excuse me for this evening. I'm sure you understand . . .' He reached over to greet the couple, kissed the woman on both cheeks, then kissed the man on both cheeks too. I stepped aside as he ushered them in, then turned to me, 'It is just so awkward at the moment.'

'Well . . . when won't it be so awkward? How's tomorrow? End of the morning? Say 'round eleven?'

'Tomorrow? End of the morning? At around eleven? All right.' He gave me another one of his smiles. 'That should be fine.'

I tried to remember the name of the place where I was staying. 'I'm at some small hotel over on the other side of town. I don't have the number with me, which I'd like you to have, so that this time you won't have any excuses . . .'

'Mr Doone,' he grinned and shrugged, 'then why don't I give you my number here and when you get back to your hotel, you can ring me. That way I'll have the number. Although I am sure that won't be necessary.'

'Fair 'nough,' I said.

He stepped inside, reached behind the door and came back with a printed card that showed his Paris address and phone number. 'There you are, Mr Doone . . .'

I looked at it, shot a glance at the number on the side of the building . . .

'You'll find they match.'

I smiled.

'Tomorrow?' he said. 'End of the morning? At eleven?'

'Yeah. Thanks. Tomorrow? End of the morning? Eleven on the dot.'

The first thing I did that night when I got back to the hotel was phone Sir Tommy, just like he asked me to. I left the number of my hotel with the lady who answered. It wasn't the lady who'd opened the door 'cause this lady spoke good English with one of those neat sexy French accents. I said thanks. She promised to give it to him.

The last thing I did that night, just before going to sleep, was phone Patsy. This time it was her daughter who answered, saying she was away for the weekend and wouldn't be home till late. I hung up, again without leaving a message, wondering who she went away with. I knew it wasn't any of my business, but I still wondered.

I put in a real early wake-up call – I wasn't gonna risk oversleeping this time – and by 9.30 found myself sitting in a café on the Avenue Foch, just a block away from his place, reading the *International Herald Tribune* and sipping a tiny cup of coffee that was so strong it almost didn't pour. I sat there for one hour and forty-five minutes, and at no time did anyone ask me to order something else or suggest that 'cause I was monopolizing a table I should take a hike.

With fifteen minutes to spare, I paid the bill, left the café, strolled over to Sir Tommy's house and rang the bell. The same woman who'd opened the door yesterday answered the door now. I asked for Sir Tommy and she said, '*Attendez une minute.*'

A moment later, another woman appeared – kinda pretty, with real nice eyes – and she asked, in English, 'May I help you, please?'

From her accent I decided she was the woman I'd spoken to last night. 'Ma'am, I'm K.C. Doone and I've got an appointment with Sir Tommy?'

'Monsieur Doone, yes, I know. You called here last night. I have been expecting you.'

I smiled and waited to be invited in.

'Monsieur Doone . . . did you not get the message? Obviously you did not.'

'What message?'

'The message we left for you this morning at your hotel. I am so sorry but Sir Tommy . . . I am afraid he is not here this morning.'

'When will he be back?'

'That . . . I do not know.'

'Can I wait?'

'Yes, of course . . . but, you know, it could be a long wait.'

'Why, where did he go?'

'India.'

Chapter Twenty-three

I took Whitestone by the shoulders and gently helped him lie back, as best he could, across the bench.

'Ya'll just stay real quiet and calm like that and . . .' I looked up towards the ceiling but in the dark I couldn't see very much . . . 'and I'm gonna get us outta here.'

'Don't do anything foolish,' he said softly.

'If I step up I think maybe I can pull myself through the trap door.'

'We've tried that once.'

More out of hope than anything else, I promised, 'I'll be all right. Ya'll just stay quiet right there.'

Supporting myself by stretching out my arms to hold both sides of the elevator, I put my foot on to the bench, careful not to step on him . . .

He offered, 'If I stand up to get out of your way . . .'

'No, it's okay. Stay there.' I only needed to boost myself enough to reach up and grab the little grated trap door at the top.

My fingertips grazed it.

But stretched like that I wasn't sure how I was gonna pull myself through it.

The little voice in the back of my head reassured me, *we'll find the strength somewhere 'cause we have to.*

'Be careful,' he repeated.

'Yeah,' I mumbled, pushing the grating real slow until it lifted away from the ceiling.

Put both hands inside the opening, the voice told me, *then pull us up like doing chin-ups.*

The grating moved higher, enough to take it off the supports that had been keeping it flush with the ceiling. And with it

balanced like that on my fingertips, I tried to slide back and
to the side.

I moved it an inch.

Then another inch.

Then there was a huge spark.

The elevator dropped.

He screamed, 'Oh God!'

My foot slipped out from under me.

A fraction of a second later the elevator came to an abrupt
stop, throwing me backwards on to the cage door.

'Dear God!' he screamed.

I landed half-sitting on the floor. 'Shit.'

And now I hurt.

'What happened?'

'I don't know.'

'Are we just hanging on a thread of the cable? We fell. The
lift fell. We could have been killed.'

'It only dropped a few inches.' I struggled to get back to
my feet.

'Don't move,' he warned. 'We're hanging by a thread.'

'I don't think elevators work that way,' I said, mainly 'cause
I didn't want to believe that maybe they did. 'Damn. I landed
square on my ass.'

'Careful. Here, sit down.' He moved his legs off the bench
to make room for me, then helped me down. 'Do you smell
anything burning? It smells like something is burning.'

I looked up at the trap door but couldn't see anything. 'I think
it was just a spark.'

'We're going to be consumed in a fire.'

'There's no fire,' I said, as much to convince me as him. 'It
was just the spark. Like last time.'

'But this time we fell. We're hanging on a thread.'

'We're gonna be all right. We just have to wait here, quiet
like, until help arrives.'

His breathing started to increase . . . 'We're hanging on a
thread . . .' and got real rapid real fast. 'As soon as we move, it's
going to crash to the ground and we're both going to be killed.'

'We're both gonna be okay. We're gonna sit here and not move
around and . . .' I tried to think of something. 'And we're gonna
play another game.'

'What?'

'That's what we're gonna do. We're gonna play another game.'

'I don't like the way you play games, Mr Doone.'

''Cause you can't win.'

He said quietly, 'I am ill . . . I'm not well enough to play another game with you . . .' Now he started mumbling. 'Not well enough . . . and now I will never get there on time . . . it's the bed I wanted . . . that's why I brought it there . . . that's the only thing that matters . . .' And his breathing kept increasing.

'What?'

'Thought I was crazy when I told them about the bed. I was born in that bed.'

'Come on, ya'll need to lie back again, all the way.' I started to move off the bench but he stopped me.

'Don't. We're hanging by a thread.'

'It's gonna be okay. I'm gonna move real slow. Watch.' I slid off the bench and kneeled on the floor. 'It's okay. Now put your feet up and lie all the way back.'

He started mumbling again. 'They thought I was crazy, but I knew where that bed should be. I knew where I wanted it and why . . .'

I asked, 'What bed?'

'What?'

'You just said something about a bed.'

'A bed.' He leaned slowly back. I grabbed his jacket and folded it under his head like a pillow, then helped him stretch his legs out and up along the side of the elevator.

'Is that better? Is that okay like that?'

'Bed,' he repeated. 'That's where we should be now. In bed. Not together, Mr Doone. Separate beds. Separate lifts too, Mr Doone . . .'

For a while he was calm, his breathing slowed and I thought it sounded like he was snoring.

I sat down, leaning back against the cage door, but my butt was killing me and being on the floor like that meant no matter how I turned I couldn't find a comfortable position. Sitting hurt so I slid on to my side, as best I could, and propped my head against the corner where the door met the wall, and for the longest time I lay kinda scrunched up into a foetal position, listening to his breathing as it grew slower.

After a time my own eyelids felt heavy and started to close.

He's asleep, I told myself.

Sleep, good idea, the voice said, *let's go to sleep.*

Okay, I said, *good idea . . . sleep . . .*

'If a tree falls in the forest . . .'

I was drifting off.

'. . . and no one is there to hear it . . .'

My head fell forward.

'. . . is there a noise?'

My chin crashed into the top of my chest. 'Huh?' My eyes popped open. 'Huh?' I looked around and realized I was still in the elevator. 'What?'

'What's the answer?' His breathing was getting rapid again. 'The answer to my question.'

'Huh? What question?'

'If a tree falls in the forest, Mr Doone, and no one is there to hear it, is there a noise?'

'Are you okay?'

'Well, is there a noise or not?' He seemed determined to know. 'What's the answer?'

'I don't know . . .'

'Think about it. If a tree falls in the forest and no one is there to hear it, is there a noise?'

'Okay.' I pretended to think about it, but all the time I kept trying to look at him in the dark and listen to the way he was breathing. 'Ah . . . I guess so, yes. There is a noise.'

'Why, is there any noise in here? In this lift? Right this moment?'

'Yeah, sure, us.'

'Besides us.'

'I guess besides us . . . no. No noise.'

'Are you sure?'

'I don't hear anything.'

'Does that mean there is no noise?'

'I suppose it kinda does.'

'I suppose it kinda doesn't,' he mimicked my accent. 'Actually, there is plenty of noise. It's just that we can't hear it. Come now, Mr Doone, if we had a radio, we could turn it on and hear music. But we don't have a radio so we can't hear any music. Still, the music is here.'

I nodded, 'Yeah, I guess.'

'So if a tree falls in the forest . . . and no one is there to

hear it, then there is no noise. Clearly that must be so . . .
just like . . . here.' His breathing rate suddenly increased and
he started to slur words. 'More Smarties . . . do . . . you . . .
where . . . could . . . more Smarties . . .'

'Are you okay . . .'

'Smarties?'

I reached into my raincoat pocket and brought out the torn
M&Ms wrapper. 'I'm sorry, there are no more.'

He began to tip forward.

Instinctively, I grabbed him to stop him from falling. 'What's
wrong?'

'If . . . a tree . . . in the forest . . .' He turned his face towards
me. 'I'm scared.'

'It's going to be all right,' I said, taking him in both hands to
make sure he wouldn't fall off the bench.

'I'm scared . . .' His body went limp. 'I am . . . going to be . . .
going to . . . be very very sick.'

And without any more warning he was, all over himself.

Chapter Twenty-four

India, the voice growled. *Yeah, sure. Why not, India? Or China? Or Timbuk-Goddamn-tu?*

I checked out of my hotel, stormed back to the Gare du Nord and piled on to the very same train I'd reserved just to get the round trip fare, never thinking I'd be on it or heading straight back like this to London.

For a boring, uncomfortable and extremely angry three-hour ride, I sat in a near-empty train – fully booked, my ass – furious with Whitestone for doing it to me again.

And just as furious with myself for letting him.

For three hours I sat in the damn train hearing his old girl-friend warning me, *never let the son of a bitch out of your sight.*

The minute I got to Waterloo Station, I went to a phone booth and called the Thurloe Court. 'Have ya'll got a room for me again, please?'

The woman there wanted to know, 'How many nights?'

I told her flatly, 'Indefinitely.'

She gave me the same room I'd checked out of two days before.

First thing I did after dumping my stuff there was phone Whitestone's house in Richmond to see if anyone there knew where he was, or if he could be reached, or when he was coming home.

The lady who answered, who sounded like the same lady who'd told me he'd gone to Paris, thought that's where he still was. Then I phoned his office, asked for him and got someone named, 'Miss DeSantis.'

'Oh . . . hello . . . I was looking for Mr Whitestone.'

'I'm sorry,' she said, 'but Mr Whitestone is out of the country. May I give him a message?'

'Gee . . . you wouldn't know when he's due back, by any chance?'

'May I ask who's calling, please?'

'My name is . . .' I looked around . . . 'Thurloe. I met him . . . the other evening, in New York, at the 200 Club dinner.'

'Oh yes,' she said.

'It was a real good speech and, well, we don't get many like him.'

'There aren't many like him. May I take a number so that I can ask him to return the call. I presume the area code is two one two . . .'

'Yeah, it is. But, no problem, I'll phone back. It's just that a bunch of us wanted to send him a little token of our appreciation. How's tomorrow? Will he be there then?'

'I'm afraid he won't,' she said.

'Otherwise . . . maybe we'll just send it to him direct. I could ship it tomorrow, you know, by Fedex, and he'll have it Wednesday. Where will he be on Wednesday?'

'If you'd like to send it to my attention here, I shall personally see that he gets it.'

'You see, ma'am, I would be . . . a little embarrassed 'bout having you open it. I'm afraid, it's a kinda jokey gift . . . a boys' kinda thing.'

'Oh. I see.'

'I hope I didn't shock you. Maybe the best thing is I just phone back tomorrow and perhaps ya'll be able to tell me when he next plans on being in London so that we can send it directly to him.'

But I couldn't talk her out of it. 'I assure you he will be the one to open it. If you would just send it to my attention . . .'

She was being too damned helpful. 'Hold on just a moment, please . . .' I needed to get off the phone with her, so I pretended to be speaking to someone in the room. 'I'm on a call . . . okay, tell him to hold on . . .' Back with her, I apologized, 'I'm sorry, I have to take another call. But, if I may, I will phone you tomorrow. Excuse me, I've got to go. Thank you for your assistance.' And hung up.

As long as I was gonna be in London for a while, I reckoned, it might be a good idea if I figured out some way to pay for it. So I asked the lady running the hotel where I could find a hardware store – there was one only a couple of blocks away – and walked over there to buy a British adaptor plug. The fella there handed me a big strange-looking thing that had three large rectangular pins in the front, and a small two-pin slot for my American plug in the back.

'It's really only for shavers,' he said.

'I want to use it for my laptop computer.'

He thought about that. 'Might work. Only a three-amp fuse in there. No good for toasters or vacuum cleaners or any heavy appliances.'

I assured him, 'I never travel with my own toaster or vacuum cleaner.'

'Then you won't have any problems.'

He didn't sell telephone plug adaptors, but pointed me in the direction of a place that did, 'bout ten minutes down the road. There, some fella assured me that adapting American telephone equipment to the British phone system was no problem, 'As long as it's BT-approved.'

'What's that mean?'

'BT . . . British Telecom.' He handed me a tiny plastic adaptor, one end of which fit into the phone socket here, the other end of which had a smaller socket to take my American plug. 'It means, you can only use an American phone here that's been approved by BT.'

'It's not for a phone.' Studying the adaptor, I couldn't understand what the problem would be. 'It's for my modem. You know, my computer.'

'Does it have a little green BT-approved sticker on it?'

'Ah . . . being American and all, I suppose it doesn't.'

'In order to use it with the British phone system, BT insists that it does.'

'And if it doesn't? Ya'll telling me it won't work?'

'It will work all right. It's just that if it doesn't have the little green BT-approved sticker, then it isn't BT approved.'

'So do I or don't I need some sort of different adaptor?'

'No.'

I stared at him. 'Ya'll saying that the same adaptor will work whether the modem is BT-approved or not?'

'That's correct.'

'Fine. I'll have one of these adaptors, please.'

He nodded. 'Three pounds, ninety-five.'

It came to almost seven bucks for this little piece of plastic. 'Kinda expensive, no?'

He raised his finger as if to say, you finally got the point. 'It's BT approved.'

Back at my room, the electrical plug fit into the socket where the lamp was, my computer power plug fit into the British adaptor, the BT-approved telephone adaptor fit into the telephone plug, my modem fit into the BT-approved adaptor, and after 'bout ten minutes of trying to figure out how to get my computer to dial nine for an outside line, I logged on to Re and pulled up my e-mail.

Besides a hill of junk – more porno stuff which I thought of forwarding to Binterman 'cause it might make me feel better, but in the end didn't 'cause I wasn't much in the mood – there were newsletters from Herbie and three messages from Debbie, all of which sounded like she was in a panic.

The first e-mail, dated Friday, read, 'We've got it. Pages of it. They didn't lose anything. Not even the five-twelve. I have copies of everything. Where are you?'

The second, dated Sunday, read, 'K.C., where are you? I keep getting your machine. I'm worried they may find out soon.'

The third was dated early this morning, New York time. 'K.C., this is serious. Call me.'

I was worried 'bout reaching her at the office, letting anyone there suspect that I was talking to her, so I e-mailed her. 'Kiddo, I'm in London, England, at a place called the Thurloe Court.' I gave her the number. 'Phone me here. Right away.' Then I rang the office.

Yolanda took the call and put me through. 'This is Debbie.'

All I said was, 'Check your e-mail,' then hung up and sat waiting for her to get back to me.

It took almost forty-five minutes. 'Where are you?'

I didn't have the heart to remind her that she'd just phoned me. 'London, England.'

'What are you doing there?'

'Long story. Where are you? Can you talk? What's happening?'

'I'm downstairs,' she said. 'I can talk a little bit. We found other sets of books. Well, Pinky did. He found it and then I copied everything. But Pinky says that may be a crime. You know, industrial espionage.'

'Doesn't sound like that to me,' I said, not sure if it was or wasn't, only sure that I had to allay her fears. 'Anyway, in the

State of New York, there are no longer any industrial firing squads.'

I guess I should have known that was the wrong thing to say 'cause she gasped. 'Firing squads? K.C., are you serious?'

'I'm joking. Don't worry. Just tell me what you guys found.'

'We found at least two more sets of books, one of which shows you didn't lose nine million, the way Maynard and Cotton have been telling people. The other shows there was a stop. The TransMare-Telco shares were dumped by the computer in the middle of the night, long before trading was suspended. As soon as they started to fall.'

'You absolutely sure 'bout this?'

'They've gone back into the accounting, taken a whole bunch of losses off Binterman's trading books and put them on to yours, all the time making it look like it came from TransMare-Telco.'

'Debbie . . .' I needed to make real certain. 'Debbie, are you absolutely, one hundred per cent sure 'bout this?'

'I'm absolutely one hundred per cent sure.'

I tried to think of what to do next. 'It's all printed out?'

'I have it hidden at home.'

'Is it safe there?'

'Everything I own is there,' she said, then asked, 'K.C., this isn't industrial espionage, is it?'

'That stuff is only about patents,' I said, not having a clue if that was true. 'Ya'll just gotta keep cool. Don't tell anyone in the office that you and I have spoken . . .'

'Can I tell Pinky?'

'No,' I said, but must have said it too fast 'cause that made her real nervous.

'No? Not even Pinky?'

'It's not that you can't tell Pinky . . .' This was making me nervous too. 'Debbie, the fewer folk who know 'bout this, the better. I'm gonna phone my lawyer right now and tell him what you've told me. I'll ask him to make some sort of arrangement to meet you so that you can give everything to him. Meantime, I don't want anybody saying anything they shouldn't which might tip off anyone at GCB.'

'They may already be tipped off.'

'How?'

'We discovered Cotton's password. That's how we got into the computer. Pinky checked the master access list. We found that too. It records every entry, notes the time and the password used. You know, so that they know who's been in there. Alex, that guy who first got into the system, says that the security people are snooping around because Cotton discovered someone used his password. Alex is scared to death they're going to blame him.'

'Does he know that it's you and Pinky?'

'I don't think so. I mean . . . I hope not.'

I blurted out, 'Debbie, don't go back upstairs. Go home right now. Get those papers. Ya'll hear me? You gotta go home right now.'

'Oh God . . . am I in trouble?'

'Promise me you won't go back upstairs.'

'I am in trouble.' She was terrified. 'Oh God, K.C. . . .'

'Listen to me. Have you got enough money on you right now for a taxi home?'

'Yes.'

'All right. Ya'll walk out that door and go home. Give me your number and your address. And when you get home, you phone me here. First thing you do when you walk into your apartment is phone me here. Ya'll got that?'

'Are they going to come after me?'

'Give me your number and address.' She did. And the instant I realized she lived in Brooklyn, I told her, 'Change of plans. Better idea. Don't go home. You got paper and a pencil?'

'Why? Where should I go?'

'Write this down.'

'I don't have any paper.'

'Then write it on your hand.' I gave her Izzy's address. 'Tell the cab driver it's right next to the McDonald Avenue Subway exit. Look for a sign that says, Jesus Saves.'

'What does that mean?'

'You'll know it when you see it. Go there right now. Don't go home. Debbie, do what I'm telling you. Just go to Izzy's office.'

'I'm scared.'

'It's gonna be okay. I'm gonna take care of everything from here. Just go to that address, right now. Go on. Hurry up.'

She hung up.

Immediately I phoned Izzy.

'Isidor Pinkus, attorney at law, speaking, may I help you?'

'It's K.C. and I hope the hell you can.'

'Why? What's wrong?'

I told him 'bout the call from Debbie.

The first thing he said was, 'Where is she now?'

'On her way to you.'

'How long will it take her?'

'She's at the World Trade Center. Thirty minutes, max. She's scared. But if those papers say what she says they say . . .'

'Where are you?'

I reminded him, 'I'm in London.'

'London? England? Oh, yeah, I forgot.'

I gave him the number of the Thurloe Court. 'Call me as soon as she gets there.'

'No wonder you haven't been home. You're in London, England.'

'She's a good kid.'

'I've been phoning you.'

'These papers she's got . . . some people at GCB might have found out that she got them by breaking into the company computer . . .' I wondered, 'Could that be something like industrial espionage?'

'Industrial espionage? I doubt it.'

'That's good.'

'Not necessarily. Sounds like straight theft. But we can cross that bridge when we come to it. First things first.'

'Izzy . . . I'm real worried 'bout her.'

'I get that impression.'

'Will you phone me as soon as she gets there?'

'As soon as she gets here I'll phone you in London, England, which is better than phoning you in New York, which is what I've been doing for several days, leaving messages on your machine that you don't seem to answer.'

'Sorry. I kinda forgot to pick up my messages.'

'So, you want to know what's new with your soon-to-be ex-wife and soon-to-be ex-brother-in-law?'

'Call me when Debbie gets there,' I said and hung up, only then realizing that Izzy wanted to tell me something 'bout Lorilee and Duke.

I decided Debbie came first.

The next forty-six minutes were sheer agony. I kept imagining the worst. There she was, standing with her back to the wall of the World Trade Center's west side entrance, and I was handing

her a blindfold, and the guard who told us crying was a fire
hazard had a machete, and he said I could offer her one last
M&M before he lopped off her head, and Maynard and Cotton
and Braddock and Binterman were all there chanting 'Death to
industrial spies', and Pinky was there crying, and the guard kept
saying that crying was a fire hazard, and I kept feeding Debbie
extra M&Ms . . .

The phone finally rang. 'Hi.'

'She's here,' Izzy said. 'She's here. Wait a minute, she wants
to talk to you.'

Debbie got on the line. 'K.C., I just got here . . .'

'Great.' I told her, 'Everything's gonna be okay now. Izzy will
go with you to your place and get those papers.'

She sounded slightly out of breath but considerably less
scared. 'Did you know he's Pinky's cousin?'

'Yeah, I know. Just let him take care of everything.'

'What do I tell them at work?'

'Tell them . . . I don't know . . . tell Izzy I said to think of
something for you. Let him give you a note like your mama used
to do when you missed school.'

'Just a minute.' She handed the phone back to Izzy.

'I'll go with her to get the papers.'

'She needs an excuse for not being at work,' I said. 'Think
of something. Then, when you see the papers, will you ring
me back?'

'Will you be there in an hour?'

'I'll wait.' Then added, 'She's a good kid and she's scared.'

'Okay,' Izzy said, 'yes. Really okay.'

With time to kill, I called home to pick up my messages.

But there were none.

Odd, the voice decided.

I figured I must have made a mistake, dialled my own number
again and punched in my code.

Again it said, *no messages*.

Now I got another dial tone, called home, waited for the tape
to say *leave a message*, then said loudly and clearly into the phone,
'This is a message.' I hung up, waited a few seconds, called home
for the fourth time, punched in my playback code and sat there
hearing my own voice say, 'This is a message.'

It works, I mumbled, and pushed it outta my head.

As long as I had my adaptors I figured I'd check the markets. But I worried that Izzy was gonna call back while I was on the line and decided the best thing to do was to keep it clear.

An hour passed.

Then an hour and a half passed.

The voice reminded me, *Izzy said an hour.*

I sat there, going nuts for another half hour, before convincing myself, *something's wrong*, grabbing the phone and calling Izzy's office.

No answer. No answering machine.

I tried Debbie's apartment.

Her answering machine clicked on. 'Anybody home? This is K.C. Pick up.' Nothing happened.

Then I tried Izzy's apartment. Answering machine there too. 'Hey, this is K.C. Anybody home? Come on, pick up.' Again, nothing.

Hanging up, I tried to think of who to call.

The voice elected, *Pinky.*

That's when the phone rang. I answered it with, 'Hey, what's going on?'

'It all took a long time to read,' Izzy said. 'This is big stuff.'

'Where are you? I've been phoning everywhere . . .'

'I'm back at the office. Debbie's gone back to work.'

'Ya'll get her an excuse?'

'She's covered.'

'So what's all that stuff say?'

'A lot.'

'Like what?'

'Like I've got to fax all this stuff to Cousin Harry because maybe I'm over my head.'

'Give me the net-net.'

'Actually I'm not too sure what it says . . . there are pages and pages . . . mostly accounts. But there's one thing I am sure it doesn't say.'

'Which is?'

'Breach of fiduciary trust.'

'You mean I'm off the hook?'

'That hook.'

'What hook is left?'

'If this is right? Maybe . . . I don't know. I shouldn't say. K.C., this could be very serious.'

'What hook am I still on?'

'Well . . . you might be on the same hook as everybody else in that company. But I shouldn't say. Maybe I'm reading it all wrong.'

'And if maybe you're reading it all right?'

'I think it's called fraud.'

'The whole company?'

'Could be. But I don't know that much about these things.'

'Tell me exactly what you're looking at.'

'A bunch of figures that represents trading in something called TransMare-Telco.'

I asked, 'What 'bout them?'

As he read them to me, the hairs on the back of my neck stood up. Someone at GCB – and long distance it sounded to me like it could be a lot of someones – was systematically running a late-trading scam.

In various parts of the world it's known as 'the weekend special' and is considered anything from suspect trading to normal operating procedure. But wherever the Securities and Exchange Commission has a say, it's definitely called fraud.

Shares linked to one of the big indexes – Standard and Poors, the Dow, whatever – were purposely getting dumped on Friday nights just before the final bell. Those same shares were then electronically mopped up at bargain basement prices any time after that closing bell on Friday but before the opening bell on Monday morning. Selling like that drove the index lower. Buying everything back on the kerb meant that the prices published in the Saturday papers didn't reflect the true value of the shares. Any electronic stops that other brokers had programmed to sell at those lower prices clicked in. Same for the foreign brokers. Unless someone in Asia or Europe knew that those shares had never really been sold, their computers could be expected to dump shares first thing Monday morning. GCB could then scoop up any remaining cheap shares in the Monday morning market, ready to unload them yet again once the big buying spree kicked in and drove them skyward.

If Izzy and I were getting this right – and I was sure we were – someone at GCB had rigged the computers to protect their own interests at the cost of everyone else, such as all their clients.

Ironically, none of this would have come to light, 'cept that they'd made a mess of fudging the books over the TransMare-Telco crash. I told him, 'Ya'll gotta take this stuff to the cops.'

'If it's what you say it is, absolutely, yes, I have to.'

'If it's what you say it is, then it's absolutely what I say it is.'

'Only one thing,' he warned. 'If this is what you say it is and the police agree, this is gonna spill a lot of blood.'

I said right away, 'Ya'll won't find my name on any of that stuff,' then suddenly thought the worst. 'Oh shit. Is Debbie there? Is Pinky there?'

'I can't tell,' he said. 'It's just codes. I hope they're not.'

'Mine is *copskid*. One word all lower case.'

There was a pause while he checked. 'No, nothing here like that.'

'How many different log-on codes are there?'

'A lot.'

'Tell me some.'

'Let's see . . . the one that shows up the most is . . . s-o-i-e. I guess that's pronounced, *swa*.'

'Someone's initials?'

'No, it's a French word,' he said. 'It means silk. I took French in high school.'

'Silk?' I started to grin. 'From a sow's ear. What other names?'

He went through a list of around a dozen, but *soie* was the only one that made sense. 'I'll call you back later tonight. You be home?'

He said he would be. 'But there's more you have to consider. If it goes deep, I mean, there are maybe twelve names that keep showing up here . . . that's a lot . . . the SEC could close the place down.' He paused, 'Do you understand what I'm saying?'

'I understand that it probably gets right back to all the guys who own the joint but that at least one of them is fooling around.'

'How do you know?'

'*Soie*. It's wishful thinking.'

'Who is it?'

'Cotton.'

'You sure?'

'I know the man.'

'But what about you?'

'My name's not there. I didn't know anything 'bout any of this. And the proof is in the bread and butter pudding.'

'What?'

'Look at the way the TransMare-Telco thing was handled . . .'

'That's not what I'm talking about. If the company goes down . . .'

Now I understood. 'How much time have I got?'

'Probably none.'

'Can ya'll make it disappear just long enough?'

'Can I? Of course. But as soon as the rabbit gets pulled out of the hat, someone is going to ask me when I put it in there. I'll have to tell them the truth.'

'If you go to the cops now . . . if they shut GCB down . . .'

'That's correct, then you're just another creditor. With what we have here, I think we can definitely prove you were wrongfully dismissed. But if there's no money, being just another creditor is not good for your health.'

'On the other hand, if we can use this as leverage for a settlement first . . .'

'I knew you were going to say that because I was thinking the same thing and great minds think alike. Except this time two great minds are conspiring to commit extortion. And even if, by some definition, it's not extortion, it is some terrible offence on my part that I don't even want to contemplate because I'm an officer of the court and trying to gain some advantage for my client by hiding a crime means they'll send me to jail with you.'

I cut in. 'Is everything we're talking 'bout protected by privilege?'

'I'm your lawyer. It's protected. But extortion or hiding a crime are moot points because we're not conspiring because we both know we don't want to go there and that whatever we do we are in total agreement that we are not going to break the law.'

'So whichever way . . . I wind up getting screwed.'

'We can't get a settlement out of them now and probably won't be able to get a settlement afterwards.'

'Maynard . . . Cotton . . . Braddock . . . what a team.'

'What do you want me to do?'

'Izzy . . . don't do anything. I'll phone you back at home tonight.'

Late that night I phoned Debbie at home. 'You all right?'

She was still pretty spooked. 'Cotton asked me where I'd

been. Izzy got his doctor to give me a note. I think Cotton believed it.'

'What's your log-on code name at the office?'

'Why?'

'Just tell me.'

'You'll laugh.'

'What is it?'

She confessed, 'Madonna.'

I told her, 'Keep your cool. Don't worry 'bout anything. It's all gonna work out.'

Then I phoned Pinky at home. 'You okay?'

'What's going on? Where are you? I've been leaving messages on your machine. I phoned you over the weekend because Debbie is real scared.'

'I know. I've spoken to her.'

'K.C., she may be in trouble. Me too.'

'I'm working on that. Don't worry. What's your log-on code name?'

'What log-on code name?'

'At the office. What name do you use to get on to the computer?'

'Should I tell you?'

'Yes. What is it?'

'Why? What are you going to do?'

'Pinky, what is it?'

'It's . . . please don't laugh . . . b-u-t-c-h.'

I told him too, 'Just keep your cool. I'll talk to you soon.'

Then I phoned Izzy. 'Get out that list of computer log-on code names. Look for Madonna.'

He did. 'Not here.'

'How 'bout, butch?'

'Not here.'

'Okay. Izzy . . . time's up.' I told him, 'Take it to the cops.'

As I hung up with him the little voice in the back of my head announced, *Broke. No settlement. No pension fund. No income. No money.*

I sat back and sighed.

The voice wanted to know, *How good does that feel?*

Real good, I said.

But I couldn't fool the voice. *K.C., we're fulla shit.*

'Cause I couldn't think of anything else to do, I picked

up the phone and called Patsy. 'Ever been real down and out?'

'Where are you? Are you still in London? How's it going?'

'I'm back in London. I've been to Paris. And it's going lousy.'

'I love Paris.'

'I didn't see much of it. He skipped on me here. And he skipped on me there. I'm waiting for him to try it again, 'cause this time I'm gonna be ready for him.'

'Down and out in London and Paris. Sounds like those poets I used to regularly read in the sixties.'

'Only thing I was regularly reading in the sixties was Peanuts. And Terry Southern. So, you ever been real down and out?'

'I wasn't too thrilled when my husband left me and my two kids for someone else. That count?'

'What did you do 'bout it?'

'What choices did I have?'

'Murder.'

'That was top of my list.'

'Why did you rule it out?'

'The only way I could think of killing him was like in that old Alfred Hitchcock television show where Barbara Bel Geddes bangs her husband over the head with a frozen leg of lamb, then cooks it and serves it to the police.'

'Barbara Bel Geddes? Wasn't she in *Dallas*?'

'Your frame of references is most revealing.'

'So why didn't you do it?'

'Because we were flirting with being vegetarians at the time.'

'Nothing wrong with being a vegetarian. I'm one. 'Cept I also eat meat.'

'A logical conclusion for someone who remembers Miss Ellie's real name.'

'Guess you do too,' I pointed out. 'So what happened when you ruled out murder?'

'I contemplated feeling so sorry for myself that I thought about becoming a bag lady.'

'Why didn't you?'

'Couldn't find the right size shopping cart to use as a closet for the kids' clothes.'

'Then what?'

'Then I did what I did.'

'Which was . . . is?'

'Get a life.'

I contemplated that. 'You're a pretty smart lady, Miss High School Principal.'

She reminded me, 'It's Mrs High School Principal.'

The next morning I woke up and announced to the little voice, *time we got us a life*.

There was a small supermarket nearby the Thurloe Court, so some time around mid-morning on Tuesday I went there and bought myself a sandwich, some Pepsis, a box of Oreo cookies – I couldn't believe the price they were charging for Oreos and wondered if that too had to be BT approved – and a couple of large bags of M&Ms. I also bought the *Wall Street Journal*, the *Financial Times*, a pad of paper and some pens. Then I returned to my room and settled in for a day's work.

I made my way through the papers, kept one eye on CNN to get market updates, and by one in the afternoon – which was eight in the morning New York time – logged on-line to muster some intelligence 'bout the upcoming day's trading.

Sifting through the back issues of Herbie's newsletter that I hadn't seen – nothing worthwhile in the Friday edition and nothing of any use in the Monday edition – I read, then reread a little paragraph in this morning's edition.

'Gone with the wind. Guatemala gold shares blown away by El Niño. Bank shares sink too. Sugar, coffee and cocoa don't mix, but a cocktail of pesticides is coming up.'

I didn't have a clue what that meant, but was curious 'nough to spend nearly forty-five minutes doing searches under the term 'El Niño' and downloading pages to read later. After that, I dialled into On-Time/Real-Time and started hunting for a few deals.

Not having CNBC to tell me where the market was heading made me feel slightly naked, but the NASDAQ wire was coming through my screen loud and clear, and after I checked real-time prices for a bunch of companies, missing CNBC didn't seem to matter so much.

The *Wall Street Journal* was reporting a rumour that TucsonBancorp was gonna acquire a small savings-and-loan in California, so I got in early, picked up 2000 shares at 7$\frac{1}{16}$th and sold 'bout ten minutes later at 7$\frac{1}{4}$. The shares stayed steady for another hour, then jumped to 7½. I reckoned that the bounce had clicked in, waited till the shares slipped to 7⁷/₁₆ths, then sold a couple of thousand. I bought back at 7³/₁₆ths, and said, *thank you, TucsonBancorp*, for boosting my trading account by $755.

Next, I spotted what I believed to be an opportunity with Atwater Marquette Micro Systems. But I dove in too fast, took a beating on 1000 shares, and handed back $215. Still, I had a gut feeling that I might be holding a decent poker hand, so I sat there watching Atwater Marquette for the rest of the day, got in just before the closing bell, made a fast ⅛th on 200 shares and clawed back another $190.

It put me up on the day, for the first time, by $730.

The voice applauded, *just 'bout buys us a BT-approved dinner.*

I celebrated in Chinatown doing *lo mein*.

On Wednesday the market turned against me and I dropped $870.

That night I dined on M&Ms and Oreos

In the meantime, I started thinking 'bout my answering machine 'cause when I called to check my messages, there weren't any, not even the one I'd left for myself. First thought was that I erased it. Second thought was, I couldn't have. Third thought was, someone else did.

It worked off a code that I punched into the phone and the only other person who knew the code . . .

I called Izzy. 'Lorilee's bugging my phone.'

'Wire tapping?'

'No. Listening to my messages.'

'How?'

'She's the only other person who knows the code. And I don't have any instruction booklet or anything here so that I can change it.'

'This is good,' he said. 'Don't worry if you get any messages from me.'

'What are you talking 'bout?'

'I tried to tell you yesterday. Your soon-to-be ex-wife and soon-to-be ex-brother-in-law attempted to get into court to get the writs overthrown. But they couldn't get their hearing moved up. It will take them a few weeks. So then your soon-to-be ex-brother-in-law called me, even more fuming, because it seems he went to your apartment with your soon-to-be ex-wife's clothes and you weren't there. He is demanding that you take them back. I think one or two tiny little shoves and they'll go over the edge.'

'Duke showed up with Lorilee's clothes?' I liked that. 'Hah, serves him right.'

'So if you get any messages from me, don't believe a word of it.'

'Why?'

'And oh yes, I also forgot, I'm seeing the US Attorney today.'

'What for?'

'For a couple of hours.'

There were no messages on my machine from him at all that day, or from anyone else for that matter. And all I got when I phoned him at home later that night was his machine. I left the message, 'What's new?'

He didn't phone back.

Thursday morning, there was a little story in the *Herald Tribune* that mentioned El Niño was flooding crops along the west coast of South America and that a locust plague was developing. Seems the bugs weren't getting fed in the flooded areas, so they were moving inland.

The only country I could picture in my head that was definitely on the west coast of South America was Chile, and the main crop they grew in Chile was . . .

I didn't have a clue.

But there were plenty of sites on the Internet that could tell me, and after sorting through a bunch of them I learned it was copper, iron ore, lead, zinc, manganese, gold and silver.

'Cept none of those were going to work. I kept digging until I found a more promising list.

Grains. Rice. Potatoes. Beans.

Then I started hunting around for pesticide companies that made products that stomped out locust plagues and also did business in Chile.

By the time the NASDAQ opened, I was taking a big position in a company called Physocide.

They opened at $3\frac{1}{2}$ and 'cause CNBC or Bloomberg or somebody else must have seen the same story 'bout Chile that I did, the shares fast shot up to $4\frac{3}{16}$.

I played them for the rest of the day, hunted 'round for

similar companies, and started thinking, real cautiously, that maybe El Niño and I could actually earn a living at this game.

When the market closed, I was up more than $4000.

That was going okay.

Finding Sir Tommy wasn't.

I'd called over to his house on Wednesday but no one there knew. I phoned that Miss DeSantis on Thursday, and if she knew it was getting increasingly clear she wasn't gonna tell me. In fact, after a few minutes, she turned me over to that guy Zachary and he as much suggested that I either leave a number for Sir Tommy to phone me back, or send the gift to the office marked for his personal attention – 'And I assure you that Sir Tommy will be the one to personally open it, because you seem to be concerned that someone might either take it or be embarrassed because, as you claimed, it's a boy thing' – or forget the whole thing.

That got me thinking that maybe forgetting the whole thing wasn't such a bad idea. Hanging 'round like this was proving nothing. So I looked up Hussein's number and called him, thinking I might just tell him that if he could get me on a flight home, anything smoking west, I'd take it.

His answer was, 'Very easy, mister, but I cannot do it from here.'

'Ya'll said they have a regular Friday schedule.'

'Yes, yes, they fly on Fridays, like I told you. But, mister, even for that, you will have to go see my associate who has a travel agency in Victoria. You will probably have to pay him some money so that he can . . . you understand . . . take care of some people to get you on the plane.'

'I thought I had a ticket?'

'You do.'

'So why do I have to bribe somebody to get to use it?'

'Because many people have tickets.'

'You mean besides being a terrible airline, they overbook their flights, then only take those passengers who pay bribes?'

'The airline business, mister, works in strange ways.'

'Give me your associate's address and phone number. I'll phone him first thing in the morning.'

The little voice wanted to argue. *We've come this far.*

But I wasn't convinced. *So far this far looks like it could be the end of the road.*

Patsy sided with the voice. 'You've gone this far. Isn't Ruby worth the extra mile?'

'Worth the extra ten miles, but no one will tell me where Whitestone is or when he's coming back and I'm kinda going stir crazy.'

'What would you do in New York that you can't do in London?'

'For one thing, get my life straightened out. There are problems with the company where I used to work. They owe me some money and it doesn't look like I'm gonna ever get it. And there's my soon-to-be ex-wife to deal with. And I gotta earn a living. Incidental stuff like that.'

'Well,' she said, 'if it looks like the company where you used to work isn't going to pay you what they owe you, will it look any brighter from this side of the Atlantic?'

'No, but . . .'

'You have a lawyer, don't you? And he's on this side of the Atlantic?'

'Yeah, he is . . . okay, you won that point.'

'How about your wife? Have you got a lawyer handling that too?'

'Same lawyer . . . and the score is now two to nothing.'

'Now what about earning a living?'

'I've got my laptop with me . . . dammit, Patsy, there you go again. You're not playing the devil's advocate, you're just talking me into talking myself into stuff.'

'By the way,' she asked, 'have you sent me my postcard yet?'

'Whoops.'

I didn't bother ringing Hussein's associate on Friday morning. But I did phone Whitestone's place in Richmond to enquire 'bout him.

Still nothing.

The little voice warned me off calling his office.

I wandered out that morning to find a postcard – bought one showing a couple of punks with bright orange hair sticking up like spikes off their heads, eating ice-cream cones – only to realize I didn't know Patsy's address.

There was no El Niño action in the market, and not much of anything else happening either.

I stayed out of it.

There were no messages on my machine – Lorilee was still bugging it – and by the time I got 'round to phoning Izzy, there was no answer at his office or his apartment.

Friday night, I remembered.

That ruled out phoning Pinky too.

So I tried Debbie.

Nothing.

I wound up taking a hike 'round South Kensington, finding a bookstore, buying a paperback novel, crawling into bed and falling asleep before I could even get through the first chapter.

Saturday morning I tried Whitestone's place in Richmond again.

This time the woman told me, 'He is due back this morning. Shall I take a message?'

'Not to bother.' I gave the air a victory punch with my fist. 'I'll ring back on Monday.'

Hoping Too Right Tel was gonna be right this time too, I spent the rest of the afternoon huddled in a corner across the street from his office, munching M&Ms.

He didn't show.

That night I phoned Patsy to reassure her that I'd bought the postcard.

'Did you mail it?'

'Didn't have your address. But if you want, I'll deliver it to you myself. You were right 'bout that extra mile. The guy's back in town. I'm counting on seeing him tomorrow. I got it all worked out.'

'That means you'll be back in the States in a couple of days. See, sometimes, the extra mile is really only a couple of hundred metres.'

'Don't understand metres. But I understand that if I deliver the postcard myself, I can save a bundle on postage.'

'What will you do with all this new-found wealth?'

'We were talking ice-cream, weren't we? Now tell me, is ice-cream at the Empire State Building kinda like breakfast at Tiffany's?'

'But I don't look like Holly Golightly.'

'Who?'

'Audrey Hepburn.'

'Neither do I.'

'Or George Peppard?'

'Why George Peppard?'

'No, you really don't know more about old movies than you let on to.'

'Sorry. What you see is what you get. Though I admit to liking Audrey Hepburn.'

'It's hardly an original thought, K.C. Doone. The airplane designer had a serious crush on her.'

'I can sympathize.' Then I started to wonder, 'Now, ya'll just said you don't look like her . . .'

'Ah. Finally. I was wondering when you'd get around to that?'

'Around to what?'

'To asking what I look like.'

'Well . . . I mean . . .' I didn't know what to say. 'Kinda natural curiosity, that's all.'

'Does it matter?'

I wanted to say no, but I knew if I did she wouldn't believe me. 'It's not supposed to.'

'No, it's not.'

'But . . . you know what the thing is? I guess we all do it. We put a face to a voice and then eventually, when we find out that the face doesn't match the voice . . . What I mean is . . . well, ya'll know what I mean.'

'No, I don't.'

'Not gonna let me off the hook, are you?'

'Nope.'

I blurted out, 'I'm just under five-eleven, been able to keep my weight down so there's no bulges, and if it's kinda dark, you know, no harsh lighting to give me away, well, if you squint a little I guess I kinda look like a young Jack Nicholson.'

There was a long silence.

'Ya'll still there?'

'If I told you I did look like Audrey Hepburn, would you meet me at the Empire State Building?'

'Sure.'

'And if I told you I looked more like Roseanne . . .'

I jumped right in with, 'Yeah, that would be fine too,' 'cause

I knew if I hesitated she'd pick up on that and anyway, I was betting on the fact she didn't look like Roseanne.

'Okay,' she said. 'Neither one.'

'Doesn't matter,' I insisted.

'How about a slightly taller version of Meg Ryan?'

'Or a shorter version of Tom Hanks,' I said. 'How's that?'

'That's good lying, K.C. Doone.'

'Ya'll want to know the truth?' I confessed, 'This time, well, this time I kinda think it is the truth.'

I couldn't believe he'd get there too early, it being Sunday and all, but just in case I decided to arrive by ten. I took up my place on that corner where I'd been yesterday, leaning against a wall where no one could see me if they came into the dead end.

Ten o'clock became eleven.

And eleven became twelve.

I hit the bag of M&Ms, managed to rip it badly and spilled a bunch inside my raincoat pocket.

I was contemplating taking off the raincoat, tipping it upside down and drinking 'em out, when it started to drizzle.

Now I huddled closer into a corner, trying to get just under the eaves of a building there, to stay dry.

Noon became one.

And one became two.

The drizzle became rain and the rain eventually wore itself out, only to became a drizzle again.

Then a big baby-blue Rolls-Royce pulled into the dead end, stopped in front of the office and the rear door opened.

And there he was.

Just like that fella Too Right Tel promised he would be.

Chapter Twenty-five

The only thing I had to wipe him down with was my own shirt, so I ripped it off, kneeled next to him, and tried to clean his face.

'Oh God,' Whitestone groaned.

His insides continued to empty out.

'Dear God . . .'

I readjusted his jacket behind his head . . . 'Come on, slide down . . .' trying to make him more comfortable.

He just lay there, groaning.

'It's gonna be okay.'

Then I realized that his groaning was really sobbing.

'It's okay.' I wiped his face again. 'We're gonna be all right. As soon as someone comes into the building, I'll get us help. It won't be long now.'

'Oh God . . . Mr Doone . . . I'm sorry . . .'

'We're gonna get help. As soon as someone shows up, I'll scream for help and we'll have the fire department get us out of here and they'll have an ambulance and a doctor . . .'

'No ambulance, Mr Doone. They steal. I know they do.'

'Who steals?'

'Ambulance drivers. They always steal.'

'No one's gonna steal anything. I'll go in the ambulance with you.'

'Then they'll steal from you too.'

'No, they won't.'

'They will.' He gasped for breath. 'They will.'

'You gotta lie quiet now. Come on, real quiet.'

'They won't get my wallet 'cause it's upstairs. They can't get my money.'

'That's good. Now just lie still.'

'But . . . you know what they will do? Steal my watch. Please don't let them steal my watch.'

'I won't. I promise.'

He reached across for his wrist, untied his watch and handed it to me. 'Hold this for safe keeping. Don't go in the ambulance. They'll steal it from you.'

I took it 'cause I was hoping that as soon as I did he'd calm down.

'Promise me you won't go in the ambulance.'

'I promise.' I shoved the watch into my pocket. 'Now, ya'll just calm down and we're gonna get outta here real soon . . .'

'They steal . . . I saw them do that on television once . . .' His voice got gradually softer and his breathing slowed.

'It's gonna be okay.' I continued rubbing his face, just like my mama used to do to get me to sleep.

And eventually he fell asleep.

Or he's dead, the voice suggested.

I fast reached for the side of his throat and felt for a pulse. It was right there, under the side of his jaw.

He's asleep, I assured the voice, then leaned back, and for the first time noticed that the stench in the elevator was sickening.

I tried to shift into a position where I could sit. And take deep breaths. And for a few moments I thought I would be sick too.

Breathe real deep and real slow, the voice instructed.

I did.

And after a time the moment passed.

I kept doing it.

And when I was sure I would be okay, I leaned all the way back and looked up towards the top of the dark elevator and whispered, 'Dear God . . . please save us.'

But if God heard me, he didn't do anything 'bout it for a real long time.

'I'm so sorry . . .' Whitestone said very softly.

'Huh?'

'I'm so sorry . . .' His voice was weak.

'Huh?' I looked around. 'You okay?'

'All of this . . . because you wouldn't give up, Mr Doone. Came all the way to London. And to France.' He started to chuckle. 'Do you believe in fate?'

'Fate? Ah . . . I don't know. I guess sometimes I do, when

something works out bad. Otherwise I think of it as . . . you know, my own skill.'

He liked that and chuckled again.

A good sign, I told the voice. 'Ya'll believe in fate?'

'Consider this,' he said. 'If I'd met you that morning in New York, and told you that I have nothing to do with those sweepstakes, you would never have come to England. Had you not come to England, we would not be here together right now.'

'Well . . . yeah . . . I kinda guess the second part is right. But the first part . . . ya'll gotta understand that those folk involved with the sweepstakes . . . I mean, I went through an entire list of names. George, Werner, Ochoa, Gonzalez. I checked on all those guys, and I couldn't find one of them. The only person who seemed to have anything to do with the sweepstakes and who wasn't also invisible, was you. So even if you'd told me you had nothing to do with it, I knew you did.'

'But I don't.'

'You do.'

'But I don't. It is true. You're referring to details. That's what I pay other people to do. Details.'

'You mean, it's not how you play the game that counts, it's whether you win or lose?' I stopped myself from getting angry. 'Isn't life supposed to be more than just the bottom line? More than balance sheets?'

'Life? Yes. Absolutely, Mr Doone. Life is much more than balance sheets. But business? And wealth creation? No, that's just a game.'

'You're good at games,' I said as gently as I could, 'cause this was no time to start arguing.

'I'm good at winning,' he nodded. 'And the way to win is to focus on winning.'

'As opposed to how the game is being played.'

'And as opposed to who's playing it.' He reached over and patted my hand. 'All those names you just mentioned . . . consider this and tell me again if you believe in fate. If I'd said to you in New York that the man named George and the man named Werner were one and the same person, would we be here trapped in this lift right now?'

'They're the same guy?'

'You see, in an odd way, Mr Doone, it's like that tree falling in the forest. Had I said that to you then . . .' He groaned louder than he was speaking. 'I am in such terrible pain . . .'

'Just stay quiet,' I said.

'I went to India for another treatment . . . but I know the treatments aren't working.'

'Lie still.' I wiped his face again. 'We're gonna get help soon.'

'They're not working. It's getting worse . . . I'm sorry, Mr Doone . . . maybe I should sleep again . . .'

'Good idea.'

And for a while he did sleep.

I sat there on the floor of the elevator listening to his breathing, trying not to get sick from the smell, waiting for morning to arrive, and thinking 'bout fate.

When the morning did show up, it sounded precisely like two women in the hallway below.

'Help! Help!' I jumped up and screamed at the top of my lungs. 'We're trapped in the elevator.'

That woke him, but he didn't seem strong enough to shout very loudly. 'Help.' It was a weak and almost sad cry. 'Help.'

'Help!' I screamed again. 'Please help. Can you hear me? Help!'

I heard a voice. 'What? Who is it? Where are you?'

Then a second voice, 'What's wrong? Who is it?'

'In the elevator. We're trapped. Call the fire department. Call an ambulance. Sir Tommy and I are trapped in here. He's sick. Get help fast. Please get help . . .'

One of the women shrieked, 'We will, oh my God, we will.'

And now I could hear two sets of feet running away.

Maybe they were gone for only a minute or two, but it seemed like for ever.

'Help! Are you there? Help!'

'I've called nine nine nine,' one of the women said. 'They're coming. They're coming.' I thought I heard her shouting to someone else, and a few seconds later I heard a man's voice. 'Are you all right in there?'

'We've been trapped all night. Sir Tommy is sick. Get an ambulance.'

'I'll make the lift work . . .'

'No,' I bellowed. 'Don't touch anything. For Chrissake, do not touch any buttons. Get the fire department and an ambulance.'

The man kept talking and I heard one of the woman shouting and then there were more voices, all of them trying to find out what was going on and who was trapped in the lift and were we all right. And each time someone asked me anything, I shouted back, 'Don't touch any buttons. Get help. Get an ambulance.'

And then I heard it.

I looked at him, grabbed his arm and said, 'Listen.'

He heard it too.

Sirens.

A couple of minutes later, with people calling to us, 'They're here, they're here,' men in heavy boots stomped towards us. Then a man wanted to know, 'How many people are trapped in there?'

'We're two,' I answered. 'Sir Tommy and me. He's sick. He needs a doctor.'

'Have you got any electricity in there?'

'No. Nothing. It's dark. And there have been sparks. Ya'll gotta know, there's some sort of generator or something just above the trap door on the ceiling. It's sparked a couple of times. We also dropped once. Not a lot. A few feet. I tried to escape to get help but the elevator cage shifted and I don't know . . .'

Sir Tommy's breathing was getting very irregular.

'Ya'll gotta get in here fast. He needs a doctor right now.'

Whoever I was talking to started shouting orders to other people and within half a minute I could hear a whole mess of folk on both floors – the one above us and the one below us – and then, suddenly, there was a small stream of light.

They'd forced opened the door above us.

'We're above the lift cage,' a voice said. 'We can see the cage but we can't come down on top of it. A cable seems to have snapped. Can you hear me?'

I answered, 'I hear you.'

Whitestone whispered, '. . . hear you . . .'

'It looks as if we're going to have to hoist the cage,' the man explained. 'This may take some time. Can you see my torch?'

A beam of light came through the trap door.

'I see it.'

And for the first time all night I could also see Sir Tommy's face.

He was sheet white.

His mouth was open.

His eyes were rolled back into his head.

'Ya'll gotta get a doctor down here right now,' I shouted.

'We're lowering down a lamp.' It appeared in the trap door and lit up the entire elevator.

The place was a mess.

Especially him.

'Put the lamp in the far corner of the lift,' the man instructed. 'Now look up because we're lowering down some water . . .'

A rope was right there dangling a bottle of Evian.

'I need towels too. And more water.' I grabbed the bottle, ripped off the cap and held it up to Sir Tommy's lips. He drank a little, but spilled a lot all over him. 'Towels. I need towels.'

'We're getting them for you. What's your name?'

'Doone.'

'Okay, Doone, my name is Nigel. And I need you to keep talking to me while we set up this hoist.'

'I'm talking to you, Nigel.'

'Who's in there with you?'

'Sir Tommy Whitestone.'

Nigel asked, 'Can you hear me, Sir Tommy?'

Tommy whispered, '. . . yes . . .'

'He's in bad shape,' I said. 'Very weak.'

'Doone, what's your condition?'

'I hurt and I'm tired. Otherwise I'm okay. But Sir Tommy's not.'

'We're going to take care of him.' There was some commotion on the floor above me before my new friend Nigel said, 'Now, Doone, I need you to stand up, if you can, and get right under the trap door. I've got a bottle of oxygen here that I'm sending down to you.'

I did what he told me to and when the cylinder came through the trap door, I grabbed it.

'You need to place the mask on Sir Tommy's face, right over his nose and mouth, and put the strap behind his head so that it's comfortable. You'll see that you can adjust it. Then I need you to turn on the valve, very slowly, but turn it on all the way. Can you do that?'

'Got it.' I took my shirt, wiped his face again, offered him another drink . . . he took a small sip . . . then fit the mask on him, adjusted the elastic strap and opened the valve. 'You're gonna be okay,' I said softly to him.

He looked up at me with his big blue eyes from behind that mask and I could see that he was trying to give me one of his Buddha smiles.

'Now, Doone, I'm lowering down another oxygen bottle. You may need it yourself. If you do, follow the same procedure.'

'I'm okay.'

'Here it comes.'

The second cylinder arrived but I put it on the floor.

'I really need those towels.'

'They're coming too,' Nigel assured me, and sure enough, the next delivery was six white fluffy towels. I put one behind Sir Tommy's head, wiped him down with one, then covered him with the others.

'You still there, Doone?'

'No, Nigel, I've gone out to lunch.'

'That's all right, Doone, I understand. What I need you to do now is help us decide what Sir Tommy's condition is.'

'Bad.'

'How bad?'

'Bad.'

'On a scale of one to ten . . .'

'Twelve. Now ya'll gonna talk about it or get him outta here?'

'Okay, Doone, I need you to stay calm and work with me.'

'Okay, Nigel, and we need you to get us the hell outta here, and get him to a hospital.'

'We're securing the hoist now. We have to do that before we can open the door below you so that we know the lift cage won't shift while we're working. This will only take another few minutes.'

'Cept it seemed to take a helluva lot closer to half an hour.

He and I kept talking, and while we did, I kept wiping Sir Tommy's face. And whispering to him, 'We're gonna get outta here real soon.'

And then it happened.

Nigel called down, 'Here we go.' I heard a loud cracking noise. Suddenly the lift door opened.

We were caught right between the floors.

And now I saw the tops of a whole bunch of heads and every one of them was trying to peer inside to see us.

A couple of guys forced open the cage door and right away a

couple of other guys crawled in. Someone helped me out, then wrapped a blanket around me. A few minutes later, they brought Sir Tommy out, strapped tightly on to a stretcher. They carried him downstairs, then outside where an ambulance was waiting.

I followed them on to the street. 'Where you taking him?'

'Charing Cross Hospital.'

A large crowd had gathered in front of the office – the police had everything cordoned off with some sort of yellow tape – and people kept shouting questions at me, like are you all right, and we've got to take you to the hospital.

But I didn't pay any attention to them. I just hurried after the stretcher and caught up to him just before they loaded him on to the ambulance.

'Hey,' I said. 'Next time I'll bring Smarties too.'

Sir Tommy looked up at me, motioned to the guys carrying the stretcher to wait a minute, then motioned for me to lean forward so that he could say something.

From under the mask I heard a very faint, 'I am sorry, Mr Doone. Usually when I spend the night with someone, I buy them breakfast.'

I grinned. 'I'll take a raincheck.'

'Another one of those Americanisms?'

'Damn right is. Now ya'll just take care. Everything's gonna be fine.'

'I hope, Mr Doone . . .' He grasped my hand and squeezed it. 'I hope after all this that your mother will be fine too.'

I nodded. 'Next time we meet . . . how 'bout some back-gammon?'

I held on to his hand until he was inside the ambulance.

'Games? That game . . . any game . . . all games . . .' He winked at me. 'You play well . . . unfairly . . . and well . . . Sir K.C.'

I never saw him again.

Chapter Twenty-six

They wanted to take me to the hospital but I refused. I said all I wanted was a real hot shower and 'bout twenty-four hours' worth of sleep in a bed. They insisted. I did too. So still wrapped in the blanket, I was driven in a police car back to the Thurloe Court.

The woman at the desk was pretty shocked to see me arriving like that. But I couldn't be bothered making explanations. I got upstairs to my room, hung out the Do Not Disturb sign, ripped off my clothes, stepped into the shower – damn, but that felt good – then crawled between two clean white sheets.

And that felt even better.

'Cept I couldn't sleep 'cause I kept thinking 'bout him and 'bout what he'd told me.

Grabbing the phone, I called Izzy at home. It wasn't yet six, his time, but I needed to tell him what I'd found out.

The number rang once, then twice, then someone with a real sleepy voice answered, 'Hello?'

'Izzy? Listen to me. Sorry to call you this early . . .'

'No . . . Izzy is . . . wait a minute . . .' I heard a woman shout his name, say something, then come back on the line. 'He's in the shower. Can I take a message?'

My mouth dropped. 'Debbie?'

'Who's this?'

'Debbie . . . this is K.C.'

There was a very very long pause.

'So-oooo embarrassing.'

'Debbie . . . are you . . .' I stopped 'cause I already knew the answer. 'Debbie . . . look, can ya'll give Izzy a message . . .'

'So-oooo embarrassing. K.C., please . . . you've got to promise me that you'll never tell anyone . . . K.C., it just sort of happened . . . sooooo embarrassing . . .'

'It's okay, Debbie . . .'

'Wait . . . wait . . . here's Izzy . . .'

He got on the line. 'This is Isidor Pinkus, your attorney. Where are you?'

'I'm still in London.'

'Is everything all right?'

I reckoned, if he doesn't mention Debbie I won't mention her either. 'I got to Whitestone. It's a long story but I spent . . . well, I just spent a lot of time with him. That guy George. And that other guy Werner. They're the same guy.'

'I know.'

'You do?'

'I found out yesterday. From Pauly in Miami. We found out because of that lawyer Ochoa.'

'How?'

'That Spanish stuff you sent me. Ochoa and the fellow named Gonzalez . . . the reason the Mexicans threw them out of the country is because they're the same people. Ochoa and Gonzalez are both really Ochoa. I had it all translated and as soon as I saw that, I told Pauly and from that we found out that George is really Werner.'

'That changes everything then, doesn't it?'

'Yes. And no.'

'You were the one who said we had to prove that they were deliberately deceptive.'

'That's right, and this does that.'

'So my mama keeps her apartment.'

'Maybe not.'

'Why not?'

'Because the company that was supposedly holding a lien on the apartment is no longer holding a lien on it.'

'Who is?'

'A bank.'

'You mean, some phoney bank in the Bahamas?'

'No. George or Werner, whatever you want to call him . . . last week . . . they unloaded all of their properties. Sold everything, the whole portfolio, to First Caracas.'

'In Venezuela?'

'They're in Miami. But it doesn't matter. They're legit. Totally on the up. The problem now becomes that the only way to get the apartment back from them is either buy it back outright which is the fastest way, or spend probably just as much taking them and George and Ochoa or whatever their names are to court, which is not only the slowest way, but might turn out to cost even more.'

'Shit,' I said. 'What now?'

'Now we have to decide what you want to do.'

'I don't know. Let me think. I've been up all night. I'll phone you back.'

'When you do, I'll tell you all about your soon-to-be ex-wife and soon-to-be ex-brother-in-law and why they want to settle.'

'They do? Why?'

'Seems she's been listening to your answering machine. Have a good sleep.'

He hung up.

'Huh?' And 'cause he was gone, so did I.

It took a while, but eventually I fell asleep and when I did I dreamt 'bout Lorilee and my answering machine. There she was, naked, standing in front of a fridge-freezer filled with answering machines . . . and laptop computers . . . and ice-cream cones served by punks with spiky bright orange hair.

When I woke up, sometime around four that afternoon, I phoned Charlotte Meissen in West Palm Beach. She was out, but my pal Wolf took the message. 'Please tell her that Alexander George and Herbert Werner . . . those two are the same.'

'The same what?'

'The same person.'

'What does that mean?'

'Please tell her I hope it means they are being deliberately deceptive.' I left my number in London.

Then I phoned Roamers' House of Funerals. My pal Grayson said his dad was in Tallahassee. I said I needed to speak to him right away. He gave me his dad's private line, then asked, 'How's your mother?'

I said, 'I hope she's hanging in there,' hung up with him and phoned her. 'You okay?'

'I don't know,' she said defiantly. 'You tell me. I've called you all weekend. Don't you ever listen to your messages?'

'Sorry, Mama, but I've been real busy and I'm not home and no, I haven't been picking up my messages. What's wrong?'

'What's wrong is that ya'll don't pick up your messages and I don't know what's happening with my apartment . . .'

'Apartment's gonna be fine.'

She started to cry. 'I can't keep living like this.'

I talked her into going to the kitchen and taking a belt of scotch. When she came back on the line she sounded better.

'Believe me, Mama, it's gonna be fine.'

Slightly juiced like that, she was now willing to concede, 'I believe you.'

Next I got Roamers on the line and told him the entire story of Whitestone, George and Werner, Ochoa and Gonzalez. He sounded very sincere when he thanked me for getting this information to him. I thanked him for taking such an interest, felt guilty that I'd kinda misled him and his son in the beginning and blurted out that the only reason I'd arranged my mama's funeral was so that I could find out from him what he knew 'bout those sweepstakes.

'That's all right, my friend . . . giving me this information means I now have a ball to run with.'

'I do appreciate it.'

'No problem. And when that saddest of all times comes, we'll bury your mama for you anywhere you want.'

Don't like the tyres you're kicking, the voice said, *we'll give you other tyres to kick.*

I hung up just in time for my phone to ring. 'Mr Doone? This is Charlotte Meissen.'

'Oh, hey, thanks for calling. Wolf gave you the message, huh?'

'No, Wolf paged me and convinced me it was urgent. What can I do for you?'

'Good old Wolf,' I mumbled, then told her the story 'bout Whitestone, George and Werner, Ochoa and Gonzalez and that the First Caracas Bank now seemed to own the properties.

'Mr Doone, when will you be back in the States?'

'This week. I guess tomorrow or the day after. As soon as I can get on a plane.'

'It may be too late for me to do anything about saving your mother's apartment. And if it is, I apologize. But you've lived up to your half of the deal, I'll live up to mine. Call me at the end of the week and perhaps I'll have news for you.'

'Your half of the deal?'

'Jurisdiction.'

There were still a bunch of Oreo cookies sitting on the dresser, I devoured them, then figured maybe I'd call in on Whitestone.

The woman who ran the hotel told me how to get to Charing Cross Hospital, but a woman at the reception desk just inside the main entrance told me that Sir Tommy had checked himself out at 10.30 this morning.

'What do you mean, checked himself out?'

She said she thought he'd been moved to another hospital. 'Try the London Clinic near Harley Street.'

I didn't know where that was, but they were listed in the phone book so I called them and asked for Sir Tommy Whitestone's room. The operator said there was no one at the clinic with that name. Now I phoned his office and figured that the DeSantis lady would tell me where he was. But she wasn't there and no one seemed to want to tell me anything. I asked for that fellow Zachary. He wasn't there either. I phoned his place in Richmond. Only the maid was home and she said she didn't know where anyone was.

Not having many other options, I went back to South Kensington, wandered around for a while, got something to eat, and later that night phoned Patsy.

'I was away for the weekend,' I told her. 'Well, not really the whole weekend, just yesterday till today.'

'Where did you go?' she asked.

'Kinda nowhere. I was trapped in an elevator.'

'Oh, how awful. Are you all right?'

'Yeah, I guess.'

She kept asking questions.

But I was still wondering 'bout Sir Tommy.

'Let me phone you tomorrow night. Is that all right? I guess I'm coming home some time soon.'

'With my postcard?'

'Yeah,' I said. 'Anything else you want from London?'

'Let's start slow. A postcard is fine.'

Start slow, the voice kept saying as I got back into bed to go to sleep.

I asked the voice, *yeah, when was the last time we started slow?*

And the voice answered, *when was the last time we had anything to do with a grown-up lady?*

*   *   *

Tuesday morning began usual enough.

I woke up early, got breakfast brought up to the room with a copy of the *Herald Tribune*, opened it to the last page, read some stuff there, and started going through it backwards, checking to see what the Knicks were up to.

All the weekend scores were there.

After studying them, I turned a couple more pages, to check out the markets. I looked over the NASDAQ – kept thinking to myself, *go El Niño* – then looked at the NYSE. Then my eyes fell on the letters GCB.

And my mouth fell open.

The headline read, 'Police Raid GCB – Broker Shut Down.'

Holy Jeezus!

The story was pretty sketchy, but said that the cops had stormed in there yesterday afternoon, armed with warrants, carted off Maynard, Cotton, Braddock and everybody else, and also brought in specialists to crack their way into the computer system.

After the initial shock of that set in, my main worry was Debbie and Pinky.

It was only three-something in the morning in Brooklyn, but I phoned Izzy anyway.

This time he answered his own phone. 'Hello?'

'I know I'm waking you. Sorry. I know what time it is. It's K.C. But I just read in the paper that they raided GCB yesterday.'

'Yes, they did,' he said, sounding half-asleep. 'I heard it too late to phone you. I was going to phone you today . . .'

'What about Debbie and Pinky?'

'What about them?'

'Paper says everyone got carted off.'

'Yes, I think that everyone who was there did get arrested. I don't know who's being held or who will get charged.'

'You mean ya'll didn't get them out yet?'

'Maybe they weren't there.'

'Huh?'

'I think maybe they decided they had other things to do yesterday after lunch.'

'You knew it was coming down?'

'It would be illegal for me to warn someone about something like that.'

I started to laugh. 'Good for you, Isidor Pinkus, attorney at law.'

'From what I understand, Pinky had a dentist appointment. Wasn't that lucky?'

'And Debbie?'

'Wait,' he said.

She came on the line. 'This is so-oooo embarrassing.'

'That's two mornings in a row, kiddo.'

'K.C., please, promise me . . . I mean, if my mother ever found out . . .'

'Want my advice?'

'What?'

'Don't tell your mother.' Then I added, 'Or his. Bye bye.' I hung up and went back to my breakfast.

Here's to GCB, I raised my coffee cup.

And our pension fund, the voice joined in.

What the hell. I shrugged, *couple of weeks ago I figured it was gone 'cause I'd blown it. This week it is gone 'cause they were crooks. So much for breach of fiduciary trust, huh?*

I sat up, finished my coffee and flipped the newspaper over to the front page.

This time the shock left me totally speechless.

Tommy Whitestone Is Dead. The headline on the left side jumped out at me. *Billionaire Dies In Same Bed In Which He Was Born*.

I actually felt myself growing faint.

The story explained how he'd had an accident over the weekend, having gotten trapped in a lift at his office in central London – there was no mention of me, or the fact that he hadn't been alone – was rescued yesterday morning and taken to a hospital, had insisted on checking out and ordered that he immediately be flown to Spain where he died of heart failure at around eight last night. The article also noted that he'd been suffering from pancreatic cancer for the past four years and had been regularly undergoing some sort of strange treatment at an alternative clinic in India.

I read the article three times, from beginning to end, then stood up and just kept walking around the tiny room.

I walked in a circle for half an hour, all the time trying to focus on the fact that it was true.

He's dead.

Suddenly, I had an overwhelming need to phone someone, to talk to someone, to tell someone about the night I'd spent with him – the last night of his life – to say to someone, *I just can't believe it.*

I thought of the nice-looking woman in Paris who'd told me he'd gone to India. I guessed she was either Kiki or Lou, but I didn't know which 'cause I hadn't thought to ask. So I found the card he'd given me with his number on it and called France. A man explained, in faltering English, that both families had gone to Spain yesterday afternoon.

I tried the house in Richmond but no one answered.

I dialled the office. Same thing there. The phone simply rang and rang and rang, till I decided that no one was going to answer it, and hung up.

It was now just after nine in London. Just after four in New York. I mumbled, *she'll understand.* 'I know what time it is and I'm sorry to wake you . . . Patsy, it's K.C . . . he's dead.'

'Who's dead?'

'Whitestone.'

'Oh, my God. What happened?'

I read the story to her and told her everything 'bout Sunday night in the elevator. 'I just can't believe he's dead.' She let me keep talking, which I did non-stop for near-on an hour, and when I'd finally talked myself out, I told her, 'Thanks for listening.'

She said, 'It's okay.'

And when I finally hung up, the little voice reminded me *she never once said, do you know what time it is?*

I slid off the bed and over to my clothes, where I'd left them in a pile on the bathroom floor.

Where's the Woollite when we really need it, the voice joked.

I reached inside my trouser pocket and took out Sir Tommy's watch, laid it in my open hand and studied it carefully.

In the back of my mind I heard him saying, *I hope after all this that your mother will be fine too.*

And now the little voice declared, *he knew.*

I stared at his watch for a very long time, then put my twenty-buck Cartier in my gym bag and strapped on the diamond-laden Rolex Oyster.

After that I phoned Hussein's associate who promised me that for a £25 bribe he could get me on a flight back to New York at six tonight.

I went to Victoria and paid him the money.

How much you wanna bet, the voice prodded, *that when we get to that airport the guy we just bribed never heard of us?*

I showed up at Luton on time.

The voice was sure, *it will never work.*

The fellow I'd bribed took my outta date Tri-State Airways return ticket and gave me a boarding pass for Allegheny Airtours flight 875 to Newark, New Jersey.

The following day Izzy faxed me a copy of the proposed settlement with Lorilee. She'd keep the house in Connecticut but I'd have first choice of the contents and any or all of our jointly acquired possessions. I'd also keep the apartment in New York. There would be no alimony. It would be a clean break.

'How come she agreed to that?'

Izzy told me, 'Maybe she misunderstood some of the messages she heard on your answering machine.'

'Like what?'

'I wouldn't know.'

'What messages did you leave?'

'Me? That would be deliberately deceitful.'

I took a stab at, 'So what messages did Cousin Harry leave?'

'Well . . . speaking hypothetically . . . if Cousin Harry were to have left certain messages that somehow led your soon-to-be ex-wife to think that she was going to get nothing because your soon-to-be ex-brother-in-law was about to get arrested for aiding and abetting a crime . . .'

'What crime?'

'You know any lawyer who doesn't from time to time aid and abet a crime?'

'How 'bout you and Cousin Harry?'

'Me? I do not aid or abet.'

Three days after that, I phoned Lorilee to say that I was coming to collect stuff. She promised not to be there. I got on the train and went to Connecticut.

The voice warned, *she will be there.*

She wasn't.

The voice insisted, *let's take everything and to hell with her.*

I walked 'round the house, looked at everything, and kept thinking 'bout my dream in the elevator.

If you walk away, who really wins and who really loses?

All I took was my fortieth birthday present, the Vacheron

watch, and the American flag that once draped my papa's coffin.

The next morning, I got back into the market. I bet on El Niño again.

The voice warned, *it's an ill wind . . .*

The locusts plagued and Physocide went up to 5⅞ths.

That afternoon, Maynard, Cotton and Braddock were formally charged by the United States Government on several counts of fraud, embezzlement and grand larceny, including various stock manipulation offences. Binterman was the only other one charged.

The voice promised, *they'll be out on bail in an hour.*

CNBC reported the next morning that bail had been denied.

Two days later, Fidel from Bloomingdale's Annex put me in touch with a legitimate secondhand watch dealer. He asked me how much I wanted for the Rolex.

The voice argued, *he's gonna rob us on the price.*

I sold it him for $41,500.

The voice insisted, *we didn't get enough.*

The next day I sent a cheque to First Caracas to buy back my mama's apartment for the price Izzy had negotiated – $41,500.

That afternoon, I blew up the deflated inflatable ice-cream cone, Scotch-taped over the holes so it stayed blown up, grabbed the postcard and made my way to the Empire State Building.

When I got there, the sun was still up.

When she got there, it was just starting to set.

I handed her the ice-cream cone and postcard. 'Hi.'

From behind her back she handed me an ice-cream soda. 'Hi.'

The little voice warned me, *this is too good to work.*

So far, the little voice has been wrong again.